The Guns of Monte Carlo

Ray Christie

Haus des Säntis
Switzerland

First published by Euro Classical Publishing under Haus des Säntis - Switzerland 2022

Paperback ISBN: 978-0-6488473-2-8

eBook ISBN: 978-0-6488473-3-5

www.raychristie.com

Book design cover by www.bespokebookcovers.com

Editing by Ryan Quinn, Los Angeles, United States.

A catalogue record of this book is available from the National Library of Australia and the Library of New South Wales.

Dedicated to my wife

Yuliana

Sancte Michael Archangele, defende nos in proelio, contra nequitiam et insidias diaboli esto praesidium

Chapter One

Florence, Italy

In a cloudless blue sky, the midday sun reaches its highest point over the Piazza di Santa Croce. The lingering humidity of the Tuscan air hugs Professor Harrington and his wife as they negotiate their path toward a lunch reservation at La Casa di Porchetta. Forty meters away, a lone special forces operator attaches himself among a group of European tourists as they wander the narrow cobbled streets.

Matt Carver from the British Secret Intelligence Service, commonly known as MI6, has the professor under tight surveillance. Far from the wild back alleys of Afghanistan, Carver casually observes the couple from their reflection in a shop window as they walk hand in hand, mesmerized by the beauty of their surroundings. He tips his Borsalino fedora slightly forward, covering his thick brow, then steps into a shop doorway for a moment to light a cigar. With his back turned to the pedestrians, he swiftly attaches a suppressor onto his favorite Sig Sauer handgun. Within seconds, he backs out of the shadow with a smoking cigar, his weapon holstered firmly inside his loose-fitting shirt. Scanning the piazza with his dark brown eyes, Carver takes a moment to enjoy the beautiful adrenaline rush. His chest tightens as oxygen and blood flood into his tight muscles. He prepares himself psychologically for what lies ahead while waiting for headquarters to deliver updates. Carver has no reason to impede the assassin due to arrive. Observe and report is his only aim. Any of the other operators from SIS could have taken this job; however, Carver has more than a mild interest. He prefers to get up close, to see how this man carries himself on the approach and execution. This unknown professional may have certain signature traits noticeable to only a handful of skilled men. Most important of all, Carver wants to catch a glimpse into his eyes during the kill. He wants to bear witness to the best special forces operator the Chinese military special missions unit can produce. Developing reliable intel on this man had been difficult for both the Europeans and their American counterparts in the CIA. Both agencies were unwilling to take the necessary steps and risk exposing themselves. The previous surveillance staff used distance, disguises, and various data-collection tools. Then the agencies would rotate new recruits into the intelligence operation every few weeks to avoid suspicion. The reports that followed contained wide-ranging information. Carver prefers a head-on approach, up close and personal, even if it means risking his life.

Meandering casually through the cobble streets, Carver puffs on his cigar while passing the Basilica di Santa Croce. He has direct sight of the professor and his wife walking carefree like a couple of teenage lovers along Largo Piero Bargellini. He arrives at the restaurant before them and walks to his table, following the smartly dressed young *cameriera*. A careful eye keeps the couple in his peripheral vision.

"*Ti ringrazio tanto*," Carver says when accepting the menu. He adjusts the position of his seat slightly, providing a full view of the piazza without being too obvious. A crowd of smartly dressed European tourists has filled the alfresco dining area. Wine bottles are being popped open with laughter and kisses shared by these new arrivals. The two subjects have also strolled in and are being directed to a table directly opposite from Carver.

The professor is sweating heavily as he unfurls a silk handkerchief to wipe himself down while his wife admires the beautiful neo-Gothic architecture, absorbing the moment and allowing herself to be swept up by her dreams. She had planned this European holiday only a few days ago, but in reality, she had fantasized about such a trip since childhood. Her husband had been working long hours, days, weeks, months, years, for what seemed like an eternity. He was finally preparing to publish his scientific research on computational complexity theory when, out of the blue, the pair were offered an all-expenses-paid trip to China as guests of Tsinghua University. Exhausted, overworked, underpaid, and feeling the effects of the relentless, wet, dull, and cold British weather on their tired joints, they gladly accepted. Excited about their first trip out of London for almost twenty years, their new sponsors greeted them warmly in Beijing. A few relaxing days of sightseeing, lavish dinners, cultural exhibitions, and special treatment by other like-minded Chinese academics and government officials had been spectacular. When their time being treated like royalty had ended, both were tearful and duly promised in their hearts to return for further research discussions. After giving more beautiful gifts, this time it was Swiss watches and pieces of jade, the Chinese intelligence officers provided the couple with first-class flights to Vienna. From there the couple slowly traveled to Florence via Salzburg and Venice, pausing at all the architectural wonders Europe affords. Unbeknownst to them, however, every move they made was closely monitored. Like a fairy tale with no end in sight, the two academics are oblivious to the horrors about to take place. Sitting within the birthplace of the Renaissance, their well-heeled lives will never be the same. Their last chapter has begun.

Three days ago, Langley sent an official burn notice to the Secret Intelligence Service in London, advising their asset had been in contact with Chinese Communist Party members. The Central Intelligence Agency's targeting officers warned them that Harrington is unreliable, and therefore they have disavowed him completely. Their counterparts from Vauxhall have sufficient reason to lead Carver on this surveillance operation, cautioning him to provide no security or support. Only to keep out of the way and allow the lamb to wait for the wolf. Other than sitting back and gaining intel on the assassin, he was ordered not to get involved. SIS and the CIA know quite well this professor will not be the last target on the assassin's hit list. After the Chinese Communist Party had gained the trust of Harrington, they would have called for him to present updates on all other research taking place and who is currently leading the research. Having Harrington on the mainland of China made it much easier for the Chinese to obtain access to his research. Careful planning to entertain the professor and his wife at various locations allowed the Chinese technical team ample time to access his lavish hotel room. This allowed hackers, from the Chinese People's Liberation Army Strategic Support Force (PLASSF), to transfer years of research material from the professor's laptop while uploading various malware inside Oxford University's secure intranet and allowing the PLASSF a backdoor to steal future findings.

The soft position of simply carrying out surveillance and data collection by SIS angered Carver. He was the man called upon when the government required a result and when politics was no longer a reasonable option. A man who acted alone under various aliases, traveling across borders from one black operation to another. They had pulled the thrill of the kill from below him in Florence. Being moments from observing the death of a traitor was nothing special, but the fact he could not prove himself against an experienced enemy was extremely frustrating.

Carver takes a long breath to readjust his mindset as he pretends to inspect the menu. His eyes sweep up from the menu in his hands to explore the windows in the buildings opposite, searching for the reflection of a lens or someone watching over the piazzas, providing intelligence. *Nothing suspicious, no snipers, no surveillance, no one acting strangely, so far so good,* he thinks to himself as he runs his fingers through his hair. Then, just as he scans the streets leading into the piazza, a soft clicking sound in his earpiece alerts him about an incoming transmission.

"Alpha five-one, this is Charlie five-two. Do you copy? Over."

Carver, unable to communicate so close to the couple, and because of the fact he resents working with other operators, simply clicks twice on his covert mic, signaling that he copies the last.

"Alpha five-one, this is Charlie five-two. Target is approaching from Via dei Benci. ETA one mike."

Carver clicks one more time, then orders a simple pappardelle dish, knowing he will not get to enjoy it. The point is to have the young, attractive *cameriera* back inside the kitchen area and out of harm's way. He can feel the gates of hell will shortly be thrust open. Calmly reaching inside his shirt, he unlocks a clip in his holster while still portraying an image of just another wealthy tourist. Carver enjoys a few more puffs of his Davidoff Oro Blanco cigar while he sits patiently for the shooter to appear. The smoke swirls high above his head before dissipating into the air of the piazza. Relaxed and comfortable, he counts down the seconds. Carver doesn't have to wait long. A couple of slow, deep breaths pass before the assassin emerges from the narrow street. With the sun high in its arc, there is a lack of shadows to provide this Chinese operator with some cover.

Now out in the open sunlight and without hesitation or fear, he steps directly across the piazza, his eyes locked on the diners, combing them for his target. *Sloppy work,* thinks Carver. *Should have gone around the backstreets and come out Via dei Pepi, extremely confident or time-pressed, perhaps.* He continues his assessment as the seconds count down. *Eyes on the target from so far out also means he is not being assisted by any observers in this location. They would have told him which table the target was at and facing which direction. Possible he has no backup, no help, and if he gets caught, he will be held at the mercy of the Italian government.*

Carver, also a true professional, has a deeper interest in this man. The assassin is dressed all in black with a flat cap and a finely trimmed moustache. He walks calmly but with confidence, then unceremoniously removes his sunglasses and places them inside his jacket as he covers the distance to his target. *He prefers to be a lone operator, just like myself.* Nodding slightly to himself, Carver rests his hand inside his shirt, a firm grip on his firearm. Ready to kill if the assassin attempts to use a hand grenade instead of the less dramatic yet showstopping bullet to the head. Carver knows the assassin will check for other shooters, for major threats to himself, as he closes the distance between them. *His primary target is bearing no threat, and neither is the wife. His brain will work overtime processing every diner.* As this man covers the last twenty meters, Carver watches the dark piercing eyes which fix on each human, like a predator. Ten meters, nine, eight…, the rush of adrenaline is flushing through Carver like bolts of energy.

Carver's team will be furious that he has positioned himself within the restaurant. *Too bad,* Carver thinks. *A ringside seat will provide further answers to the ever-increasing amount of questions SIS has about the Chinese and their new ventures into global assassinations.* Five meters to go and Carver's heart rate is banging hard in his chest. Time appears to slow down as he watches the man reach into his jacket to pull out his carefully selected weapon of choice. Just then, the two men lock eyes. The Chinese man suddenly freezes, a look of unease crosses his face, a moment of uncertainty. *Is it doubt, or a test?*

Carver, with one hand on his weapon, tucked under his shirt, the other hand playfully rolling his cigar between his fingers, stares directly at the assassin with a poker face. What feel like minutes pass, suddenly, as if someone fired a starting gun. The assassin's face, like his body, sparks back to life. He quickly pulls out his firearm, grips it in both hands, and adopts a shooter's Weaver stance. His non-shooting leg in front and slightly bent, directing the weapon toward the professor as he flicks off the safety. Then suddenly, and at the worst possible time, the *cameriera* arrives at the professor's table, menu in hand, unknowingly blocking the shot, instantly becoming an unwanted obstruction.

The assassin does not miss a beat. He fires one bullet into the youthful girl's head, killing her immediately. The cerebrospinal fluid bursts from the exit wound, covering the face and upper body of the professor. As the *cameriera* falls forward into the lap of the professor, it provides a clear line of aim. He fires two shots, the rapid double tap of a specialist. One round hits the frightened professor in the forehead, the next his eye socket. The whole restaurant instantly erupts; the diners start screaming at the massacre before them. Some run for their lives, toppling over each other as plates and wine glasses smash on the ground. Other less mobile diners sustain injuries from being trampled on in the mass panic in those initial few seconds of death. Those patrons that are in control of their bodies, but too unfit or overfed to run, take cover under the marble-topped tables. A couple are in shock and can do nothing other than sit there quivering. For no obvious reason, the assassin turns the gun to the wife and puts one in her head. As he does so, Carver has to control himself not to return fire. His blood had begun to boil the moment the assassin shot the young waiter. Without realizing it, Carver had drawn his gun, exposing the barrel, and flicked off the safety. But this is not his dispute. Not yet.

The carnage has begun, with the yelling and shouting soon following in uncontrollable bursts. Obscenities in numerous European languages are unleashed in crying sprays of those full of courage from the Tuscan wine. As if to marvel at his performance, the man remains there, facing the professor, feeling nothing when removing another life. He slides his weapon back under his clothing and is about to turn around and flee, then he remembers. He looks directly at the one man who did not flinch, the only person who failed to be scared, neither cowering beneath the tables nor stumbling like the rest of the hateful Westerners. Sitting there smoking a cigar with his grip on a firearm, observing. The killer's head dips slightly to avoid the direct sunlight on his face, affording him a clearer view. *Who the hell is this guy?*

Carver's heart races. A Mexican standoff has occurred. He is bracing to pull out his firearm and tap holes into his opponent. *Just reach for your gun, let me finish this, you scumbag.*

"Alpha five-one, this is Charlie five-two, let him walk, over." The satellite overhead provides Carver's chief with a bird's-eye view.

"Bullshit, this is your lucky day, you son of a bitch," Carver mutters under his breath as he slowly resets his firearm into the holster under the vigilant eye of the executioner who just wiped out innocent civilians in cold blood.

Carver's stomach turns over as he watches this evil excuse of a man smile back at him while slowly shaking his head. When the assassin turns and walks off, Carver can no longer remain there, as people are struggling to revive the dead. He gets up and crosses to the young waitress. Her life meant nothing to the man who blasted her, purely an insignificant obstruction. Staring into her childlike face, now mutilated and ghastly, he has to fight the urge not to run after the assassin. He knows his day will come; the intelligence agencies will make certain of it. If not, Carver will do what he does best to seek vengeance, by going rogue, with no rules or limitations required.

As he moves the girl off the professor, something causes him to turn around. His famed instinct warns him the day is simply beginning. Through the blue backdrop and slight wisps of clouds forming in the Italian sky, he glimpses an object floating through the piazza. Carver has no time to warn anyone. With a sharp breath, he launches himself over the tables and rolls to the corner of the restaurant, where he pulls a table down in time before the blackness envelops him. What seems like hours is not even minutes. Carver lies slumped in a pool of his blood under the restaurant rubble and the flesh of diners. The glass and shattered marble pierce his injured body, and the silence in his head abruptly ceases as horrifying screams penetrate his blood-clogged ears.

"Alpha five-one, this is Charlie five-two. What is your situation? Over."

Chapter Two

Port Hercules, Monaco

A close-knit secretive unit formed of ex-Jiaolong Commandos, known as the Sea Dragons, swims along the sandy bottom of Port Hercules, La Condamine. The target location is eighty meters from the *Golden Tiger*, a custom-built, one-hundred-foot Italian vessel registered under the name of Eddie Wu, a Chinese billionaire.

Twenty more meters to swim and then Xuedong, the point man, stops. Checking his GPS, he gives the signal toward the hull of the *Ischia*, seven meters above. The sun has yet to set, so the men keep themselves directly under the vessels to remain out of view. Above them, the sounds of Rachmaninoff, sweet laughter, and high heels clicking over the teak floor on the main deck are drowned out by mechanical noises emanating from the engine room deep inside the boat. As Zhang arrives at his position, he feels the hull and notes how the engine is purring steadily, faintly muffled by the noise coming from the LAR V Draeger rebreather equipment attached to his chest.

Zhang chose this advanced scuba gear as it will eliminate any air bubbles popping to the surface of the glistening calm water in the marina above, which would reveal their location. With the covert approach successful, the four-man team goes into action, applying skills they developed within the Chinese special forces. Assassinations off the coast of Indonesia, the Philippines, and Vietnam are these elite units' specialties; now they can add Monaco to their area of operations. Within seconds, the first two commandos take up position under the stern, at the port and starboard edge. While Zhang, the demolition expert and leader of this newly created death squad, organizes the attachment of a highly explosive device under the bow, Xuedong provides security twenty meters due east, toward the harbor entry. Concentrating on a low-frequency sonar device, he scans for any underwater countermeasure vehicles. VIPs with a price on their head employ their own security practices, particularly during anchor in locations such as Africa and South America because of kidnapping and piracy attacks. The Monaco Grand Prix weekend, however, presents an element of safety, one which the Sea Dragons have exploited. The target had been under surveillance for months by the Chinese military counterintelligence unit as he prepared his scientific research on quantum physics.

Now a weekend of hedonistic adventures provides a window of opportunity to eliminate this problem for the Ministry of State Security, with the bonus of causing chaos within the United Nations. The clear salt water of the marina is recorded at eighteen degrees Celsius, considered warm for the men who are all trained in Arctic warfare diving. Zhang sways back and forth, navigating the current before placing a suction cup on the hull, securing himself as he hurriedly makes his measurements. Careful attention in locating the most lethal area is paramount to his success. In doing so, he reminds himself that this part of the operation carries the most risk. Getting too close to the waterline and being spotted would cause the entire mission to fail. Zhang's breathing becomes more rapid now as he carefully attaches the bomb, positioning it correctly to ensure the direction of the blast will rip straight through the hull into the bedroom. He is confident his target will die from blast injuries because of the high amount of explosives he has packed.

Zhang's backup plan in the event the bomb does not wipe out the target immediately relies on location. To be overcome by injuries and powerless to move, he would then drown in the sinking vessel. Unlike in the street, where he may be lucky enough to survive and wait for medical attention before he bleeds out. Now the bomb is hot, so the ruthless commander of the kill team removes the suction cup and descends to the floor of the marina, where he awaits the others to regroup on his position. From the corner of Zhang's eye, a ghostly shape glides past him about four meters overhead. *A school of fish, perhaps, or maybe a shark!* Zhang had ignored to study the Mediterranean marine life from the intelligence-gathering unit. He now acknowledges that a mistake.

Prepared for a possible shark attack, he pulls a blade out from the sheath fixed on his thigh, then the Chinese special forces operator rolls onto his back and lies flat on the marina bed, providing a complete visual above. He rotates his head all around himself, checking for it. Nothing! He again glances at his wristwatch. Zhang knows his team should make their way back now. At last. Within ten seconds, two commandos come into view and settle into a defensive position as instructed, hand signals confirming all clear. Zhang waits another ten seconds, then ten more. *There is something wrong.* Xuedong Wang was his loyal second-in-command. He spent the previous five years conducting high-risk operations with this man throughout the South China Sea. A strong commando and someone who can handle himself in life-or-death situations. Zhang swims out without him. *The team cannot risk wasting time in the marina.* He gives the hand signal to move out, and the three men swim a meter above the sand back to the airlock hatch on the *Golden Tiger*. There is considerably more work to be done on this mission, and their leader knows he can't do it alone.

***

Zhang can visualize the overweight target walking the short distance from one of the many VIP areas ringing the Grand Prix track to the yacht, supported by a Victorian rosewood cane, buckling under his load. The obese academic will be on board within minutes. Greedy, pompous, and deceptive, the functional alcoholic will order his Scotch whisky from the bar. Then he will single out one of the new escorts, provided courtesy of a sleazy official from the International Council for Science. The intelligence provided earlier by the Chinese informant within the United Nations Security Council confirmed the target will again make his path to the master suite at the bow of the vessel, as he has done on preceding nights. After his moment of pleasure with the inexperienced girl, he will switch into the black-tie formal wear for the dinner reservation at Le Louis XV.

Zhang, needs to be ready also; a champion swimmer, he maintains a stable pace, mindful not to disturb the silt as he follows the route back to their vessel. *The device is set, and they briefed Xuedong on timings, his hard luck. This mission is too important to worry about one man,* Zhang reinforces his decision, a man committed to the plan.

The *Golden Tiger* had been commandeered weeks earlier in the Mediterranean by Zhang and the Chinese special forces naval commandos. The specialized team navigated the vessel to a dry dock in Italy where they strengthened the hull, then fitted a lockout hatch underneath and installed an underwater airlock, a feature used in submarines. This presented the raiding party with a covert hatch to come and go easily under the water's surface unnoticed to perform these types of missions. Zhang ensured the modest hospital and galley on board were well stocked with stores and with military encrypted satellite communications installed. After which, the team secured their berth in Monaco's expensive marina, two days before the prestigious and thrilling Formula One Grand Prix.

Thinking about the situation as he climbs into the airlock, Zhang's notorious temper rises from within. He suspects Xuedong's navigational wrist unit system failed badly, or his breathing system may have malfunctioned. *Tough luck.* Zhang will deal with Xuedong if he makes it back. Equipment maintenance is each man's priority. Failure is no excuse, he warned them.

The Chinese military's finest soldier, Zhang Xiaopeng, owns outright control over his team and its finances, equipment, and methods of operation. Choosing outright aggression and violence ensures any critics within the Ministry of State Security remain silent. Tall and lithe, though graced with granite-solid muscle, he developed his frame for operational requirements rather than visual aesthetics.

Removing his face mask and breathing system from his recently shaved face reveals his sharp cheekbones, epicanthic folds on his wide-set eyes, and a flat face, which ensured Zhang wouldn't be destined for a television career. The offspring of a lieutenant general, Zhang suffered a harsh childhood. Under the one-child policy, he was physically and psychologically abused. To make Zhang a dominant leader, his father felt that destroying his spirit every day was the foundation. What he created instead was a barbarous monster. The Chinese military quickly discovered that a combination of bright intellect and the gratification of taking lives without question was an asset to this secretive special forces unit. Considered a maniac by his associates, Zhang cared little as he stomped over them continually in his quest to be the toughest, putting the mission first, never failing to get results, and maintaining silence about his duty—that is what mattered most to the hierarchy in the Chinese military: secrecy. It wasn't a shock when he was singled out by General Zhou Kai, known as the Black Bear. The general rewarded him with the position of commander of a black ops unit, which he called the Gray Wolves, a modest but deadly special missions unit that specialized in assassinations. They were phenomenally successful in several high-risk operations month after month.

With the formation of this advanced kill team and with the endorsement of the Black Bear, Zhang is now afforded unrestrained authority and unfettered access to foreign and domestic targets. This unique breed of assassins will tolerate no one in bringing dishonor and failure back from missions. Neither will he support his men to perform on their own or modify a plan. The potential for spies to penetrate and cripple his objectives can never be underrated. Zhang wants those around him to know what he requires from his team. As a point, he has made the ultimate judgment. Zhang will execute Xuedong on the spot once he returns. *Obedience is key to survival.*

Chapter Three

Place du Casino, Monte Carlo

The distinctive roar of the high-powered Formula One cars signals the start of the race. All eyes are now fixated on the Monte Carlo–to–La Condamine circuit. Monaco's population has grown by one hundred thousand visitors for this annual contest. The millionaires, their entourages, and exclusive security details, arrived via private jets and luxury yachts from all corners of the planet.

Once they are nestled in their seats, decorated in gold and diamonds, sipping crisp champagne, and smoking thick cigars, Carver can carry out his mission. He steps out of his hotel suite and adjusts his earpiece, then dials the number allocated to a SIM card inserted in the first audio surveillance device. His concentration peaks while listening attentively to the faint voices against the backdrop of the race. Ending the call, he then activates the second device. Equipped with an exceptionally sensitive electret microphone, he can make out the drivers for the VIPs in the garage arguing about McLaren switching from Renault to the Mercedes-Benz engine.

As Carver waits patiently for the elevator, a door opens then closes softly to his left. From the corner of his eye, he assesses the potential threat. Drifting his hand aside from his waistband where a Sig Sauer P365 sits firmly, he lingers for a lady to cross the plush carpeted hallway. Now standing slightly behind him, Carver can revel in the essence of her fresh Carthusia perfume washing over his body. He steps away from the elevator and spins his body aside and motions for the lady to enter first, as a gentleman would do.

This act gives him an opportunity to carefully evaluate this attractive girl and the room from where she came. Once inside, Carver adjusts his Kilgour jacket as the doors close softly. The elevator music plays a loop of Valse Lente, properly fitting the situation. The girl then shifts her head lightly to face Carver and says, "*Je vous remercie*," the words ever so gentle. She smiles confidently as she acknowledges him, tenderly removing her eyes.

Carver notices a slight Italian accent and replies, "*Il piacere è tutto mio,"* my pleasure. The charming woman tilts her head. A saucy smile appears, then with a flick of her head, she turns around, facing the doors once again. With only a few centimeters between them, the scent of her freshly washed body is enticing.

Once they arrive on the ground level, Carver watches as the girl walks off across the marble floor toward the exit, causing a stir among the bellboys who stop and enjoy her beauty. Carver stays behind to hold the elevator doors open for an old woman, then strides out and proceeds through the luxurious lobby in the direction of the staff stairs heading down to the garage.

He enters the private car park by the stairs, which provides a little extra time to check the area. The elevator is the chauffeurs' and staff members' preferred means of access, those too lazy for the steep steps. Carver had studied previous intelligence on these hotels, although he made his plan ever since stepping foot inside the hotel.

With no one monitoring the stairs, he moves with poise and energy. His heart rate rises slightly as he immediately searches for and counts the valet drivers and car mechanics. Their faces are captivated by the Formula One race playing on a television, hoisted high on their meal room wall next to the amenities.

He then dials the third SIM number and, once connected, listens anxiously for any signs of movement or voices. The silence brings a smile to his face. *Perfect.* The car is clear, the personal driver now seated comfortably with his colleagues. Carver removes his Sig Sauer and holds it low, crouching down as he makes his way past the bays of Rolls-Royces, Bentleys, and Aston Martins until he finds the target vehicle. He then carries out a quick bomb inspection, quickly checking for how high the car rests on its axle, exposed electrical wires, fresh paint, a modified body shell, holes or damage under the car, any familiar odors of explosives, or irregular devices strapped to the frame. The search turns up nothing of interest, so he rings the first SIM number and listens to the men watching the race again. From his pocket, he extracts a copied keyless remote, which was provided by his technical team. When he clicks on the unlock button, it deactivates the internal and external lights on the car. Next, he clicks once more, which deactivates the alarm and unlocks the heavy doors. His firearm is pushed back into his waistband before he climbs into the rear seat.

Carver quickly does a thorough check and ensures the electret microphone, which was placed there by the British Special Reconnaissance Regiment (SRR) the day before, has not been tampered with. He removes a carbon steel surgical blade from within his French sleeve cuff and carefully slices along the seam under the headrest then peels the leather upward, exposing a soft sponge. He thinks back to his training on such procedures and applies the required force before making deep incisions to this weight of sponge. Carefully, he removes a portion and places it into his jacket, then fills the gap with a modified mobile phone. Once neatly tucked down, he pulls the supple leather covering back down. With a tube of glue, he squirts a line along the broken seams at the base of the headrest and clinches the leather in place until the cyanoacrylate sets. After a visual inspection around the car's seat for sponge dust or sliced threads, he quietly slides out of the car and gently presses the door closed and resets the lock. Retracing his steps back up to the lobby without drawing attention, Carver sucks in the adrenaline.

The British Special Air Service (SAS) operator, now working for the Secret Intelligence Service in a specialized unit, craves high-risk adventures. His normal pastimes relate to unknown women, extreme sports, and fine cigars. In no specific order. Matt Carver is the quintessential man one would find in fine cocktail bars from Paris to New York. Tall with slightly long, dark wavy hair brushed back with a quiff, he dresses in expertly tailored suits covering a defined V-shaped muscular back and huge chest from years of physical exercise and military operations. Always working the room with a wide, friendly smile covered in a neat stubble beard, his deep blue eyes capturing the attention of the opposite sex. An interesting, magnetic, and charismatic man, who, because of his past, gets invited to many formal dinner parties among the British high society.

Carver, with his masculine qualities, sharp intellect, and professional etiquette, can blend effortlessly into the London Stock Exchange, MOD Whitehall back offices, arms trading with Arabs in the Middle East, or as captain of the rugby team, leading his old university chums to yet another final. Born in London with both parents serving as diplomats meant his childhood was spent living overseas. This allowed Carver to study different languages, cultures, and traditions and to form interesting friendships as he grew into his late teens. Coming back to the United Kingdom, he attended Oxford. From there, he studied philosophy, politics, and economics. After lectures, his professor would talk about the Cold War and mysterious tales of adventure. Unbeknownst to Carver, his ethics of war teacher was on the SIS payroll, and Carver himself was being evaluated as suitable for recruitment into the intelligence world.

These sessions fanned embers of anticipation within him, so much so that he began reading extensively about the diverse styles of warfare. When sitting late every night in the Bodleian Library feeding his mind with military strategies, black operations, and intelligence work, this created adrenaline rushes he came to crave. Carver became desperate for adventure. As a leader of men, he realized what needed to be done. He wanted to be part of the elite, a band of brothers, and a force of strength. After handing in his final exam paper, he strode straight into an army recruitment center. Initially, the intel agencies were too slow on their approach.

Carver's outstanding military career covered twenty-five years, the last twenty in the Special Air Service. During that time, Carver's technical expertise, courage, academic curiosity, creativity, and capacity to think critically aroused the awareness of the gray men. Someone quickly organized an approach with an offer to join the men and women at the "circus." Back then, the well-established and experienced spies used the sobriquet for the military intelligence, section six. Carver gladly accepted, and from then onward, with a hand-selected group of reliable men, he carried out his duties in a covert paramilitary arm of the Secret Intelligence Service, used solely for "critical actions."

From time to time, this involved collective cooperation with the American Central Intelligence Agency (CIA), the German *Bundesnachrichtendienst* (BDN), and their French counterparts, the *Direction générale de la sécurité extérieure* (DGSE). Carver, however, cares little for partnerships or positions of influence in geopolitical circles. He now lives for the rush. No longer in the jungles of South America and the dust bowls of the Middle East, his new combat zones are now merged with distractions of the familiar smoke and mirrors from power-hungry politicians, drug barons, narcissistic billionaires, honey traps, and countless special forces operators and intelligence agents with various aliases backed up by their manicured legends.

His lifestyle fees to match his personal "legends" are afforded to him by the unaudited offshore accounts of "Foreign Consultant Fees," located in the Cayman Islands, Singapore, Switzerland, and Belize. Any opportunities Carver finds to grace the magnificent establishments throughout Europe or Asia, which are integral to a mission, he accepts readily. Over the years, this specialist has been less bothered about the target, but more about the thrill of the hunt. The skillful planning and tactical guidance from mission support are thrown out the window. Carver prefers an unorthodox attitude to warfare. The legalities surrounding the assassination of a crooked politician, terror leader, or high-rolling international drug lord are not his to fret about. A perfunctory level of confidence in the Intelligence and Security Committee (ISC), with the backing of Harrison Woodward, openly known as Harry, is not the finest insurance policy. But taking risks is part of Carver's career. Reducing the cost of damage and international headlines is a concern solely for the pipe-smoking, gin-drinking, ex-naval officer and crusty-old SIS chief, who signs paperwork with the letter *C*. For it is he who will feed the prime minister excuses as to why cities burn while bodies pile up at the hands of his most prized student.

***

The adrenaline coursing through his body during an operation is incomparable to anything he had been exposed to growing up. Tonight, Carver plans to relax in excellent company, surrounded by the deep sonorous and mellow notes of a cello, smooth scotch, and an earthy cigar. Exiting the lobby, he makes his way south through La Condamine, heading toward Saint Nicholas Cathedral.

On Rue des Remparts he cuts down an alleyway, then doubles back to check for a tail. He repeats this countersurveillance move a couple more times until he finds himself in the narrow streets well inside the old town, Monaco-Ville, known as *Le Rocher*. A small café allows him the convenience of grabbing an outside table to observe the area. Lights and shadows move around as the tourists stroll past with their cameras and phones held high. Ordering a dish of Stocafi without looking at the menu, he then orders a bottle of champagne to accompany the Monégasque favorite. Careful not to draw attention to the slight bulge of the Sig Sauer in his waistband, he carefully sits down and unfurls a napkin from the table over his lap. Removing the firearm discretely, he places it under the white linen and runs his fingers through his hair. His breathing feels relaxed, yet small beads of sweat have surfaced on his forehead. Despite Carver's powerful level of fitness, his heart rate has elevated slightly. The injuries sustained in the bombing at the Florence restaurant are only partially healed. He mops away the perspiration just as the waiter returns with a bottle of Laurent-Perrier in an ice bucket. Carver instead opens a bottle of sparkling water and grabs a handful of ice. Slugging it down, he thanks the waiter as she fills his glass. Suddenly, his heart skips a beat when he views a figure in the distance, dressed in a crisp pink blouse, navy shorts cut just above the knee, and a pair of brown flats, her blond hair secured in a knot bun.

"I didn't think you would take in the sights when there are better things to be doing in Monaco." Not one for small talk, Sarah approaches the table and plucks a menu from a passing waiter. Carver lazily uses his foot to push a chair outward, for this beautiful interruption to sit on, while looking beyond her to check for her security detail.

"A true romantic." With a feigned smile drawn across both their faces, Sarah takes the seat and pulls it tighter to Carver. To others, it appears they are a couple making up after a trivial quarrel. In reality, Sarah has appeared in the middle of an active operation to gather much-needed details. She leans in to fake a kiss and whispers softly into his ear. "We have lost contact with the bird."

Carver kisses her affectionately on the cheek as he mulls over the situation. Having no surveillance drone above following their operation is not a significant deal. He prefers not to have his bosses breathing down his neck. However, there is more to this than a basic systems failure. The SIS does not have technical errors; their research and high-quality build and maintenance of these multimillion-dollar machines are remarkable.

"That's very impressive, but you are reporting this to the wrong person. I'm no engineer, plus you know how much I hate those things." He looks around as Sarah scans the menu. "How long has it been down?"

"About one hour." Sarah beckons the waiter and directly places her order of bouillabaisse and a Coke. Sarah Fontaine, SIS director of operations for East Asia. Cambridge-educated and ten years in military intelligence. After coming out of language school with strong marks, she spent a couple of years working the embassies before being headhunted for her present role. Carver thought she would look more at home playing polo and attending the Royal Ascot races. But as things were, she was his boss, kind of. Harry had warned her to simply provide but don't advise or manage his best nonpolitical weapon.

"Unthinkable, a Coke, seriously." Carver shakes his head. "Some things never change. You embarrass me, Sarah." He takes a quiet breath after a slight chuckle, then asks a question that is bothering him. "What about the waiter in Florence?"

"Gabriella. Her name is Gabriella. Yeah, we made sure the family received the money. Of course, they would not understand who sent it. We can't do much better than that, wrong time and place."

Carver repeated the name *Gabriella* in his head. Of all those who died in the café that day, her death affected him more than any other. This was the first time an innocent, young, and beautiful face was taken away in front of him. Despite anger in his voice, Carver spoke softly, "Gabriella was in the right place. It was her place, and she had every right to be there. It was my fault. I should have taken him out."

"Have you completed all the paperwork for tonight?" Sarah, looking for a way to change topics, was referring to the current operation and soon-to-be assassination of one high-ranking Chinese diplomat.

Carver pours Sarah a glass of champagne, then takes a sip of his own. *It's a suspicious look for people not to be drinking alcohol in such an establishment,* he thinks. "Drink that, sit back, blend in, and look sexy."

Carver watches as a priest ambles past them, rosary beads in his right hand and an unlabeled bottle of wine in the other. The priest keeps his head down as he turns toward Rue de l'Eglise and disappears out of view. Carver checks his watch.

"I'll take that as a yes, clean and tidy, okay, there will be no eyes on you, street work only, I have assets at your disposal, let me know where to place them, and I'll provide you with their call signs ten minutes before the operation begins." Sarah maintains eye contact; however, she is reading other messages written all over Carver's face. She knows the Florence bombing affected him, and as that operation was done and dusted, there will be no mention of it again.

"That won't be necessary. The Chinese are all over town scoping the place. I don't want uninvited people coming to my party." Carver is now worried the street workers, or, in official words, the surveillance operators tailing the subject, will get caught up in his plans, or worse, get spotted.

As a Middle East expert, Carver now works on the Asian threats. He needed a change. Long hot days and nights in Lebanon, Syria, Iraq, and many other places had become repetitive. A kill job is the same, but the location is everything, and with a personal vendetta fueling his appetite, old Harry came through and provided him with the access to unleash his fury. Several safe houses and apartments around Europe are available to him, plus the locations of arms and various specialist equipment limit his contact with the technical staff within British intelligence. Carver, however, still stays in luxury hotels where possible. This way he can rub shoulders with his high-profile targets as they arrive in Europe to bribe politicians, carry out assassinations, conduct their industrial espionage, infiltrate universities, and weaken Western democracies. And as a bonus, he can spend time with Sarah, when, of course, she is not all wound up and busting his nuts about something.

Her bouillabaisse arrives, and the glass of Coke with ice. Carver sits contently, watching as she gently rips up pieces of bread to dip into the stew. The smell of saffron, fennel, and orange peel drift across his nose. A moment of romance just as quickly drifts away again as the scent of fresh gun oil rises from his lap. Carver questions if he will ever be capable of enjoying a romantic meal without a firearm close to hand. Not unless he takes out the Chinese assassin. The man who appears to him at night from the darkness, walking across various piazzas and boulevards, removing his sunglasses, and aiming a gun at his head. As usual, the gun never fires. The man walks closer and closer each night until Carver wakes up fumbling for his weapon, drenched in sweat.

Carver can't bear it any longer. He tries pressing Sarah again on him. "Anything further on our Florence friend? Address, workplace, married, girlfriend, sporting associations, favorite coffee shops. What do we have on him?"

"Not the time or the place, but trust me, as quickly as we have a profile, you will be the first to know it. Now, let's eat, as I have to get back to work."

With the food and drinks finished, Sarah leans over and gives Carver a decent kiss. "Take care and keep the comms on. We don't have eyes on you, however tracking works." Carver sat there with her sweet taste lingering in his mouth, watching his on-and-off-again girlfriend walking elegantly away. The slight bulge of a firearm under her blouse stirs him back to life. He checks the time once again on his expensive A. Lange & Söhne watch. With a private thank-you to the British taxpayer for furnishing him with the correct look, he then quickly pays the bill and walks off for his meeting with the priest.

Chapter Four

Langley, Virginia

A large black Chevrolet Suburban with tinted windows speeds along the George Washington Memorial Parkway, weaving through the traffic. Ten kilometers to their north, large unwelcoming gray slate clouds drift low in the sky. Winds have now whipped up into a frenzy, showing no patterns as fat droplets of rain smash into the windscreen. The driver manages the highway as he forces the revs higher on their approach toward Langley. His priority right now is to make good time, as the airplane his boss needs to board has been held on the runway for them. Since leaving the White House on Pennsylvania Avenue several minutes ago, his boss has not spoken a word.

The director of the Central Intelligence Agency, Cain Hoffmann, looks out over the Potomac River as he waits anxiously for his phone call to be answered. His third attempt in as many minutes. The encrypted phone has only one contact number saved. This belongs to his top operator in the field, Sean Flynn. His last known location, provided over twelve hours ago, was an eight-figure grid reference that placed him six miles off the coast of France.

The CIA paramilitary operations officer was tasked with yet another seek-and-destroy mission, this one more delicate than anything attempted before. Hoffmann knows how the Europeans will react if he is caught orchestrating an assassination. Without informing their counterparts, it will set their intelligence sharing and logistics cooperation back years.

Hoffmann rubs his temples gently, trying to ease the migraine that has gradually built up since he met with the president. The last time Flynn missed his check-in call was during an operation in Kandahar, Afghanistan, a few months ago. That time, Flynn was subject to a blue on blue, almost blown away by a drone strike in a friendly fire incident. The drone pilots mistook his maneuvers on the ground for a nearby Taliban commander. The sovereign city-state of Monaco is a world away from Flynn's usual hunting ground, which is the reason Hoffmann is concerned. Chasing the Chinese, if caught, has the potential to initiate World War III. Hoffmann slips the phone into the inside pocket of his dark navy suit, switching it for his official one. After a couple of rings, his call is answered. Hoffmann gives his orders, "Cancel London, I am going to Berlin. Make certain we have a team meeting me on my arrival."

"Of course, sir, I have a fresh rotation in place. They are presently being briefed. I'll have the men head straight to the airport." Liana Peviani is seated in the conference room deep inside the counterterrorism center at Langley. The room itself is a structure made of glass, raised off the floor much like a fish tank and surrounded by an electromagnetic field, available to merely a handful of people. The room is used solely for high-level meetings, which provide the safest assurance that their conversations are protected from eavesdropping.

"Sir, I am in the glass room with Olszewski. He wants to have a drink with you. It's about your meeting with the president." Val Olszewski is the director of national intelligence. A man that Hoffmann doesn't trust, yet legally the DNI serves as the head of the United States intelligence community, which means Hoffmann is answerable to Olszewski. In the eyes of Hoffmann, Olszewski is simply another obstacle for Flynn. His top CIA paramilitary operations officer is now taking part in Hoffmann's private special missions unit. Targeting the recent breed of Chinese special forces now operating completely outside their motherland. The black ops units comprise well-experienced tier-one operators, detached completely from their previous regiments.

These secretive units are what the DNI is unaware of, and within dark spaces, Hoffmann can disguise many secrets. Flynn is one of them. Seated in the speeding Chevy, Hoffmann slowly shakes his head; he recognizes only too well that politicians like Olszewski are extremely self-centered and too narcissistic to be in the business of supporting the brave, those that extend beyond the call of duty to do things only a few men can do. Controlled aggressive killers like Flynn need to be protected from others within the intelligence community. Then they will have the freedom to carry out their magic.

He will be a piece of dog shit stuck on your shoe, was how Hoffmann described Olszewski to Liana when she first came to work for him. *Keep him at arm's length and tell him nothing, and whatever you do, never mention Sean Flynn, okay?*

Hoffmann uses Liana, his charming and knowledgeable assistant, to handle as many meetings as feasible with this man. It is arduous work and lengthy hours for the new intelligence staffer. Her grades at Harvard and her postgraduate studies at Lomonosov Moscow State University highlighted great potential for a career within the intelligence community. Not least her expertise to deflect concerns and queries from sensitive topics, such as the operation currently being conducted in Monaco. A welcome addition to Hoffmann's small team looking after the likes of Flynn.

Stealing a glimpse at the speedometer, which reads ninety miles per hour, Hoffmann takes hold of the door handle to brace for the sweeping left turn down to the CIA building as he thinks of his response to Liana. During Hoffmann's career path, he brushed shoulders with Olszewski more than once, noticing how he constantly placed his goals ahead of his staff, many of which were fired by Olszewski. The asymmetric style of warfare required to fight the modern wars meant stepping outside of the rules of engagements and into the gray areas. Hoffmann knew Olszewski would use this to his advantage, citing various American rules of law. Flynn, who has made a life of working within the gray side, would be a man Olszewski would despise. And it was Hoffmann's job to ensure he will never catch wind of his existence. For this particular reason, he kept everyone on a need-to-know basis, much to their annoyance.

"Is Pope in the room?" Dallas Pope, the deputy director of the CIA, will again cover for Hoffmann. A star quarterback during his college time at Ohio State University who went off to West Point, Pope served as an officer in Iraq before joining the company. He was a patriotic man with strong morals, a veteran that put his country before personal political ambitions.

Liana speaks slowly and deliberately, something Hoffmann drilled into her in critical times, as it allowed both parties an extra moment to think. "He just stepped out but will be back in shortly. Something is up with the director of the National Reconnaissance Office. Between him and General Glassford of the NSA, he is quite busy."

"I don't care how busy he feels he is. Grab him now and have him deal with Olszewski. I have other matters to deal with. Olszewski only requires something sensational for the President's Daily Brief. I have already briefed the president, so I don't want to waste his time with the maggot. Just sort out Berlin and grab your bag and passport. You have made the team."

Liana doesn't know what to say. Her mind is racing. Her boyfriend has reservations for the Blues Alley jazz club tonight. She needs to take her puppy to the vet for vaccinations. Yoga is organized for this afternoon with her best friend, and she is to inspect a new apartment tomorrow morning. "Sorry, sir, you mean me? Do you want me to come to Berlin? Operational!"

Hoffmann is about to hang up when he hears the tail end of her reply. "Yes, congratulations. Hope you kept a bug-out bag handy, as they taught you in the Farm."

Bug-out bag handy! Shit. A mixture of fear and excitement runs through her veins, and now she struggles slightly to remain composed. She has a bag containing a change of clothes, a couple of burner phones, some US dollars and euros, makeup, and a modest first aid kit. None of the extra magazines, gun-cleaning kits, topographic maps, paracord, multi-tools, and all the other equipment that the CIA taught her about but she never dreamed she would actually need. "Yes, of course, sir. What time are we leaving?"

"Three minutes. We are pulling into the car park. Also, get my bag from the office and meet me downstairs." With that done, Hoffmann hangs up as the Chevy pulls sharply into his car space. The smell of burnt tire rubber, overused brake disks, and gas fumes from the hot exhaust highlight the pressure the vehicle was under.

Three minutes . . . goddam, three bloody minutes . . . Running out of the conference room, she spots Dallas Pope in the corridor on the phone. Excitedly she spins around and yells to him on her way past, "I'm going to Europe; deal with Olszewski for me, darling, so sorry."

The long reach of the CIA is enormous, extending to every corner of the globe. Partnerships with the Secret Intelligence Service are paramount to success throughout Europe because of the contacts the intelligence officers have made from its beginning in 1909. Now Hoffmann needs to call in some favors, or at least come clean on a few things with men he can trust.

He moves inside to a secure room with small, enclosed cubicles and grabs a bottle of water from a vending machine, then walks to the cubicle at the far end of the room. Once inside, he closes the door softly, then grabs the receiver and dials a number from memory.

"Harry, old chap, thank God to hear a friendly voice."

Chapter Five

La Condamine, Monaco

As Carver walks casually along Rue Emile de Loth, he stops briefly to look up when he hears a solitary yellow wagtail calling out in flight. Unable to catch a peek of the little bird, he sits down at a fountain and dips his hand into the water then runs his fingers across the back of his neck. The water cools his body nicely, and now freshened somewhat Carver continues his tourist stroll. When he reaches Rue de L'Eglise, he finds the stiff and rough oak door slightly ajar. Carver moves through it and instantly finds himself within a massive Roman Byzantine–style cathedral. He spots the priest on the gallery above the narthex and quietly ascends the steps to accompany him. The priest looked to be admiring the seven thousand pipes on the grand organ and makes no acknowledgement of Carver's presence. They stand in pure silence, which is something the two men do whenever they meet. It is their hidden speech. One of deeper reflection. Carver thinks he understands the spiritual part of it, but in reality he appears somewhat misplaced. Happy, though, in his own world, beside a man of wisdom and compassion. Perhaps, Carver considered the probability, the priest is seeking to propel purpose, faith, hope, or confidence in the tortured soul standing beside him. A few more profound thoughts run through Carver's mind just as the priest slowly turns and picks up his hand.

"*Sancte Michael Archangele, defende nos in proelio, contra nequitiam et insidias diaboli esto praesidium . . .*"

It was always the same: *Saint Michael the Archangel defend us in battle, be our protection against the wickedness and snares of the devil.* Carver slowly opens his eyes as the priest blesses him.

"*In nomine Patris, et Filii, et Spiritus Sancti. Amen.*" The priest raises one hand and draws the sign of the cross as he releases Carver's hand with the other, leaving behind a key. With a placid smile and a modest bow, the father turns and retreats toward a narrower side door. Carver, feeling energized, even though at peace, makes for a different exit from the one he first used to enter the cathedral. Once outside, he makes his way to Rue Colonel Bellando de Castro.

After conducting a countersurveillance move, Carver removes the key from his pocket and enters a door leading off from the street. Now he is under the watchful eye of a security camera that captures his every move. Once he climbs the steps to the top-floor apartment, he carefully opens the front door and listens for any signs of activity. Satisfied there is no one around, he moves inside and gently closes the door behind him.

Carver drops the key on the hallway table before entering the security alarm code. Once the code is accepted, he walks into the open area of his apartment across the decoratively patterned white Calacatta marble floor. Thick veins with gold hues run through the expensive thick slabs. Brass edgings border the rooms, highlighting the quality construction of Carver's two-bedroom residence. Crystal chandeliers hang down from high arched ceilings and wainscoting wall paneling containing silver and bronze finishes conveys a world of old-money success. Mirrors feature heavily, adding a sense of space, while green, orange, and purple wallpaper creates a vibrant display. Pierre Le-Tan artwork hangs in the corridor separating the living space and kitchen as Persian rugs provide refuge from the cold floor.

With the coffee maker now filled with his favorite Bazzara Dodicigrancru beans, Carver turns up the brightness and volume on the monitor linked to his camera system. This provides an unrestricted view of the street and internal access to his property. Moving to his office, under a painting by Andrea Vicentino, he pulls a piece of wood paneling from the wall. Setting it to the side, he then withdraws a large metal box from its position and places it in the center of the room.

Once the lid is removed, an olive-green military-grade plastic crate is exposed. A lifetime of memories is contained within. A smirk turns to a full grin as he reaches for his favorite sniper rifle. The Arctic Warfare Covert (AWC) rifle is complete with a Schmidt & Bender scope. An excellent weapon in urban environments. The short barrel with a folding stock allows easy transport while the detachable compressor reduces noise levels.

Injuries sustained in the Florence bombing meant he could not get up into Val Lumnezia in Switzerland to hone his accuracy on the weapon. One of the remotest areas in the European Alps is Carver's playground. He conducts regular excursions so he can maintain high standards in mountaineering techniques, while retaining his skill set in sniping without being interrupted. After this operation in Monaco, Carver plans for the weapon to get tested in all degrees of extreme climates. Next to this rifle sits a police scanner, which he removes and takes to his office desk. He connects it to the apartment's internal audio system before coming back to the kitchen to collect his coffee.

On the kitchen counter lay several packages, graciously delivered by the priest hours earlier. The relationship between Carver and the Catholic church is complicated, roughly based on the good fighting evil. Modern weapons systems and assorted hardware, logistics, and intelligence are the tools of his trade. To ensure he has access, SIS supplies him with the crucial equipment and specialized workforce, although Carver prefers to establish his own networks and reliable technical resources without paper trails. Donations to the needy and diverse security work provided by Carver, throughout South America, Africa, and Southeast Asia, support the Catholic church in managing their missionary work in relative safety while offering himself access to their international networks.

Once he takes a sip of the strong-bodied coffee, he then slices through the parcel tape with a carving knife, dumping the contents on the counter. Carver charges the new burner phone and sets the speed dial to the phone numbers of the SIM cards that are assigned to the audio devices back in the private car park of his target's hotel. Unwrapping another parcel, Carver finds the keys to a car and a hotel room pass card, a small one-hundred-milliliter bottle of Amouage perfume containing a knockout chemical, just in case, and fake security passes from an engineering company. A GPS locator is in the larger parcel, complete with several trackers, for attaching under cars and waterborne vessels, plus sophisticated photography equipment. All directly taken from the stockpiles of the Special Reconnaissance Regiment at RHQ Credenhill, Hereford.

Satisfied that they have delivered his list of goodies, he quickly strips and cleans his firearm. Carver glances up every so often at the surveillance monitor, which is showing several pedestrians ambling along the street outside. Among them, he notices a couple meandering arm in arm, with an unhealthy interest in his front door and pink façade of his building. He immediately takes a screenshot before they pass out of view, adding it to the hard drive of various people shuffling past his apartment.

When Carver notices a pattern or similarities, he typically delivers the images to the SIS for analysis. On purchasing the accommodation, he carried out extensive security additions, hindered slightly because of the tough heritage laws in Monaco. The heavy walls and bulletproof windows and blast-resistant doors give him an obvious feeling of safety. However, Carver understands the fact that foreign actors could easily hack various government agencies to obtain his identity and address.

Before going out for the evening, Carver has a shower and then packs clothes, GPS trackers, and the collapsed rifle into a black canvas bag. He adjusts the timer settings on various lights, the radio, and the television to turn on and off at different times, then throws the rubbish out. Back inside, he takes a mental note of settling the maid's monthly wage, goes through the contents of the fridge, switches his A. Lange & Söhne watch for a Garmin, then eventually sets the security alarm just before he leaves his apartment.

Leaving via the back exit, Carver quickly makes his approach to the supplied car parked in a cul-de-sac off Avenue Saint-Martin. A few minutes' drive takes him to a lofty vantage point overlooking Port Hercules. Once he parks the car at Chemin des Pêcheurs and pedestrians have slipped out of view, Carver heads into bushland on Avenue de la Porte Neuve. Previously, he had studied this area for a spot overlooking the marina in the event a backup plan is needed. More notably, he also has a commanding view into the hotel room his target is vacationing in. A shot from this distance would be comfortable for Carver. Although his plan is not just to deliver a statement; he wants to divert the suspicion far from the desks of SIS. To use explosives will appear more like the style of the Mafia or a strike by either Mossad or the Russians.

Carver moves into a concealed position by gently crawling through the bushes, making no noise and being mindful not to break any branches. After completing his reconnaissance in the observation post, he will ensure no traces of his presence. No footprints, snapped twigs, flattened grass, or other telling signs of activity. The only thing he cannot hide from is his thermal signature. For this reason, Carver plans to stay here for a limited period. Enough time to get eyes on and play witness to this bloodshed. Removing the rifle from the bag, he attaches the stock and unfolds the bipod; a small mesh cover is placed accurately over the scope to eliminate any reflection to potential observers who may look up in his direction and get alerted by the sunlight or other artificial light shining off his glass scope. Carver decided earlier that the rifle will serve two purposes on this rare evening. Primarily as a backup in the event that the target sits in the passenger seat, avoiding the device in the car's headrest. Or in case of a failure of the mobile phone circuitry or Monaco's Telecom service frequency, and likewise the possibility of HQ requiring someone else taken out at short notice. The last thing Carver wants is to be running around town getting a weapon and finding a position to eliminate another Chinese spy. Especially on this weekend when there are copious amounts of champagne, oysters, and beautiful women to share it with.

Stretching out into the prone position, Carver lies on the ground and spreads his legs wide with the inside of his feet flat on the ground. Nearly all of his body is in contact with the earth, producing a stable platform. Next, he settles the weapon in a position where the barrel has an unobstructed line of sight through the vegetation toward the hotel. Next, he makes minor adjustments of his body position to adopt a consecutive line with the butt of the weapon securely on his right shoulder. He places the crosshair of the scope onto the hotel and counts along the row of windows from left to right, then up to the correct floor. From here, he makes the basic elevation and windage adjustments. Turning the turrets on the scope, he ensures the bullet's point of impact will be the same as his point of aim. With the scope focused and his weapon zeroed to the hotel room, he checks all three windows of his target's suite. All curtains and windows closed, Carver now shifts his attention down to the street level. Staring through the scope, he examines the crowds mingling, some drinking, others smoking, all enjoying the warm sun on their faces as he lays in the dirt with insects crawling all over his body, checking him out. Slowly moving his hand into the bag, careful not to disturb the bushes, he pulls out his phone and inserts the earpiece into position. Once he dials the numbers allocated to the microphone devices, he will have live intel on the movement of his target.

Carver glances down and taps the dial button. A slight adjustment of the volume is made before resuming good eye position behind the scope. The microphone device automatically connects, which provides Carver with audio from inside the vehicle. Silence. Another glance to check the time on his Garmin; he estimates another fifteen or twenty minutes and the target should take off for his meeting with a British subject. Someone who will be dealt with appropriately and in a more legalized manner in a court of law. A long stretch in prison will be his destiny instead of getting murdered on foreign soil for auctioning off state secrets to the Chinese government.

Nothing surprising in this by foreign powers, thought Carver, but the extent of their activities was rubbing him the wrong way. More so was the annoyance of feeble administrations in the past who were reluctant to strike back. Beijing is offering huge economic favors to those that seek to reinforce "partnerships." Industrial espionage is a cancer to the UK and the Western world, and when the Communists started gaining access to defense technology, it was time for the military to lead the response. No longer could the politicians ensure the safety of the British population, and no longer could the people sit back as one powerful country grows stronger each day by plundering their universities, defense, and research facilities. Over the years, corruption saturated those in power on an unprecedented level. Spies are provided with jobs in British firms and delegation teams, with their financial packages, and ensured unfettered access to top-secret material, which China then uses to replicate or to create defensive capabilities of the British and American technology. The UK found themselves unbalanced on the back foot. As throughout history, the intelligence agency calls for men such as Carver to end it. To seek and destroy those in control of the spies, to eliminate the threat and reset Western powers.

Before SIS handed the responsibility over to the spec ops unit, they were presented with evidence containing phone taps and electronic transfers of money into accounts. The data transfers of secret information back to Beijing had been intercepted by the Government Communications Headquarters (GCHQ). Plus covert surveillance on several high-ranking men and women from the Chinese Communist Party, during their numerous trips to London on secret meetings with diverse professionals. Describing themselves as partnerships under various front organizations, these parties could amass decades of research and designs, allowing their country to leapfrog over all the United Kingdom, European Union, and American technology.

Carver could not wait to put a few of these men and women to sleep. He felt he owed it to his country. After years of engaging in wars so that foreign nations could live in harmony with their neighbors, he finally felt he was doing something greater to safeguard the future of Western democracy.

Carver keeps the live audio running from within the target vehicle so he can now concentrate on the hotel. After completing a sweep of the three hotel windows, he quickly drops his aim down to the street level and checks the guests going in and out. He searches for a packet of between six to eight men, all business associates of the target. A weekend in Monaco at the Grand Prix, flights, five-star accommodations plus an open bar, courtesy of the "United European and Chinese Friendship Department." Just one group from a multitude of front organizations run by the Chinese Ministry of State Security. Carver recalls information from a top-secret dossier provided from a joint investigation by the CIA and SIS of their Chinese counterpart agency named the 'Intelligence Bureau of the Joint Staff of the Central Military Commission.' The names and faces of which he memorized, locked away in his head, like a deck of playing cards, each face being revealed then covered by the next face. One of his many talents was reading cards, a skill he expects to put to work once his target sits in the rear seat to receive the justice. When the target is settled, Carver will dial the memorized number of the mobile phone hooked up to the explosive device to trigger it. He will realize instantly if the device detonates, as the audio will be lost. The sound of police and ambulance sirens will be heard distinctly from his position. Once this develops, Carver will pack up and hit the casino. The slight matter of stashing his weapon and grabbing a shower and a fresh change of clothes will happen with speed.

Carver's breathing has now slowed. The crosshair moves up and down ever so slightly with the tempo of his lungs. If or when he's required to pull the trigger, he will do so when he fully exhales within the rest period, with an empty lung, just before inhaling. The crosshair will rest perfectly on the target long enough for the finger to develop a delicate squeeze on the trigger. Once the weapon fires, Carver will follow through with the finger squeezing on the trigger before releasing it gently forward. By the time Carver slides another round into the chamber, the bullet will have found its target and a judgment will be made to deliver another shot or to gather up and move.

With no spotter, Carver checks the wind speed himself, using the flags and sails on the yachts berthed in the harbor below. As his bullet will pass over the harbor a few feet above their masts, he can calculate the wind drift adjustments easily. The wind won't be a factor. The distance is within the operating capability of the Urban-designed sniper rifle. The shorter barrel limits the long-range accuracy. Tonight, if required, to take a shot into the target's room, through the glass, will not be simple, but is well within Carver's area of expertise. Rotating through his checklist, he focuses on the far left of the three windows. This is the dining room, according to the intelligence brief, and is where the target would be expected to have a few drinks while enjoying the view of the harbor in the evening. The Schmidt & Bender scope attached to the rifle allows an expanded view, capturing all windows. As Carver maintains strict concentration, a muffled bang roars out from the harbor. Through his left eye, he immediately spots a yacht rocking uncontrollably, with people falling overboard.

The pressure of the explosion causes surface ripples that gradually broaden outward. Carver has observed, heard, and felt the blast waves from enough explosions on land and underwater to appreciate that this was no engine failure or a cooking accident in the galley. With his eye on the scope, he quickly scans the yacht and notes the name *Ischia.* He spots those on board now moving frantically to escape as the vessel takes on water and sinks slowly. Some men on the neighboring yacht throw life buoys toward the passengers in the water. Smoke has developed, growing from the galley. Carver adjusts his weapon back to the hotel and catches sight of a group of men running down the street. His target is being protected. The members of the security detail on either side of the target have their shooting hands placed just inside their jackets. Hands on their weapons. The lead man clears the bystanders on the footpath, making room for their VIP to pass while the other close protection officer looks to be making a call. Carver keeps the crosshair on the target as he runs down the street. If the target's security detail changes their escape plan and uses a backup car to take off from the street, Carver will have to take the shot. He has a clear line of sight, about eighty meters of road before it sweeps off to the left.

He flexes his trigger finger and prepares to shoot as a car pulls up. Waiting patiently, Carver hopes he will not have to take the shot. The report from his weapon will not be significant, although a rapid extraction from his observation post to the cache location for his weapon and clothes will not be smooth. He isn't keen on walking around with a sniper rifle after using it, specifically in his own backyard.

His life in Monaco and surrounding areas has been pleasurable. He prefers to operate in Asia, Africa, and the Middle East where he doesn't have to worry so much about being traced, as his travel patterns are well disguised. Using bombs provides him with a satisfying degree of separation, and as an expert assassin for the secret services, he chooses his methods carefully. The British technical support team hacked the security cameras of his hotel, allowing him to walk into areas while the technicians paused all recordings of his activity. The same happened with Monaco's live traffic cameras and webcams. Carver welcomes this level of protection, which is paramount in covering his operations. Although he was advised by SIS not to request camera blackouts for long periods, Carver wanted to use what he could to his advantage. Activating the bomb when he was within a casino or another well-heeled establishment would ensure he was covered from being a suspect. From his observations of the target, Carver's luck looks to be holding. The security detail is now walking toward the hotel entrance, disappearing inside toward the grand lobby, just as Carver hears through the static in his earpiece.

"Copy that, the car is ready, car park clear," said one of the security guards.

Splendid news. Carver's excitement intensifies. He can just about make out the voice of the driver speaking from outside the vehicle as they prepare to extract the target. He pushes the earpiece deeper into his ear and listens to the sound of the car door opening and the soft sound of leather being squashed as the driver takes his seat in the luxurious and customized BMW 7 Series. Carver visualizes the driver, starting the engine and rolling the car out into the waiting bay area next to the elevator doors in the hotel's basement car park.

Under the cover of thick scrub, the smell of salt water mixed with explosive chemicals enters Carver's lungs from the harbor below. The red and blue lights, complete with their various sirens of the emergency services half a kilometer away, attract the attention of all. Armed police, along with the fire department and paramedics, work methodically to treat and haul away the injured. Meanwhile, Carver maneuvers the barrel of the rifle toward the hotel car park street exit, listening intently to the audio from inside the car. He makes out the relaxed breathing of the driver, then the distinctive sound of him racking the slide, chambering a round inside his firearm. Suddenly he can hear loud footsteps, then the car doors being ripped open. The beeping sound of other cars unlocking rings out in the background. Carver's adrenaline pumps heavily.

He needs to be certain that the person who entered the car is his target. Without voice recognition software, he has to use his expert judgement. Tonight's operation, like many of Carver's ops, is without approval or knowledge of the foreign secretary, the Joint Intelligence Committee, and all the various ministers. Once he pulls the trigger or flips the switch on a bomb, the British can deny all knowledge. If Carver gets arrested, there is no accountability. His trust in the usual departments would bear no fruit. Only the prime minister and Harry Woodward can assist. Which, if required to, would end his career in this covert black world. Carver listens for any confirmation of his target, anything.

"*Ni hao ma?*" The target, an obnoxious, short, and stocky Chinese beetle-like man with thick glasses, a flat nose, and sunspots on his balding head has spoken. Carver listens to the phone call and the purr of the high-powered engine of the BMW. He notes the increase in the revs as the car ascends from the basement. *That's enough.* Carver is content with his verification. He grabs the phone and speed dials the mobile embedded in the headrest. *What's the worst that can happen?* he asks himself as it makes the connection. The static noise proves success in the device coming from his earpiece as the audio device has been blown to pieces inside the BMW. Carver rapidly packs away his rifle and moves out of his observation post. He gently pulls up some of the undergrowth with his fingers, removing signs of the flat area where he was laying. Crouched and concealed among the shrubs where they meet the street, he waits for a couple of minutes for any signs of activity. Satisfied there are no pedestrians nearby, he then casually walks out toward his car.

A short drive later, Carver arrives at Sentier du Bord de Mer off Avenue Marquet, a remote car park where he stashes his weapon for pickup by the priest. Removing the SIM cards, he takes a lighter and burns them on the ground, then throws the melted plastic over the rocks into the water. He then changes into fresh clothes and adds a splash of Kilian cologne to cover any traces of the fumes from the burnt plastic. His car is now clean of any evidence, allowing him to make the short drive back over the Monégasque–French open border without worry. As the emergency services deal with two unexplained explosions on the biggest weekend of the year, Carver's only interest is a night at the casinos with good company, which will round off a hard day's work. Satisfied with today's events, he figures his briefing will wait until tomorrow morning. He will wait until then to learn more about the unsettling bomb in the yacht. He suspects Israelis; if so, there won't be much intel. Tonight, though, is all about the Casino de Monte-Carlo. Carver considers a night of Dom Pérignon if Sarah shows up. If not, it will be glasses of Balvenie single malt, a tasty Davidoff cigar, and some card counting at the blackjack table. The night is only beginning.

Chapter Six

Port Hercules, Monaco

The open sundeck provides the guests on the *Golden Tiger* with a spectacular view of Monaco in all its glory. The rising sun appearing over the horizon casts long shadows across the harbor and surrounding streets as the sixty-two-meter-high monolith, known as the Rocher de Monaco, soaks up the bright orange glow. The police keep an enormous crowd of onlookers back from the area as the emergency services wait to begin the clean-up operation. The fire department is busy assessing damage to the pier while the detectives shuffle around trying to make sense of what happened last night. Police continue filling their notebooks with witness statements while their tactical scuba divers comb the sandy bay looking for bodies and evidence linked to the bombing. A salvage team slowly makes their way across the water with a large pontoon crane to remove the sunken *Ischia* once the permits have been signed.

Zhang, sporting a pair of dark sunglasses, barefoot and dressed in a white bathrobe, is relaxing with another cigarette to accompany his glass of oolong tea. As he signals the attention of a stewardess, he looks on with amusement, enjoying the fuss and dedication of those involved in the spectacle being played out across the harbor. He pays particular attention to the television network vans that have arrived, watching how the technicians quickly extend their antennas and satellite dishes while the correspondents apply makeup between sips of coffee from takeaway cups. It's a race between Deutsche Welle TV, France 24, and BFM TV. He grabs the remote and turns on the small flat-screen television, selecting the same network as the one parked on Avenue J. F. Kennedy. The rolling news ticker at the bottom of the screen reads: "Bombing in Monaco considered an act of terrorism." A grin slowly emerges across Zhang's face as the cameras show a row of bodies covered with white sheets getting strapped to trolleys and prepared to be loaded into the backs of ambulances. The death toll stands at seven, with an unconfirmed number of persons reported missing.

The young, blue-eyed, blond-haired stewardess arrives by his side with a platter of boudin noir, *jambon de l'Ardéche,* and *bûche de chèvre*, with some freshly baked *brasillé* complemented with *miel des Cévennes* and freshly sliced apples. The pig blood sausage, dry-cured ham, goat cheese, and sweet pastry did nothing for his appetite. In fact, it looked like leftovers to him. If it wasn't in a bowl of noodles, he wasn't having it. Waving her away like a foul smell, he turns his attention back to the television. A news reporter crosses to a colleague who was reporting from a hotel around the corner. This is the location of a second bomb attack. In bright red letters, the words "Police suspect the two attacks are linked" flash across the bottom of the screen. Zhang's grin quickly disappears. He turns up the volume to listen to any information that may be of importance. Shortly, he will attend a briefing with his boss from the Ministry of State Security, and he wants to have full knowledge of all the carnage in Monaco.

Zhang was woken from his sleep by the early-morning message. The order was simple. Remain on the boat out of view and prepare an action plan. This left him fuming, as he really needs to be on the streets to find the real perpetrator who was behind the other bombing. Not only has one of his unit members disappeared, but Zhang was here in Monaco when this Chinese VIP was executed. Zhang's job is to use the intelligence offered to him to locate the threats in Europe, safeguard their people, and eliminate the enemy. He can feel his stomach tightening as the cursed weight of failure threatens to derail his very existence. Thinking back to his childhood and how his father would ridicule him for the slightest wrongdoing sickens him. Far from his hometown, that same feeling is squeezing the wind out of his lungs as he fights to control his breathing. Beads of sweat form on his forehead as he paces on the deck. Zhang tries hard never to visit the memories of his past for fear of self-destruction. Glancing around at the hotel windows surrounding him, he has an uneasy feeling. After flicking his cigarette into the harbor water, he sets down his empty glass of tea and hurries down to the lower deck. Zhang grabs a pile of invoices that were left clipped together in the admin tray by the service crew. Removing them from their paper clip, he selects one with the familiar red-and-green lettering of the *Casino supermarché*. He slides onto a seat and harnesses the pent-up anger within himself and turns this feeling into one of determination. With deep concentration, he compiles a list of equipment he will require. *The first phase of this next operation is going to get messy.* Alone and comfortably immersed in the task at hand, he silently talks to himself as his scribbling intensifies. Zhang can feel his confidence rising. *Many fat pigs are going to pay for this.*

***

Eddie Wu was not forewarned the minister of state security was boarding his yacht. When he hears the footsteps on the gangway, he turns around to see the man himself. Eddie's heart almost stops. A self-made billionaire, he wants nothing to do with China. Though he'd been happy to use their factories, cheap labor, straightforward business arrangements, and accessible logistics to kick-start his road to unimaginable wealth. Originally, his businesses dealt with supplying Europe with cheap goods, from electronics to clothing, then he made bold moves into software development. The big money was in video games, ripping off the US by copying their software and selling it into China. Goods come out and software goes back in. It was a win-win deal. So far, he'd evaded the attention of the extended members of the Chinese Communist Party, as those that mattered were well rewarded with substantial deposits into their Swiss bank accounts every month. As the morning sun warms Eddie's thick neck, he feels far from calm. Other players have entered the arena, and he fears his luck has run out. With a hesitant step forward, he reaches out his hand to meet this unwelcomed intruder. "Mr. Lin, it is my utmost pleasure to have you aboard my boat."

Grabbing Eddie's fat hand, Danny Lin gives a limp handshake. Years of sitting behind a desk have made his thin muscles soft and weak. "Thank you kindly. I judge from the flat expression you were not expecting me, and for that, I apologize." Pointing over his shoulders toward his security team, he continues, "My staff arrange things, and because of security protocols maybe they thought it was best left for myself to speak to you directly; however, I was time-pressed this morning, what with the murder of a good friend of mine only a few hundred meters from here. I'm sure you are aware of that!"

The last conversation Eddie wants is one of bombings, particularly as his undesirable guest downstairs may have been involved in one of them. He avoids Zhang like the plague, hoping any minute he and his men will leave. "I learned from the news there was a terrorist attack. I heard the explosion on that boat across the harbor." Eddie flicked a switch on the table, alerting the galley crew to bring food and drinks. "Terrible, really, we are all saddened, not something you would expect in a place like this. Actually, we are planning to move out later this morning once we get supplies on board."

Danny Lin isn't listening; he doesn't have to. He will decide what cooperation people can provide and what will happen if they fail to do so. As head of the Ministry of State Security, the MSS, his power is something unimaginable to the standard civilian. Danny considers Fat Eddie, who stands uncomfortably before him, shifting his weight from one foot to the other, to be someone who should know his place in the pecking order. Danny makes himself at home. Removing his suit jacket and placing it neatly over a white leather barstool, he then picks up a remote control and switches off the television, then turns his back toward Eddie to observe the clean-up operation taking place.

Eddie is lost for words, unsure what his involvement has anything to do with the MSS. He thanks God when he sees the stewardesses coming up with a tray of drinks. The two Swedish girls have no idea who these new arrivals are or their intentions, so they carry on as normal, setting down glasses and preparing the table for breakfast. It is common for Eddie to eat each time new guests arrive; this is nothing surprising. What is surprising to the girls is that the six men who don't speak split up, with two staying at the stern, two at the bow, and the port and starboard being manned by the remaining two. Surrounded by what look like characters from a John Woo movie, the girls find the atmosphere somewhat disturbing. Last night was frightful for them, and now they feel uneasy with weird-looking men dressed like those who shop at a charity store. The matching and poorly fitted dark suits, complete with cheap black sunglasses and plastic shoes, provide a style severely out of place in Monaco. Isabella, the more experienced of the two stewardesses, looks over at Eddie for approval of her intentions. *The yacht crew agency mentioned nothing about tending to the needs of tacky Chinese gangsters when I was recruited at the beginning of the season!* Her mind races. Eddie catches her staring at him, and with a nod of his head, Isabella carries on preparing the table.

"This is what will occur." Danny Lin speaks without turning. "This boat will remain here. It will stay until I give you permission to leave. Is that clear?"

"Yes, of course, Mr Lin. I didn't mean I would move out without consulting you. I mean, I was only thinking there could be other attacks, I just thought . . ."

Danny turns. With his hand raised and finger pointing at Eddie, he abruptly cuts him off mid-sentence. "No, Eddie, no . . . who told you to think?"

Eddie can feel a lump gathering in his throat. Determined not to show fear, he averts his gaze and looks instead at the girls working quickly. The cutest one of the two, the younger blonde wearing pink bike shorts and a white blouse tied above the waist, brings from the galley a tray of freshly cut fruit and lays it on the table.

Danny moves over and picks up a piece of watermelon from the tray. "Give us peace, you two." Stuffing it into his mouth, he moves to the coffeepot and pours himself a glass. Eddie, trying to remain composed, opens a bottle of San Pellegrino sparkling water and takes a mouthful.

Danny is much shorter than Eddie, slim, with no shoulders, a pencil neck, and balding at the front. Despite this lack of visual strength and a limited ability to present as an intimidating figure, he makes up for it with his deep voice and dark, piercing eyes on top of a hooked nose. Once the girls leave them alone, Danny wipes his mouth with a napkin and takes a seat at the table. "I came here today to make sure you are doing all you can to help the Ministry of State Security."

Eddie pulls out a chair and sits down, pouring his bottle of water into a glass tumbler as he does so. "Yes, of course, it is my duty to help."

"Don't interrupt me." Danny squeezes a piece of lime over the fruit platter, taking his time before he speaks again, making Eddie sit there quietly until spoken to, a method he uses to show control. "Your guest who joined this fine vessel a few days ago will need your assistance. You will provide him with accommodation, a car, cash, and whatever else he needs. He works directly for me, which means you work directly under us all. Are you clear on that?"

Under the table and throughout the boat, Eddie has listening devices installed by a security firm working out of London. Mainly to listen to the secret conversations of his well-connected business associates that he invites on board at every opportunity. Despite the evidence collected from the table this morning, there is nothing he can do. The MSS will put him in a Chinese prison if they even suspected a hint of disobedience. "Certainly, anything he wants, I will be happy to deliver."

"And the rest of your guests, what have you done with them?" Danny slides a cigarette out of a pack and lightly drums the tip on the table, a behavior that Eddie finds extremely annoying.

He thinks back to the dreadful night when Zhang and a small team of special forces boarded his vessel under cover of darkness. The shock of a dark figure standing over his bed, a gun pointed at his head, is something Eddie will never forget. Forced to comply with their demands, they ordered him to have the captain set a course for Marina di Carrara, Central Italy. Embarrassed yet full of rage, he put on a display of deep regret when he announced to his guests over breakfast that the yacht had developed engine issues and would therefore be out of service once in port. Offering to pay for flight tickets to destinations of their choice, Eddie arranged for limousines to pick up his three hugely disappointed business partners when they arrived at Carrara.

For the next few days, he was stuck with Zhang and his four-man team. Scoundrels who gave nothing away about their plans. No small talk, no apologies, no manners. Eddie's staff, however, were amazing. Captain François, in particular, simply shrugged his shoulders when told of the change of plans. The unpleasant guests on board who were not like anyone he'd catered to before did little to upset the man.

François, the wise man, asked no questions. He was at the end of his working career and was simply biding his time for retirement. Ex-French navy, now a long-term employee of the private sector, a red-faced, white-scruffy-haired, Negrita rum–drinking joker and a terrible golfer. Eddie knew once they all arrived in port, François would entertain them by hitting the bars and golf courses, in no particular order. The two cute stewardesses from the yacht agency, along with the deckhands, engineers, chefs, and various others, were all looking forward to a break from their normal duties. Generous sums of money were handed to each of them by Eddie, who booked their accommodations in Hotel Rondine, a beautiful location overlooking the Tyrrhenian Sea.

When Eddie found out about the plan to fit an escape trunk under his boat, he was outraged. *No sane person would destroy the structural integrity of a magnificent yacht for this reason.* After saying this to Zhang at the shipyard, the Chinese special forces goon quickly produced a knife and had the blade resting under Eddie's throat before he realized what was happening. Zhang slowly slid the metal blade across Eddie's skin, making a thin red cut.

Subconsciously, Eddie lifts his hand and feels the lightly formed scar with his fingertips before explaining to his new enemy about the men on board.

"Good work, Mr. Wu, you will be well compensated, and of course I will officially recognize your assistance in state affairs." An attempt to be more businesslike falls on Eddie's deaf ears. He knows only too well what his position is within the Chinese Communist Party. A low-level pawn, one that can be sacrificed in a power play, so others can grab the glory.

Danny finally lights his cigarette. Holding it at the very tips of his fingers, he blows the first puff of smoke across his shoulder. Then he remembers the commotion from across the harbor. Standing up with his head held high, he marches across the deck to get a better view. "Zhang, Mr. Wu! I believe he is downstairs. Please fetch him for me. I have a lot to discuss."

Chapter Seven

Bordighera, Italy

Two black Audis, each filled with three men, roll to a stop beside each other in a car park off Piazza del Capo. Their orders are simple: rendezvous with Sean Flynn and provide support. The passenger in the lead vehicle gets out and stretches his legs. Only two days ago, he was operating in the streets of Jalalabad, Afghanistan. After receiving a brief call via his satellite phone, Jackson and his men were flown to Germany, then onward to Italy, where they met a local CIA officer. Not much was known about this European operation. The CIA man in charge of their movements was cagier than any other spook he normally worked with. *This ain't no place for Taliban. What the hell are we doing here?* Jackson was born for adventure and excitement.

Now standing in this coastal town in Italy, he feels far from satisfied. Searching around for a café, he thinks back to previous missions he and Flynn were lucky to survive. Despite having the utmost respect for his fellow paramilitary operations officer, Jackson will be extremely pissed if Flynn took him off the battlefield to protect some limp-wristed, obnoxious, narcissistic, and overpaid head of state on a goodwill visit to some shithole. Jackson feels a slight change in the morning breeze, a soothing warmth. He no longer misses this sensation. His body is used to the harsh climate of Afghanistan. However, one thing he misses is the smell of the ocean. Only meters from the car park, where he can hear the waves breaking over the pebbles next to the coastal road, he breathes in the fresh salty air and allows himself a moment of civilian life.

"You don't get any prettier in your old age."

Briefly startled, Jackson doesn't notice Flynn walking up from behind him. He can only shake his head as he looks at the muscled-up figure walking out of the shrubs that separated the car park from Corso Francesco Rossi. The two men embrace as if they scored a winning touchdown at the Super Bowl.

"The last I heard of you, you took off with some warlord's cash across the Wakhan Corridor," says Jackson, who holds Flynn by the shoulders at arm's reach so he can get a good look at the CIA legend.

Flynn laughs hard, his square jaw displaying bright white teeth. He has a short neck with a head covered in wavy blond hair. Standing at six three, his gigantic frame holds thick solid muscles designed for hard work. Before joining the military, he was on a pro surfing contract with Quicksilver. Throughout his career, he still maintained the easy, carefree style. A surfboard was never far out of reach when around water.

"Well, you shouldn't listen to gossip, especially when it's about bags of dope money. It's great to see you, man.

You can thank me later over a beer for taking you away from the cold mountains."

Jackson's eyes light up. "I enjoyed that place, away from all Langley bullshit."

Jackson turns and walks Flynn toward the closest Audi.

"We haven't been told jack shit, by the way. Your mate dropped us these two vehicles, which we gave a quick inspection of, and a box of gear I guess you ordered."

Flynn takes a few seconds to meet and greet the other men, all US special forces, before giving an impromptu briefing.

"Right, men, myself and Jackson will take one car with the gear in it. I need one of you to head down to the pier, opposite the La Cambusa café, where you will find the boat I arrived in, named *Carpe Diem.* In the galley, you will find a Chinese special forces guy. He's in a bad way. I got what I need for now, but I need one of you to get to work on him."

"Are you shitting me? Here in Italy, how are we even meant to take him out of here? It's full of tourists and locals." The other men are thinking the same thoughts, but none of them will voice anything.

Waiting for a couple of Italians and their children to walk past them on their way to the shore, Flynn then moves to the rear of the Audi and inspects the goods. The men follow and wait patiently for his reply.

"Just take the boat farther down the coast, find an old farmhouse, or take him into the woods. I don't care. Just extract the information from him. Tell me as soon as possible their other targets and who's involved. I want names, places, and timings, and I need it quickly."

Jackson nods. Being the most experienced of the new arrivals, he speaks to the team rapidly, providing his orders. They decide that the ex-Navy SEAL, along with another, is to take the boat to Termini. The other men will commandeer a van for their prisoner and move him without attention to a CIA safe house.

"Let me work on finding a proper location. Just get moving, guys. As Flynn says, we need to get on this bloke, squeeze him for info, and contact us on these." Jackson hands out encrypted phones.

As the men set about inserting SIM cards and programming specific numbers, the ex-Navy SEAL named Mike asks, "Once we get what we want, what will we do with our guest?"

Flynn gives the man a wink as he climbs into the driver's seat and starts the ignition.

"Burial at sea; it's what his mother would have wanted." Laughing at his joke, he closes the door and drives himself and Jackson out of the car park.

***

As Flynn dives, Jackson takes out a road map and opens the page at their location. Placing his finger on the grid square, he grumbles, "Okay, Flynn, kinda hard to give directions when I don't know where the hell we are going."

The spec ops guy was always ready for a fight, growing up on a ranch outside Houston, Texas, where his father bred Brahman bulls for the rodeos. Toughness was in his bloodline. Short and wiry, with huge forearms built up from wrestling with those beasts, Jackson bears a resemblance to a younger Sylvester Stallone. Now sporting an operator's beard with toughened skin on his nose and around his eyes, due to long exposures on the mountains, this gave him a look of an Everest survivor. He suffered many injuries messing with bulls, from broken bones to gashes from their horns. Yet years of this lifestyle made him feel more alive. Bucking bulls was a way to let off steam, which differed completely from Flynn's love for surfing. Two highly capable men driving through Europe on a mission. One man has the plan, the other is along for the ride. Neither of them would swap this life for anything.

"I'll let you know exactly once I get hold of Hoffmann. Hold the wheel a minute." Flynn takes his hands off the wheel to click a sequence of numbers into the sat phone before taking control of the car once again. The navigation screen on the dashboard was disconnected earlier. Jackson prefers the old-fashioned style of using paper maps and being offline. Likewise, Flynn is more content with his own navigation than what the Audi multimedia interface can provide.

The two men are sitting in silence when the phone rings. Once answered, Flynn flicks it onto its loudspeaker before setting the device on the center console as he joins the SS1. He drives carefully, paying attention to the speed limit northbound on this historic road built by the Romans, which connects Rome to Imperia in northwest Italy, on the Gulf of Genoa.

Cain Hoffmann's voice crackles faintly through the encrypted device. "Good morning, I presume it is morning time for you? And where the hell in God's name have you been? I was worried sick."

Turning the volume up on the handset, Flynn checks his rearview mirror. "Morning, boss. First things first, where are we going?"

"Berlin. What's your ETA on that?"

Flynn looks at the needle on the gas gauge, then at Jackson. "I will give you that soon. Any info on our targets? They shouldn't be too far away."

"Our analysts reckon they would have left just before the bomb went off, well clear of Monaco. The NSA has chatter, leading us to think they will move to Berlin. The Chinese have several safe houses there, full of intelligence officers and friendly academic and research facilities. It will be like finding a needle in a haystack. Once they hit Berlin, they could disappear anywhere," says Hoffmann.

"ETA thirteen hours," Jackson mutters in the lull of the conversation.

"Hoffmann, I am working on a piece of intelligence at my end." Flynn trusts the director of the CIA, but he knows only too well what information Hoffmann wants and what he prefers not to know. The abduction of a member of the Chinese military followed by his interrogation, torture, execution, and the dumping of his body in the Mediterranean is something Hoffmann would appreciate not knowing. War crimes are something the Western nations are held accountable for, and it's Flynn's job to protect those upstream. No one wants to be sitting in The Hague like a common criminal.

Flynn pulls the car over to the side of the road and takes the map from Jackson. Placing it against the steering wheel, he studies the lay of the land while waiting for Hoffmann to reply. It was only by good fortune that Xuedong had swum a little too far from his team when providing security, enabling Flynn to strike him with his speargun loaded with rocuronium bromide, paralyzing him and allowing his capture without a huge struggle as the Chinese team planted their bomb on the *Ischia.* His priority was to drag his opponent back to an advanced SEAL delivery vehicle, which was being manned by Team Six. They would assist by taking the prisoner to a ship a few miles offshore for "processing." Much to Flynn's annoyance, they couldn't extract the correct information to determine when the bomb was going to go off or who was the primary target. Then, as luck would have it, his plan hit a snag. JSOC commanders gave the SEALs other taskings.

Flynn, with decisions to make, hung on to Xuedong a while longer in the hope he would be more cooperative on dry land. Directing the CIA fixer to charter the *Carpe Diem*, and deliver it to the navy ship, allowed Flynn to keep his new pet. The high-priority link to the Chinese team. He'd wanted to get Xuedong on land to provide him with some hope of survival, but he was being too damn difficult. Bruised and bleeding, he offered nothing.

European operations had been on the increase for some time, with a lot of hard-core operators coming out of other theaters looking for action. Flynn knows what he needs: a well-experienced team to break this shit bag down. Twisting his wrist to look at the time on his black Suunto watch, he thinks, *Shit, it could be a few hours before they get anything out of him.*

Hoffmann takes a few minutes before answering, "Your mission was to observe this team, find out why they are on the *Golden Tiger*, and report back. Anyway, what's your gut telling you now?"

"I think in a few hours I'll know more about the Chinese team; I will move in and check them out, build on the profile I have on them. Learn more about their intentions then work on a plan to take them out. If that's what you want? I think after last night we would have full cooperation from Europe," says Flynn.

"That's what scares me about you. It's not Afghanistan, this is the middle of bloody Europe, and it's the Chinese we are dealing with here. Monaco is full of television crews from all over the world. We have eyes in the sky and are watching developments closely. We blocked other satellites from gathering intel before us. The Brits are already asking questions, much like the Israelis. What we found was interesting, though. The Chinese minister of state security has arrived. With him, he will have close protection, not just his security detail. I mean that of politicians and business leaders. Any sign of aggression toward the Chinese will see the Europeans backpedaling, fearful of their trade deals. We need to watch and see who is moving, track them, and build our own picture of what is happening," says Hoffmann.

Flynn checks his mirrors while whispering to Jackson, "This has deep shit written all over it." Jackson has been thinking the same thing.

"You mean to tell me the MSS is in Monaco, and because of him, we are to stand back and observe? If he is there, then his purpose is to protect their hit team. Who else, other than the Chinese president himself, carries more power? I could bet on my life that those guys are still in Monaco, and if they are, that means they are in no rush to head back to China. I'll go one step further by saying this team is on a mission, Hoffmann, so expect more deaths of high profiles."

Hoffmann doesn't reply for some time. Flynn knows he will discuss this with his advisors.

"If you had called me like you were supposed to, I would have briefed you on this new information. Anyhow, it's causing a stir at the Pentagon. I have Olszewski breathing down my neck, which is why I needed to get out of Washington. I'm heading to Berlin. You have forty-eight hours to build some credible information. The president will take scalps soon, he needs to know what the hell is going on," Hoffmann replies curtly.

"Copy that." Flynn reaches down and switches the phone off as Jackson unboxes a couple of Glock 19s. Passing one over, Flynn inserts a magazine into its place, chambers a round, and secures the weapon into his new covert waistband holster. He then folds the map neatly and passes it to Jackson.

"Okay, what now, Flynn?"

Flynn looks at his appearance in the rearview mirror, rubbing his face and running his fingers through his hair while trying to stifle a yawn.

"I haven't slept for two days, so . . . now we sleep until the boys get some intel for us. Monaco will be crawling with Chinese spooks. I want to know what the hell we are walking into. Find a place where the boys can tie up the hog, then book us a hotel with decent food and a good bar."

Chapter Eight

Saint-Jean-Cap-Ferrat, France

The sultry voice of a voluptuous maid singing a French love song floats across the room. "*La solitude que je redoute, Qui me guette au bout de ma route, Je la mettrai dehors . . .*"

As Carver stretches his arms and legs, waiting for the blood to circulate, he listens peacefully for a moment while she prepares his bath. Gently rubbing the sleep out of his eyes, he checks again to make sure his jacket on the nightstand beside him fully covers the firearm. The stack of cash sitting next to a glass of water is a testament to his successful night in the casino. Although, despite the winnings, Carver feels deflated. Throwing back the white sheets, he makes his way to the window. He disconnects his phone from the charger and turns it back on again, wondering if there will be any missed calls or urgent messages. From his balcony in the La Voile d'Or, Carver looks out over the port towards Monaco Bay, a scenic thirty-minute drive away. He found the mood inside the Monte Carlo bars somewhat depressing because of the bombings, plus the lack of good company. For that reason, Carver felt like a change of scenery, at least until

Sarah provided him with his next job. Carver had tried calling her in the hope she could meet him for dinner and, perhaps, if he were lucky, a night in this wonderful hotel. To take advantage of his unrestricted credit card, he booked a room with the sea view. After a few attempts trying to get through to Sarah for non-SIS related issues, he gave up and switched the phone off. A lonely late-night swim in the ocean was the last thing he did before falling into a deep sleep, allowing the salt water to be absorbed into his body.

Now a hungry feeling absorbs him as the Rémy Martin clears from his head. Carver considers going for another swim before breakfast to reignite the fire in his head. As he stands in his birthday suit, completely unaware, he watches the sunlight glistening off the ocean as the yachts begin their charter operations. His encrypted phone buzzes twice, breaking his attention and sparking life back into his body. He picks it up and stares at the screen; a wide smile crosses his face. A sense of happiness fills him with pleasure when both messages bear Sarah's name.

"Sir, your bath is ready. I left extra towels. Would you care to eat in your room or perhaps downstairs?" The maid stands in the doorway, trying but failing terribly to keep her eyes up to meet his. The temptation to glimpse at the naked hunk before her is too much. Hands resting behind her back serve well in pushing her curves toward him.

Unaware of the sexual tension and his state of dress, he catches her eyes. "Thank you. I'll be down after my bath. Reserve me a table by the window, okay, facing the water." Carver pulls five hundred euros from his stack and places it into her hand. The look of confusion on the maid's face should have been expected. "Listen carefully, please, I am a very private man, a businessman who has many competitors looking to steal my ideas. Will you keep an eye out for anyone suspicious that is asking about me or trying to get my details from the hotel?"

"Yes, of course, sir." Squinting her eyes slightly, the maid tilts her head to one side and quietly mouths the word, "Russians!"

Carver smiles. "The Russians, Arabs, North Koreans, Pakistanis, Afghanis, the list is endless. I am hoping to invest in Rajasthan, India. Their textile markets are quite competitive. The Chinese are all over the place trying to disrupt these trade deals to the EU. So, please, I think maybe the Chinese will spy on me."

The maid's eyes open wide. With a wink, she points a finger to her lips. "Oh my, yes, I will watch out for you, Mr. Bond."

Laughing at her joke, Carver writes his mobile number for her.

"Don't mention this to anyone, darling. When I stay here next time I will reward you again, okay?"

Thanking him ever so pleasantly, she slowly slides the money down the front of her top, exposing herself deliberately in the movement. Then, with a moment of hesitation, she backs out of the room, stealing a final peek at the mysterious man as she closes the door gently behind her.

With one grade-A observer paid, he returns to the message from Sarah.

Sorry I cannot meet, working late, another time, ok?

Carver checks the sent time of the message, 22:50. He deletes the message and quickly opens the next one.

I have unwanted company across the street. Once I shake them, we can meet. There are urgent developments we need to discuss. Message sent 05:35.

Typical Sarah. Carver shakes his head. *She's one early riser; five in the AM and she would be up and ready for her morning routine, then laptop open and back to work by zero five twenty.* Carver thinks about her "unwanted company!" As an experienced SIS operator, she was used to spies tracking her. Although on this rare and highly sensitive deployment, it's a situation that needs terminating. Sarah would follow the standard protocols in such circumstances. Within a short period, those conducting the reconnaissance on her will be under surveillance themselves. Carver returns to his state of affairs. As the brain fog evaporates, Carver realizes for the first time he isn't wearing any undershorts. Rolling his eyes, he remembers how the maid behaved earlier. *Let's not embarrass me anymore.* Pulling on his shorts, he quickly gets ready for breakfast.

Down in the breakfast bar, Carver grabs a copy of *Le Monde* as he heads to his table on the terrace. While he waits for his semi-cooked red tuna, Tarbouriech oysters, and Roquefort to arrive, he checks the view outside for any threat. Next, he opens the *Le Monde* and places it on the table, then skims over the headlines. Once he checks the news, he dials a number on his phone and sits comfortably, observing the locals and tourists around him through the dark lenses of his Tom Ford sunglasses.

While speaking quickly on his phone to the priest, Carver catches a man, twice, looking in his direction. A badly dressed man accompanied by a woman, both Asian, both with untouched breakfast plates and lacking the normal grace and calm manners expected of clientele in such a location. Finishing his call, Carver resumes reading an article in the paper. When the food arrives, he leans to the side, allowing the waitress more space to position his plates and orange juice on the small table. This angle provides him with a direct view of his new friend a few tables to his right. Carver spots the man holding some kind of object under the table, partially concealed by a napkin. Unsure if it is a phone, camera, or microphone, Carver now prepares himself for a busy morning. Enjoying his meal while enjoying the view across the Mediterranean, he considers his options. He orders a pot of coffee and sends a message to Sarah. *I have company as well. Let me know when you are free.*

The soft sounds of a pianist playing "Clair De Lune" ease their way from the speakers across the terrace. In this world of the rich and famous, Carver feels at home. The adrenaline now running through his body, however, is a gentle reminder that death is closing. As the coffee arrives, he inhales the aroma of the magic beans then sets about fueling himself. Carver notes how his friend still hasn't touched his food, a sure sign they are waiting for him to leave. *Test time.* Carver gets up and heads over to the waitress, presses a fifty-euro note into her hand as he shakes it, then quietly asks her not to clear his table, as he is only using the bathroom. Carver then heads off in the direction of the car park. He waits a couple of minutes, then walks back toward the terrace. *Bingo.* As predicted, the Asian couple got up to follow and are now exposed. *Too late.* Pretending not to notice, Carver passes them and walks back to the table and takes a seat. He sips some more coffee, finishes another article in the paper, then leaves. Once in his room, he rechecks his bag and gets ready to leave. Before doing so, he contacts one of the technical support team for SIS, his go-to guy for hacking, Tommy Taylor. A PhD student from the University of Birmingham, a clever geek of a kid who gained access to FBI files when he was only fifteen. Working out of GCHQ, he loves the live action, the quick-fire requests under pressure, and the kickbacks that support his crypto trading. Carver loves the guy, as he is happy to work off the books, avoiding the legal authorization from his seniors.

"Tommy, it's Carver. Listen, I need you to give me a list of hotel check-ins last night and this morning at La Voile d'Or. Look for a couple of Asians traveling together, and tell me who they are and anything else you can dig up, okay?"

"Copy that, Carver, mate. I'm guessing you want this right now?"

"Yes, send it," says Carver.

"Shit . . . okay, I'm on it. You owe me some super-hot Israeli software, okay? Next time you are in Tel Aviv I will send you a shopping list."

Carver shakes his head. "No can do, hurry, Tommy, I'm standing by." He busies himself by checking his weapons, putting a round up the spout of his Sig Sauer and then securing it and attaching a covert three-inch neck knife to his waistband. He leaves a fifty-euro note for the cleaner as a reminder. As he looks out the window to check the crowd downstairs, his phone buzzes to life. "What have you got?"

"Wow, man, lucky you are still breathing. The names I got, James Lee and Ying Yue, these are nasty pieces of work. They joined the Ministry of State Security about twenty years ago, always work in pairs, posing as a married couple. Devoting their whole life to smoking out Chinese double agents. Lee works on European research with CERN, the *Conseil Européen pour la Recherche Nucléaire*. For years he has been sending the particle physics research findings and details of leading scientists and technology back to Beijing; as you can understand, not everything is shared. Ying Yue works for SAP in Germany, a huge enterprise software developer. Think of annual revenue of around thirty billion euros, the third-largest software company. She has an enormous mansion at Walldorf in Baden-Württemberg, while he has many properties in Switzerland, Paris, and London. His principal home being Cologny, Geneva. It looks as though the Chinese Communist Party is heating things up, and these two have become big players. When the Chinese president Xi Jinping started the military-civil fusion policy to build China's economic and military strength, all high-profile and well-connected Chinese were called back for training."

"Cut to the pointy end, Tommy, I don't want a history lesson. Are they an immediate threat or not?" asks Carver.

"Carver, put it this way, they are not there to observe your movements, they are there to end them."

Moving over to one of the other windows, Carver asks, "So, why them? Why not send an operator to take a shot? Why send a couple of scientists?"

"Maybe they blend in better. You would see a threat coming a mile off unless you are losing your touch, getting old, I guess."

Chuckling at the young man teasing him Carver, decides now is the time to move. "Right, that's great work, Tommy, I appreciate it. Check who they are reporting back to and contact me anytime, and I'll see what juicy software I can get my hands on for you later."

Pressing the red end call button, Carver slides the phone into his pocket, his bag fitted securely over his two shoulders, then he loosens his shirt slightly. He is ready, ready for a couple of scientists. *Today's bloody threat picture has changed radically*, he thinks.

Moving swiftly out of his hotel room, he takes the stairs down to the lobby. Carver thinks of how these two academics are preparing to take him out. It won't be by force. He can only guess it will be something toxic. *Shit! The coffee. Could they have poisoned me?* Carver walks to reception and proceeds to the security room he noticed before. Walking inside, a startled staff member asks what he is doing. Carver has no time to discuss his theories. "Europol, I am leading an investigation." He flashes the

Sig Sauer, and the bright-eyed young security officer gets all excited.

Within a few minutes, the helpful staff member scrolls through the footage and plays it back at high speed. Carver only needs to check if they approached his table on their exit. As they both watch the footage, Carver silently picks up a set of keys from the wallboard. "No, nothing. They didn't go near the table," he mumbles. "Excellent work, young man."

Without hanging around, Carver walks to the car park, eyes scanning all around. He would prefer to go on the hunt for them and wipe them out, but this mess he could do without. Carver clicks the car key remote repeatedly until it is in range and the matching car is revealed. The white BMW is in a parking spot, tight to the curb.

As Carver reverses out, he spots the Chinese man sitting in a car at the exit, speaking into his mobile phone. "Okay, surprise me, science man," he whispers to himself while shifting the car into drive and proceeding toward the exit. As he is about to pass the car, Carver suddenly brakes and jumps out and hurls himself into the passenger-side door of James Lee's car. With one swift movement, Carver drives his fist into the side of Lee's head. The next strike is a direct jab on his windpipe. As he struggles to breathe, Carver frisks him quickly, then checks if the woman is nearby. "Who sent you? Why are you following me?" Nothing. Carver grabs the man, one hand around the throat, with the fingers digging into the pressure point in Lee's neck. With the other hand, he fishhooks him by sticking the index and middle finger into Lee's mouth and grabbing a tight hold of his cheek to control his head. With complete control, Carver drags Lee by the head into the stolen BMW, then quickly delivers a couple of hard strikes into his kidneys. He roughly places Lee into the rear footwell and tramples on his legs and arms, kicking them into position, then pushes back the driver and passenger seats, squashing the prisoner firmly in place. With a quick look inside Lee's car for any intelligence, Carver then drives out of the car park with his new friend. Tapping *Sasso di Bordighera* into the GPS calculates the trip at just under an hour. He knows the place well, plus getting away from the issues in Monte Carlo is a smart move because of the high presence of law enforcement. Now in France, the local law enforcement would be on his trail, if not for the stolen BMW then for the kidnapping of a distinguished scientist. The crossing into Italy will buy him precious time.

Carver thinks back to Sarah. *Could she have the same threats?* His heart skips a beat, knowing he is not there to protect her. *First things first, Carver, find an ideal resting ground for this human cargo. Once all information has changed hands, then go for Sarah.* He checks the rearview mirror for a tail, then hammers the engine to life. As he approaches Avenue Claude Vignon, Carver shakes his head at the shit predicament he is wading through. The muffled cries from Lee subside as Carver checks his watch. "Lucky I drank lots of coffee, Mr. Lee, we are going to have a long chat, buddy. No one in China cares about your little shiny ass. You belong to me now, okay?" No reply.

Carver grabs his phone and with one hand steering the BMW northward, he types an encrypted message to Tommy: *Mate, delete all camera footage in the hotel. Track me and disrupt the cameras on my route to Italy, ASAP.*

Chapter Nine

Port Hercules, Monaco

Eddie finds Zhang down in the galley with his head almost inside the fridge. He's picking through the cold meats, eating what he recognizes and discarding the rest. Stepping into the galley, Eddie lets out a small cough. "Ah, Mr. Xiaopeng, sorry to disturb you, but Mr. Danny Lin is on board and would like to meet with you."

Momentarily startled, Zhang pretends not to notice as he rolls up a few slices of prosciutto and dips them into a freshly opened jar of Amora mustard. Sticking them into his mouth, with a traceable sign of regret, Zhang quickly grabs a fresh glass of oolong tea to wash down the horrible food. "Disgusting," he slurs.

On the worktop, Eddie notices the invoice from *Casino supermarché,* the list of goods is by now indistinguishable because of the notes from a ballpoint pen. A list of items and requests. He quickly scans a few lines, some written in Chinese, others in English. Eddie stands there peeking from the corner of his eyes until words became recognizable. *Laser microphone, Mossberg shotgun, FLIR thermal camera, M4 Carbine, hiking boots, clothes, cigarettes, ammo, Glock 19 . . .*

Zhang takes a step toward Eddie and motions for him to step aside. Grabbing the list on his way past, the top Chinese spec ops operator climbs the stairs to the deck so he can meet the boss. Eddie doesn't know what to do. He finds himself in a difficult situation. At the beck and call of the Chinese Communist Party, he has no option but to serve them; otherwise, his family will end up dead or in a remote prison on false charges. He looks at the head of Zhang disappearing from view, then Eddie starts the climb up the stairs. *Logistics, that's all I'm doing, unaware of anything, providing logistics for Chinese diplomats. It's all cool, Eddie.*

Danny Lin and Zhang Xiaopeng have taken a seat on the open deck, arrogantly flicking more cigarette ash on the teak deck. "Some iced tea, Eddie, like a good boy," howls Danny while pointing his crooked finger at the table in front of them.

Danny is on the phone, not talking, simply listening, while Zhang takes the list he was working on from his pocket and notes down a couple more items.

"Okay, no problem, I will fix that right away." Setting the mobile on the table, Danny turns his head to look at Zhang. Without speaking, he simply lowers his eyebrows and slowly shakes his head.

"What's up with you?" Zhang's voice speaks with an attitude. He will allow no one to think they can intimidate him. If the man in front of him wasn't high profile, Zhang would have leaned forward and slapped his face.

"I'll tell you what's wrong. One of our spies has no head, Zhang. Someone blew it completely off his neck.

That's not nice, is it? And I am just off the phone with a dear friend to tell me they abducted her partner from under our noses. He was working on a lead, a potential target," says Danny.

Zhang doesn't answer. Feeling somewhat underdressed in his white robe, he stares at Danny, daring for an accusation. He would be justified in protecting his dignity. He is the most highly trained killer Beijing has produced.

Danny eyes Zhang with distrust. "Listen, Zhang, I didn't come here to apply pressure. Neither did I break my engagements with the scum at the UN this morning to engage in idle chitchat with a man in a fluffy white robe. I came here to see what the hell happened last night?"

"I completed my orders last night, mission complete, target eliminated, so drop the attitude, Danny. I respect your position and I hope you respect mine, otherwise only one of us will leave this boat." Zhang noticed movement from Danny's security. They had been listening via covert earpieces. The one on his immediate right loosens his arm and moves it closer to his waist.

Danny notices too. With a smile, the director of the MSS takes a deep breath and does the annoying slow shaking of his head, much to the displeasure of his fellow countryman. "Well, mister hotshot. I understand you lost a man, and I also lost two men. Three for one night is not great, is it?"

Danny stubs out his cigarette and lights another, dropping the lighter onto the table. "Either the Americans or British, we don't have a full picture yet, but one of them has stepped up to the plate and is now protecting their assets, which causes us many dilemmas. If we back off, then they win, and we lose. We lose respect, and our president will look weak. If the president looks weak, our heads will be on a plate. It is now or never, Zhang, now or never." Danny emphasizes this point by stabbing his finger on the table with each word. "You have full authority to go after whoever is stopping us."

"How can I go after ghosts? I need intel, Danny. Also, I'm doing this alone, no more people holding me back." Sliding his list across the table, he looks up to see Eddie approaching with drinks.

They sit in silence as Eddie nervously places the drinks on the table. Once he carries out this duty, Eddie excuses himself and is about to leave when Zhang speaks. "Eddie, in my room there is a black bag on the bed. Bring it up here, will you?"

Skimming his eyes quickly over the list, written on the back of the invoice, Danny lifts his head, looks at Zhang, and gives a nod. "We have some Russian contacts who will assist with this. Give me about five hours and everything you need shall be delivered to the consulate in Zurich."

Despite needing to use the bathroom, Zhang pours himself some iced tea. He can feel a dryness in his mouth. A sign that tells him something is wrong.

In the marina, the local authorities have cleared some yachts to leave their berths. The multimillionaires, tycoons, magnates, bankers, and other big shots unperturbed by the previous night's entertainment have now expressed their rights, via their legal teams, to enjoy the delights of the Mediterranean Sea. Zhang could get used to this life. But not the food. As Eddie returns on deck, holding a black bug-out bag in both hands, Zhang can see how weak and unhealthy this man really is. Unaccustomed to carrying heavy items, he lays the bag down next to the table with a groan of an eighty-year-old man.

Zhang, with all the speed and grace of a soldier in the field, strips off the robe and unpacks the bag. Within a few minutes, he is fully dressed, passports, multiple credit cards, and wads of cash at his disposal. Danny speaks silently toward the mic hidden under his collar. Shortly after, one of his security team approaches Zhang and hands him a ten-millimeter Smith & Wesson 610 revolver. "What's this shit? Am I going to the gunfight at the OK Corral? Danny, are you serious? What the hell?"

"Hey, work with what you have. Get in contact with Zurich. Ask for Jürgen. Once he receives the items, then you will meet him. Anything you need, go through Jürgen and him only. He is looked after by us financially, and it goes without saying, he is less obvious than any of our countrymen."

"What about the yacht? And Eddie, can he be of any help?" Zhang speaks as he secures the trusty revolver in a holster, then straps it firmly under his shirt.

"I don't trust him. But for now, I need this down at Saint-Tropez. You are not the only wheel in motion. You are only a minor cog in an enormous piece of machinery, Zhang." Danny stands up to meet Zhang at eye level. "Remember that always . . ." Danny stoops down to pick up his lighter. "We have immense talent coming through the military now, young and motivated, patriotic, guys with superb control over their temper. These guys are the future . . ." Danny pauses a moment to light his cigarette. Blowing out the first draw, he sucks in and inhales deeply. As he exhales, his head explodes in a ball of blood, brain matter, and pieces of skull.

Zhang screams with fright, then suddenly his training kicks in. He drops to the deck and looks in the sniper's direction. From the shock and confusion, Danny's protection team race over and one of them draws their weapons on Zhang, screaming at him to throw away the weapon.

"It wasn't me, you fool. Look at the exit wound, look at the blood and shit all over me." Zhang is flat on the ground, wiping the gore out of his eyes and hair. His black leather jacket would be easy to wipe clean, but that's the last of his worries. The security guys figure it out and begin barking orders into their mics. Backup teams can be heard in their black vans roaring up the street from all directions.

Zhang, still on the deck with Danny, visualizes the sniper laying in position, with a fresh round chambered. His breathing would be stabilized, then the crosshair begins its search for the next target. Zhang can't wait any longer. *I need to get off this boat, right now!* Quickly, he springs to his feet and dives for the stairs leading down to the galley. A bullet rips through his lower leg and the searing pain causes him to cry out. Down in the galley, he has some cover. Grabbing a towel, he ties it around the entry wound as a temporary tourniquet. Slipping on his blood, he can hear the commotion on the deck above. The guys above are taking cover.

Through the pain, Zhang screams out for his backup crew. “Hey, guys, get weapons, there’s a sniper out there.” His remaining security guys come racing out of their rooms. They had followed his orders well when he had ordered them to remain out of sight, but now he needs to put them into the fight.

“Go up there and get me a location on him,” orders Zhang.

As they make their way up to the deck, Zhang moves quickly to the airlock hatch to prepare for a dive. Hearing the men screaming above, it is quickly apparent the sniper is hitting his targets. He knows the shooter will be busy for the next few minutes, trying to wipe out all targets on the yacht before making his escape. Offering the men as a distraction is a dirty tactic by Zhang to help make good his escape. He considers the idea of going after the sniper, but with the closing law enforcement due to surround the area and his own injuries, it would be futile.

Working quickly to get dressed, he grabs the medical kit, ammo, and other pieces of gear, then secures it all in a waterproof bag, which is fastened tightly to his body. One last check on the makeshift tourniquet and he is ready. As with countless times before, he slows his breathing as he enters the underwater airlock hatch to launch his attack. He feels it in his gut; he feels death closing in. Now with the president’s backing, and the whole of the Chinese Communist Party behind him, he will stop at nothing to bring war like no one has seen before to the streets of Europe. This time is like no other. This is vastly different . . . it has now become personal.

Chapter Ten

Shanwick Oceanic FIR Airspace

Cain Hoffmann spent the first leg of the seven-hour British Airways flight to London Heathrow on his phone. Ever since the report came in detailing the attack in Monaco, the director of the CIA had many questions for his men on the ground. Val Olszewski is screaming for information, as he needs to brief President Lancaster. So too is Gary Duval, the CIA deputy director of operations. The sweat builds on Hoffmann's brow as he repeatedly insists he knew of no live missions in Monte Carlo. That part is almost true. It is outside of his job description to plan and run operations. As the CIA's top man, his responsibilities are more political in nature. However, Hoffmann is not a simple person. Scribbling notes and passing them to his aide, Liana, he then scrolls through the phone searching for the next man on the list. Ken Herber from Task Force Orange, the JSOC moniker for the US Army's Intelligence Support Activity. The special missions unit had been collecting vital intelligence on the Chinese Communist Party and their special forces operators and training areas. Herber was proving to be a great asset for Hoffmann; tipping him off before writing up his operational reports allowed Hoffmann to be ahead of the game. The director of the CIA had a unique style with the top-tier units across the US military, passing out one of his encrypted cell phone numbers to the commanders of each SMU so they can keep him in the loop without waiting for the painstakingly slow chain of command. When it came to the movements of these Chinese operators, Hoffmann wants to know every detail.

"I was expecting your call," Herber answers immediately, the voice strong and direct.

Hoffmann keeps his voice to a whisper, knowing Herber has a specialized earpiece attached that will amplify the slightest sounds. "Have you anything for me, Herber? I need names, locations, and their skill sets." While waiting for a response, he checks the plane's position again. Touching down for a quick transfer at Heathrow will give him a moment to stretch his legs and grab something better to eat. He leans over to speak. "Liana, check somewhere in the terminal I can grab a steak or ribs, please."

"Eating well, I hear." Herber lets out a chuckle before continuing. "Okay, from what my unit has established, as of thirty minutes ago, there is a huge group of Chinese diplomats, business leaders, and various political figures staying in Monte Carlo, spread out across a couple of hotels. Some men from defense also, but not operators or anyone capable of doing actual harm. What I have heard is, one of their VIPs has gone missing. From the chatter and hurried meetings, this is causing quite a stir."

"Since the shooting of their minister of state security, who are they pointing the finger at?" asks Hoffmann.

"Well, take a guess! Americans . . . that's the first cab off the rank for them. We picked up a conversation between one operator to Zhongnanhai in Beijing, asking for permission to go on the offensive. Beijing's top man, Danny Lin, was on that boat to protect something valuable. He would not allow the Monaco authorities to get aboard. Now we need to piece together what it was he felt threatened by and why no other high-ranking diplomat could have been used instead," says Herber.

Hoffmann thinks for a moment before replying. "Zhongnanhai, that's their equivalent of the White House. Do you know who they spoke with?"

"Not yet. Our analysts are working on that. More important was the response. There was a direct order from a general. We traced the call to the Regent Palace in the northwestern corner of Zhongnanhai. 'Lie low in the grass before you strike like a cobra' was the message, plus the same old garbage about the West not showing them respect and how they need to show the world their true strength . . ."

"Just wind back a bit, Herber, if you will," Hoffmann cuts him off. Signaling the stewardess for coffee, he then hesitates slightly before adding, "'Strike like a cobra.' Who was that message meant for?"

"We believe the unit that carried out the bombing in the marina. Expect more of the same, Hoffmann. We traced many calls to the *Golden Tiger*, the yacht owned by Eddie Wu. The bodies that came off the boat didn't match up with various witnesses. The sniper did a great job dispatching those on board. But one got away," says Herber.

"Okay . . . do you have a photo of him?" Hoffmann is like a child preparing to open his Christmas presents; so many presents have been presented and he's not sure which one to open first. He speaks again before waiting for an answer, "If these men that did the bombing in the marina, and the sniper, are not bothered about making deaths look like accidents, then yes, they are sending a message and you are right, we will expect more."

"You know as well as I do, Hoffmann, Monte Carlo is full of Chinese honey traps. They are crawling over the men here, loads of Russians in the mix, as they have their agenda. Those girls are proving more popular. I have men out ready to grab one of the Chinese, which may lead us to their bosses."

Blowing over his piping-hot black coffee, Hoffmann dares for a sip before replying. "Shit . . . always fiercely boiling . . . Herber, now let's get down to the sniper. What can you tell me about him?"

"From the position where he took his shots, I can say he is well trained, calm enough to stay in position and take out everyone on the yacht except the young girls. My laser range finder gave the distance at 846 meters. There are two of them. Don't forget the spotter; he would be a top-tier shooter as well. They rented the apartment he took the shot from at the beginning of the year. The neighbors said no one ever moved in. The local cops are still working on the few leads they have. I will monitor their system in case something of interest pops up," says Herber.

"Do that. I'm stopping in Heathrow to connect with the Berlin flight. Send me the image of our suspect ASAP, and try to get access on the boat or find out what you can about it. Also, keep your ear to the ground for any more high-rankers loitering about Monte Carlo."

"Planning to, Hoffmann," says Herber.

The two men disconnect their phones just as the seat belt lights illuminate. Hoffmann's flight is approaching Heathrow. "Liana, let's have some lunch."

***

The migraine starts again just as his meal hits the table. Liana skipped the Concorde Room and choose the Fortnum & Mason bar for Hoffmann and herself. She pulls out a couple of barstools deep within terminal 5 in Heathrow as Hoffmann lays his laptop and phone on the cold marble bar top. Liana reads through the menu and begins talking to the handsome bar staff. Hoffmann wonders if Liana thinks she's on holiday. He makes a mental note to mention it to her, but for now he's hungry. The food will ease his migraine and, with any luck, some alcohol will hold it off a bit longer. Waiting for his Glenarm sirloin, he sips on a glass of ten-year-old tawny port. From his trouser pocket, he removes the smaller burner phone used for Flynn and Flynn only. Slowly spinning it with his finger on the bar like a bored child, he contemplates phoning for an update. Figuring it won't be answered, he places it back in his pocket.

"My old friend, imagine bumping into you here."

The posh voice behind him is instantly recognizable. He spins around on his barstool to catch sight of the man calling on him. Then he rolls his eyes once he sees Harry Woodward. Hoffmann never thought his British counterpart would have tracked his movements. "Harry, you sneaky devil, always breathing down my neck." With a hearty laugh, the two men shake hands before Harry takes a seat beside Hoffmann.

"Passing through without dropping in to say hello, Hoffmann! I thought I'd catch up with you, make sure you are eating well." Harry eyes the medium-rare steak being served, the steam rising in a spiral before disappearing into the wide expanse of the busy airport terminal.

"Nice airport, but not for talking shop, Harry. Is there somewhere we can go? Once I finish this, of course."

"Sure thing. How about Berlin? I have a plane waiting. Take your time, we have a lot to discuss."

***

Harry Woodward, the SIS chief, leads his American counterpart, Cain Hoffmann, onto a private Gulfstream G700, registered under an obscure company made up by the Secret Intelligence Service for sensitive flights. Harry studies his old friend's face as they walk up the steps. He can see a couple of extra lines around the eyes, a few hairs protruding from the ears, and the beginning of a sunspot on his temple, which he didn't have when they last met only six months ago. *Holding secrets takes its toll on the human body. I know only too well.* Harry keeps his thoughts to himself as they lower themselves into the comfy leather seats. The captain's voice flows clearly over the speakers, providing the current temperature, flight altitude, wind speed, time of arrival—the standard information ignored by those on board. The two-hour flight to Brandenburg Airport in Berlin will give the two men enough time to get their stories straight before meeting the German and French spy bosses.

Removing his shoes and sliding them in front of him, Hoffmann then wiggles his toes with satisfaction before speaking. "When was the last time you were in Monte Carlo, Harry?"

"Jesus, probably six or seven years ago, before I became the chief of the circus." Harry loads his Roush pipe with Amphora tobacco as he continues down memory lane. "I spent a lot of time in Vienna before that, flew in and out of Monaco every few months to meet a few Chinese high rollers with gambling issues. Back then it was the Wild West in intelligence work—Russians, Chinese, Arabs all coming to splash their cash and connect with their dodgy cohorts. They all took their woman. Used them to weaken the men. Usually worked, sometimes. Not long after that, SIS started recruiting gay men. That threw a spanner in the works for quite some time, especially with the Arabs. Over time, they all adjusted their personnel, if you know what I mean."

Hoffmann sits back and closes his eyes for a moment. He enjoys listening to Harry; he speaks his mind and covers complex issues with simple schoolboy explanations. "Boy, it's great to be out of Langley. You know, Harry, the repercussions of this sniper are going to be unimaginable. There are already fingers pointing at us. Probably you guys as well. We need to find out who is behind this, and fast. And by the way, notice I never asked if it was your team that did it."

The puffs of smoke rise from the pipe as Harry works the lighter across the top of the chamber. Keeping the lighter in his hand to work the pipe as needed, he then slides a hip flask out of his inner pocket. "You did ask! Just then, and no, there are no British sniper teams in the area. If any unit guys are there, then it would be entirely coincidental," says Harry.

The British always play their cards close to their chest with their intelligence and special forces operations. Hoffmann doesn't expect Harry to give the go-ahead on such an act of war, so he drops it. "I am getting an image soon, hopefully, of the suspect involved in the yacht's bombing in Port Hercules."

A stewardess, an SIS staff support member, lays down an ashtray and a couple of empty glasses. Harry hands her his hip flask. "Be a dear and refill that please and bring a bottle to us."

Harry works his lighter once more on the pipe, sending a cloud of smoke upward where it blows throughout the aircraft by the air-conditioning.

"We would have had some images to share, which would be useful to you, but for some unknown reason our bird in the sky got blinded, some kind of electrical interference. How's that for bad luck, Hoffmann?"

Hoffmann knew this was coming. Lifting his hand toward Harry, he nods slowly. "I hear you, yes. Apologies for that. It was one of those moments when we needed to ensure the Europeans had no eyes on our target. Someone in the European Union Satellite Centre is sharing or at least had been sharing information with China by giving them their taskings and findings. Now they are scared. Worried about their political future."

"You mean to tell me another European Union decision-making organization is discussing our foreign and security policies with China?" Harry looks around for the stewardess and his bottle of gin.

"You don't sound surprised, Harry," says Hoffmann.

"Well, you wouldn't believe the conversations some of those in the United Nations and the EU are having with the Chinese. They think it's all about cheap televisions and knock-off clothes. GCHQ has to recruit and train more staff for the joint technical language service to pick through all the reports. The United Nations is being tapped on the shoulder by us Brits with some unsettling questions. We have been watching this for some time, and it is clear to see that the Chinese leaders are fearful they will lose this critical connection. The Central Military Commission of China has sent out its orders, threatening those who are about to end the years of providing much-needed intel to their defense organization," says Harry.

A nonsmoker, Hoffmann has always enjoyed the aroma of pipe tobacco. Tasting the passive smoke in the back of his throat, he unravels what Harry has just said. "War on drugs, war on terror. It blindsided us, Harry. Now the Communist Party is caught out and now making moves, but how deep are they? And how will we recalibrate and maintain order?"

Ah, now we are in business. Harry watches calmly as the stewardess fills the two glasses and sets down a bucket of ice in the aisle. A box of cheese, cold meats, pâté, olives, nuts, dates, berries, and chocolates in little baskets is set down beside the two men.

"Thank you kindly, dear." Passing a glass over to Hoffmann, Harry then takes a sip of gin and repeats the words, "Recalibrate and maintain order . . . well, my old friend, we cut off the head of the snake and every other damned snake that takes its place."

Hoffmann doesn't speak, a smile on his face as he sits back, nursing his gin. *This will be interesting.*

Chapter Eleven

Sasso di Bordighera, Italy

Carver reverses the BMW into a field off Str. Gardiora, a narrow mountain road on the top side of a deep valley in the Italian hills. The untended and overgrown olive trees give him the presumption he won't get disturbed for some time. His passenger has made little noise on the quick journey across the border, and Carver hopes the Chinese spy has a will to live that outweighs his morals. Exiting the car, Carver walks back to the roadside and waits. Listening for any sign of a tail or perhaps an inquisitive local. Standing there in silence for a couple of minutes, taking the opportunity for a quick leak. Enjoying the breeze on his face, he scans the area to plan escape routes. In the event of being compromised, he will put his survival, evasion, resistance, and escape training to good use, making light work of the difficult terrain through the mountains. The smell of burning wood drifts up the valley, and he can hear the sound of Livorno chickens scraping the earth for food. Other than that, there is complete silence. This is not ideal; Carver can't risk his cargo screaming out and alarming the neighbors up the valley. *Time to get to work*. Carver approaches the car and slides the front seat forward, allowing James Lee to wriggle around and stretch his body slightly.

"Good morning, Jimmy, this is your chance to live . . . Who sent you?"

Lee scans the area with a look of bewilderment. When he finally locks eyes with Carver, he cries out, "Where am I? I am a scientist, why have you kidnapped me?" Attempting a delay tactic in this deadly situation.

"Wrong answer."

Carver violently pulls Lee's arm until it is sticking out the door. Without warning, the SIS man strikes down on it with his heel, using the full weight of his body, snapping both the ulna and radius. Prepared for the scream, Carver quickly shoves Lee's face into the backseat of the BMW, somewhat muffling the sounds. After a few minutes, Lee's energy is sapped, his wailing subsides, and his heartbeat slows slightly as he realizes life is within grasp. Carver times his next action well. Once Lee has a glimmer of hope in his eyes, Carver rams the Sig Sauer into his mouth, chipping a couple of teeth on entry. He then repeats the question.

Once the barrel is removed from his mouth, Lee painfully mumbles, "General Zhou Kai, it was he. He sent me, the Black Bear."

Committing the name to memory, Carver then presses Lee on the general's details. After a few minutes unpacking the specifics of the mission the general had sent him on, and re-questioning to look for gaps, Carver then asks about the attacks at the marina.

Lee looks Carver in the eyes, the man likely to call time on his life. Seeing no mercy, Lee then stares beyond him out into the field, lowering his eyes to the ground as a realization comes over him that his life is about to end. A man of dignity, of patriotism to the Communist Party, a man of wisdom. He was never to expect such a situation would happen to him. It embarrasses Lee when tears roll down his eyes, but he tries as much as he can to hold his head high and speak through broken teeth about what knowledge he has. As he does so, Carver takes the man's wallet and searches him for any intel. A clear sign of what lies ahead.

"Tell me about the woman."

Carver knows he hit a nerve. Leaving this bit of information until the end would test the truthfulness of James Lee. The Chinese spy, about to be dispatched in the Italian countryside, has one chance to open up.

"Tell her I love her. She followed my lead, she helped me rise within the party. Her name is Ying Yue. Our service to the Communist Party took away our chance to have a family. For that, I admit, is my only regret. Tell her that, please."

Carver climbs into the car, closes the door, and takes his weapon out. He wraps Lee's jacket around the muzzle, and without a goodbye and at point-blank range, he pulls the trigger. The sound is muffled from the outside world slightly by the jacket and the doors of the BMW. Carver figures the sound won't attract much attention, but the flames will. As he torches the vehicle, he immediately takes off across the valley. Sanremo on the Italian coast is around seven kilometers from his position. Carver weaves his way through the thick bushland while breathing lightly. He has multiplied his focus and determination with the fresh information. Next, he makes a quick call on his phone. "*Santuario della Madonna della Costa,* oh-two-hundred." With the all-important rendezvous point sorted, Carver now gives some thought to the two names.

General Zhou Kai, the Black Bear, and Zhang Xiaopeng! The scumbag from Florence. The two names repeat themselves with every footfall. *Zhang.* The assassin who nearly blew Carver apart at the café. *The worthless human who mercilessly took away the innocent life of Gabriella.* That killing cut Carver to the core, more than any other death he was a witness to. *She should have been off-limits.* The young waitress was yet another face who will visit him at night. His mind races, his speed intensifies while the anger brews inside him. A list of items he requires to enact his revenge keeps him focused as he pushes his way through branches and drives his feet into the steep mountainside climbing over another ridgeline.

Carver arrives at the edge of the small coastal city at nightfall. Sticking to the backstreets, people's gardens, and small vegetable plots, he slowly makes his way up to the church unnoticed. Set high above the city with views over the port of Sanremo and the Ligurian coast, the land provides him with a huge vantage point. After doing a recce of the rendezvous location, he finds a suitable place to lie up and wait for his contact driving up the steep and winding road. A couple of hours later and right on time, he can hear the old Renault van making progress as the engine revs around each tight bend. Once the vehicle gets to the front of the church, Carver watches from the darkness as the driver flicks a lit cigarette out the window.

That's the signal. The embers dance off the cobblestones as Carver runs from cover and enters the rear doors of the van.

On the floor of the old Renault Trafic, a black bag sits waiting. Carver opens the zipper and immediately withdraws an MP5. He loads a magazine, then swiftly checks the working parts before lifting the weapon into position, covering their exit. Scanning the darkness as the Renault works its way down the hill, Carver almost hopes someone will try to ambush them. The driver, an SIS support staff, one of many called into action for Carver's planned hit in Monaco, is quick to respond to the request for help. They keep the old van in storage for such an event, similar to many others dotted around the Mediterranean. Carver makes plans to drop the driver off along the way, as the van will be used to get to his next objective.

***

A cool Mediterranean night passes swiftly as Carver grabs a little sleep in the back of the Renault. The old work van doesn't look out of place in the Piazza Eroi Sanremesi, as a lot of renovation work is being carried out in the middle of the city. Carver watches the cars coming and going, shopkeepers grabbing their coffees at the cafés nearby before opening their various stores. He leaves the van as they display the open sign on the glass door of the men's clothing shop, which is a short walk across the car park. Selecting his garments, he goes to the cashier and pays with little fanfare.

As he retreats to the van to change his clothes, he scans the area for any threats. Back in the Renault, he picks out a burner phone from the black bag provided by the staff. He also tops up his mag with another round and puts an extra mag into his pocket, then lastly gives himself a spray of cheap aftershave. The bags provided by SIS in these situations typically contain a weapon with ammunition, cash, a hat, sunglasses, lock-picking tools, spare phones with SIMs and batteries, a grooming kit, first-aid supplies, and a GPS tracking device, which can be sewn into his clothes. Carver slides the phone into his pocket, then sits there observing the car park for a few minutes before getting out. Clad in clean, casual clothes with a rare feeling of anonymity, he too goes to locate a suitable spot for breakfast.

On entering Caffè Ducale, Carver quickly assesses the building before selecting his seat at the rear, a small table facing toward the street. Ordering eggs, hard cheese, porchetta, orange juice, and a coffee, he then inserts a new SIM card into his phone. Powering up the phone, he notices it only has 40 percent battery. *Shit!* Carver navigates the phone through the basic prompts until the reception kicks in, then he makes a call to Sarah. With an eye on the street outside, he feels his heart banging harder against his chest. *Unwanted company and urgent message to discuss.* The message that Sarah sent him yesterday morning bounces around his head as he tries to piece all the parts together. She answers the phone after it rings several times.

"Good morning," says Sarah.

"Hey, how are you?"

"Carver? Wow, I'm glad to hear you are okay. Where are you? We need to meet up."

"I thought you had company. I was quite busy myself, had friends pop round unexpectedly."

Carver can hear Sarah typing on a laptop with seagulls squawking in the background.

"That's true, well . . . I had a moment there when I needed to reorganize some things. A few friends helped me out, and now I am free. The boss is in Berlin. He has asked me to fly up there and for you to continue on your project."

The young waitress comes over and puts down Carver's fresh orange juice and coffee.

"Okay, forward me the details." *What the hell, you cheeky* . . . Carver observes movement outside the café, a couple of Chinese tourists, maps in hand, now entering and heading toward a seat at the far side of the room.

"I will do that now. And, Carver . . . I wanted to catch up with you, don't think this is all work . . . okay? You know that, yes! Maybe we can have a holiday, just the two of us, after things wind down a little." Sarah's voice is full of hope, probing and teasing combined. Despite her attempts to connect with Carver, she has lost his attention and understanding. He requires messages to be clear, black and white, highlighted with keywords circled in red, when it comes to women. He prefers simplicity, but this morning he focuses his mind on his new friends.

"Sounds great. Let me know how you want things handled. I'll check in again on this number soon. Bye for now, Sarah," says Carver.

Sarah switches the phone off and sets it on the table. She sits there looking at it in deep absorption. Her security guys are busy moving gear about and getting in position as the deckhands unhook the mooring lines and prepare the vessel for sailing.

***

Carver sits forward on his chair eating his poached eggs, followed with mouthfuls of porchetta, trying hard not to shovel it in quickly. He gets up halfway through his breakfast to fetch the *la Repubblica* newspaper from an adjacent table. From the corner of his eye, he notices the couple have a phone positioned toward his table. *Sending my image back to HQ, sneaky pricks.* Carver returns to his table and finishes the meal with slices of hard cheese as he plans his next move. His head gently sways to the sounds of “Nessun dorma” coming through the bookshelf speakers behind him. Comfortable and relaxed, he offers no sense of danger. As he flicks over to a new page in the newspaper, he casually takes his phone and sends a quick message. He turns slightly in his chair to stretch his legs and notices that the café staff are now busy cleaning up and preparing food out the back. Carver drops a fifty-euro note on the table, grabs his orange juice, and stands up before darting across the room toward the Chinese couple. Without warning, he flicks some of his orange juice in the woman’s face then throws the rest onto the guy’s face. With this distraction, he quickly swaps his empty glass for the phone that the couple had positioned on the table then leaves the café.

Once outside, he races back to the van, scanning the car park and surrounding streets for threats. Carver takes a quick glimpse at the screen on the phone, and what he finds isn't a surprise to him. A Huawei phone with all the standard apps displayed. Whoever was watching him quickly disconnected the link. *No doubt discussing options as their surveillance operators have been compromised.* Carver considers his limited options. Now back at the van, he collects the black bag and slots the phone into the side pocket on the door for the SIS support guy to come and retrieve. The MP5 sits nicely on top of everything inside the bag, with his favorite Sig Sauer now fixed inside his waistband. Locking the van, Carver turns and walks up the street.

Within a couple of minutes, he reaches Panificio Pasticceria Semini, the small patisserie providing the street with a fresh aroma of sweet delights. He continues walking with his head down and casually turns into the alley next to the bakery and climbs the steps, looking for a vantage point to observe for other surveillance officers. With no followers, he decides not to enter the main street again. He instead makes his way up the steep hill, jumping into gardens and bursting through homes, apartments, and shops when no other route is possible. A few screams and half-hearted arguments are left in his wake as he gets onto Giardini Regina Elena, a small street with about half a dozen cars parked neatly in a row.

Taking out a lock pick, Carver walks past the cars, then drops to his knees at the passenger door of a Volkswagen Golf and works the lock. Once inside, he jams his feet against the bottom part of the steering wheel and, with his hands pulling the top of it, he breaks the steering lock. Freeing the wheel in both directions, Carver then rips off the plastic cover under the steering column and the ignition cylinder so he can strip the battery and starter wires. Pushing the gear stick into neutral, he then cuts the power wires from the cylinder and connects the exposed copper wires. Carver looks up to check that the lights on the dash have lit up. Once happy, he then cuts the starter wires from the cylinder, strips them also, then sparks the two wires together, allowing the engine to start. Within moments, the engine settles down into a pleasant rhythm. Carver manipulates the exposed wires into a safe position, then completes a quick check all around the car to ensure no one is approaching. Backing out of the street, he quickly drives the Golf down Via Galileo Galilei, keeping a check in his rearview mirror while navigating through the center of town. Lifting his mobile phone, he selects the new message. Sarah has provided him with the next job. *Saint-Tropez, Hôtel de Paris Saint-Tropez, Charles Walcott.* With a shake of the head, Carver estimates it will be almost a three-hour drive in this traffic. *Bloody hell, here we go again . . .*

Chapter Twelve

Shanghai, China

General Zhou Kai is unaccustomed to waiting in line. His American contact sent instructions to meet alone at the Long Bar in the Waldorf Astoria, built on the banks of the Huangpu River. As the Black Bear stands towering over the new Chinese elite who are pushing their way toward the mahogany bar, he can't help but notice the growing Western needs of these spoiled kids before him. As they discuss their wealth and ambitions, the men hold aloft their glasses of vintage champagne, showing their Swiss watches dangling awkwardly from their limp wrists. The girls are no better, busy admiring each other's new European designer labels while swaying their heads to French jazz, a language they do not understand. The general hated the place. *Fashion does not equal sophistication.* As he stands there watching, he feels like asking these young ones what their country means to them. *Would they go to war? Could they even make it past basic training? Impossible. There is no better time than now to push ahead with my plans.*

When the general approaches the bar, a smart young kid who is busy cleaning the marble top with a towel greets him. As he catches his eye, the young guy hesitates slightly before nodding and, without asking for the general's order, calmly goes to retrieve a bottle of baijiu. On his return, the general simply barks at him to follow. Walking past the crowd, he makes his way to the far corner of the room, where three leather chairs face a small and well-polished table. To the side stands a floor lamp about six feet high with half a dozen bulbs shining brightly. Reaching inside the glass shades, the general unscrews half of these to darken the corner. "Put the bottle down and fetch another glass and a bucket of ice. When my guest arrives, don't come with the menu. Simply provide some light snacks and don't come back, do you understand?"

"Yes sir, as you wish." With no more to add, the young man sets down the bottle of a fifteen-year-old Kweichow Moutai baijiu and a thick whiskey glass, then turns on his heel and leaves the grumpy and rude old man.

Growing more and more pissed, the general takes the bottle and pours himself a glass. *They have the thirty-year-old on display and perhaps the fifty in the back, yet they give me this.* Wallowing in his anger, he lifts the glass and purposely spills a few drops on the ground, a private ceremonial act, then takes a large gulp. As he sets his empty glass down, he checks his watch.

***

From the other side of the room, Val Olszewski observes his contact, the imposing figure whom the Chinese Communist Party fears yet respects. The one man who holds the power of influence, almost as high as the Chinese president himself. General Zhou Kai, the Black Bear, the chief of the Joint Staff Department of the

Central Military Commission (CMC). The man who holds all the cards. All foreign adversaries know only too well his dangerous reputation. Agencies such as the CIA and SIS have a desk devoted to the man, yet solid and credible intelligence is difficult to obtain. In the military and political circles throughout China, the rulers think of him as an intelligent yet cunning man. With a wild look in his deep-set eyes set behind thin gold-framed spectacles, sporting thick black hair parted neatly, and no sign of wrinkles, he appears much younger looking than his sixty-eight years, fifty-one of which were spent serving his country around China, then the world. All the top leaders in the Communist Party remain loyal to his position of power, such as the chairman of the Standing Committee of the National People's Congress, the CMC director of the Political Work Department, and, just as important, the majority of the other generals, including those from the PLA Air Force and admirals of the navy. These top dogs have direct control over their men and machinery of war, who will gladly obey the Black Bear without question. Any high-ranking politician that wanted ambition would also fall into line quickly when his name is merely whispered.

Olszewski recalls the time when he and the general were first introduced, a brief moment almost five years ago when he was working for the CIA. The location was the grand lobby within the St. Regis Amman in Jordan. Both men came head-to-head as Olszewski was with his entourage of intelligence staff sent by the White House to discuss Jordan's interest in the purchase of Wing Loong UAV drones from the Chinese. Olszewski was in the middle of a conversation with a senior engineer from the Chengdu Aircraft Industry Group, concerning China's industrial espionage work. An offer to the engineer was in the making. Olszewski was explaining that they needed someone inside CAIG who could verify how they came about their research and designs when they were suddenly approached by the man he now knows as the Black Bear.

"Do not speak to the Americans. Get back to your room." Violently grabbing the engineer by the arm, the general pulled and pushed him across the lobby. At the elevator, he shoved the panicked and remorseful man against the doors and slapped him across the face. Thick red blood poured from the engineer's nose, broken and now slanted to one side on his face. The general was fuming. Once he had the engineer sent on his way, he turned to face Olszewski. Watching the huge Chinese man walk back across the lobby, Olszewski began shifting his weight nervously from leg to leg, unsure what might happen. A security team comprising Navy SEALs and Delta Force operators took up position in front of Olszewski, speaking silently into their comms.

"I want a word with your boss," said the general, without looking at the men. Olszewski motioned for them to step back.

As the general got closer, Olszewski took a seat on a lounge chair and waved his hand at the one opposite him. The general nodded and lowered his enormous frame heavily onto the white leather.

"I know who you are; I know all about you. I also know what you were trying to do, Mr. Olszewski. If you want something, you go through me and only me. If you turn one of my countrymen to work with the USA, I will get rid of them and anyone close to them."

During their brief discussion, Olszewski alluded to the general that they may be able to assist each other through their careers. To judge each other and their intentions, more meetings were organized over the next few months. Over the years that followed, they grew powerful and rich together. Thinking back to that time, Olszewski never remembered seeing or hearing anything about the senior engineer. He simply vanished.

***

As he walks across the room, Olszewski is neither satisfied nor cautious about the location where he meets the general. This location is not entirely within the rule books, but rules matter little to him. Ever since he started providing the Chinese with intelligence from within the CIA, and later as the director of national intelligence, luck appeared to follow him everywhere. The Chinese Communist Party members are embedded within almost every country in the world, and their spies had infiltrated all major companies, universities, and joint organizations from the United Nations, World Trade Organization, and International Monetary Fund, to name a few. Every so often, Olszewski is provided with some juicy intel to disperse around the intelligence community. The financial incentives provided to him are more complicated to receive than the regular monthly intel, provided courtesy of the general. Olszewski receives those via diplomatic pouches delivered from the Chinese embassy in Washington, DC, to him during his well-loved acupuncture sessions. The United States swaps the intel for similar projects, keeping them informed of China's intentions related to various African and Southeast Asian countries, plus weapon sales and advances. Olszewski doesn't consider himself a traitor. In his eyes, he is still providing a service to his nation, plus keeping the Chinese onside is worth it considering their rapid military growth. *No one else is doing anything about them, so why should I?* The same mantra rolls around in his head as he approaches the table, his hand outstretched to meet General Zhou Kai, the infamous Black Bear himself.

Rising to meet the American, General Zhou Kai speaks quietly, "Good evening, Mr. Olszewski, it's been a long time. How was your flight?"

"Fast . . . This is all very sudden, General, what is it that cannot wait?"

The two men sit as the waiter arrives with another glass and several small dishes of food. Once he leaves, the general replies, "No doubt you have been following the issues we are having in Monte Carlo. Someone out there is causing headaches for us. We are not in the business of street combat, and I hope you can do all you can to prevent a full-scale war."

"Monte Carlo, and what about Florence? . . . None of that was at the hands of an American. To be frank, General, I think you are barking up the wrong tree. I too am short of answers. We are trying to piece together the crimes and connect the dots."

The general thinks about his response as he pours two glasses of baijiu and hands one to Olszewski. Sitting back in the leather chair, he slowly shakes his head. "Crimes. No, not crimes. This is terrorism, and someone needs to be held accountable. Our minister of state security had his damned head blown off, Olszewski. This is a huge red line. Someone crossed it, and there must be payback. I need names, and I'll respectfully ask for your agencies to stand down. Let us sort this out."

Olszewski hasn't slept in over twenty-four hours. When he received a message the previous day that the general wanted to see him in person, Olszewski's time was spent arranging meetings in China, South Korea, and Japan, an attempt to mask this particular sit-down as the primary reason he left Washington somewhat abruptly. All the major networks have been constantly ramping up the speculation of a war. Olszewski had watched the rolling coverage on the long flight over to Shanghai via Seoul, himself trying to piece it all together. Phone calls to Cain Hoffmann provided little intel. *That ass is hiding something from me.* He rubs his temples slowly to ease a migraine that occurs whenever he thinks of the director of the CIA. Olszewski takes a sip of the baijiu to relieve the annoying pain. The Chinese alcohol delivers him instant relief and sparks a plan. "Okay, General, one for one. That way we settled the score; the big wheel of gray warfare can keep turning for another decade."

The general refills the glasses and takes an oyster from the platter in front of him, sucking it down his throat, followed by a bite from a spring roll before wiping his mouth with a serviette. He looks around the room as he chews his food, then directs his gaze to Olszewski, where he gives a nod of agreement.

"Grab a pen . . ." Olszewski waits until the general is ready before speaking quietly. "Ken Herber from Task Force Orange is our top man in Europe, Army Intelligence Support. This is one sharp operator; I believe he is one of the CIA director's go-to guys when the shit hits the fan." Olszewski makes a decision and offers Herber to death row. This callous act fails to stir emotion within him, and neither will it bother his dirty friend, who easily believes the lies. The psychopath plies his trade of deception and death using skills perfected over the years. A feeling of peace now consumes his body. Olszewski's breathing is as relaxed as it has ever been.

"Where is he now?"

"Monte Carlo. I will provide you with his movements as I receive them." Olszewski is sending this lamb to the slaughter with not an ounce of pity. Finishing his glass of baijiu, he too starts eating. Selecting a steamed pork bun from the table, he splits it in half while waiting for the general to supply him with a name to take back to the United States.

"You think he took out my intel officer and then the minister? Both attacks?"

Swallowing a mouthful of the pork bun, Olszewski then looks around briefly before responding. "That's exactly what I am saying. I don't have the motive behind the tasking at this point, but someone deployed him there with all the equipment in place. If they removed him from the picture, I know all players will return home to have a rethink. That will buy us some time."

General Zhou Kai sits back and thinks about this. Watching Olszewski fill his mouth while eating from the various dishes in front of him, the Black Bear can see no sign of guilt or dishonesty. *Ken Herber, Task Force Orange.* He heard some rumors about the secretive special forces unit. *It would be beautiful to eliminate their top man. That would shake the most powerful military in the world. Perhaps then they would take notice not to mess with China.* "Okay . . . I will return what I know." Sliding his notepad into the breast pocket on his shirt, he offers someone in return. "The man you Americans should look at is Eddie Wu."

Chapter Thirteen

Monte Carlo, Monaco

It is almost lunchtime when Flynn receives a call informing him that the Navy SEALs extracted what information they could from the Chinese commando before dispatching him to the ocean floor. Flynn and Jackson during this time hadn't ventured too far from the soft surrounds of the Crystal Bar located within the Hôtel Hermitage Monte-Carlo. "Okay, Jackson, settle the bill. I have a meeting with the team at the Sainte-Dévote Chapel. You provide rear security and check for anyone following. It's only a few minutes' walk." Flynn rises to his feet and makes a quick pit stop in the bathroom, briefly stepping into an empty stall to recheck his Glock. Once finished, he starts his journey from the hotel, finding his way onto Avenue de L'Hermitage alone. The sun is scorching his face and a trickle of sweat makes its way down his barreled chest. Covering the short distance from the Hotel, Flynn casually checks the cars and entryways to the shops. An uneasy feeling consumes him. Despite being a highly experienced and professional operator, he trusts his gut more than intel. Now he is within a short distance of the meeting and his interest in obtaining critical information to set out a plan is accelerating, although he needs to be careful because of the unknown knowns regarding the Chinese strength.

He takes a moment to allow cars to pass as he crosses the street and moves toward the chapel. Once he passes under the road bridge, Flynn waits for his ears to adjust from the din of traffic to that of footsteps, vegetation rustling, or the sliding of metal against metal as a round gets loaded in a firearm. With a deep, slow breath, Flynn walks to the entrance of the chapel and peers inside to the darkness. Stepping toward the holy water font, he wets his finger and blesses himself as his eyes adjust from the brightness outside to the darkened interior. Without trying to look out of place, he stands next to a bench full of candles and lights one, then glances down between the long row of benches. He now spots his team close to the pulpit. He assumes they are taking time to have a word to God, releasing their faults and asking forgiveness. Flynn slowly makes his way down the aisle; the quietness and coolness is a stark contrast from the busy streets outside.

The Navy SEAL who was tasked with dealing with the interrogation and dispatch of the Chinese commando turns his head toward Flynn and nods. Finishing his prayers a few seconds later, he gets up and motions toward the side of the chapel. The two men stand under a supporting arch to begin the debrief. "Well, Mike, what did he say?"

Mike looks serious and somewhat hesitant before speaking. "The China man was good. He held out for ages. What we got was a mixture of lies and what I believe to be some truths."

"Go on," orders Flynn.

"Well, we have a small team of guys killing off a few spies no longer useful to them. They want to get rid of their contacts before they get picked up and interrogated by our agencies. I pressed him on further targets, but he was in the dark. He told me a man named Zhang held all the information. He was the leader, and all information came from someone he referred to as the Beast," says Mike.

Flynn stands there watching the main doors of the chapel as he listens. "The Beast! Sounds fake. Did you check him for any implants?"

Mike nods. "We found one and destroyed it. Once we did that, we moved location. Then I stripped the skin off his wrist and started snapping his carpal bones. That's when he started singing to us."

"Anything about Berlin?" asks Flynn.

"Nothing. He mentioned Saint-Tropez, he was unsure if that meant an operation was being planned or where they operate from. He was losing a lot of blood. It may be where Zhang is. The last thing he said was a warning. The cheeky bugger told us to leave Europe as his comrades are rising up. Then his lights went out."

"Okay, good work. I need to speak with Hoffmann; he wanted me in Berlin, so I'll scrap that plan. Saint-Tropez it is, then. Right, from here, I want you and your men to make your way there once it gets dark. Split up and find out what you can and update me. I'll come later tonight with Jackson once we tie up loose ends," says Flynn.

"Sounds good." With the conversation finished, Mike turns to face his men. With a slight nod, they all rise and make their way toward the exit.

Taking out his mobile, Flynn dials Hoffmann. *Saint-Tropez, better than the bloody Korangal Valley in Afghanistan.* The phone rings twice before he can answer it. "Good afternoon, boss, I have some information I need analyzed."

"I was waiting on your call, Flynn. We are in the dark here. Berlin is the second largest intelligence agency after our own, and we have nothing. I hope you have something for me?" Hoffmann sounds like he hasn't slept since leaving Washington.

"Give me all you have on the Chinese presence in Saint-Tropez. I'll be going there with little intel." Flynn can hear Hoffmann barking the location to someone in the background.

Leaning against the cold stone wall within the chapel with his mobile phone pressed to his ear, Flynn flinches at the loud bang. He isn't prepared for the deafening explosion. It blows in the arched windows around him, slicing his face and hands, ringing in his ears, drowned out by the distinctive sound of screaming coming from outside. A further blast occurs, followed by another. Someone has thrown devices into the chapel, so he has no option but to get out and into the fight. Penetrated by small shards of stained glass and pieces of masonry, he is angry the war has started without him. As he sprints, he switches his mobile phone for the Sig Sauer. The sound of rapid gunfire from outside the chapel begins suddenly and becomes louder the closer he gets to the thick oak doors, which took the brunt of the blasts.

He pulls on the heavy door slightly, offering himself a view of the courtyard. To his horror, he sees a couple of his men lying in heaps, their limbs twisted awkwardly because of dislocations and fractures. A call from one of the SEALs to his comrade ordering a retreat is cut off as a bullet penetrates his skull. Flynn traces the shooter's vantage point to somewhere on a high wall east of his position, an estimation of about forty-five meters. *He has us trapped . . . Jackson, where the hell are you?* Flynn hesitates as he thinks of Jackson. *He is protecting us!* He quickly scans the higher ground, noting the high number of shrubs offering concealment, then the large building set up high on the rocks, which contains several windows facing down to the chapel's courtyard. *Impossible to launch a counterattack, unless . . .* The seconds it takes Flynn to come up with his plan are cut short as the thuds of bullets hitting the door, inches from his face, force him to duck back inside the chapel. Remembering his interrupted call to Hoffmann, he reaches into his pocket and pulls out the phone. He's still on the line. "Hoffmann, we are under attack at the Sainte-Dévote Chapel in Monte Carlo. Get eyes on and have medical come in for the men."

With that said, Flynn doesn't wait for further discussions. He has a man to kill. Turning his phone off for tactical silence, he drops it into his pocket and races to the rear of the chapel to the other exit. Flynn will not wait to get ambushed while trapped like a wild animal in this concrete shell. He knows that if another improvised explosive device gets hurled inside the window, his death will be certain in this house of God.

With full-on aggression, he bursts through the rear exit and holds his Glock up, sweeping the area while moving low and fast. Within a few paces, he makes it to a steep wall about thirty meters high, one filled with bushes and shrubs adjacent to the chapel. He secures the weapon before jumping up to grab a handful of branches in both hands. With powerful back muscles, Flynn hauls his body up easily, ensuring a good foothold, then he works a path up the wall while staying underneath the vegetation. Halfway up, he stops and listens.

The men on the ground have ceased shouting orders; he hears no sounds of magazines being reloaded or boots scraping. Nothing, only the sound of birds in the trees and traffic on the road bridge, which passes high above the chapel courtyard. Soon the sirens will start, ambulances and the law. Flynn knows he won't have much time, so he presses on upward. Another ten meters will bring him to the base of a rustic building with pink paint cracking and peeling off. The large and majestic residence is covered by bright terracotta tiles with French windows set inside white Monaco masonry arches, which rise high above him. With one hand on a piece of stable rock and his foot jammed against the trunk of a small shrub, he continues his ascent.

From the corner of his eye, he notices a flash of light. Glimpsing down, he finds a piece of brass. Then another and one more. Shell casings. Flynn pieces together the attack. *The shithead started with crudely made explosives, then made his getaway up this path. He then returned fire when the SEALs refused to die, interrupting his attempt to flush me out.* Flynn keeps his anger under control, knowing his men fought to the death, allowing him time to get out. He needs to settle this. When war becomes personal, the potential to accept risks is heightened.

Flynn grabs a couple of shell casings and shoves them into his pocket. He clambers up the last portion of the hill with anger. He knows these attacks are not like the Middle East, where street fights can last for hours or days. This one took seconds. Now the attacker will make his escape, and Flynn knows he will lose him if he doesn't act rapidly.

The request to reposition the satellite may take some time. Knowing that Hoffmann will have issues with that presents Flynn with no other options but to continue his pursuit. He gets to his feet and pulls out the firearm and sweeps the area. All clear. Looking to the ground, he checks for snapped branches, fresh footprints, crushed plants or grass, any markers to highlight which direction his prey has run. Then he finds something that brings a moment of joy. Dark red venous blood, almost a velvet color, runs downward along the rock. The trail of blood of the wounded. Flynn considers the obvious route through the well-maintained grounds, hoping to find a quick path out onto the street. He focuses on all potential ambush locations while approaching that position with caution.

With ease, he climbs over the wall onto a redbrick pathway, which weaves its way around the large building. Flynn keeps close to the wall and moves forward quietly, firearm raised and ready to shoot. In the corner, he steps around and sweeps once more. *Blood* . . . More of it than before, soaking into the sandstone wall separating the manicured grounds from the walkway. As Flynn approaches, he notices the shrubs behind the wall have been disturbed. Closer now, he sees the first of the body, a black Hi-Tec boot, then a trouser leg, an arm . . . *JACKSON! Shit. Shit.* The procedure of checking for a carotid pulse is pointless. Jackson's neck has been slit wide open, exposing his windpipe. The knife has been left in place, rammed upward from the base of his skull, severing his brain stem. *My CIA buddy survived countless gunfights around the world. Never would he have guessed Monte Carlo would be his last battle.* Flynn flicks some sweat out of his eyes. *This guy is good.* With no time to offer a prayer or last words for Jackson, he drops to one knee and again brings his Glock up to sweep the area. Flynn thinks about the amount of blood around Jackson's neck that had stopped flowing. Jackson's heart can no longer pump the life-supporting liquid to his brain because of the damage, and CPR would be useless. *Time to move on; he's a minute ahead of me.* He jumps up to his feet and runs quickly inside the monumental building. As he runs through the corridors toward the street exit, he is aware of a group of people already on the floor. Members of the public and staff run in all directions as some hide while others stand around in shock.

Flynn sprints to the door leading out to the street while ignoring these helpless victims, panicking and screaming as another armed intruder passes through their private retreat. Weapon up and ready to fire, he rips the door open and steps out onto Avenue de la Costa. The property sits on the outer side of a hairpin bend with a narrow one-way street passing by at a steep angle. Flynn scans the street on the right, which is the approach road from the bottom of the hill, and then it turns on the hairpin in front of him, rising steeply. About forty meters away, on the top side of the street, he notices a man crouching behind a row of motorcycles. Without hesitation, the man fires twice, then steps farther back behind the motorcycles to take cover. Flynn feels a sudden stinging pain shooting from his left shoulder and down his arm. *You bastard! You got me.* Lifting his right arm, Flynn steadies it against the hood of a car with his firearm pointed up the street. Waiting for his shot. Flynn can hear the noise of a motorbike engine being started, echoing off the high stone walls on the narrow, winding road. A few moments later, a fireball erupts, then another. *The bastard is blowing the fuel tanks on the bikes.*

With his view obscured, Flynn needs to switch positions. He quickly races to his left across the road, then maneuvers for a better shot, trying in vain to ignore the pain coursing through his body as the toxic fumes of burning fuel and plastic enter his lungs. Through watery eyes, he moves toward the fluttering flames and smoke. Barely identifying his target, he drops his knee on the tarmac and lifts his weapon with one arm to take aim. The assassin pulls on the throttle and the front wheel of the black Kawasaki bike lifts sharply. Once the wheel touches down on the tarmac, the rider leans forward and pulls the throttle once more, keeping the powerful bike under control as he races out onto the road. With some awkwardness, he manhandles the bike by swinging it from side to side, weaving up the hill, making the shot from Flynn difficult.

A slight squeeze on the trigger, then another before he sends off several more controlled rounds through the flames. Flynn can only look on in anger to see the killer of his men disappear.

Chapter Fourteen

Saint-Tropez, France

Carver gets out of the cramped car and stretches his long legs, stiff from the run through the Italian mountains. Sliding thick fingers through his long dark hair, he reminds himself to make a hot shower his top priority. Putting two hands on the roof of the stolen Volkswagen, he rocks it gently and listens to the sloshing of fuel in the bottom of the almost empty tank. The fuel gauge sits in the red, and the risk of breaking down on the outskirts of a coastal city would draw too much attention.

Carver dumps the car in the backstreets and makes his way to a small area of woodland where he makes camp among its dense bushes. Once under cover, he turns on his mobile phone, then calls the priest, followed by Sarah. The last message he received read: *Saint-Tropez, Hôtel de Paris Saint-Tropez, Charles Walcott.* Charles Walcott, his old legend. The clean identity he uses when the proverbial hits the fan. Until SIS can come up with another decent legend, and preferably another distinguished gentleman doing business throughout Europe, Carver feels content slipping back into the cover he so desperately needs.

The phone rings once before getting answered. “Hey, have you made it there yet?” asks Sarah.

“Straight to the point, as usual.” With a laugh shared by both, Carver continues his impromptu briefing. “I am on the outskirts, a bit of vehicle trouble. Also, I am staying right here, as I want to know what I am walking into before I move.”

Wasting no time, Sarah relays her intel to Carver, bringing him up to speed on the attack in Monaco. “Listen Carver, whatever knowledge Cain Hoffmann gave to Harry Woodward, it was filtered somewhat before it made its way downstream to me and others with the appropriate clearance. Nonetheless, its paramount that we do not take a backward step, more importantly, we still have the clearance to operate and bring this fight back to the perpetrators. That means you need to turn up the pressure.”

“Wow, that’s heavy stuff, attacking a group of hardened men . . . Do you think it was our guy? Zhang! Using explosives appears to be his thing,” says Carver.

“The latest intel from Sean Flynn, CIA, confirms it was Zhang at the chapel. His men also picked out Zhang during their briefing before he slaughtered them. Apparently, they had their interrogation party with one of Zhang’s henchmen. So yes.”

Carver sits for a few seconds, weighing all this. “Okay, so where is Zhang and also this guy Flynn?”

“Zhang took off on a motorbike, westbound. He could be in France, but we believe he is coming to Saint-Tropez. Unless his mission, whatever it could be, has been called off. And Flynn, well, he is getting patched up somewhere. I need to get in contact with him, so that is something I will work on," says Sarah.

"How likely do you think it is they would call it off? I mean, they must not call it off. If he goes back to China, it will be hard for me to kill him. Hard, but not impossible. We need to let him move freely."

"From the aggressive dialogue and deniability coming from Beijing, I gather we have reached a new turning point. Whoever is leading the charge is doing so off their own back," says Sarah.

"How so?"

"For one, the American president has recently come off a call with the Chinese president, who claimed he was in the dark about these European operations. Something had worried the Chinese president and our intel confirmed he was now under protection in an undisclosed location due to fear of a coup. The NSA has also confirmed the same."

"Shit. Who would have the balls? Sorry, I mean, who would have the military support to start that? You know this could lead to an outright war?" says Carver.

"Yes, I agree with you. A war is what they are after. Why? That I cannot answer. But we must find and take out Zhang. We are speaking to our European counterparts about the correct dialogue used by all parties. It's imperative that all EU members hold steady and allow us to do what we do best."

“Hold your politics for Whitehall, Sarah, all I need is intel, then let me do what I do best. Give me another target, a big one to draw this piece of vermin out.”

“What makes you think he will come after you?” says Sarah.

“He went after the American special operations guys, correct? How did he know about them? I’m telling you, the Chinese have eyes all over Europe. Someone is using them, and this information is being passed back down to Zhang. That’s how he hit the men at the chapel. If I pop up and wipe out one of their big guys, he will be on my tail. After their minister of state security got killed, he will stop at nothing to eliminate all suspects.”

Carver can visualize Sarah as she makes a quick decision. Her eyes will be focused, lips turned tightly inward, slowly sucking air into her mouth. Then her shoulders and back will straighten and the slow nodding of the head will begin as she irons out her plan.

“Okay, I have someone in mind that will hurt them. Change your phone and get back to me. I’ll add a new number to call in your Vauxhall voice mail . . . Take care, Carver.”

Turning the phone off and almost satisfied at how the morning has gone, Carver rests until nightfall before starting his walk on the last few kilometers to Saint-Tropez. Laying comfortably under a palm tree, Carver ignores his mild hunger and waits until the tree crickets and cicadas begin their nightly calls before setting off.

***

With the sun dipping below the tree lines, Carver gets up and exits the woodland. He moves briskly along Chemin de Sainte-Bonne Aventure and scopes out easy properties on both sides of the small lane. A genuine need to change his appearance as best he can constantly plays on his mind. Carver looks for an easy opportunity. He listens as children splash playfully in a swimming pool, dinner plates clink loudly, a cat meows for leftovers, and a radio churns out relaxing songs from Vincent Scotto, suitable for a night under the bright stars above. The sounds float effortlessly over the privacy walls surrounding the villas as Carver walks past, his Sig Sauer pressed comfortably against his body.

He walks farther along before stopping to peek over a wall into the next property and spots a little white dog basking in the last of the warm, humid air of the evening. Dogs are the pet hate of trespassers, and in this location, the police would be called and on the scene within minutes of anything suspicious. Carver shakes his head and moves on, knowing he cannot hang around. He takes a left onto a smaller lane. Fifty meters along, he finds what he is after, a low wall offering a full-frontal view of the small property on one level. With a quick check for noisy neighbors, Carver pounces on top of the wall, then lowers himself gently and backs himself in behind an overgrown bougainvillea. He utters a curse at the thorny vines scraping into his thick skin, then waits a few minutes, observing the windows, looking for movement. From this location, he can see no water bowls for dogs and no children's toys in the large grassy yard surrounding the pool. His spirits rise slightly.

After the killing of a Chinese citizen yesterday, the desecration of his corpse, car theft, and breaking and entering on a residential property, Carver forbids himself to count jail time, which the French and Italian courts would hand down if arrested.

"It's not over yet," he mumbles as he pulls the bougainvillea off his body and moves across the property. Double-checking that his phone isn't switched on, he moves against the corner wall of the villa. Peeking inside to a room, Carver sees a perfectly made double bed, an old-style wooden armoire wardrobe with a couple of matching antique chairs. The room has double French doors leading out onto the yard, with no signs of home security fixed into the old wooden frames. Carver tries the handle. Locked. He gently uses a tension wrench partnered with a lock pick to slowly test and manipulate the pins. His hand keeps enough torque on the tension wrench while he sets each pin. Within seconds, the door is open and he enters.

He closes the door behind him to allow all sounds in the house to be heard clearly. Silence. Carver walks over to the wardrobe and opens it slowly, suspecting the old rusty hinges may creak and squeal loudly. Much to his disappointment, he can find no outer garments suitable to change his appearance. There is no time to waste, so he quietly heads into the hallway to check the next bedroom. He stops to listen before gently opening the next door a few millimeters. When he determines it to be empty, he then makes his way to the wardrobe. "Merci, Monsieur," he whispers. Much to his surprise, he pulls out a lightweight gray Haglöfs jacket. A smile creases his face as he spots a brown tweed duck-billed hat resting on the base of the wardrobe, which is quickly placed on his head. Carver tucks his long and unkempt hair neatly inside, changing his appearance remarkably.

Okay, time to move, Carver tells himself as he retraces his steps, ensuring no signs of a break-in or disturbance. He pauses slightly at the corner of the villa and checks for movement on the property. Taking a slightly indirect path to avoid the bougainvillea, he hurries back to the outer wall and peeks over the top, expecting to find the lane empty. *Shit!* Carver's heart skips a beat as he spots a black car parked fifteen meters from the villa, blocking access to the main road. Two men walk slowly toward the property, one on each side of the road, holding their firearms with both hands, their barrels pointed downward and slightly in front of them as they comb the street. Carver slowly reaches into his bag and retrieves a silencer for his Sig Sauer and screws it in place. The footsteps on the loose gravel from the other side of the wall provide him with the direction and speed of these two threats. Their faces were neither French, Italian, nor German; from what Carver could see, the men looked Asian, and not friendly.

"This night is going to get messy," he whispers to himself before correcting his stance, preparing for an ambush as the men creep past. The noise of the insects almost drowns out the unwelcome newcomers on the other side of the six-foot-high brick wall. Carver thinks quickly about the layout of the street, planning the primary escape route and at least two others, depending on how the situation plays out. He can hear the men talking silently into their comms. The man closest to the wall where Carver is hiding stops and gives an order to his partner. Their words are deliberate and not rushed, with no hesitation or fear. Hunkered down in the shadows, Carver waits for the men to make their move. When he sees the silhouette appearing over the wall, his plan changes. Choosing the same entry technique and location as Carver, the first of the men drops from the wall and immediately aims his firearm at the property.

The man starts sweeping it slowly from right to left and back again before giving the order for his comrade to join him. Once the second man is on the wall, Carver knows he will have holstered his firearm. The man needs two hands on the white-painted brick wall so he can control his drop and not cause any noise from the bushes below. Carver is only two meters away, his weapon aimed at the first man's temple. Any moment now their eyesight will adjust to the darkness, and the advantage Carver has now will be lost. As a mosquito feeds on his wrist, the faint sounds of Vincent Scotto are heard far off in the distance, the happy family enjoying the cooling Mediterranean night. High above, a blanket of stars illuminates through the palms of trees while the acrid stench of stale cigarettes drifts the short distance from the target to Carver's gun barrel. The SIS man fires once, then he sweeps the weapon slightly right to the second man, who has yet to draw his own. Double tap and back to the first for his second subsonic round in the back of the head just before he topples over. Job done.

The muzzle report sounds no louder than a slap across the face. Despite this, Carver still waits a few seconds to listen for any changes in the neighboring properties. When satisfied the coast is clear, he drags the bodies along the wall and attempts to stuff them behind the thickest part of the bougainvillea. As the thorns rip into his skin, Carver removes a set of comms from one man and inserts the device in his ear, then checks the volume level. Next, he searches their pockets for any signs of identity. Finding nothing except bundles of cash, which he pockets, and spare ammo, he quickly prepares to leave the area and put as much distance as he can between himself and the dead. Suddenly, a thought crosses his mind. He removes his phone and takes a picture of both men, closing his eyes each time the flash sparkles to save his night vision. He attaches the photo to a message and sends it to the SIS tech kid, Tommy Taylor. Only one word is required: *NAMES?*

A quick check over the wall and with a strong pop and vault, Carver lands on the other side with his firearm drawn before his feet touch the ground. He runs over to the black car, an Audi sedan, and checks inside for anything of interest. The keys are still in the ignition and there's more than half a tank of fuel. Muttering to himself about his predicament, Carver jumps in the driver's seat and gently closes the door. Selecting reverse, he releases the parking brake and backs out of one problem and heads into town to create another.

Driving for several minutes toward Saint-Tropez, Carver has spent the time rifling through the glove box, center console, side pockets and under the seats and checking every crevice he can find, looking for intelligence on these men. The car is clean. Not trusting if listening devices have been fitted, he reminds himself not to make any calls. Carver hopes the Audi has a tracking device installed, which could draw out Zhang. He decides to hold on to it instead of dumping and switching vehicles. With his eyes peeled, he navigates his way along the coastal road toward his meeting. With little traffic on Avenue Gén de Gaulle, he knows finding a parking space won't be a problem. Driving past a row of two-story townhouses painted in pastel yellow, mauve, creamy mint, and peach, he loops around Place Blanqui, parks, and returns on foot. The streetlights give off a dim yellow glow, casting long shadows from every object in their path, distorting facial features to the less vigilant observer. His large profile stands out, however. Carver shuffles along, stooping slightly with his new hat pulled down over his thick brow as he nears the back of the property. Once he walks past a hundred meters, he then doubles back to check for followers. Carver then scoots up the external steps to the second-floor entrance, which was built over the garage. Someone has switched the rear security light off, the only one in the row of five apartments that sits in darkness. With his Sig Sauer in his right hand, and the suppressor still attached, Carver opens the rear door with his left and moves slowly inside. With a quick sniff of a recognizable scent, he stands in the small kitchen and waits for the occupant to present themselves.

"My dear boy," says the priest in his calming voice as he steps in from the small living room that attaches directly to the kitchen.

Carver relaxes and turns his back, unsure why he is slightly embarrassed in the priest's presence with the tools of his trade. He tactfully removes the suppressor and holsters his weapon.

When he turns around, the priest stands there smiling, a set of rosary beads in one hand and a glass of wine in the other. "Are you knocking off the altar wine again, Father?" The two men laugh before the priest slides an old leather-topped barstool from under the breakfast bar and offers Carver a seat.

"I'm sorry to arrive early. I got myself a new car."

Chapter Fifteen

Zermatt, Switzerland

The air at this altitude is crisp and clean. Overhead, a deep blue sky covers the town from one horizon to the other. Red geraniums are displayed neatly in every window box and church bells ring peacefully, marking each hour at one of the highest ski resorts in Europe. Now in a better mood than when he first arrived in Switzerland, he relaxes his guard and finally opens the patio doors to enjoy the view of the Alps and the Matterhorn. The highest summit in Europe bearing down on Zhang makes him feel insignificant to the power of nature. Despite the distance from himself and the mountains in front of him, the Matterhorn sends a shiver downs Zhang's spine. He thinks back to the tough and inhumane winter warfare training courses with the Russian Spetsnaz that they ordered him to complete before achieving his commander's position. Staring at the huge mountain face, he wonders briefly if any of those men fought in such inhospitable environments. *Give me the streets of Europe any day*, thinks Zhang. Retreating inside, he cranks up the room temperature and tops up his glass with Graubünden wine, then takes a seat at the dining table to clean and dress his wounds. With more alcohol in his body, Zhang feels comfortable in these strange surroundings, and every so often he considers what the risks could be for him venturing outside to stock up on more food and wine of his liking.

***

The eight-hour drive, finishing with a train trip from Täsch, two days earlier to this chalet in Zermatt was more painful than time-consuming. Leaving the sovereign city-state of Monaco, then crossing from France to Italy and onward to Switzerland, caused no issues. It was the burning sores from the bullets embedded in his back that bothered him. After the gunfight in Monte Carlo, Zhang rode his Kawasaki sharply along the coastal road, making good distance as the blood seeped out of his back and slowly made a path over his aramid-lined cargo pants.

A couple of hours after leaving Monte Carlo, Zhang stopped briefly at Savona in Italy to make a quick phone call to General Zhou before dumping the device. He also took the time to check his wounds and do what he could to stop the bleeding. After attending to himself, he followed his plan and turned north before hitting Genoa, then crossed into Switzerland, where he would finally patch up his wounds and access whatever help he required from the huge Chinese diaspora that had flocked to Europe. During that phone call, the general promised Zhang he would find him suitable accommodations, instead of using hotels or guesthouses. Ordering him to stay low for a few days then wait to be contacted later, the general had named several high-profile Chinese businessmen and their families living throughout the country. Zhang thinks about these so-called compatriots.

The escapers who shun China and take advantage of the Western schooling and lifestyles. In his eyes, these men should get pulled into line and made to assist with any demands he makes.

***

On entering this strange property in Zermatt, Zhang quickly checked each room, and the windows and doors. Security was good. Visualizing how an ambush could occur and what cover he would have from each part of the chalet helped him work out his defense. When he figured out the inside, he took a walk around the chalet, scanning the land for possible sniper positions and escape routes. Once he was satisfied with his plan, he returned to the kitchen and began the task of stripping down and cleaning his cowboy-style ten-millimeter Smith & Wesson 610 revolver.

With that job complete and without a break, he prepares to treat his wounds. Noticing a rack of wine in the dining room, Zhang skims the labels, then slides one out of its place and wipes the bottle free of dust before moving to the kitchen. After pouring a glass of the Bündner Herrschaft, he takes a large swig and grimaces at the taste, then swallows a bit more to feel numb enough for the upcoming pain, but not that numb to lose accuracy in a firefight.

Zhang lays the contents of a trauma kit over the table, then he carefully peels the bandage off his lower leg to assess, clean, and reapply a sterile dressing. The damage from the sniper's bullet could have been worse. The shot missed the bone and, despite the pain, he is sure full mobility will return in a few weeks. The good news is there are no signs of infection because of the well-maintained quick-clot dressing he applied shortly after escaping the sniper attack on the *Golden Tiger*. As Zhang carries out his self-treatment, the sight of his blood and torn skin makes him think back to those on the boat. *Eddie Wu! Did he make it out alive?* He forgot to ask the general. *And what about the cute girls?* Putting their faces to the back of his mind to join countless others, he continues with his medical work. The riding gear did a lot to protect the bullets from doing damage to his back, which penetrated his body but not deep enough to cause problems, as all internal organs were intact. No longer could he wear the expensive leathers, not only because of the bullet holes, which would attract attention, but also because of the fact that Zermatt is vehicle free. When he dumped the motorbike at the train station in Täsch, he also discarded the leathers in the deepest bin he could find.

Zhang takes another gulp of wine and is now in combat readiness mode. They had drilled this into him through years of specialized training. With his shirt removed, he then twists his arm around his back while delicate fingers clutch the set of medical forceps ready to do what should be carried out in a trauma ward. All he can see is his bloodstained back reflected in a large mirror taken from the bathroom. With no hesitation, he delicately extracts two pieces of lead from beneath his tight skin and bites down hard through the pain. He drops the lumps of bloody lead one by one on the glass table. Zhang realizes how lucky the shootout had been when he finds two other bullets that had lodged in his motorbike helmet and failed to penetrate it. Despite the luck he had received, it does nothing to prevent his thumping headache for the rest of the day. Once he washes out his wounds with iodine, a level of confidence returns.

Zhang wants to keep his good fortune and make sure no infections take hold, so he takes out a prepared syringe full of antibiotics and, without drawing breath, he flicks off the cap and sinks the pin into his flesh then presses down steadily on the plunger. With all wounds treated, he neatly dresses the area and hopes the medic, which the general had promised, will show up sometime soon. The next procedure is to find enough energy required to make himself a meal. They mostly stocked the kitchen with local food with very little imports except for a couple of bottles of soy sauce. Zhang is determined to try his best to eat as much as possible over the next few days. To restore his energy for the upcoming operations ahead will mean consuming a high number of calories. After about ten minutes of forced eating, he finally lays his fork down on the mostly empty plate of pasta and sausage, which is a mix of beef, pork, and spices, known locally as *landjäger*. Zhang sets the plate on the floor, then swings his legs up onto the sofa and within seconds is fast asleep, his newly trusted 610 revolver gripped loosely in his hand.

***

The next few days pass slowly. He enjoys the taste of the local wine, maybe a bit too much, and he is even getting used to the raclette cheese and the various strange cold cuts of meat that were left in the fridge by the family before they were ordered out by the controlling powers. On one afternoon he receives a delivery, more food and some toiletries, all of which are left at the front door. When he hears the doorbell ring once, Zhang goes into a panic. He quickly grabs his firearm and scrambles to the window so he can peek out at the uninvited guest. From behind the thick navy-and-gold curtains, he can just make out a man retreating down the concrete path before scuttling away toward town. Zhang looks at the paltry amount of food left by this man and the contents of the fridge; with a disappointed feeling, he considers breaking cover and walking to the shops himself so he can pick his ingredients. More cheese and wine too.

***

He sits comfortably on the terrace, a smile on his face, a glass of wine in one hand, a cigarette in the other, and a bag of groceries from Migros supermarket lying by his feet. Zhang thinks about those simple orders from the general a few days ago. *Allow the dust to settle so new targets can be located, then resume your attacks.* The new Chinese hit men arriving in Saint-Tropez will look after the British and Americans who are sent to stop the assassinations of their people. *Their corrupt countrymen!* thinks Zhang. He can't work out why the Western governments would send in their special forces to save such vermin that turned their backs on their people. The general put it to Zhang that even with the CIA and SIS breathing down their necks, it is a requirement that they push ahead with the plans; the men and women who spilled the secrets of the West need to be killed as a priority to prevent them revealing details about the Communist spy network covering Europe.

His constant checking of the wounds every day lifts Zhang's confidence in his health. Scars will form and join many others around his body. Even better is the fact he can resume physical training once again. No way in hell he could be an office guy, and on the doorstep of beautiful hiking trails, Zhang decides it is time to burn some calories. Despite his eagerness to move on with the next job, killing some weak-minded spy working for China but now compromised and no longer useful, he desperately wants to go after the tier-one guys. The best of the best. He needs to show the general he is China's ultimate weapon. The finest assassin China can ever produce. A man who can deliver on the mission and instill fear in their Western enemies. Even if it means disobeying orders.

Chapter Sixteen

Saint-Tropez, France

The orders had been blunt: spread out and attempt to cover as many targets as possible. Intelligence reports are coming in thick and fast. Now it is Ken Herber's job to follow one of the leads on Zhang and report back. Carver will keep a low profile in France, waiting for a list of high-profile targets to eliminate. This is a crude plan, as the deaths will cause such a fury within the Chinese Communist Party, meaning Zhang will receive directions to intervene. The CIA has its resources spread across France, Spain, Italy, and Germany, as do the SIS and the French DGSE. The Russian SVR made provocative moves in Eastern Europe, and various Islamic terror groups used the distractions in Monte Carlo to rearm cells to support their new European enclaves. Sarah Fontaine finds herself in the middle of this mess and is yet to have ideal answers. All she has to work with is a couple of tough-as-nails operators who now have their skin firmly in the game. She has not established the exact decisions yet, as her composure is straggling and the voices in her head sound confused.

Sarah sits with her hands covering her face as a cigarette burns in an ashtray. Keeping her eyes closed, she massages her tanned forehead with her fingertips, trying to stir life into her frontal lobe. She needs to come up with a plan. One that will solve the problem of continuing death and destruction. She needs to find a list of targets important enough to draw out Zhang. As the attractive director of operations from SIS sits there, scheming and questioning a multitude of decisions, she feels exhausted. She tries to piece together the events that unfolded during the week, from Florence to the *Golden Tiger* yacht to the car park bombing . . . *Tick, tick, and tick, yes, all accounted for.* But the real question is: *The sniper, who the hell was that?* She keeps asking herself the same questions that Harry, her boss, is asking. As she lifts her head to look out over the port from her table on Quai Jean Jaurès, a thought crosses her mind about taking a puff from the cigarette. Her coffee, now cold, needs replacing. She signals the attention of staff then quickly picks up the cigarette and inhales a lungful of the smoke. With the cigarette hurriedly set back down into its position, she closes her eyes as the nicotine floods her lungs. Instantly, the feeling of relaxation washes over her body as she holds it for a second before exhaling the smoke over her shoulder, then orders a fresh coffee from the waiter.

Sarah rubs her hands along her thighs, then squeezes her leg muscles to help the blood flow through her tired body. Once the dizziness passes from the nicotine, her mind sharpens slightly. Sarah now remembers about her messy hair. An expensive navy silk hairband is taken from the pocket of her white shorts, which she uses to wind her blond hair up in a neat bun, wrapping it in place.

Only a short time ago, the attractive SIS assistant director of operations was woken rudely from her sleep. A full two hours of forgotten dreams, the much-needed silence shattered by one of her mobile phones. Harry had provided Sarah with another bouncing ball to follow.

With no time to spare, either to shower or make herself somewhat pleasing to the eye, she leaves a rented seventy-foot yacht and heads to dry land. The intelligent woman juggles this current black operation with the level of secrecy and daring acts of warfare required, mostly on her own. The past few days have taken their toll on her. She realizes her ability to work alone carries with it a level of stress that is hard to quantify. *Vauxhall Cross in London is where I should be. At least I would be surrounded with my staff, not doing fieldwork and being on call twenty-four hours every bloody day.* As she questions her position and the current situation, she can feel her temper rising, which is unusual. A feeling that something is not right overwhelms her. *Is it Carver? The fear I might lose him, never see his face again, feel his warmth?* She tries to shake herself free from distractions. The consequences of falling in love with her top operative cannot happen. *Could it be true?* She reaches over the table, grabs the cigarette, and sucks deeply on it. The lungful of smoke, more than she meant to inhale, causes her to cough wildly. As she attempts to muffle her embarrassment and attach the cigarette back to the ashtray, a couple of locals briefly take a glance over before returning to their breakfast.

"You could have asked for one. I have a whole packet."

Sarah looks up suddenly, then drops her head, embarrassed by getting caught. Once the CIA operative, Sean Flynn, left the table to take a call, she couldn't help but try a smoke to help calm her nerves. "I'm sorry, I don't smoke . . ."

"It's fine," says Flynn as he takes his seat once more. "I don't smoke either, only on operations; I find it helps me think."

Regaining her composure somewhat, Sarah sits upright and adjusts her yellow boatneck blouse so it sits evenly on both shoulders. Then she opens the screen of her laptop. She motions for Flynn to retake his seat once again just as a fresh glass of coffee arrives. Flynn orders one more for himself, including a plate of eggs, cheese, and bread.

"I have never been debriefed by SIS before. Europe is way different from Afghanistan. You know, Sarah, I could live here," says Flynn.

Sarah is busy entering the passcodes to launch the encrypted programs SIS uses to send and receive their data. "You want to live in Saint-Tropez? What's wrong with Arapahoe County in Colorado?"

"Very impressive. You read my files. And no, not necessarily Saint-Tropez. I mean somewhere around the Mediterranean. It's beautiful here, less bullshit than in the States." Flynn had made his way to Saint-Tropez almost immediately after Zhang got the better of him, hoping to catch up with the Chinese assassin to finish what he started. When he made his usual check-in call to Hoffmann, he was told to find this SIS woman and assist where possible. All CIA contacts are considered compromised, so they will funnel all further orders through to him via the British.

One thing Flynn wasn't told about was her beauty, the blond hair and tanned skin, high cheekbones, and an athletic body. She has it all. He watches her typing on the screen, her lips moving softly as she reads the words appearing on the screen. Flynn turns his face away and looks out toward the port and the street in front of them, more of a distraction for himself and to remind himself of the threats they now face.

Sarah tilts the screen away from the sun glare and finally locates the page she's looking for. The updated information was sent by her boss, Harry, which includes updates from GCHQ, including the photo of Zhang and some notes taken from the Russian military. "Okay, Flynn, as Harry Woodward and Cain Hoffmann have both signed off on this information and you, for want of a better word, are seconded to SIS, I am free to discuss this with you."

"Wow, do I get to meet the Queen?" says Flynn with a chuckle as he takes a smoke of the cigarette.

"You are looking at her . . . now, be sensible for a minute." Sarah slides her chair closer to Flynn and turns the laptop so Flynn can look at the dirty piece of work who took out his team. "It looks like Zhang has moved up to Switzerland. We have tasked one of your Intelligence Support Activity guys with locating him. He is already on his way there to get eyes on. Meanwhile, back at the ranch," Sarah says with her eyebrows raised and finger pointed toward the ground, "we figure out a way to draw Zhang to us. In the event it isn't him in the Alps."

Flynn sits and stares at the face of Zhang on the screen. He reaches over to the track pad and, using two fingers, scrolls through each of the photographs taken by various agencies over the years. "Good work . . . I won't forget that face." With the face committed to memory, Flynn sits back in his chair and lights another cigarette. They sit in silence for a few minutes, Sarah punching the keys on the laptop, Flynn organizing his mind. The waiter comes and lays the food and coffee down on the small bistro table. Sarah moves her laptop and arranges the table and cutlery. Flynn takes little notice of the food being delivered.

Then he speaks, "If he is in Switzerland, I want to go up there and take him out."

"You don't have a team." Realizing what she said, Sarah quickly changes tack. "Sorry, what I mean is, Harry said you were off the books. The guys sent to help you out are no longer here. By the way, I have sent their bodies to Germany and hopefully they will be in the States by now." Sarah watches as the sad news of his men being repatriated back to the USA sinks in. She reaches over and touches his forearm. "I know it's hard, and I am sorry. Therefore, Hoffmann has agreed for us Brits to take full control. He's concerned about how Zhang ambushed you guys; something isn't right on your side."

"He used the word *ambushed*?" Flynn casts an eye over the port, his blue eyes squinting from the warm sun. He watches as men and women tend to their million-dollar yachts, carrying supplies on board, some hosing fresh water over the deck while others inspect their sails. He takes another pull off the cigarette, then continues. "I had an inkling something was wrong; Zhang couldn't have got past Jackson so easy. Luck only goes so far, plus he had explosives ready. That was planned. He isn't working alone, and whoever is supplying him intel has information that is too close to home."

"What are you saying?" asks Sarah, although she knows what he meant. Her analytical mind has already covered most of this. The only problem she has is a lack of knowledge about possible suspects within the huge American intelligence community.

"We have a leak, someone supplying the Chinese."

"That's why it is in our hands, Flynn. You shouldn't be using your network, not until your side gets their ducks in a row. Let us Brits handle this end. You are on the team, same side, just a different team."

Flynn runs his hands through his blond hair, then rubs the three-day growth on his face as he figures out his role. "What if our army intel guy is working with the Chinese?"

"Only one way to find out. If he comes back saying there is no sign of Zhang, then we will know he is bullshitting us, and SIS will take a deep interest in him and his crew. I will keep the CIA in the dark until we can fix it. Only Cain Hoffmann and you will be in the loop. Meanwhile, we can cause mayhem here, in France, or wherever we find decent targets to draw Zhang out, make him flustered, force him to break cover and screw up. I believe . . ." Sarah taps a few keys and looks over her shoulder before closing the laptop cover. "The Chinese government has a loose cannon. One of their generals, nicknamed the Black Bear, is pushing for war. And it's also confirmed that CBS, the Central Security Bureau, has moved the Chinese president for his own protection."

So, there it is. We now have two targets. Zhang and the Black Bear, not the Beast. He nods to himself in silent confirmation. Flynn then stubs out the cigarette and takes a drink of his coffee before speaking. "I heard that name from Mike, one of the SEAL guys. Although it sounded fake to me. What do we have on this general?"

Drinking the last of her coffee before it loses its heat, Sarah sets the cup down and checks her watch before replying. "We are still working on that. Eat your meal before it gets cold. I must ask, who did you call?" she says while reaching into her small backpack to pull out a new phone.

"Jackson's better half . . . I wanted to call her instead of some stranger from defense." Flynn pushes the eggs around on his plate, then stops and rips off a chunk from the fresh warm baguette and smothers it with butter before putting it in his mouth.

Sarah says nothing. She takes his phone from the table and removes the battery and SIM card, then places it all in a small bag to be destroyed after their meeting. Sliding a new phone across the table, she sits back and gives Flynn time to get used to his new boss. "How's your shoulder? You don't appear to be in pain."

Flynn shrugs his shoulder. "It is clean. Was a ten-millimeter; unusual gun for an operator, a bloody revolver, but yeah, I never felt better. Thanks for the medic, by the way." Sarah moves her lips, about to respond, then stops as a man walks past on his way out from the café just as a new couple arrives hand in hand and sits at a table next to them.

"We can cause mayhem." Flynn breaks the silence.

"Excuse me?" Sarah looks at the muscular frame of Flynn as he chews quickly on his eggs, his wavy blond hair shielding his eyes slightly.

You said, "We can cause mayhem here to draw Zhang out. Is that me and you?"

With a stifled chuckle, she shakes her head. "Sorry, I should have explained. I will run you and your British counterpart, Matt Carver. Personally, I don't want all my eggs in one basket. You would understand that."

Finishing his meal, and with a drink of coffee, Flynn then lifts the phone and puts it in his pocket. He wipes his hair back behind his ears as he leans back in his chair to take in the view. "Well, Sarah, I would need to meet this guy. You know how it is. As a fellow professional, I want to check him out."

"If you had been paying attention, you could have. He was the one who delivered your eggs and coffee."

***

Carver picks up some breakfast of his own at a small café on Rue Henri Seillon and retreats to the safe house the priest organized for him. The holy man had led an interesting life, beginning his career in the SAS, and as part of E Squadron, he worked frequently with the Secret Intelligence Service officers. Intrigued with their work, he began a new career as one of their operational officers. He did his fair share during the Cold War and in various Middle Eastern countries, then he turned a corner in his life and went off to Italy and received the sacrament of holy orders. From there, he began living the religious lifestyle, with just a touch of guidance on the moral forces in the world.

Walking along the narrow one-way cobbled street, Carver's thoughts return to Zhang and his whereabouts. Sarah had briefed him previously on the suspected injuries he had and the subsequent healing time. Carver knew that the healing times quoted by any civilian doctors were a lot longer than combat medics or those doctors employed by the military to keep a man in the fight. Intensive surgery could be sought weeks down the line. Zhang, in Carver's view, could be up and running in a few days. Which is what he told Sarah. *Expect another killing any day now.*

Carver also had help from Tommy Taylor, his expert technical hacker, the geek whose job it is to keep him untraceable. Tommy assured Carver the local police didn't have a photo or any surveillance footage on him, neither did any of the Euro agencies. And it was Tommy's job to scour the usual investigative bodies and make all data disappear when it popped up. When Carver rolls out on a mission and requires protection from cameras, he calls on Tommy, who acts accordingly by hacking into the various networks to shut down the streets. It is a great partnership and one that has paid off and allowed Carver the anonymity a man of his profession requires. However, Tommy is only one man. Patriotic, yes, although Tommy has his own life and it isn't guaranteed that the geek would be in front of a computer 24-7.

Not a guarantee, thinks Carver as he walks past his apartment and loops back a second time before entering. Having continuous cover is only a luxury, so Carver uses Tommy only when necessary. *No point burning the young man out,* he thinks to himself.

Moving up the rear steps, Carver stops and scans the area one more time, his hand gripping the Sig Sauer in his jacket before entering. Sitting down at the dining room table, Carver takes from his jacket a few photos, each with locations and timings on them. His first target: A portly man of Chinese origin; his legend purports him to be of Malaysian Chinese origin. Li Xing-fu, born in Kuala Lumpur to a political family who was sent to Europe at a young age to gain his education in a Swiss boarding school, then in Oxford, where he earned his PhD in the field of medical science.

Carver flicks through some notes summarizing his political ambitions and donations to various groups, all of which are noted as front organizations used to influence the Europeans. He flicks through the first page to learn about his Chinese Communist Party membership, multiple trips to Zhongnanhai, and financial records showing transfers back to Beijing. The detailed report also lists his love of braised pork belly, Sichuan hot pots, and jiaozi and how he came third in a badminton competition in high school. Nothing of genuine interest, so Carver casually skims through the pages, looking for a reason to feel good about what he is about to do.

Suddenly he stops at one page and has to read the title again as he can't believe his own eyes. Genetic bioweapons and coronaviruses. Casting his eyes over the page, he reads the summaries under titles such as "advanced infectious disease programs," "artificial manipulation," "microbiology," and "molecular genetics." *Bastard. Yeah, that will do it.* Happy with the target that Sarah selected, Carver now works on a plan to wipe this creature off the earth.

Chapter Seventeen

Zermatt, Switzerland

Not wanting to be visible in his movements, Ken Herber chose a room in a traditional wooden chalet at the far end of town with a room that faced the main street. The accommodation had three floors, with the ground floor comprising a restaurant, bar, and hotel lobby. Tourism was booming throughout Zermatt and the visitors have occupied or had booked almost all rooms in the small Alpine town. Hotel staff offered Herber a couple of different rooms on both floors. As the American casually checked the views from each, he pretended to make a fuss over which room offered the best views of the morning sunlight. He knew in which side of the building he needed to be staying the moment he arrived on the street, and they granted his choice with no suspicion of the real purpose of his stay.

The intelligence support operative spent the better part of the day setting up his surveillance equipment and adjusting the focus on the long-range cameras. He fixed the primary camera on Bahnhofstrasse, which translates to *railway station street*. This was the cobbled street that runs north to south from Zermatt's train station to the

Matterhorn Museum. Once night falls, Herber will move out and set up other remote cameras, also supported with facial-recognition technology that will be linked to his laptop back in his room. Notifications will alert him once Zhang passes within eight hundred meters of any of the lenses. As Herber is the first man on the ground, the CIA tasked him with gathering as much intelligence as required to organize the shooters to come in and take care of the problem. Dispatching a target would come easily to Herber. He utilized his skills in Afghanistan and Iraq when the SEAL teams and Delta unit guys found themselves under heavy contact, and it was his job to take the target out, then provide covering support before evading capture. Here in the mountains of Switzerland, it is easy to switch off mentally and enjoy the moment. Dozens of tourists meander past his lodgings, carrying their shopping bags and snacking on large bars of Swiss chocolate or chunks of cheese. *This place is on a different scale,* thinks Herber as he makes the finishing touches to the lens. Covering the end of the Nikon glass with a fine black cloth to avoid reflection, he thinks back to his nights on the slopes of the Hindu Kush mountain range in Afghanistan. *Goat head curry tasted like shit . . . good times, though.* Shaking his head at the thought of past meals, he continues quickly on his work. Within seconds, he links the camera to his laptop using the HDMI cables, then he switches on the camera before launching the related facial-recognition software and . . . *bingo.* Sharp quality and a live view of around two hundred meters of the Bahnhofstrasse. Herber watches the laptop screen as tourists walk along the infamous street, browsing happily in the windows at the latest Swiss watch, reading menus framed in glass boxes next to restaurant doors, and marveling at the beauty all around them. Unaware that in a room high above, their faces on the screen are enclosed within a green box while the software rapidly calculates for a match. Herber sits behind this screen and waits patiently for the sun to drop behind the Alps so he can set up a couple more cameras. He then gets to work by cleaning and testing the slide action and spring on his Glock once more before setting it down on the bed beside his small day pack. With nothing more to do, Herber lies down on his queen-size bed and catches some sleep.

***

The sun is about an hour away from setting, and now the cool wind stirs. The drafts easily find the gaps through the thick wooden windows, which cause Herber to rise from his bed and fetch a blanket from the cupboard. Weary from the long day and the thought of working throughout the night motivates him to stay fueled. From the bedside table, he grabs the phone and dials reception. A hot meal and coffee organized. He then lays out some cameras and checked that they are all fully powered. The next job is to clean their surfaces with alcohol wipes to remove his fingerprints. Sitting back on the bed, he wraps himself with a thick red blanket as his laptop screen is busy processing the faces in the street down below.

Herber's head drops forward as he momentarily falls asleep, his senses dulled as he recalibrates his mind to the situation in front of him. Then he hears a sound that momentarily startles him. A few more knocks on the door. "Coming," shouts Herber as he picks up his Glock. Holding it under his blanket to hide the noise of metal on metal, he gently racks the slide. With a round in the chamber, he holds his weapon with both hands close to his chest and tiptoes to the side of the doorframe with his back against the wall. "What do you want?"

The young hotel staff is confused. *The man ordered only about ten minutes ago and already forgot what he ordered.* Opening the lid covering the food, the man inspects the meal and relays the order. "Sir, I have your papet Vaudois, tartiflette, leckerli biscuits, and the pot of black coffee you ordered, correct? Yes . . ."

It takes Herber a few seconds to translate and confirm in his head what he selected from the in-room menu. *Leeks with sausage and potatoes, another plate consisting of more potatoes, bacon, onion, and cheese with some biscuits.* He will carry the biscuits in his pocket tonight, a handy snack when he creeps around the village and rooftops to set up his surveillance cameras. *Oh . . . that smells good.* The waft of sausage and bacon is sucked into the room between the gaps in the heavy wooden door. Herber can taste the meal in his mouth already. "Thank you. Just set it on the floor. I am wet from the shower, and I'll pick it up soon."

Herber listens as the young man lays the tray on the wooden floorboards next to the door. "I will charge the meal to your room. Please enjoy and good night."

"Thank you again, good night." Herber waits until the young man walks down the hallway and past all the other rooms. The creaking staircase to the lower floors signals his departure. On his floor, European tourists booked several of the rooms, mostly Germans and Italians. The hotel kept the last two end rooms for the seasonal tour operators who lead hikes up to the Matterhorn and the scenic two-day trails to Grächen.

When Herber checked in, he found a hiking brochure displayed on his bedside table; as a promise to himself, the Edelweiss trail is earmarked for later. Once he pins down the target and studies his movements and behavior, he will send his intel briefing back to his command. As soon as some other shadowy team finally dispatches Zhang and his tasking is complete, Herber will take a break from work and head off to tackle the twenty-kilometer ruck march to test his fitness in the real world.

First things first: get a meal down, then start work on the cameras. Herber slides the Glock inside his waistband then slides open the lock on the wooden door. Turning the handle clockwise, he gently opens the door and peeks out into an empty hallway. Opening it farther, he can now check the other end of the hallway. All clear. *Stop being paranoid, it's not Kabul.* With a smile on his face and a rumble in his stomach, he looks down at his feet. Placed on the red foot mat with a hotel receipt next to the tray, his hot meal is hidden under a silver dome. Next to it sits a large steel flask of coffee, one mug, cutlery, and a small carton of milk. Bending down, he lifts the dome off the hot meal, and the rising steam carries the welcome flavor of a home-cooked meal. With a smile on his face, Herber thinks how lucky he is. *Operational life has never been this good.*

Chapter Eighteen

McLean, Virginia

Val Olszewski has been back in Washington just for a day when he schedules an urgent meeting in his office at McLean Drive, no more than a ten-minute car ride from Langley. In attendance are Dallas Pope and General Glassford, two men who wield dominant power in Washington. Their feelings sit extremely low this morning; an uncomfortable presence engulfs them as soon as they step into the soundproof office of the director of national intelligence. Pope looks around the walls, which lack some personal touches. A few pictures of the director with different presidents, a golfing trophy, and a couple of plaques he can't be bothered to read.

He has a flashback to junior high when he was often called into the principal's office to receive some form of punishment. Both men are not happy, and their unwillingness to cooperate is written across their faces. The latest slaying in Europe of their top operators hits these patriots hard. The last thing they want is to sit in this office and discuss the potential fallout with the Chinese. Their principal goal is getting back in the fight.

After the handshakes, Olszewski shows them to their seats. The leather armchairs are positioned in front of his large desk, each with a small side table. A built-in mahogany bookcase towers behind them, filled with leather-bound books, and under their feet lies a thin Turkish rug that looks more than a hundred years old. "You see, gentlemen, on my trip to Asia I had the fortunate chance to ease relationships with important partners. In ten years from now . . ." Olszewski stands up from behind his desk and moves to the drinks cabinet. While the two men sit with their arms folded across them and stay silent, Olszewski continues his prepared speech. "In ten, twenty, maybe fifty years from now, if we are lucky, our great country will be in a difficult position. China is rising economically, and therefore militarily, and likewise India, Indonesia, Russia, and many other nations." He stops speaking as he prepares some drinks, giving time for his words to sink in. With a finger of Tyrconnell whiskey poured into thick tumblers, he walks back and hands the men their drinks.

"Bit early, is it not?" says Pope with raised eyebrows as he looks across the room at General Glassford for his opinion. The deputy director of the CIA seldom drinks, and when he does, the location is a lively sports bar or one of the agency's little-known bars tucked away in a backstreet in downtown Washington. Not in an office of a man he does not trust. Pope reluctantly takes the whiskey and swirls the amber liquid around in its glass, careful not to spill any on his light gray suit. The color of his tailored jacket closely matches his hair, which is more silver than gray, neatly parted on one side and cut close on both sides, the top slicked over with expensive gel. Glassford shrugs his shoulders and without waiting for a toast or special announcement slugs down the expensive whiskey and sets the tumbler on the small brass and wooden table next to him. Olszewski thinks about refilling the general's glass but decides against it, as he knows the whiskey will get wasted once more.

"Depends which time zone you are operating in. My head still thinks I'm in Asia," says Olszewski with a slight laugh as he resumes his position back behind his desk in a brown leather chair. "Which is why I have made the unusual invitation for your delightful presence here today. I know you all have busy schedules and, what would you say? This gathering may be out of whack with usual protocols . . ."

"It means you either want recognition of a successful operation, or you screwed up, or someone did, and there is a major cover-up planned," Glassford cuts him off abruptly. He didn't come all the way over from Fort Meade to listen to some wannabe politician lecture him about failed operations. Glassford views Olszewski, the man behind his oversize desk, as someone who does all he can to hamper the investigations from the National Security Agency and throw away months of investigative work on a whim, only to feather his political ambitions. The reason for Glassford's outburst is not lost on Pope; the general is a straight shooter and very protective of the men and women under his command. The director of the NSA knows what it takes to get credible information. His organization is the world leader in the art of cryptology. Their game is outmaneuvering adversaries either on the legal path and sometimes in the abstract version of legal. All information has to be carefully sanitized before lands on Olszewski's desk, which creates headaches in the real-world threat environment. These two men are always at each other's throats, and Pope finds himself a ringside seat.

"My business is not getting people killed, our patriots walking out of churches and getting ambushed in the street, a one-man killing machine waltzing around Europe doing what he wants, and we know nothing about him." Olszewski fires off his response without worry. As the boss in the United States intelligence community, most of his colleagues fear him. But not the general.

"You lowlife," shouts Glassford, his face becoming redder with each word passing his lips. "You accuse me of not doing my job. Every time you advise the president on upcoming intelligence matters, we hear nothing back; we provide all the facts and your office wastes much-needed money required by us for the real work. You only arrived after 9/11, and ever since you have tried to justify your existence. Factually, you may be the boss, but we should only report to the defense secretary, not some limp-wristed bureaucrat . . ." Glassford takes slight a pause if only to think what else to say to help hammer his point home.

Olszewski finds the opening he is waiting for. He leans forward against his desk with his two arms outstretched and his hands open. "And what have you come up with? Time and time again, the Chinese, North Koreans, Russians, and Iranians have hacked into our vital systems, from oil refineries to our shipping industries and banking, only to mess around with our heads, or steal data, knock them offline, and cause millions in cybersecurity action plans, then they retreat to their little holes. Has your magical agency ever shut them down? Or at least provided names of the men and woman whose fingertips dance over the keyboards, their superiors, or those bankrolling the bastards?"

Pope is loving this. He has never seen Olszewski squirm, then explode in a fireball before, and he wants more of it. Sitting there watching two heavyweights squaring off, he can't wait to share the gossip with Liana and Hoffmann over a quiet beer.

Olszewski has a feeling Glassford will go down the path of accusing the DNI of being a waste of time and money. But in his opinion, the facts stand up, the NSA can't operate without proper oversight, and the CIA can't manage the entire intelligence community. *It is my job to protect the future of this goddamned agency.* The words ring loudly in Olszewski's head as he tries to portray that very image. In reality, his mind is focused on his private dealings with the Chinese general. Being on top of everything is critical. He desperately needs Glassford and Pope on board, so he has access to real-time information to pass along to the Black Bear. Hoffmann is too cunning, too convoluted. It is pointless to attempt getting inside the man's head. *Calm the waters, Olszewski, don't give these men a reason to look under every rock.* Olszewski takes his glass and swallows the remaining whiskey. He stands up and walks slowly back to the drinks cabinet, using his well-practiced theatrics to provide some extra time so he can process his thoughts and attempt to claw his way out of this mess. "Look, gentlemen, I know we all have important jobs to do, some more than others," he says, his comment directed at Glassford. Olszewski looks into the man's cold gray eyes for a moment longer than necessary.

"Well, just don't be asking for more resources and leaving us on the breadline." Glassford's tone matches that of Olszewski, a sign that their tempers have settled, allowing business to begin.

Pope, sensing an opportunity to push for an explanation regarding this meeting, speaks softly. "Now that you two have stopped locking horns, maybe we could all be enlightened to the present situation. Why exactly are we here, Val?"

Olszewski considers the direct question while trying to hide a look of desperation. "Remember back in 2002 at a press briefing when Rumsfeld acknowledged the limitations of intelligence reports?"

Pope sits motionless, wondering where the director of national intelligence is heading with this, while Glassford simply stares at the floor with a look of boredom drawn across his face as he rubs an old scar on his bald head.

"A failure to look in places is one thing, but if we don't know what to look for, then we become ineffective." Grabbing the bottle of Irish whiskey from the cabinet, he walks over and refills Glassford's glass. Pope has only taken a small sip from his but now accepts a top-up. He has a sinking feeling he may need it.

"The great unknown unknowns are what I have been discussing with the president. We are the best at acquiring intelligence from all corners of the world. Furthermore, gentlemen, our success in choosing and maintaining high-value sources to keep the information flowing is unmatched. Well, the British and Israelis would argue that, but more to the point, gentlemen, the nation will most likely share their appreciation for your service much like I do if they knew the half of it. However . . ."

Glassford was waiting for this. *The DNI never blows smoke up your ass for no reason, here it comes.* The head of the NSA tries to remember any potential failures he was involved in or the multiple times he bypassed legal approval, which led to him testifying before Congress. *What has this shithead got me on?* Glassford takes a sip of whiskey and locks his steely eyes with Olszewski's.

Olszewski returns to his desk and continues his speech. "The world is becoming increasingly complex. Western nations have become divided. Mistrust of governments is at an unprecedented level, and scrutiny of our work by lawyers and the press is perplexing. We strive to protect the nation. Which is why I have had to take an alternative approach in advising the president on what our greatest threats really are. Recent meetings I undertook, both formal and informal, were to find those 'unknown unknowns.'" Olszewski taps on his desk with his finger softly when saying the final two words.

Glassford keeps his poker face despite the machinery inside his brain spinning out of control. *Who the hell does this man think he is? If he screws up, I ain't going down with him.* Glassford waits for an explanation of why the top intelligence boss would take it upon himself to do what thousands of men and woman in the intelligence community are doing every minute of the day.

Pope, on the other hand, nods agreeably, saying it's a novel approach and one that could save resources. He doesn't believe it, though.

"I have the backing of President Lancaster, and also . . ." Olszewski moves his eyes from Glassford to Pope, "Gary Duval."

Pope considers the deputy director of operations a mean son of a bitch. The man appears to have no soul. Unmarried, a decorated war veteran with no known family, he didn't socialize with colleagues or follow any ballgames. He never owned a pet or even a plant and has no attachment to anything that would invoke an ounce of care for another living thing. All Pope knows about him from their limited conversations is a mild interest in history and classical music, and that he'd paid off his huge house in Spring Valley, the upmarket area of Washington, DC. As the deputy director of CIA for operations, nothing happens within the clandestine world without his approval. The Special Activities Center, and more specifically the Special Operations Group, is his pride and glory. The feared paramilitary arm. Questions regarding his management are met not just with suspicion, but with downright hostility. Pope knows enough about Duval from countless warnings by Cain Hoffmann to keep his distance. The recent events in Europe will come as a shock to Duval. This is his bread and butter, and Hoffmann is running his own black operation behind his back. No doubt Duval will be enraged, looking for answers to hide his embarrassment for skilled operators being stolen from his group to work on unapproved missions.

Pope doesn't blink at the sound of Duval's name. He simply nods, then takes another sip of whiskey, this time almost sinking the lot down his throat. He is moving into uncharted waters and needs to play this carefully. His mind races about what he needs to do and how to summarize it. *Hoffmann needs to be called first. The head of the DNI is making his own moves with the backing of the president and Duval. This could undo years of carefully placed assets in the middle of our own black of the blackest operations. The SIS would need to be notified also . . . a real shit storm!* Pope draws a list of people in his mind that will be required to pull back until they figure out who Olszewski is talking to, and why.

Pope feels a headache building as he ponders over Olszewski's explanation of unknown unknowns as one of complete vagueness. *If Duval gets the freedom of approval to mobilize his men, that will complicate the entire mission.* A couple of years ago, Hoffmann wanted a small discrete team of only five or six operators. Not hundreds. He had handpicked the best under the nose of Duval and used them sparingly. Now, with Olszewski and Duval on the scene, they have kicked the gates of hell open. Pope puts the glass to his mouth and swallows the whiskey in one large gulp. *This shit is going to get messy.*

Glassford's heartbeat is returning to a somewhat normal pace, thankful he is not being accused of some other political bullshit charge so he can continue to live life in his usual mild state of anxiety. Although, this recent development of Olszewski causes him some concern. He has been around long enough to know when more headaches and bullshitting will be required in the months ahead. Retirement is looking ever so attractive to the four-star general as he looks directly at the bottle of whiskey perched on the desk.

Chapter Nineteen

Paris, France

The gray skies open and the heavy rain begins falling in the early morning, continuing without pause throughout the day and into the night. Carver's wet clothes and soaked shoes do little to hamper his spirits. Even the fierce wind, which comes in uncontrolled bursts, each one lifting sheets of water out of the Seine River, only causes a momentary blink of his eyes. The torrential rain biting at his ears and mouth only makes his focus more intense. Once locked onto his target, the weather conditions simply fade away. His adrenaline looks after him, warming his body better than any arctic gear.

A walk past the property in the fourth arrondissement yesterday offered no actual intelligence, and what Carver could understand about the man's behaviors from another walk late last night drew little conclusions. The only intel Sarah provided suggests the man normally finishes work around seven. Shortly after, he returns to his first-floor apartment on the Seine—more accurately, on the small island named the Île de la Cité. This is also home to the Notre-Dame Cathedral, the Sainte-Chapelle, and of a higher concern the Paris police prefecture, all of which results in top security in the fourth arrondissement. The intel explains that the blinds on his first-floor apartment will be pulled shut around eleven, and it details him as a late starter for work, often leaving the apartment at nine or ten in the morning. As Carver considers the best way to get close to the target, he begins by elimination. *The streets are too busy in the morning, there are too many cameras dotted around the parks, plus the response time by the police is fast because of the required protection of one of the most expensive neighborhoods of Paris.* That leaves Carver with only two options: break into the apartment and conduct his business up close and personal or take a shot using a sniper rifle from the gardens south of the cathedral. The problems Carver faces with the rifle option are that the relentless rain will cause visibility issues, a streetlight next to the windows causes a blinding effect, the angle of the shot from a low-elevation shooting position is not perfect, and the glass may be ballistic proof. He notices a lot of recent repairs to the façade of the building, likely because of the renovations after the Notre-Dame fire. The high temperatures from the flames and hot gases would have caused extensive damage to the neighboring properties. Carver accepts that the first option is usually the best option.

Dressed head to toe in Parisian black, Carver walks along Rue du Cloître-Notre-Dame with a black cap pulled down and the collars on his jacket upturned, shielding his face and neck from the driving rain. His hands are stuffed deep in his pockets as he walks past the six-story sandstone building, his eyes scanning the street and passing cars. Carver walks past the apartment and heads north around the rear, then he loops back into position to check if he is being followed. As he walks closer to the apartment, his thoughts turn to the new working conditions. His shrinking team now comprises Harry Woodward, Sarah, and the new kid on the block, Flynn. All others have been sidelined, even Tommy. The small mission unit is one of Harry's best-kept secrets. On a small team, there are many advantages for Carver when working alone, although the potential for capture by the French police will result in him serving time without the British government bailing him out. Sarah confirmed that the same arrangement goes for Sean Flynn. Both men are out on a limb, working alone in high-risk operations in Europe. Mainly because it is in Europe; the same predicament wouldn't apply too much in the Middle East. Sarah also spoke briefly about new actors probing the involvement of top-tier special ops guys in Monte Carlo. This is the reason Harry has cut his support. Carver is thankful he made contacts over the years without SIS knowing. Contacts he cultivated in the event the government turns their back on him. Tonight may be one of those nights. Checking the time on his wristwatch, he reaches into his top pocket and pulls out a small flashlight. Spinning the filter to the red lens setting, he holds it in his left hand as he approaches the address. The rain keeps hammering down, leaving the pavement free from pedestrians. One or two cars pass by every few minutes, their headlights reflecting off the wet black road, the drivers fixated on the street ahead. A Tuesday night in Paris is a typically quiet event, one that will allow Carver to do what he needs to do without an audience.

The Haussmann building contains six apartments, one on each floor. Li Xing-fu owns his three-bedroom apartment, which is on the first floor. To enter the building, there are two doors. The first is a metal-framed outer security door with glass panels, then behind that is an eight-foot-high original heavy oak door hung with huge cast-iron hinges. A security camera is built into the intercom system, complete with audio. Carver had already decided on a different entry method while making his second walk past the building. The famous Parisian architect Baron Georges-Eugène Haussmann designed many of the buildings spread throughout the city. The floor, which Xing-fu lives on, is known as the noble floor, the most decorative of all. Inside, it has the highest ceiling in the entire building. From the outside, the ornate cut stonework around the windows complete with a wrought-iron balcony is a familiar sight. The ground floor begins with the horizontal sandstone blocks on the façade, with deep gaps between the neighboring blocks, which rise like a natural ladder to each floor toward the forty-five-degree pitched roof. Carver estimates the distance from ground level to the bottom of the balcony is no more than ten feet. He walks around the corner and takes another glance at his watch before placing the slimline flashlight between his teeth. In an attempt to leave as little trace as possible, he slips a pair of surgical gloves on, then makes sure his hair is tucked tight beneath his cap. In his mind, he figures the police have a three-minute response time in this postal code.

Carver takes a last quick scan along the street, then runs over to the wall next to the front door of the apartment. The sandstone blocks offer decent gaps, allowing him to wedge his left foot in tight and, with his hand, he grabs a higher block and pulls himself up in one fluid motion. Spider-Man climbing up the front of the building only takes a couple of movements. Then he stretches out his right arm and grabs hold of the thick iron bar at the base of the balcony. Next, he moves his left foot into another gap in the sandstone and his cold leg muscles push hard while his arms provide the extra help to haul his body higher up the façade. Once he has steadied himself, he takes hold of the top bar on the small balcony with both hands, then he gently yanks his body up and over the railing. The size of the balcony just about fits his crouched body. Now in position, he takes a moment to gather himself. He swiftly checks his surroundings and makes sure nothing fell from his pockets or no part of his clothes is snagged on the building. Carver looks back toward the street for potential witnesses. The adrenaline is flowing and his breathing is relaxed. Safe so far with no signs of trouble, he then turns his ear to the glass doors and listens for any sounds coming from inside the apartment. He can only detect silence. Paris is sleeping. He directs the red light coming from his flashlight to the frame, which holds the decorative French balcony doors in place. Carver sweeps the light across the top, down both sides, across the bottom, and between the gap where the two door panels connect. Satisfied there is no alarm built into the frame or the doors' old antique locks, he almost cheers with joy. His hands wrap gently around the door handles, turning them both slightly to check if they are locked, which they are. Carver moves onto his house-breaking training he received from the SIS and removes a long screwdriver from his cargo pants, then jams it between the two door panels next to the lock housing. With steady pressure, he leans on the screwdriver, listening carefully for the cracking of the old hardwood frame. He pulls back on one door slightly until he can hear metal scraping. The door lock is free of the keeper and is finally unlocked. He instantly puts the screwdriver and flashlight back in his pockets, swapping those tools with his firearm.

Slowly and carefully, Carver opens the unlocked side, then moves inside the darkened room and drops into a crouch. His firearm is raised to eye level as he sweeps the room. Once his natural night vision adapts to the dark room, he moves delicately deeper into the building. His ears are pricked and listening for anything that might signal danger as he slowly advances toward the bedroom. Much to his excitement, the adrenaline is pumping. Carver would love to sit down and enjoy the feeling, although he knows the seconds count; he needs to move. If a silent alarm is triggered, he has about a minute left to get out of the building.

He opens the first two doors, one a bathroom, the next a bedroom, which is converted to an office. He looks at the distance between each door and decides on the larger room to check next. The door opens softly and Carver feels the warmth immediately on his stony face, seeing one enormous lump laying in the bed accompanied by the snoring expected of a fat and unhealthy mammal. *A creator of deadly viruses is no better than a terrorist; all human lives mean nothing to this lump of waste.* Carver's thoughts race through his head. *The huge number of deaths, innocent families ripped apart, Western economies destroyed, and this filth lays in Paris sleeping soundly.* He's almost disappointed this man isn't armed and firing a volley of shots at him, but neither were his victims who died from his virus.

Carver slips the handgun back into his jacket and pulls out the screwdriver. *A bullet is too quick.* With no hesitation, Carver drops his full weight onto the scientist, grabbing the man's cheek with his left hand and forcing his head into the pillow while the screwdriver plunges into the base of his skull. Carver stabs repeatedly like a man possessed, severing the spinal cord and ripping the brain to pieces until there are no signs of life. Xing-fu doesn't even have time to scream. Carver ceases the attack then turns without a thought and walks into the bathroom. Once in the shower, he uses a steady stream of hot water to wash the screwdriver and remove all the blood and gore from his hands. Under the sink he finds a spray bottle of disinfectant containing bleach. Flicking the nozzle to "on," he bolts over and sprays Xing-fu on the face and all around the bed, then backs out of the room spraying all the way behind himself as he retraces his steps back to the balcony. Carver glances down onto the wet street, the rain coming down even harder and the wind howling up the street. No sirens or alarms blare from within the building or surrounding streets. With a sliver of confidence, he backs out from the room and onto the balcony. Once Carver climbs down from the small ledge, he hangs from the iron railings then drops the last few feet, splashing onto the wet pavement and immediately walks toward the Seine.

Carver is pleased with how the assassination went. Normally, something like this would be planned well in advance. Weeks if not months of surveillance and a killing to make it look like a robbery gone wrong, a suicide, or a simple motor vehicle accident. But not now. Ever since Zhang entered the playing arena, the rules changed. Up close and personal, real gruesome wet work will attract the media. The Chinese will not be able to let it go. Revenge now replaces diplomacy.

"The job is only half-complete," Carver says to himself as he crosses the empty street on Quai aux Fleurs and takes the Pont d'Arcole bridge over the river and off the island. A couple more minutes tramping through the rain, which is coming down almost horizontally, and he makes it to a side street called Rue Adolphe Adam. After moving past a row of small European cars, he arrives at the small Renault Alpine rental. With no time to spare, Carver reaches down under the wheel arch and dislodges the key fob. His large bulky frame is not suitable for quick entry to such a compact car. However, he quickly climbs into the driver's seat before ripping up the carpet on the passenger side. The rental invoice sits on top of his European Union passport under the name of his legend, Charles Walcott. Farther along the footwell just under the dash, he retrieves a stack of cash, a driver's license, and various credit cards. The French sports car, similar to the German Audi TT, was selected because of its small size for navigating European backstreets. Parking is also a problem in Paris, and Carver didn't have time to drive around looking for a slot to fill a larger vehicle.

Once the engine is started, Carver checks the illuminated lights on the dash for any issues. All clear. Once he moves the car out from the side street, Carver flicks the wipers on double speed and watches as each blade wipes the rain clear from the windscreen. Navigating through the streets of Paris causes no confusion or drama. SIS trained Carver on the fastest routes in and out of many European cities in previous programs. He is familiar with many of the backstreets, dead ends, one-way streets, the locations police would set up roadblocks, and the suburbs where he could purchase a weapon.

A few more kilometers and he is now driving east on autoroute de l'Est. Four hours until he reaches Luxembourg, and his timing will have him in a position to watch his next target wake up and have his breakfast. Looking down at the dash instruments, Carver finds the water temperature of the car now at the midway point. He reaches down to the heating controls and selects full heat. The cap is pulled from his head and with one hand he squeezes tightly to force the rainwater free from the fabric. Placing it back on his head, he once again tucks his long, dark hair under the duck-billed cap. With an eye on his rearview mirror, Carver keeps the car just under the speed limit. The tank is full of fuel, although he needs to make a quick stop. Once he is clear of the city, he pulls the car off the motorway and arrives at small sleepy village called Pont-aux-Dames. All the lights are off as he drives through the main street looking for a country lane. Finding the perfect dark spot between a row of thick hedges, Carver pulls the car to a stop and kills the engine. Clambering out of his seat, he walks to the back of the car and opens the small boot. Inside is a black duffle bag and a Heckler & Koch SA80 A2 rifle covered by a hotel towel he stole earlier. Parked under a huge oak provides some relief from the torrential downpour, although the rain falling from the black clouds still negotiates a path through the leaves and branches, forcing Carver to work fast. Stripping out of his soaked clothing, he unzips his bag and removes a fresh dry set. Standing barefoot in muddy puddles on this small country lane, he waits until the car heater dries his feet before sliding on his dry socks. Moving to the driver's door, he throws these socks and dry runners into the front of the car and then shoves his old wet clothes deep into a thick hedge, well out of view.

His last task before closing the boot and getting behind the wheel is to take a leak. The wind is swirling and howling around him, taking his stream of urine on a joyride. He can smell the strong odor of coffee as he empties his bladder into a puddle in which he stands.

***

Large, beautiful houses line both sides of the wide street, and old-fashioned lamps hang over the cobbled parking strips illuminating the tidy paths to each home. Luxembourg, one of the most expensive cities in Europe, a place where not much happens yet a place that is home to a man on Carver's list. Sitting in his car with the engine turned off, the rain splatters the windscreen and aluminum roof, sounding like tiny drumbeats. The side mirrors offer him a protective view behind him and, out the front window, he can clearly view the target's property. There is a BMW parked in the driveway, the porch light is glowing, and all curtains are closed tight, shielding them from the harsh weather. Carver enjoys the warmth of the car as he replays the conversation he had with Sarah two days ago regarding the soon-to-be-slayed Ma Guozhi, a tall, thin man with a receding hairline who is never seen wearing anything other than his trademark black suit, white shirt, and red tie with a Communist-red badge of loyalty pinned on his left breast. A respected member of China's National Security Commission, his official job is acting as a successful attorney assisting foreigners investing in China, while his real motive, as a Chinese intelligence officer, is getting access inside foreign companies, understanding their business practices, secrets, and goals. Guozhi collates all information and sends it back to Beijing for a detailed examination. They then select suitable businessmen for enhanced probing. Their bank accounts, emails, private messages, circle of friends, and whichever professional memberships they belong to are all investigated. Even their character and vices are explored for exploitation if required. Once a suitable person is confirmed, the devious Guozhi will make his moves to turn the Westerners against their own companies and government parties. Their allegiance and commitment to work with the Communist Party will be rewarded with the financial success that would take them a hundred years to accumulate in their current path.

The ten years living in Europe have been kind to the fifty-nine-year-old spy. His future, beginning from childhood as a young princeling, was always destined for greatness. He was born into a wealthy and exceedingly privileged family because of his father's political position. Now deceased, his father had been a prominent member of the Politburo who ensured the young Guozhi had all the right connections and a lucrative career path was therefore guaranteed. Raised in a rich suburb in Beijing, he enjoyed the services of a personal driver and maid. Throughout his school years, his marks were always exceptional because of the countless hours of private tuition. His loyal wife, a piano teacher, and their three young children rotate family life between Zurich, Berlin, and Luxembourg. When they are out of town, the mistresses arrive regularly, much like the deliveries of fine wine and the local freshwater crayfish.

Without Tommy Taylor at the desk to hack into the various devices within the man's home, Carver will have to go in blind. Living in Luxembourg, the Chinese spy has no access to private security or bodyguards because of the low crime rate in the country and the probable speculation by the locals about why a Chinese lawyer would need heavies around. Now he is forced to live with nothing more than security cameras and the phone number of the local police station.

What makes Carver somewhat confident on this early morning is the fact that Guozhi will be at home by himself. The little intel he accessed brought up travel bookings for his family. They were scheduled to fly from Luxembourg yesterday to Heathrow on one of the wife's frequent shopping trips to Harrods.

Squeezing his hands into a fist to promote blood flow, Carver acknowledges how well Sarah did her homework, selecting this list of high-value targets. Creeps that he has no issues with dispatching. The thorns in the side of Western democracy living in the open and carrying out their gray warfare in total peace. Carver thinks about how he will close this account. *Guozhi will have eaten his last crayfish and caressed his final escort for this life.* Screwing the suppressor onto his Sig Sauer, he checks the time on his watch. "Four twenty-five," he mutters to himself. Because of the fluid nature of these assassinations, Carver has to plan such executions on the hop. Each hit will be slightly different due to the time of day, access to the target, escape routes, and security concerns. From inside the Renault two-seater sports car, Carver looks down the street and considers the best options to kill the man cleanly. *Option one, ring the doorbell and put a bullet in his head when he opens the door. Option two, break in and slice him. Option three, shoot him through the kitchen window or wait for him to leave for work and kill him outside.* Carver decides on his second option. He will check out the property, then look for a way to disable alarms, get into the house, and finally kill the spy inside. A simple repeat of Paris is preferred, as ringing the doorbell at an early hour could raise too many warning bells that could prompt Guozhi to call the police and hide within the large two-bedroom house. If the man was allowed to leave the house, it would present too many variables as well. To kill Guozhi within the house provides Carver with an area of privacy and cover. The element of surprise in the early morning, when the man is not fully wakened, will be another advantage, allowing Carver to do his business and get out of the country without the local cops hard on his tail.

Time for the last check. He inserts a fresh magazine into the firearm, then slots it into his jacket. Next, he tests the red light on his flashlight, then from his black bag he takes out a lock-picking set, a bump key, and a small wrecking bar. Grabbing the signal jammer, he turns the knob to green. Carver slides it into his jacket and zips the pocket tightly. All alarm systems or cameras linked to Wi-Fi and Bluetooth networks will be blocked from transmitting their data. At the very least, it will prevent notifications on Guozhi's mobile phone giving him a heads-up. Carver catches a glimpse of himself in the rearview mirror. Not a pretty sight. Blackness covers the bottoms of his eyes due to lack of sleep. Dry lines crease his face, and the long dark hair needs shampoo. The heat from his foul-smelling breath creates a fog in the mirror. After this hit, Carver will have a little time to recuperate before his next target. A hot soapy shower, teeth brushed, and a few hours of sleep is all he craves. The drive from Paris to Luxembourg was boring; no takeaway coffee or food joints were available at such an early hour. *Guozhi won't mind if I grab something from his fridge, I guess . . .*

Carver looks down and checks the time once more. *Four thirty, it's time to move.* With a final deep breath to fire up his adrenaline, the SIS assassin reaches up to deactivate the internal light before opening the door. He swings his legs out and gently closes the door behind him and walks in the direction of the target's home. The key fob is left untouched in his pocket. If he clicks the door lock button, a soft tone will sound and the indicator lights will flash, alerting the neighbors of a strange car in the street. The rain is still coming down hard, somewhat less than Paris a few hours ago, but enough to make someone look out of place without an umbrella.

Moving swiftly along the cobbled footpath, Carver crosses the street just before he approaches a streetlight. All the houses are of a similar age. Built during the eighties, they covered their roofs in black-and-gray slate with a steep pitch. The second floors have dormer windows, and their gardens are well established, with huge trees or manicured hedges marking the boundary between neighbors. Some have ivy creeping up the sides and most of them have garages built under the house and not to the side due to the limited land size. Carver takes a final, somewhat casual glance around before walking up the side of the target's house. After several meters he crouches down, keeping his body tight against a thick bushy hedge measuring roughly five feet tall by three feet deep. One that is perfectly rectangular due to a recent trimming by the contracted gardener. Inching closer to the front left corner of the house, he scans the brickwork and eaves for cameras, cables, or motion sensors. Spotting a couple of security lights facing the front of the building, he pushes his body deep inside the hedge and crawls through the middle of it until he reaches the side wall. Underneath him, as he slithers through the vegetation, the cracking branches and rustle of small leaves are not audible over the sound of the rain and moderate wind pushing through the street. Carver shivers as the water runs off the leaves and trickles down the back of his neck. Now his knees have become soaked in the fertilized soil and his hands are filthy. After clearing a path through the muck, he gently parts the branches and looks out at the side of the house. Through the darkness, he cannot see with certainty if there are security cameras or lights, so he slowly frees himself from the clinging branches, careful to keep the noise down, as this area is sheltered from the wind. From this side, being on the west of the house, he has access to three ground-floor windows. The dull yellow light cast from the street fails to reach this side of the house behind the vegetation, forcing Carver to wait a few moments to allow his eyes to adjust to the darkness before assessing the wall and roof for any obstacles. He moves at a snail's pace when approaching the wall and uses the red light from his flashlight to check the frame of the first window for any security alarms. The old wooden windows have never been updated. On checking the frames, he spots how they have been roughly repainted over the years, with the hinges and seals covered as well. He checks all three windows and finds that they all are free of security alarms and all but one is secured. With a beam of red light shining into the room, he can see what looks like a washing machine, dryer, ironing board, and various baskets. An old handle secures the window frame, set into a notch, which keeps it locked, but also allows some wind to travel into the house. Carver decides to enter the house here, as the rear of the property will most likely have security lights at the back door. He quickly slides on a pair of gloves and secures his flashlight before removing his small wrecking bar from his jacket. The wrecking bar is better for houses such as this, as it will break through thicker and tougher material. Slotting the sharp edge between the gap next to the lock, he pushes upward, allowing the old dry wood to crack slowly before giving way. Next, he pushes the window up as far as it will go and wedges the wrecking bar into the frame, holding it in place. With his two hands gripping the windowsill, Carver heaves up and slips through the window. Once inside the room, he pulls out his suppressed firearm and holds it at the door in front of him. His ears are pricked for anything suspicious or alarming. With nothing to worry about, he moves closer to the door and, with his left hand, he slowly turns the handle and opens it inward, offering him a view of the hallway. Once he steps out onto the carpet, he looks both ways and walks to the front of the house so he can plan his departure. The front door opens directly to the outside. There is no porch door to contend with. Yellow streetlight filters through the small glass panels above the door, giving off enough light to see what locks are fitted. Once he unlocks the door, he checks the front room.

On entering the large living space, he is surprised by how bright it is, as the streetlights do well in penetrating the thin curtains. Looking around himself, he is immediately awestruck by the sight before him. The place is like a museum, an art collection fit for a museum. As he strolls around the furniture holding his weapon with both hands, he can't help but check the contents surrounding him. Retrieving his red flashlight and putting it between his teeth, he drifts it across the furniture, starting with an antique brass Victorian oil lamp next to a seventeenth-century wainscot chair. Antique books on Roman law sit in an enormous bookcase. Italian marble urns and rare German porcelain vases are displayed behind a glass cabinet, and several oil paintings hang beautifully on the wall. Finally, he stops his search to focus his thin beam of red light in the middle of the room where he spies a French Empire coffee table with green marble and ormolu. *Sarah would absolutely love that,* Carver thinks to himself as he checks the weight of it. He slots the flashlight back into his pocket, then continues to clear the rest of the ground floor before going up to the bedroom to dispatch Guozhi.

Don't forget the table . . . and some food, he reminds himself as he treads softly down the hallway to the rear. Once in the large kitchen, Carver gives it a quick once-over. They have renovated the property with an extension on the back to allow for a large dining table with double doors leading out into a garden pergola. No expense has been spared in fitting this modern kitchen. White cupboards sit underneath black granite bench tops that wrap all around the room. Brass lights drop on thick chains from the ceiling, and the floor is covered in white-and-black marble. The huge island in the middle of the room contains both a double sink and a huge industrial-size cooking range. Carver eyes the fridge with suspense. He makes a mental note to raid it before fleeing.

Carver checks his watch and realizes he left his car almost ten minutes ago. Getting quickly back to business, he checks the back door then the next couple of doors leading off the kitchen. The first leads into a pantry while the second leads into a small servant space used for cooking the foods with strong odors and washing the dinnerware out of view from the guests. Once these areas are checked, he turns to make his way to the stairs leading to the bedrooms. Suddenly his heart bangs against his chest. He feels the presence of someone before he hears the shouting.

"STOP, STOP, STOP . . ."

More wild yells come from the hallway, then he feels a burst of movement coming directly behind him. Spinning around and dropping onto his left knee, Carver fires two quick rounds before rolling behind the kitchen island to assess the situation. What happens next is unbelievable. Multiple shooters all fire aimlessly, their bullets smashing into the cabinets, causing small fragments of marble and granite to slice through the air. The sound reverberates off the marble floor, causing an earsplitting sensation, and the sour, acrid smell of the gun smoke soon fills the room. Trapped, surrounded and outnumbered, Carver knows his options are limited. Shoot to the death or throw his firearm across the room.

"To hell with this," he mutters to no one. He scuttles to the other end of the island and tries to count the number of men he is up against. Carver guesses there are about three in the hallway and one more in the dining room that he desperately hopes is bleeding out. All he can do is wait for the remaining shooters to reload. That way he has a lesser chance of getting hit when he returns a volley of direct shots. Carver checks his weapon as a habit, ready to unleash just as the rates of fire decrease slightly.

The shooters appear to be unsure of his exact location within the large kitchen, and because of the lack of fire being returned, they cease firing altogether. With his head ducked down and in a crouched position, Carver spins around softly and prepares to spring up onto his knee and shoot with controlled aggression. He would rather wait until all men are in the room and try hitting each of them. Despite the ringing in his ears, he can make out a man issuing commands. Unable to understand the Chinese language, he knows exactly what they will be planning.

The smoke is still thick and combines with the toxic dust dropping over his body. Each breath he inhales, this damaging concoction sinks deep into his lungs. The need to cough is almost overwhelming. Suddenly Carver realizes this is his best chance to launch a counterattack, as the men wait for the dust to settle. *Disco time.* Carver takes a couple of deep breaths through the material of his clothes, then lifts his weapon to head height and quickly stands up, ready to fire.

As he peers through the darkness, he can only see thin ribbons of light from the hallway cutting through the dust. Shadows rock back and forth between the light, which tells him the three men are loitering nervously, waiting for the right moment to launch their attack. Carver moves his right foot out and rests the heal on the marble floor, then rolls forward slowly. He inches closer to the men, keeping close to the kitchen cupboards. About eight feet from the hallway, he strikes using the element of surprise. Carver launches himself across the floor. With his body crouched, he fires at the first of the men, keeping the weapon fixed on their chests. He hits one with two quick bursts, then jerks immediately to the left.

The remaining two men predicably open fire into the darkness of the kitchen. Carver uses the noise for cover and can move freely without being heard. Positioned at the doorframe, he waits again, stalking his prey. This time, the men use more advanced tactics, entering the room quickly with flashlights now attached to their weapons. The number-one man, the tallest of them, steps in and immediately turns to his left to the heavy side of the room, the uncleared sector. The stocky number-two man steps in to begin his clearance from the counterclockwise direction, taking the easy corner first on the weakest side. Both men expect Carver to be positioned in a hard corner, an area of the room that they cannot see. The tallest man moves cautiously about ten feet away, walking past the island where Carver had been moments ago. In perfect sequence, the stocky man sweeps his flashlight quickly to the right corner toward the wall about three feet away, expecting to find nothing before continuing along. His lack of preparedness is displayed on his face when a knife is thrust into the center of his throat. The effectiveness of the attack is instantaneous, taking the stocky one out of the fight immediately. Carver rips the knife out of the man's neck, which allows the drowning to begin. The dying attacker is standing in shock, busy sucking blood down his windpipe, when he is grabbed by Carver and used as a shield as the bullets fired by the tall attacker enter his back. After a quick burst of gunfire, the tall man realizes with horror he is shooting his own man and immediately ceases firing and jumps back. Carver instantly lets off a burst of rounds before finding cover.

When the remaining gunman realizes all his men are killed, he becomes enraged. Without a trace of fear, he races around the kitchen island and swings his weapon wildly to find a clear sight of the British enemy. His finger is squeezing the trigger to unleash a dozen rounds when he unexpectedly receives a hard impact on his cheek.

Carver fires again; this time the bullet hits the man on the top of his head as he drops to the ground. Carver stands up from his squatted position and fires two more shots, one into each of the last two men. The blood begins pooling slowly across the marble floor.

A deep breath boosts the adrenaline flow around his body, doing its magic inside him. The kitchen is a mess, and he looks to his left to find a few bullet holes in the fridge. Hunger has somewhat left him for now. Carver spends the next action assessing the dead. He rushes into the dining room and finds the one he shot in the dark. Still breathing. Carver makes good use of his Sig Sauer once again. He quickly checks the dead body. A feeling of disappointment fills him, although it isn't much of a surprise not to find any identification or communication devices. The same for the other three.

Carver knows the clock is ticking, due to the fact that the unusual roar of gunfire in this quiet street will certainly alarm the neighbors, so he needs to work sharply before the local police arrive. He loads a fresh magazine and sprints upstairs two steps at a time. On reaching the landing, he kicks in each door and clears all rooms. With a string of curse words to himself, he finds empty beds in all of them. *Someone tipped off Ma Guozhi!* Carver shakes his head at this shocking revelation as he runs down the stairs, noticing he has left a trail of bloody footsteps everywhere. In the hallway, he glimpses himself in a huge mirror. Dark wet blood drips from his clothes down onto his shoes.

Carver fears the public attention. He desperately needs to sort this out, and quickly. With a quick change of direction, he races back upstairs and hurriedly rummages through the cupboards, picking out any large, dark clothing he can find before making his way to the front door. Unsure if these men had this house under surveillance ensures Carver keeps the weapon in his right hand, ready to use, with the new clothes tucked under his left arm. He opens the unlocked door smoothly and runs back to the Renault Alpine. After a few seconds, he has the car weaving its way through the small streets, and once on the motorway, the engine screams to life as he makes his way toward Germany.

He bangs his fist angrily on the steering wheel as he feels the world closing in on him. Sarah will need to provide answers, otherwise he is on his own. He knows they will launch a manhunt operation shortly and will continue until they find him. Carver runs his fingers over the steering wheel controls and switches on the radio, then searches for the local stations. Realizing it's too early for news reports, he kills the connection. *I need to get in contact with Sarah, and Tommy . . .* Carver thinks about the need to bring Tommy back on this case, and if Sarah won't approve it, then he will do it anyway behind her back. Shaking his head softly while checking the rearview mirror, he notices his breathing is slowly returning to normal. Feeling cold in his chest and stomach, he glances down toward his clothes. The sight and wet feeling of so much blood surprises him. He momentarily thinks some of it could be his own. Doing a quick head-to-toe check, Carver realizes he is still wearing the surgical gloves. His mind returns to the possibility of getting pulled over by the police. With no protection from his government, the situation would lead to a lengthy prison sentence. Staying on the main roads is too risky, so he makes his way to Schengen, a short thirty-minute drive using all the small back roads. He finds a parking spot on a quiet area along Rue Robert Goebbels, a small two-lane road that passes the Château de Schengen. The beautiful building surrounded by immaculate gardens is used as a hotel and international conference center that is conveniently situated on the three borders of Luxembourg, France, and Germany. Carver looks over the Moselle River, which separates the château on the Luxembourg side from Germany on the other side, then he checks the time. The sun is due to rise soon. Far off on the horizon, its soft rays of gold and purple battle against the gray skies above. High trees and streetlamps casting long shadows obstruct a clear view along the winding path that skirts the riverbank. Puddles and wet grass reflect their light orange glow, forcing Carver to squint his tired eyes to trace the empty path south until he can find nothing but darkness. The river flows from the north to south for a couple of kilometers before weaving its way southwest through France; with a slow current, Carver thinks of it as a last-option method to escape if the police show up. From the car, he cannot tell if any threats may linger deep in the shadows. No vehicles are driving around during this early part of the morning, so he grabs his fresh clothes and the gun, then leaves the Renault and walks down to the riverbank. After wading into the chilly water, he strips the Sig Sauer down into its separate parts.

Carver is careful to only use weapons that have their serial numbers professionally removed by an SIS gunsmith contractor. As he holds the firing pin assembly and barrel in his large hands, he thinks back to his training and understands how these parts could still connect him to the house. He realizes how a search of the area will be conducted by police divers if they catch him nearby. The forensic ballistic examiners will quickly conclude this was the weapon involved in the homicide. With no other options, he takes this extra precaution, hoping they will never find these parts.

Holding the firing pin in his teeth, he drops under the water and then rips into the riverbed with his bare hands. Scraping away the rocks and pebbles, he then buries the small metal rod and its spring a few inches deep before covering it with the pebbles and pressing down on it with his feet. Next he swims downstream about one hundred meters and removes his clothes and washes the worst of the blood from them before wrapping each piece around rocks and dropping them into the middle of the river. Each time he submerges his head into the cool water, a welcome shiver runs through his body. Pushing his fingers through his long black hair, he removes any carbon residue from the ammunition and the shards of black granite that came from the kitchen countertops.

Once washed, he steps out and quickly heads back to where he left his clothes. He quickly slips on a tight blue T-shirt and a black sweater over his wet body. Finally, he steps into a pair of blue jeans, which he finds a struggle to fit over his large legs. The small clothing will have to do. His waterlogged shoes, which he tried to wash, will be replaced later. Back behind the wheel, the blowers are on full power. Seconds later, Carver crosses the bridge into Germany. Despite wearing dry clothes, his wet body from the river seeps through onto the seats, making it somewhat slippery. The wetness is the last of his concerns. To change his appearance will come easy; Carver considers that the car is his biggest and more immediate dilemma. Over the next couple of hours, he needs to change vehicles, put distance between himself and Luxembourg, eat something, and get answers from Sarah.

Carver fiddles with the radio station and tunes into 100.7 where the early-morning news is just breaking. A very nervous presenter speaks quickly with a note of fear in her voice: *"This morning a horrible massacre has taken place in a quiet suburb in Luxembourg. Police are on the scene, and the reports we are receiving suggest an armed and dangerous gunman is on the loose."* Carver looks into the rearview mirror, his dark eyes looking for threats. Time has run out. If the neighbors describe his car to the police, it won't be long before they find him. This knowledge sends a rush of blood from his heart that is felt heavily on his chest.

In front of him, a small yellow van makes its way along the country road. Carver pulls his car to the other side of the road, immediately downshifts, and plants his wet shoe onto the accelerator, passing the van at high speed. *The autobahn will have cameras; I need to make a quick decision.* As Carver adjusted the stream of hot air from the fan on the car's dash to his wet hair, a horrible vision suddenly causes his breathing to stop while his heart bangs angrily deep inside him once again. The red-and-blue lights flashing in his rearview mirror warn Carver that this day is only just beginning.

Chapter Twenty

Berlin, Germany

Buchanan has a sharp eye for detail. He picks up on something crucial that others simply miss. Some call it lucky; others say it's a form of obsessive-compulsive disorder. Chris Buchanan couldn't give a rat's ass. During high school, he was known to be guarded and socially awkward, which developed into something more sinister. He reached a point in his life where it was either gang violence or enlist in the army. Choosing the latter, he finally found his true purpose in life as a member of the American army's lesser-known special forces unit, the Intelligence Support Activity. He was trained as a specialist HUMINT operative, or in civilian language, human intelligence. Buchanan spent years on the ground gathering intelligence, either undercover or running agents, and also carrying out surveillance on terrorists or hostile forces. During his years working within the ISA, he did some "knob turning," meaning signals intelligence, or SIGINT. This meant tracking cell phones and radio and electrical communications plus using various other cool techniques in order to provide a clear picture for the shooters to move in—an area where Buchanan finally ended up. Months of training by the battle-hardened 1st

Special Forces Operational Detachment, otherwise known as Delta Force, allowed him to be a "shooter," a full member of the direct-action element within the Intelligence Support Agency.

His work was tough, dangerous, and thrilling to the point where he couldn't tolerate the thought of living a mundane life. An opportunity arose by chance during a tour in Iraq when he bumped into a mysterious man named Gary Duval. Buchanan figured he was CIA. The man had a habit of appearing in the middle of a briefing, then disappearing without being noticed. He was never introduced or acknowledged by any higher ranks. One night after a difficult operation, Buchanan, exhausted and sleep-deprived, arrived back at a private bar at the far end of the major army base. The sizeable room was arranged with a seating area in front of a large flat-screen television for the PlayStation. A kitchen area at the back allowed them to chomp down on a quick meal instead of making the trek to the canteens. Next to the dining area, a small bathroom had been installed, and a selection of mismatched armchairs with a tattered couch sat behind a few coffee tables. Pinned proudly to the wall was a large American flag, the finishing touch to their home away from home. The room could accommodate about thirty people. Each rotation of troops added to the luxury and comfort over the years. Setting his weapon down, Buchanan walked over to the fridge and pulled out a beer. Hooking his finger under the tab, he cracked it open and collapsed on the old leather couch. With closed eyes, he took a long swig of the cool, velvety-sweet amber liquid. The feeling was overwhelming. Three days of water rationing left him dehydrated. His tongue was as dry and rough as sandpaper. Slowly opening his eyes, which took time to refocus, he half-expected the other crew members to be arriving. Instead, he found a man sitting in an armchair at the far end of the room, dressed in khaki pants, boots, and a dark blue long-sleeved shirt. A black bag sat on one of the other armchairs and a laptop rested on his lap.

The man nodded. "Tough night?"

Buchanan considered asking the man how he got into this secretive part of the base. This was the home ground for the Intelligence Support Activity guys, and from time to time the Delta guys, or SEAL teams, would meet up here for a drink, depending on who had the most beer. Buchanan let it slide, figuring he had no energy to engage him. All he was interested in was the condensation running down the side of his Budweiser and onto his thick fingers. He didn't have stamina for a pep talk or to sit there discussing what he had just witnessed. All that was on his mind was a few cans of beer and a feed before hitting the sack. No need to wash. Buchanan never showered on operations.

"Something like that . . . tough week," was all he could muster.

"Do you know who I am?" asked Duval.

Before answering, Buchanan lifted the can to his heavily bearded face and took another drink. Letting the beer gurgle into his mouth caused white froth to cover his moustache. Wiping it away with his left hand, he looked up and replied. "I presume you are a spook. I saw you hanging about here and there. Only someone within your organization can move freely around base and access our briefings."

"Well, those are fair observations . . ." Duval lifted his laptop, clicked a few keys, then shut the cover. "However, I prefer the more hands-on approach to problems."

Over the next few hours and several fresh cold beers, Duval found a man with no proper direction in life other than to do harm to bad people. Buchanan was someone that Duval could use to create his own team of badass hit men.

***

At five feet nine and close to 180 pounds of hard muscle, his body is used to rough living. He feels neither the freezing cold nor the intense heat within harsh environments, and no matter what food he eats or how little of it he gets down his neck, the thick muscles stay on his bones. The rugged man from Wyoming feels more at home when perched high on a mountaintop in Afghanistan or sneaking around a bombed-out city. Other men in his unit get off watching a ball game, sitting in a strip joint, or rebuilding a car engine, but Buchanan gets his kicks observing a main supply route for days in some hellhole in Africa or hiding under rubble within the ruins of a derelict building in Syria waiting for a terror group to show up. Buchanan would be sharp and focused on every second of the operation, his finger relaxed on the trigger, his mind on the job. Each moving thing is processed scientifically, much like a biologist staring through a microscope into their petri dish. A car sitting low on its suspension or driving slower than others on the road—Buchanan may suspect the driver is carrying a bomb, slowing down to finish the last prayer before bursting through the gates. Perhaps a pedestrian that looks out of place would be missed by his colleague beside him. A man with a deadly intent walks differently than someone relaxed, his gait tighter and more measured. All these small behaviors add up, and in a remote village or a built-up cosmopolitan city, Buchanan is like a wolf looking for a weak link.

Several years on from meeting Duval, his life is full of adventure. The chain of command is small, the budget is massive. Duval provides the taskings, and Buchanan and his men plan and carry out the operation. The latest information supplied by Duval for this operation is sketchy at best and bordering on an international scandal at the worst. For this very reason, Buchanan places himself in front of the two monitors fixed to the side of the panel van. He needs to be sure his target doesn't slip past them.

His fingers on his left hand type commands on the keyboard while his right hand is fixed on a small joystick. Covert cameras are installed on the exterior of the Mercedes-Benz Sprinter. Inside, Buchanan delicately maneuvers their angles until he is presented with a high-definition view of the pedestrians walking past. Dave Kenn, another member of the CIA Special Operations Group, had parked the surveillance vehicle a few hours ago on Unter den Linden. Between Starbucks and Dunkin' Donuts, three men remain hidden from view in the back. Kenn casually walks off and positions himself in the street somewhere nearby to conduct countersurveillance. An earpiece and a covert mic attached to his collared shirt provide Buchanan with an advanced warning system.

The location was easily decided on as a great vantage point to wait for their target. Approximately one hundred meters in front of them sits the huge American embassy, which is next to the famous Brandenburg Gate. Connecting these locations to the American junk food is the expansive Pariser Platz, an open space named after the French capital; but more importantly, the main entrance of the embassy opens directly on to the square.

Observing Pariser Platz and the surrounding area, the team knows they won't have to wait long. Buchanan, the most experienced in surveillance, leads this special mission unit and received his orders directly from Duval. Inside the van on Buchanan's left is Tony Marchetti, an Italian American who resembles a mafioso with his greased jet-black hair and gold chain hanging over a white T-shirt. Behind him sits Chuck Lambert, bald with a long brown beard and sporting a baseball cap, dressed neatly in black cargo pants and a navy shirt.

Lambert passes the time by cleaning weapons and testing the various surveillance equipment. He is the tallest and strongest of the four, despite his thin frame. He came from Delta Force, while Marchetti and Kenn arrived shortly after from DEVGRU, known as SEAL Team Six. All of them had heard about the work of the CIA Special Operations Group through whispers. This extra level of romantic secrecy was a driving force for their transfer.

Dave Kenn, however, is a strange one, having spent time with the FBI before deciding to test himself in the military. He is more calculated during each stage of planning for their operations, always looking for things that can go wrong. Buchanan feels it best to have a focused man on the outside observing while the rest of the men concentrate on their normal duties.

The high van has a high roof and is fitted on all sides with a layer of soundproof material. Access between the driver's cabin and the back is tightly sealed, so even at night they can have the internal lights on without being noticed from the street. A ventilation system supplies them with fresh air-conditioning, which means they don't have to sit and sweat in the midday heat.

A camp-style toilet allows them to do their business without resorting to empty bottles or plastic bags. All in all, it is a regular setup, nothing unusual about how they operate the various electronic equipment or set about their tasks. Despite this, the tension inside the van is heavy and tempers rise.

"We are too close to the embassy, Buchanan . . . spying on our own people is screwed up, man." Lambert mutters this mantra for the umpteenth time.

Buchanan is growing tired of his team second-guessing him. "Think about it, Chuck, this is Germany, for Chrissake, not some sandpit hellhole. Hoffmann's security detail expects friendlies in the area. Duval has us marked down conducting counterterrorism duties on a need-to-know basis. If there are any suspicions, he will let us know."

Buchanan never takes his eyes off the screen. He expected his men to question the plan when he first laid it out a couple of days before. Over the past forty-eight hours, they tracked Hoffmann and Liana as they made trips around Berlin. During the week, Hoffmann had spent most of his hours in meetings deep inside the Zentrale des Bundesnachrichtendienstes, referred to as the BDN.

The German equivalent of the CIA is the second largest intelligence agency in the world. The agency began during the Cold War, and during that time a tight partnership between the BDN and CIA blossomed. The BDN possessed a well-informed knowledge of the communist states within the Eastern Bloc, which was crucial information for the Americans. This massive building in the heart of Berlin is the German headquarters of the Federal Intelligence Service, which is the largest intelligence building in the world, a place where Hoffmann feels secure and relaxed.

His counterparts from the British Secret Intelligence Service and DGSE from France also are in the city, therefore causing quite a stir from the media. They have stationed network vans and their crews outside the BDN headquarters on Chausseestraße in the Mitte district of Berlin for days, searching for answers to the two bombings in Monte Carlo and the church massacre.

The British released a bland statement to the press acknowledging the terrible crimes that took place in the "sovereign city-state of Monaco. With strong European and American partnerships, we will leave no stone unturned until we have brought the perpetrators to justice." It was the standard spiel given to word-hungry journalists who will undoubtably create inflamed versions for their clickbait-loving subscribers.

Lambert taps his foot annoyingly on the soundproof floor, then he stops and removes his headphones and rubs his eyes, slowly coming onside with this dodgy operation, although he has some doubts. He looks over and probes Buchanan once more. "Well, what makes you think she will drop her guard?"

"This is her first assignment. For her, Europe is a dream location in a safe environment. Liana and Hoffmann have been in Berlin for days. So far, they have ventured out for coffee at Starbucks and had lunch twice at Quarré. The formal meetings have winded up, which means Hoffmann will get down to the informal meetings. Those partnerships he has built up over the years with the puppet masters of Europe, men behind the politics and those that dictate who leads their nations and who shall be laid to rest."

Lambert ponders this for a moment. "Okay, I somewhat get it, but Liana . . . where does she fit in?"

"She doesn't. Liana is simply the bait. As for her role and the rest of the time spent in Berlin, her duties have come to a dead end. Hoffmann will let no one venture near his close and private contacts. These men and woman only deal with people of influence and value. A handful of people that have proved their worth over the years. Liana will be free to roam the city, to learn it and perhaps set up her own contacts. Prompted by her peers to build up her own network, in doing so she will venture far from the nest . . ." Suddenly Buchanan holds his finger up and blurts, "Action up, lads, we have movement."

Lambert places the headphones neatly over his bald head, then adjusts the sensitivity of the long-range microphone, which is directed at the front entrance of the US embassy. Tony Marchetti simultaneously reaches over the small narrow desk and grabs the team phone and selects the last call. When Kenn answers, Marchetti confirms to him that "your order is ready."

Marchetti quickly pulls on a black cap and a dark gray jacket, then slides himself between the thick black curtains separating the workstation from the rear doors. The material allows him to open the doors and exit the van, protecting the sight of his CIA teammates inside. Just before he opens one of the two rear doors, he checks his equipment. "Starbucks floor, over."

Lambert, on hearing Marchetti's comical radio check, replies quietly, "Starbucks counter, ready for your order, please."

With a chuckle from Marchetti, he gently opens the door and steps out and onto the streets of Berlin. Knowing Kenn will come past in a counterclockwise direction from Bundesstraße, Marchetti moves into Starbucks, confident that Liana is covered. He eagerly places an order and walks over to the window until his order is ready. Resting somewhat comfortably on a barstool, he spies a coffee-stained copy of *Berliner Zeitung*, left on the window table by a couple of students, so he grabs it to help with his cover. Casually flicking through it, he finds the newspaper doesn't cover the event in Luxembourg. The Parisian assassination is mentioned in one paragraph, with limited information. *Still early days,* thinks Marchetti.

He keeps his mind on Liana and what information she may hold about the British man helping the unknown American assassin. Duval had expressed the pressing need for this Brit spy to be put in a grave and to find the identity of the American during a highly volatile phone call to Buchanan in the early morning. The Berlin team had been wakened from their safe house in Neukölln and told to carry out this operation on a need-to-know basis.

This is not too surprising, but something doesn't sit well with Marchetti. His mind keeps wandering to the facts presented hours earlier. *Kidnapping our own people in Europe, under the noses of all the major intelligence agencies based in Germany. The British embassy is right around the corner, filled with SIS men, and not far from them is the Russian embassy, with their "take no prisoners" attitude. When it comes to assassinations, their SVR heavies are not to be messed with.*

Rocking his head back and forth to the techno coming through the wall speakers, he thinks how this op could turn into one big clusterfuck. He would be much happier on the streets of Turkey or Yemen, but Europe is too close to home. Nonetheless, the payday that Duval kept promising them had come true. Yet Marchetti knows little regarding the complete picture, other than that a handful of Chinese wanted to start World War III. Their aim is to push and probe before striking at the heart of the UN, ripping the United Nations Plaza in Manhattan to pieces, forcing the Western nations to strike back.

Duval had mentioned to them all previously how he had insider information on the Chinese renegades' intention and that he could get all his team on their payroll if they assisted in some fashion. This had annoyed

Marchetti at first. Accepting bribes from a foreign nation was not what he and the men in the van signed up for years earlier when they first put on a uniform. Although over time, as they read and studied the political landscape, their support for these politicians dropped spectacularly. They often discussed how the politicians were lining their own pockets and seeking to secure positions of importance, only to create a magical future for themselves and their families that existed only in the most memorable dreams for others. Marchetti thinks back to a night in Istanbul when Duval asked the men about retirement. *You want to be running around defending your country for a bunch of ungrateful pricks? Those who will sooner cast you aside in order to protect their election hopes? Leave you to rot in a hell-forsaken place? There are no rescue teams in our line of work; that red line has already been crossed once you signed up for this unit.*

All the men agreed, Marchetti included, and when Duval spoke softly in the dusty bar in the heart of Kadiköy, the men inched their heads closer. *Okay, listen up, men, as I will never repeat this. The Chinese Mafia has a couple of issues; therefore we need to help them with that. For our help, they will reward us well. Otherwise, you can sweat your asses off for fifty years and not come close to what they will give. I hope you all have your bolt-holes and new identities for when that time comes, and it will come, either with or without you. Be rich and safe, or run the rest of your life looking over your shoulder.*

Those words rang true. *The time has come.* Sitting in the coffee shop, Marchetti realizes there is no going back. After all, they had successfully transferred the money to his accounts in Belize, the Cayman Islands, and Zurich. Each man received five million US dollars distributed evenly across their bank accounts for their help in finding both the SIS and CIA man, with a further ten if they can kill them both. *No one's life is worth that,* thinks Marchetti. *Although my new life in Puerto Vallarta in Mexico is awaiting, I will slot anyone for that price.* He cannot get this dream lifestyle out of his head. Once his team can track down the two targets, he will man up and do what comes naturally. Step one is information, and from the side of his eyes, Marchetti watches her walk into view. Kenn flicks to life on the radio. Marchetti acknowledges the transmission with simply a click on the device, sending a buzz across the network.

Once Liana arrives in the café, she immediately orders a coffee to go, speaking German almost fluently. *Fast learner,* Marchetti notes to himself. As she stands looking out over the platz, the look on her face is almost angelic. Long black hair tied up, expect for two strands cascading down both sides of her oval face. A long red wool coat that is secured firmly with black lace buttons, protecting her from the changing weather patterns. Underneath, a cream white skirt meets a pair of black knee-length boots with a gold zip running up the outsides. Marchetti views her attire in the glass's reflection. She designed her style not for boardroom meetings or media conferences; instead, it is more suited to upcoming photographic opportunities, which she would have planned ad hoc. He inhales long and slow, and his well-refined Italian nose catches the light scent of bergamot and neroli from her expensive perfume through the heavy aroma of roasted coffee beans. Marchetti regains his focus and flips over another page while pretending to read an article. He secretly hopes she gives up what they want instead of having to resort to violence.

Time is something they don't have, and sitting in the soft surrounds of Western civilization, he promises to himself to treat her better than his usual subjects. When Liana steps out of Starbucks, her cardboard coffee gripped in her hand, she walks with the carefree attitude of a woman lost in the moment. The perfect time for the men to act. Marchetti waits until Kenn passes by the window to lead the pursuit. A few more sips of coffee as he checks for a tail on Kenn, then the Italian American CIA paramilitary operations officer folds the paper neatly and leaves the shop to take up a secondary position on the soon-to-be victim.

Liana meanders a lonely path west along Unter den Linden, stopping at Bebelplatz for a few photographs before continuing. Next she crosses Schloss Bridge, her camera resting against the sandstone columns with the ninety-eight-meter-high dome of the Berlin Cathedral neatly in her viewfinder. After a couple of snaps, the mandatory self-portraits begin.

"Excuse me, madam, allow me to take one for you," says Kenn.

The polite offer from this smartly dressed man is too good to pass up.

"I would very much appreciate it," remarks Liana. "How did you know I wasn't German?"

A large smile spreads across the dark-haired man as he takes the camera from Liana's outstretched hand and, with a sneaky wink, responds softly, "Germans do not interrupt their busy schedules to talk with handsome men on bridges, now, do they?"

Laughing uncontrollably and unable to suppress her blushing, Kenn seizes the opportunity to capture her beauty against the baroque architecture of the glorious cathedral. Once Liana composes herself, he takes a couple more photos from various angles, then walks over to hand over her camera.

"All this photography work has made me hungry. How about you, little American model? Would you care to join me for a bite?"

Feeling somewhat flattered, she almost considers it harmless. However, her time is limited and Berlin has a lot of sights to offer. When she places her hand on the camera and locks eyes with the charming man, she never even notices the van that has rolled to a stop over her right shoulder. "Sorry, you made me laugh and gave me a memory, but I will pass on this . . ."

Before she can get the last of her excuses out, Kenn pulls her into his body as if to kiss her. The shock of what is happening causes time to slow down. A sharp pain now burning in her stomach is too much to bear, and the stranger's hand muffles a scream. Dave Kenn is a professional in high-risk abductions. Wasting no time, he bundles the lightweight frame of the CIA officer into the side of the Mercedes van assisted by Marchetti, who, like Buchanan, had timed their arrival beautifully. A handful of pedestrians witness the event. It baffles some, while others figure out quickly that the girl is being kidnapped. When the van door slides shut, the wheels are already in motion. An older man on the street screams at others to call the police while a younger woman fumbles with her phone, attempting to call the authorities. Lambert, from inside the van, has already switched on the cell-jamming device, preventing anyone within one thousand meters from accessing the network.

Buchanan navigates along the planned route, sticking to the speed limit as Lambert listens for updates on the police radio. The short distance through the streets of Berlin take less than two minutes before they reach an underground car park. Two levels below street level, the men transfer the drugged-out Liana to the back of an old taxi. Buchanan sets the timer in the back of the van. Lambert takes up position behind the wheel of the taxi with Kenn in the back. Buchanan will drive a backup car with Marchetti and follow the prize to the next destination a few blocks behind.

Chapter Twenty-One

Zermatt, Switzerland

The cell phone buzzes once before it is quickly answered. Zhang sits on the balcony overlooking the town, wrapped only in a blue-and-green-striped towel. Sweat slowly runs down his chest and back. The renegade Chinese assassin arrived back to the chalet after a quick run, then endured a cold shower. Despite stepping out of the cool mountain water over ten minutes ago, it surprises him that the sweating hasn't stopped. The recorded message lasted only thirty seconds. Zhang only spoke a few coded words, allowing the voice-recognition system to proceed, then he memorized the information. When he walks back into the large living room, the place is empty apart from the nervous-looking Jürgen sitting on the couch, staring into the fireplace. On hearing the Chinese man enter, Jürgen turns and speaks. "Is there a problem?"

"No, why would you say that?" Zhang asks, his demeanor changing slightly as he spots a look of fear in his eyes. The jittery young man from the Chinese consulate in Munich is unaccustomed to receiving a phone call in the middle of the night, then getting tasked with delivering a diplomatic bag almost six hundred kilometers away.

Casually tucking a loose strand of long blond hair behind his ear, the German national stands and gives a shrug of his strong shoulders. "I mean, this is not very normal, getting called with such urgency to come here. I had a lot of explaining to do why I didn't come into work today."

"Don't worry, you are working, your duties are to assist with Chinese diplomatic affairs, and that's what you are doing . . . yes?" Zhang gives the confused lad a smile as he walks across the room to his package. They stamped the large black bag with the words "Diplomatic Bag, The People's Republic of China" in bright yellow letters. Underneath is a series of letters and numbers followed by a line of Chinese characters, which are a translation of the English words. Zhang lifts the heavy bag and walks into the kitchen with it. Once there, he sets it on the granite bench top and checks the plastic tamper-proof fasteners on the opening of the bag. Sliding the second drawer open under the bench, he pulls out a large carving knife and slips it between the plastic zip ties. With a flick of the wrist, he slices the plastic in two just as Jürgen walks closer. The suspense of its contents prove difficult for Jürgen to simply ignore. Zhang nods his head approvingly as he acknowledges the interest the young German shows in this secretive delivery. The items were sent to him on the orders of the Black Bear. The general used his corrupt contacts throughout Eastern Europe, built up over the years, to ensure that when the time comes, he could call on those under his wing to supply whatever his heart desired.

Zhang stops short of opening the mouth of the bag and instead looks up at Jürgen with a wide smile and says, "Hey, what's the word for *surprise* in German?"

"We call it *Überraschung*," says Jürgen. With another step forward, he is now standing right in front of Zhang, with only the bag separating them. His eyes fixate on the top of the bag. The excitement creeps over him. For years, he handled these bags and never got to see their contents. The more secretive the deliveries he was part of, the higher the fees he requested to keep his mouth shut. Illegal activities assisting the Chinese were hugely beneficial for both parties. The Chinese enjoyed the low-profile German national moving around, attracting no attention when delivering pouches, gifts, or VIPs. For Jürgen, the financial transactions into his private Swiss bank account helped to pay for his many expensive skiing competitions. His plan is to become a professional alpine skier, although the adrenaline rush of racing downhill at speeds of over one hundred kilometers per hour is not unlike the feeling he is experiencing now.

Reaching into the dark black bag, Zhang gropes around until he grasps a small black case. Opening it carefully, he places his fingers around a black-and-silver cardboard box filled with fifty rounds of ten-millimeter ammunition. Slowly removing it from the black bag, Zhang teases the wide eyes of his spectator. Then, in one swift movement, he flips it around and watches the eyes of the German as he reads the words "Sellier & Bellot, handgun ammunition." The moment has come for the assassin. Jürgen's jaw drops and his eyes narrow as they meet the blackness of Zhang staring back at him.

With a frightening shriek, Zhang cries out, "*Überraschung*, asshole," as he grabs the carving knife and lashes out at Jürgen's throat. He sinks the eight-inch knife deep into the young man's windpipe. Zhang immediately lets go as his victim reaches up and grabs the handle with both hands. Consumed by horror, fear, and unbelievable pain, Jürgen has lost all ability to understand what is happening. He drops awkwardly to the ground and his long legs kick out. Drowning in his own blood, choking from a lack of air getting into his lungs, and bleeding profusely, the man is a lost cause. Within a minute or two, his life will slip away.

The noise of the German laying on the kitchen floor making such a racket is too much for Zhang. He lifts the black bag and walks into one of the other rooms so he can check the bag in peace.

***

His sweating has eased slightly. The latest injection of antibiotics was enough to eliminate any concerns he had. Zhang conducts a last walk around the chalet before moving out. Whoever owns the property can deal with the dead body in the kitchen. Zhang isn't a cleaner. The only items he takes are the man's car keys and a room key. The small car park at the train station in Täsch is his destination. Although, there is another loose end that requires his attention.

Bahnhofstrasse is almost empty of tourists heading into the late evening, most of whom have taken their positions behind heavy wooden tables draped with red-and-white-checked cloth in these fine restaurants of Zermatt. The succulent Swiss cuisine topped off with velvety smooth wine and crisp German beer will ensure it traps their focus within their comfortable surrounds. No one will pay much attention to a lonesome man walking through the street sporting a backpack and a scarf around his face with a hat pulled low, fending off the biting wind and fog tumbling down the icy slopes to the streets below.

On entering the chalet, Zhang makes a beeline immediately for the staircase. Moving up two steps at a time, he quickly reaches the correct floor. Walking softly along the corridor, he takes a mental note of the room numbers as he finds number seven. The room that was booked earlier for Jürgen. With the key already in his hand, Zhang unlocks the door and steps inside. Closing the door quietly behind him, he sets the bag on the bed, then inspects the room. Once satisfied, he moves back to the door and waits.

Standing at the doorway, Zhang's concentration never falters. He listens intently to every noise, trying to decipher its meaning. A number of times, he opens the door ajar to peep out into the hallway, only to find a random tourist coming home or a staff member attending to room service duties. After another forty minutes, he hears movement again. Someone is knocking at a door. Slowly he twists the handle on the door, then, as the few times before, he eases the door back, allowing a slight glimpse down the hall. When he spots the same staff member carrying a tray of food, his heart races. *Perhaps I will strike lucky,* he thinks proudly to himself. With one hand reaching into his jacket and the other on the door handle, he is almost sure of the outcome. Zhang closes the door slightly so it will not look suspicious from the hallway. As he can hear reasonably well, there is no reason to spook anyone. He can hear the well-spoken staff member repeat the room occupant's order, "Papet Vaudois, tartiflette . . ." There are a few seconds of silence following that which concerns Zhang. He can't help himself, so he eases the door inward, creating a millimeter-wide gap. Just enough to observe the tray being placed down on the floor, then the room boy standing up, turning and walking toward the staircase. Slowly, Zhang closes the door once again. Knowing that his opposite neighbor will likely have a firearm ready, perhaps he may come out and check the hallway before returning to his room with the meal. The seconds feel like minutes, slight noises become amplified, and his sensory organs are in overdrive from the savory food across the hallway. Parts of him just want a shootout, to get it over and done with.

Okay, enough. Zhang can't wait any longer. He eases the door open once more, just in time. He can see the American, the greedy American, reaching down for his meal. *His last supper*, Zhang mumbles in his own mind as he withdraws a Taser from his jacket and points it at his target. Swinging the door open, he clasps both hands on the thick-handled Taser and squeezes the trigger. Two electrode darts shoot out from the device, trailing thin wires behind them. One dart pierces the man's cheek and the second one lands on the neck. Instantaneously, every muscle in the American's body violently contracts, his brain momentarily interrupted in sending electrical signals to his body. No longer able to keep his balance, Ken Herber falls forward and crashes heavily on the wooden floorboards. Zhang knows he must act quickly, as the effects of the Taser won't last long, and he cannot stand there Tasing him repeatedly. He dashes across the hallway and presses down on the Taser once more. The rapid clicking sound comes to a stop when Zhang pockets the taser. Now he quickly drags the limp body into the American's room and drops him on the worn carpet. He quickly slams the door shut then retrieves a short iron bar from his jacket and strikes down hard on Herber's shoulder. Herber tries to scream but the Taser is activated once more. Back to the paralyzing pain party once again. Once the clicking stops, the iron bar is used, this time connecting with his kneecap, shattering the joint completely. Just as before, the Taser is fired up once again, then the bar is used on his rib cage. Zhang stands up and notices the sweat dripping from his forehead and landing on the back of the American. He feels somewhat wobbly on his feet and slightly disorientated. Ken Herber is out of action. The American breathes heavily, a noisy raspy sound rising from his throat. One of his ribs had broken and pierced his left lung. The man is in a world of pain. Zhang takes a moment to collect himself and look around the room for any information that may be of interest. His search finds various pieces of camera equipment, much of which is uninteresting, so he refocuses his attention and turns to Herber and kneels down beside him. Ken Herber is coming around, and when he locks eyes with Zhang, he somehow builds up the power to spit a mouthful of blood and saliva into the Chinese man's face. Zhang quickly recoils in horror. Disgusted with this, he quickly swings down with the iron bar and cracks Herber's head open. The shock of the man's head bursting wide open disturbs him even more. *Shit, shit* . . . he curses to himself as he jumps to his feet. The smell of blood, spit, and whatever splashed from the American's skull is revolting. He searches around the darkened room and grabs a red blanket that is lying on the bed and uses it to wipe the filth off his face. He then drops it on Herber and curses at himself again for losing it so quickly. Unable to get answers from the dead man, he ignores his mistake and gathers up other items of bedding and places them in the middle of the room. He looks up and spots a red led light glowing in the center of the room. He reaches up to the smoke alarm and removes the cover and snaps the battery out of its housing. Then he takes a lighter from his pocket and flicks the spark wheel. With the fuel ignited successfully, he holds the flame at the corner of a blanket. Once the fire takes hold, he repeats the process in a few more areas. Satisfied the fire is spreading, he leaves the room and closes the door.

With no one in the hallway requiring his attention, he crosses the hallway and, from his own room, he collects his bag and makes his way out of the chalet. Back on Bahnhofstrasse, he hurries toward the train station at the north end of town. The sweat is still on his face despite the cool air, but his mind is clear and the nausea feeling has left him. He succumbs to the urge to not look behind him. Turning his head over his shoulder, he can make out the faint glow coming from behind the curtains. Within minutes, the whole chalet will burn to the ground. Picking up his pace, Zhang needs to get to the car at Täsch. The clock is ticking, and his schedule is full.

Chapter Twenty-Two

Monte Carlo, Monaco

The lack of information is both infuriating and worrying. She would expect something like this from Carver. That is the annoying part. He knows how much she cares for him. Her true feelings. Yet he never contacted her after the operations as instructed. This was when the wave of anger left her to be replaced with deep concern. These two waves ebb and flow every few minutes, once again testing her ability to get on with business despite the potential nightmare that may exist. When her thoughts of fury and anxiety overlap, it's like someone is etching the pain into her mind. Sarah Fontaine fights the natural urge to tap out and faint in an embarrassing heap. Instead, she looks straight ahead and stares at her reflection in the beveled mirror across the bar. Her mouth drops open slightly, stunned at the sight of her sunken eyes, no longer carrying any signs of joy or pleasure. Her skin looks pale with a texture of rough leather. Removing the olive from her drink, she knocks the liquid back like a lumberjack after a hard day's work. She sets the glass back on the coaster and attracts the attention of the charming barman for her third drink. Perched on a black barstool with soft padding covered in royal-blue suede, her tanned legs crossed elegantly and a purse in her lap, Sarah looks like a picture of sophistication. Dressed exquisitely in a new low-cut black cocktail dress with matching heels, a gold chain with a solitary diamond sitting an inch above her cleavage line, and her beachy blond hair swirling down her back, the young SIS director is performing a role far beyond her job description.

The Casino de Monte-Carlo is Sarah's temporary hunting ground for a couple of nights. She is wading into unchartered territory and approaching these problems from a different angle. Patiently observing the elegantly dressed man pour some gin, vermouth, and ice into a mixing glass, she thinks back to the breaking news that flashed across the television in her hotel room last night. Breaking news continued throughout the day on all the major channels, covering many various events taking place all over Europe. However, the murder in Paris last night appears to be, from what Sarah can tell, a successful operation by Carver. Despite the manner in which the target was eliminated, the few news reports she found on Paris detailed a gruesome scene. Many of the mainstream channels described it as a robbery gone wrong. *The Chinese won't believe that for one minute*, she thinks.

Now in front of Sarah, the barman strains the martini into a chilled cocktail glass, drops a green olive into the mix, and places her drink down on a fresh coaster. "Mademoiselle."

"Merci, Monsieur." Taking the drink in her hand, Sarah strokes the condensation on the side of the glass as a thought crosses her mind. She takes a casual glance around the room to find the usual clientele expected in such an extravagant spot, one of the oldest casinos the world has to offer, and one that attracts the rich from all over the world. Stunning artwork, decorative moldings, and plasterwork highlighting the Belle Époque architecture is revealed in all its glory by the huge and elegant crystal chandeliers that hang from the high ceilings. Elaborate brass and gold touches mixed with the marble columns and floors highlight the attention to detail in the interior design. The place is a hive of old money charm.

Despite French being the official language in Monaco, within the surrounds of the bar she can pick up many others, mostly Italian, German, English, and what interests her the most, a few people speaking Mandarin. A group of men huddled in conversation sit facing each other on small armchairs at the end of the bar. A few minders sit farther back, blocking a pathway, or at least attempting to provide some resemblance to a protective detail around their bosses.

Sarah wants to meet one of these Chinese men. The identity of the marina sniper and his intent are troubling her. Sarah considers the possibility that Eddie Wu can provide a clear picture of what has unfolded since. Eddie has remained out of view ever since his release from the police interviews conducted by the local authorities in Monaco. The only surviving Chinese man on the *Golden Tiger* resulted in many theories around Europe and especially back in China. High-ranking intelligence officials within the Ministry of State Security in Beijing immediately demanded his return to face an internal enquiry. He had answers, and Sarah scrambles to find the right approach to such a private man. There is one way she momentarily considers, not as something she would do, but as a last-ditch effort if need be. Goose bumps spring up on her arms, and she shudders at the thought. *No, not going to happen,* she mouths to herself as she swivels her head to her right along the bar.

On the third barstool sits a beautiful young woman with long, wavy dark hair. The stunning and delicate brunette would not look out of place on the front cover of *Vogue*, thinks Sarah. She wears a dark green dress, cut just above the knee, with a split running up her left thigh. Both shoulders expose her bronzed soft skin, with her neckline presenting a string of pearls and a reasonable view of her ample bosom, which results in timely bar service. In Sarah's opinion, the woman's dress choice would keep the conversation dignified while still allowing a slice of sensual thoughts. *What's her story?* she thinks. *Could she be one?* There was only one way to find out.

"Do you mind if I join you?" Sarah asks as she approaches the woman and points to the barstool next to her.

The beautiful woman turns around with a note of surprise on her face. Quickly giving Sarah a discreet once-over, she then smiles and gently nods. "Be my guest."

Sarah extends her hand and introduces herself as Barbara Edwards, using the made-up name that matches her room reservation and the ID in her purse. The lady provides the same: Francesca Vecchiarelli, a threat intelligence analyst working as a contractor for Intesa Sanpaolo, Italy's largest bank. Sarah commits this to memory, even though it would most likely be false.

Francesca buys their drinks and asks Sarah the usual questions surrounding her career, family life, and her business in Monaco. After a couple more drinks, the two women relax as the alcohol lubricates and loosens their guard.

"I wish I had a rich man to take care of me. Instead of spending my time moving from hotel to hotel in search of business deals, which can become boring and draining," remarks Sarah. Pointing to her face, she adds, "Look at me, exhausted from tripping around. When I get back to London, I sleep, wake up, write reports, eat, and go again. I have nothing at home. I cannot commit to even a simple plant because of the stresses of my work."

Francesca's hazel eyes widen and her laugh fills the room. She uses her hand to cover her mouth as she tries to contain the hilarious description Sarah had painted for her. The increasing alcohol seeping into her blood amplifies her mood. "Oh, poor you, my love, I'm so sorry to laugh, I was picturing in my head a lonely plant waiting for the beautiful English woman to return."

The two women laugh some more as the waiter arrives with fresh drinks, some canapes, and a handwritten note for Francesca. He sets the empty glasses on a silver tray, bows his head, and quietly leaves the table.

Francesca lifts the note and reads its contents. She takes a quick glance over to the far corner of the room and, with a slight giggle, she pushes the note neatly into the top of her dress before looking back toward Sarah.

Sarah's eyes once again find their natural sparkle. She is full of enthusiasm and cheekiness as she slides her tongue back and forth between her lips at the sultry Italian. A laugh erupts, and when the noise subsides, Francesca takes the note out from between her breasts and slides it across the table for Sarah to read. Somewhat unfazed with another offer, although Francesca views the inclusion of the English girl between the sheets as promising, this night may develop into something more exciting. She picks up her cocktail glass and, with a flirty smile on her face, she seductively runs her fingernail slowly around its rim.

Sarah reads the handwritten scribble on the piece of paper. *A moment of your time for a large financial gift, VIP room at nine o'clock.*

Like two schoolgirls behind the bike sheds sharing secrets, Sarah plays her game flawlessly, understanding perfectly that her new friend is either a high-class escort, a money trap operating for one of the many intelligence agencies, or an industrial espionage contractor for the commercial industry. Sarah continues her new role as a supporting friend and shakes her head as she giggles at the pitiful nature of the invitation, holding it up and waving it between each of her perky breasts. This prompts Francesca to slowly open her legs and roll her eyes to the back of her head. Sarah roars with laughter for some time, and eventually, when the laughter eases, she holds her ribs because of the pain. Tears roll down her cheeks, and as she straightens up, she realizes this is the most fun she's had in weeks. Slowly sitting back up, the two girls attempt to compose themselves. Francesca fixes her dress while Sarah adjusts her hair and repositions the sparkling diamond on the gold chain, then moves it back into the center of her chest.

Francesca is the first to speak. "Those seedy Asian nouveau riche," she says, holding two fingers up and twitching them when she utters the French words. "Always targeting young single women in decent places like this, they believe money conquers all morals."

"Tell me about it," adds Sarah, attempting to convey herself in a similar position. "I know their kind, power created by wealth, mainly through corruption and slavery treatment of their own people. Then treated like royalty by the very people they oppress. The parvenu disgust me." The SIS woman allows her feelings to settle on the young Italian as she spins the olive around her glass using the small cocktail stick. A feeling of wickedness is rising within her.

"Well, what are you going to do about it?" asks Francesca.

Sarah considers the question and how she should play her next move on the frisky brunette who sits across the table from her.

A cute grin slowly emerges across the Italian's delicate face, her gaze turning lustful as she waits for a response from this new sharp-looking woman from London. A woman that Francesca thinks may introduce to her an assortment of fresh connections. Her time in Monte Carlo is coming to an end, and a friendly face in a new city like London sounds perfect. The highly attractive and sharp-witted honey trap deals not specifically in threat intelligence but rather a plethora of information. The best-paying clients for the information she gathers vary widely, from industry competitors to journalists, scientific researchers, and the Italian intelligence and security agency, or Agenzia informazioni e sicurezza esterna. Over the years, she has built up a network of regulars who fly in for business trips and invite her to spend time with them on their yachts, in their penthouses, or as tonight would attest, for a week's accommodation in the finest hotel that Monte Carlo offers. One of her regulars paid up front for her room and allowance before arriving for the Formula One Grand Prix the week before. Arriving from Moscow with jewels and the finest champagne, the young and filthy rich cryptocurrency entrepreneur was smitten by the tall, busty Italian. The pair hit it off the previous year in Basel when she met him at the annual watch fair. A couple of nights later, while oiled up with Bollinger and tied to the bed with her lingerie, he escaped from his world filled with paranoid suspicions. Lying in bed with his skinny arms wrapped around this beauty, the wealthy Russian described his business methods and future ventures. It felt good to talk about himself to what he considered a "dumb escort." The brief moment of preeminence and showboating felt good during those moments for the young man, who was very much unaccustomed to the murky world of espionage. Francesca lay there committing every word to memory and, as the Muscovite succumbed to the alcohol and fell into a deep sleep, she rolled over and considered a list of people that would pay handsomely for this knowledge. Since that lustful night, Francesca has carved out a comfortable life for herself, roaming around European cities collecting information from a selection of industries. Her victims are vast and ever-expanding and so too are the buyers. London would launch her "career" to new heights. Perched on a stool in the exquisite bar that joins the Casino de Monte-Carlo, a new idea is forming; her mind is clearing the fog that arrived via several martinis. *The time has come*, she thinks, having a trusted partner, someone to watch out for her during the high-risk nature of infiltrating the high rollers. Tonight, could be a test for the English woman. *Is she up for a piece of action? The thrill of the hunt for valuable information and the rewards that follow?*

Sarah sits there calculating, her mind racing. She floats her gaze back to the men and watches as the barman pops another bottle of expensive champagne. The man in the middle is unmistakable. The top dog decorated with a gold chain and a couple of diamond rings on this fat fingers and a Swiss watch dangling like a bracelet. His face is easily recognizable. For days, the images had been popping up on her intel briefings. Eddie Wu stands out like an old friend. She knows her inner voice is prompting her to act. Teasing and caressing her mind, pushing her to do something that morally disgusts her. Yet, as she sits here in the surrounds of wealth and glamour, her mind is cast back to the last time she saw Carver. *Where is he? Bleeding out in a ditch somewhere? Arrested or killed by the enemy? Or is he living it up with hookers in the backstreets of Paris or Budapest or God knows where?* Her head spins, slowly at first, then quicker and quicker, as suddenly the room freezes and time stands still. The situation now becomes clear, as if everything is laid out perfectly at her feet. Sarah is blessed with the tools she needs in order to manipulate a man. The facts are in front of her, and such answers need to be extracted, no matter what it takes.

Looking up at Francesca, she takes a deep breath, and before backing out, gives the Italian a sexy wink and whispered, “What’s their best price, honey?”

The night has just become interesting, she thinks as her heart rushes. "Are you serious?" the foxy Italian queries. Her sultry eyes beam with a naughty display of excitement.

"Of course, my love, on one condition, we stay together." Sarah can't believe she's uttering these words. More surprising is the ease with which they leave her wet lips. The thoughts she is having contemplate two different circumstances. One is to get inside Eddie Wu's room using her sexual energy and, once in the room, to put on a display with the hot-bodied Francesca. No matter what it takes, Sarah has one motive, to search his room, plant a listening device, get his mobile number, and, if possible, check his potential for future recruitment by the service.

Francesca doesn't take long to respond. "It will be my pleasure to stay with you." As a grin appears and a blush forms on her smooth cheeks, she looks forward to the delicate touch of a woman. "Okay, honey, why don't we offer a night of passion to the one who carries the most attention. Make it worth our while, yeah, just don't judge me, okay?"

A sincere look creeps over Sarah's face. "Oh God, no, I would never dream of it. To be honest, I always wanted to do something like this, but I never had the nerve to carry it out." Sarah looks over at the men. Her eyes fix directly on the big guy in the middle. She draws a tactful smile and instantly knows Eddie is going to give answers tonight one way or another. "If you don't mind, I want to go and freshen up." Sarah picks up her purse and walks in the direction of the ladies' room, leaving Francesca to iron out the details. Once in the bathroom, the intelligence director immediately goes into the far stall and slips out a Zanco Tiny T1 mobile phone from her purse. She types a quick message and hits *send*. Next, she takes care of her personal business while waiting for the reply. After reading the confirmation, she removes the SIM card and wraps the phone in tissue paper, then flushes both items down the toilet. Before she heads back to the bar, she touches up her lips in front of the mirror. Staring at her reflection, she shudders at what Harry will say when he learns of her involvement. "Cross the bridge later," she murmurs before opening the door.

Sarah rejoins her new Italian friend back at the bar. As they sit closer together than before, Francesca allows her hand to rest on Sarah's leg. With no objection, her fingers gently stroke the smooth skin, slowly slipping farther inside her dress.

"It is my pleasure to meet you lovely ladies tonight. I am sure we will have a great time together." Eddie Wu stands next to Francesca, watching her hands intently as they caress the tight thigh of the stunning blonde.

"I am sure we will," responds Sarah with a smile. "Sorry, I haven't introduced myself." Reaching out with her manicured hand, she offers it to Eddie. "You can call me Barbara."

Eddie takes her hand, and with a warm smile, he says, "You can call me Eddie."

"Oh, wait a minute," Sarah adds with an air of suspicion and excitement. "You were on the news if I am not mistaken. Regarding that horrid shooting last week, right here in Monte Carlo!"

Eddie is not surprised his name is well known. All the major news networks and social media tools are in overdrive, discussing possible motives and suspects. Eddie himself had been questioned on multiple occasions by every law enforcement agency in Europe. Once the police arrived on the *Golden Tiger*, his shoes were removed. He was then made to wear a forensic crime scene suit, then finally his hands were secured inside paper bags. All to preserve evidence, as the first responders did not know at first there was a sniper. A full search of the yacht was carried out to find the murder weapon, and when the covert hatch was discovered, fitted underneath, Eddie was the prime suspect. It took a few days of interrogations, ballistic experts, and crime scene investigators to establish what actually took place. Eddie had an expert legal team flown in from London to secure his release, on condition he stayed in Monaco to answer any further lines of enquiry. The last thing Eddie wanted was to appear guilty, so he settled in and booked a few rooms for himself and his entourage. The days were long, filled with breakfast, brunch buffets, a light swim in the pool, fine wine after an early dinner, then scotch, cigars, and some female company.

Eddie sucks in his stomach and puffs up his chest somewhat to appear well built as he grasps the situation. This night is special. These genuine beauties had ventured into the bar, half-drunk and in need of a good time. They look rich, educated, and well-presented, typical in this part of Europe, but in Eddie's eye, they have something extra. The look emanating from their faces is one of nervous excitement and naughtiness, unaccustomed to the authentic life of an escort. Both their behaviors portray a shy virgin bride on their honeymoon night who will desperately unleash years of dreams and desires. This is what Eddie lives for, he wants to be the receiver of everything they have to offer.

He sizes up the woman that had picked his name from the media. *Barbara*, he says to himself. Her blond hair is amazing. He wants to feel it in his face, to taste it . . . "Yes, what a terrible day that was. It was terrifying for me. My staff also, those poor girls . . . hopefully the police will catch those responsible. Criminals and thieves need to rot in prison." Eddie then lifts his large hand and waves to the barman, a sign that the conversation on that event is over.

Over the next hour, the two women probe and tease the rich billionaire. Francesca moves softly from topics of business to sexual desires and loops around to exciting upcoming conferences throughout Europe and entrepreneurial ventures she has heard people discussing, hoping to launch Eddie into disclosing something interesting and sellable. Sarah plays her hand differently. She sits back with her elbow resting on the bar while wrapping her blond hair slowly around one of her fingers. This prompts Eddie to spend more time talking about himself as she observes his nonverbal signs to both of them and also to his security detail, which lingers back at the table of the other men. When she decides Eddie has trusted his company enough, he signals to his men to give him some privacy. Sarah notices this and asks politely, "Why do you need the security men? If you are innocent, then there is nothing to worry about!"

Eddie looks at his men, who now have made their way to the bar and ordered themselves a proper drink. "Well, my dear lady, some in the Chinese government may or may not want me dead. I am afraid there are some rogue elements who are not following party lines and are pushing for a war. They see me as a money-making machine. And I for one will not finance a bunch of terrorists."

It was suspected by SIS that Eddie is not part of a war machine. Intelligence gathered by the British suggests he is a simple capitalist who wants nothing more than to shine in the open market. Sarah figures the big man wants to use his entrepreneurial skills to build a successful empire and amass a fortune on which he can live life in peace.

"That's understandable, I guess, though will you have built up many enemies by refusing such help?"

"Something like that," Eddie remarks, his face growing solemn and his voice scratchy.

Francesca notices the mood turning gloomy and immediately jumps in. "You poor thing, Eddie, it must be very hard for you. Perhaps Barbara and I can help you relax." As she speaks, her fingers run along his bulging waistline, then downward to his front pocket, where she slips her gentle hand inside. "Perhaps we could retire to somewhere more comfortable," she adds.

Eddie can barely contain himself. Unable to wait a moment longer, he tells the young barman to disregard his order. With a few awkward smiles and words of encouragement, the three make their way across the street to one of the best rooms in Monte Carlo.

***

Sean Flynn had spent the day being debriefed by members from the Intelligence Support Activity prior to their departure. Their tasks in Monte Carlo had ended following the decision by both the SIS and CIA to limit the amount of personnel until they did some internal housecleaning. A traitor is among them all and it is going to involve a lot of manpower to smoke them out. Flynn is in the private sports club sharing a meal with the four men who all sit heavily on the armchairs looking disappointed to be leaving. Their time in Monaco has been entertaining, particularly their accomplishments at picking up the honey traps, which had become a competition between the men. Earlier, they all enjoyed a workout together, followed by a swim and sauna. During which times Flynn discussed and carefully analyzed relevant pieces of information.

One crucial piece, however, is still outstanding. Ken Herber has yet to provide an update regarding Zhang's whereabouts in Zermatt. A huge question mark hangs over Herber's head regarding his loyalty, and Flynn knows the outcome if the ISA operative cannot produce the actionable intelligence. Herber will find himself on a CIA hit list, and it will likely be Flynn's job to kill him. Blowing out a mouthful of smoke from his thick Partagas cigar, he knows it won't be enough to relax his present mood. Unable to have a drink with the boys, he looks on with a forced smile as they retell their version of events about the countless women they picked up over the week. Suddenly, his phone vibrates against his chest. Reaching into his top pocket, he pulls out a little shit phone that Sarah gave him. After reading the brief message from his new British boss, he quickly replies back, then disposes of the phone into his Americano.

"I'll be back later, boys," he says as he stands and slips on a black denim jacket. Outside, he jumps on a black Yamaha and makes his way from the gentlemen's club, Thirty-Nine, to the hotel in Monte Carlo a few minutes southwest. Once on the side street, he parks and uses the back entrance, avoiding the more public entrance. He walks past the elevators and gives the reception his motorbike helmet, then collects a room key. He must have missed them by a couple of minutes, as the perfume lingers in the elevator he is now standing in.

Despite the two heavies who followed him, Flynn is professionally relaxed. The Russian men quickly dropped their attention toward Flynn once his finger hits the button for his chosen floor. When the doors open, one goon gives the departing Flynn a sly smile as he walks out and down the corridor to his room. *The heavies are no doubt protecting some oligarch on the top floor*, thinks the American. As soon as the elevator doors close behind him, Flynn turns and makes his way to the fire escape stairs.

When he reaches the top floor, he slowly eases the door out and checks for the Russians or anyone else providing security. He figures the Russians must have returned to the lobby, so he is free to move out from the concrete stairwell. Flynn is well aware the hotel cameras will record every movement, although there isn't much he can do about that now. He just needs a few words with Eddie without the distraction of having to deal with his bodyguards. Flynn's thoughts turn briefly to Sarah. He hopes she is doing okay. Her message was brief, only revealing to him she was invited to his room. Luckily, the ISA guys had been busy scoping out the hotel. They had provided Flynn with Eddie's room number and a description of the layout.

The electrical power box containing the various fuses and colored wires was explained to him in great detail in case he needs to cut the connection to the room. Although that was unnecessary tonight, and Flynn is thankful. The risk of electrocuting himself by fiddling at a fuse box in the corridor under pressure is not something he is interested in.

Getting closer, he notices something. The sight of the room door ajar, a pair of hotel slippers preventing it from shutting, means Sarah is in control of the situation. As he walks closer, he swings his head over his thick neck to the other room doors, making sure they are all shut tight. Once he makes it to the door, Flynn slides his hand inside the denim jacket and grabs the grip of his Glock 19, easing it out slightly with just enough room so he can screw on the suppressor. Now with his silenced handgun, he does all he can to slow his breathing while checking the doorframe. From deep inside the room, he can just make out a faint, high-pitched voice. A woman's voice, or perhaps the radio is on. He can't be sure. Holding the weapon against his chest, he eases into the door, so it slowly opens. Flynn senses every move he makes. He tries to picture the situation inside the room and considers Eddie's reaction or if he has a couple of minders hanging out in the lounge area. He knows the bedroom is to the right, just off the lounge through a set of sliding double doors. From Flynn's position in the hallway, he can make out a faint yellow glow coming from the bedroom, which spreads along the floor of the lounge. Crouched against the white-painted wooden panels that cover the entire wall, Flynn disregards the expensive oil paintings that hang along the hallway and the plush cream carpet underneath. These soft furnishings almost wash the feeling of danger away. Luckily, the noise-absorbing carpet allows for the six-foot-three CIA assassin to inch silently toward the lounge.

Now the female voice has become distinguishable. *Oh shit.* Flynn takes a back step and hides his muscled frame back against the wall in the hallway. From there, he listens intently, almost closing his eyes to help with his focus. *There it is again! An Italian accent.* Flynn waits as he struggles to comprehend the situation. *Where the hell is Sarah?* An urge of panic now emerges. Standing in the shadows with his weapon held low, he is about to decide to leave when a laugh breaks the silence. Now he can clearly hear an Italian voice and another woman laughing. *Sounds like Sarah.* Flynn now moves with a gut full of purpose, stepping silently out of the hallway and into the lounge. As he gets near the sofa, which faces the television, it forces him to move against the wall. Opposite him is the balcony, and tonight Eddie had pulled the blinds open, displaying the harbor and sea views. Flynn works his way around the room, keeping to the walls until he reaches the double sliding doors, which are not fully closed. Stepping closer to the gap, he swiftly checks for shadows or anything that may reflect from his body, then he peers into the room. Lit with the bedside lamps and some light coming from the en suite, it is bright enough for him to recognize the fat lump on the bed. However, his eyes don't linger on Eddie for too long.

His chin drops when he sees Sarah kneeling over the Italian, who is spread out on the bed next to Eddie. The naked Chinese billionaire is gagged and tied to each of the four posts on the king-size bed. His bulging eyes are fixated on the partially clothed blonde who, with the Italian, are putting on one hell of a show. Flynn is mesmerized as Sarah reaches around and removes her black lace bra and drags it teasingly across Eddie's face. Then she swivels around, facing the double doors, and gently slides off the Italian girl's thong and lays it on Eddie's chest, who is now moaning and panting. As Sarah keeps up her performance, Flynn thinks about searching the room, although as hard as he tries, his legs refuse to budge. This sight is almost hypnotic. Until Sarah looks up at him standing there. The naked English spy almost shrieks with fright. Then there is a short, embarrassing moment when she simply freezes as they both lock eyes on each other.

Sarah wishes she were alone with the beautiful Italian. She had never experienced the touch of a woman and was about to do something deeply private with Francesca. Knowing Eddie was leering over her body was disgusting, and the thought of Flynn watching her from the doorway was embarrassing at first, although this has now evolved into a new level of excitement. As she sinks her face down between the tanned legs of the Italian, her eyes move toward the door. As Sarah gazes into the shadows toward the CIA assassin, her tongue sends the Italian into multiple spasms. The Italian wants to delay it, so she pulls Sarah's face up and gives her a deep kiss, then flips her over so she can return the serve. Flynn breathes heavily and slowly retreats away from the door, deeper into the shadows. He takes a deep breath as he tucks the weapon under his belt and stands there trying to ignore the screams and cries from Sarah, who is undergoing this new experience. Clearing the fog from his mind, he reminds himself of why he is in the room. Lowering to the floor, he crosses the lounge out of view of Eddie and the Italian until he reaches the small desk in the corner. He grabs a briefcase sitting on the table then, using a small red-light pen to illuminate the pages, he sifts through the files, looking for anything interesting. Once complete, Flynn works his way around the entire suite, carefully searching for any evidence linking Eddie to Zhang. Finding nothing of interest, Flynn knows it's time to act fast. One of his best methods to find answers would be more physical in nature, and the American isn't considering the sexual approach like the women. With his decision made, he goes back to the hallway and secures the door, then checks the girls again, just for a moment. Next, he unlocks the balcony doors and walks into the bedroom, his weapon in hand.

"I hope I'm not disturbing you, Mr. Wu," says Flynn.

A scream from Francesca, as she rolls off Sarah, is slowly followed by a pathetic howl from Eddie. Sarah, startled at first, simply sits up in bed, her body glistening with sweat.

"Quiet, please, I am not here to harm you. I want to speak to your boyfriend for a few minutes." Flynn can see Eddie's eyes look toward his bedside table. A couple of phones lay there beside an ashtray.

"Don't bother, Eddie, I don't want to shoot off your hand." Flynn looks at the girls and tells them to get dressed and stay in the bedroom. He watches as they tweak their lingerie along their slender skin while Eddie wrestles, trying to free himself from the bedposts.

After a few moments, Eddie realizes he is simply making the knots tighter. Spread-eagled and naked as a man stands over him is unbearable. The embarrassment is horrifying, and the feeling of vulnerability is a position he swears he will never find himself in again, no matter how beautiful the women are. "What the hell do you want? Is it money?"

"Money!" laughs Flynn as he walks over to the window and looks out over the yachts in the marina. "If I wanted money, I'd go down and rob the casino."

"Well then, you must have got the wrong man. I have nothing of interest. I am just a businessman who sells video games in China, that's all."

"Is that right? Wow, I must sack the people giving me information, then." Flynn looks over at Sarah, then looks out into the lounge. The others missed the cue, although she understood what he meant.

Gathering up their belongings, the two girls walked past Flynn wearing their undergarments toward the lounge room. Flynn closes the double doors behind him and walks over to Eddie.

"Zhang, he is out there somewhere killing Americans. He was on your boat. You know where he is, and you are going to tell me. Otherwise, I will strangle the life out of you and make it look like a sex game gone wrong." Flynn can see the horror in his eyes. Something isn't right. Eddie doesn't look like a killer or a man who moves in those circles. Instead, he is trembling like a leaf.

"Please, you must understand. I know nothing about Zhang. He kidnapped me, ordered me to work for him. I already told the authorities all about this. You must believe me." Eddie's voice trembles with panic and fear.

"Okay, you know nothing. How silly of me to think otherwise." Flynn holds his arms up in the air. Shaking his head with a look of sarcastic disbelief, he walks off to the bathroom and has a look around. When he comes back out, he has a large white bathrobe in his hand. "I thought you would tell me everything. Zhang's address, his American contacts, who gives him orders from China, who pays him, who provides him with weapons." Flynn stops and looks around the room as he thinks of something. "Did you ever watch the old American television crime drama called *Columbo*?"

Eddie looks at the American with a look of confusion. "No, well, I mean, I know the show, but I never watched a full episode."

Flynn walks over to Eddie and bends down over the bed. "That was a great show. However, Eddie, I never understood why Columbo didn't use better methods."

Eddie doesn't like where this is going. "What do you mean?"

"Like this." Suddenly Flynn manhandles Eddie and wraps the bathrobe around his thick neck. "You see, Eddie, there are faster ways to get information than ringing doorbells and asking everyone unusual questions."

Eddie tries to kick out the moment his throat gets squashed. Whatever air is left in his lungs is now trapped. The heavy bedposts hold tight as Flynn tightens his grip, watching Eddie's eyes almost popping out of his face.

"Columbo should have tried this, Eddie, what do you think?" Flynn laughs as he counts the seconds.

Francesca is panicking in the lounge room. "Let's run, come on, Barbara, please, he must be CIA, we need to leave."

"Calm down. He said stay here, baby, there might be more of them outside. We just wait and hopefully we get money from Eddie to stay quiet. If he pays these guys then he will pay us a lot, yes?" Sarah speaks with sincerity; she feels sorry that Francesca was dragged into this. However, she can't let her leave without confirming her silence. Sarah helps the sobbing Francesca get dressed, then the two of them go out and sit on the balcony, away from the choking sounds coming from the bedroom. The pair looks out over the million-dollar yachts berthed in the harbor and Sarah takes Francesca's hand. The night had been a dramatic mix of two worlds.

Chapter Twenty-Three

Freudenberg, Germany

The red-and-blue lights spin quickly in the dark, covering the country road with a techno theme. Carver is in no mood to discuss his night with a couple of cops known as the Landespolizei. He needs to lose them and disappear.

Chasing the prime suspect in a multiple homicide is the biggest case the two young police officers had ever come across. As they follow the car at a safe distance, the radio sparks to life and multiple frantic calls back to their station relay all the important information. Details on the suspect's car, its license plates, its direction of travel, and any threatening behavior displayed from the suspect are provided. Backup is organized and their instructions are simple. Keep your distance, do not approach until backup arrives. Heinrich, being the most senior of the two, knows what that means. The special response group known as the Spezialeinsatzkommando, or simply the SEK, the German SWAT teams, will be tasked to take down the suspect and they will receive no recognition. A promotion is too far down the line, possibly another three years, and with a baby on the way, Heinrich wishes for a higher income. The urge to run the suspect off the road and conduct an arrest is incredibly inviting. Next to him sits Günter. The younger man is also eager to do something exciting. His reasons don't reflect promotional purposes; instead, it is the testosterone flowing through his body. He wants to get physical and bring this murderer down. Heinrich bangs the steering wheel with his fist. "Shit . . . this is the biggest bullshit, Günter, the SEK will be the tough guys, not us."

Günter has the radio in his hand and is just about to provide another update as he watches Heinrich get wound up. "Well, we should take him out before they get here. Just say he tried to ram us," adds Günter.

A smile creeps over Heinrich's face. The young man is strong. "Let's get closer and see if we can force him to make a mistake, yes?" says the promotion-hungry Heinrich.

Carver watches the cop car in the rearview mirror. He knows they won't chance taking him down on their own. The clock is ticking until a more specialized unit arrives. Carver doesn't want to wait around; the odds are already against him. Being arrested and thrown in jail is not appealing to him. He needs to act, and act quick. The cop car has dropped off. Now it is about fifty meters behind him. Carver scans the road ahead, looking for something that can help his situation. The country road is leading into a small town where the streetlights illuminate the sky. He knows there are plenty of options to consider and multiple roads to choose from.

Carver searches his brain for possible ambush points where they could set up. As he comes up to the end of the country road, he suddenly notices the cop car racing up behind him. *What the hell are they playing at?* Carver thinks. Half alarmed and intrigued, he can only concentrate on his own actions as his eyes search for an escape route ahead of him. Then, as luck would have it, a plan forms in his mind. Up ahead is a warehouse. The floodlights illuminate several lorries, which are picking up or dropping off their goods. It matters little to Carver what they are doing, as long as they are mobile. He glances back up to the rearview mirror then, unexpectedly, he slams on his brakes.

Günter lets out a yell just as Heinrich jerks the steering wheel violently. The wheels screech on the wet tarmac. The car fails to get a grip and slides a few meters before crashing into the back corner of Carver's small Renault, causing a loud bang.

Heinrich moves his neck from side to side. The pain is manageable but there is a worrying scratching sound coming from his collarbone. As his vision comes back, he looks across to young Günter, who is slumped over the airbag, slightly groaning. Heinrich can see blood running down the white airbag onto Günter's blue shirt. As he pushes the young officer back into his seat, he notices the police radio had slapped forcefully into Günter's face because of the impact of the airbag. *The burst lip will heal,* thinks Heinrich, who then starts to come around. Slowly at first, as his brain starts sending messages to his body, prompting him to speed up, yet it takes Heinrich a few moments to understand the urgency. Then he remembers about the murderer. It was him that caused this. "Günter, get your weapon out," shouts Heinrich. "Let's get this animal." It is a struggle for Heinrich to get from the car.

His seat belt got caught around his holster and the airbag. Finally, he removes himself from all obstructions and jumps out. Heinrich then drops to a crouch with the weapon pointed at the smashed-in Renault. Shouting commands at the suspect does nothing. Heinrich looks over to Günter, who by now has joined his comrade and tells him to move forward and inspect the vehicle. "I'll cover you," offers Heinrich. A few tense moments go by until Günter stands up and puts the weapon safely in his holster. "He's gone."

***

Carver's back aches; his neck can only turn halfway to the left or straight ahead. Plus, his left leg and hip are throbbing. The impact of the crash was heavier than he expected; nonetheless, the drastic measures worked. When the cars came to a standstill blocking the country road, he was out and running, slowing only to find a suitable hiding place in the hedgerow outside the warehouse yard. The lorries were leaving the yard to distribute their goods to the other states. He only needed to catch one without being spotted. On seeing the first lorry to leave the yard come out of the large metal gates, Carver ducked his dead down into the dirt. Once the lights passed over him, he hobbled up and made his way alongside the trailer. Carver only had seconds to attach himself before the driver maneuvered through the gears to increase the speed, which pushed Carver to fight through the pain. He ran alongside the lorry and frantically cut a one meter tear through the large plastic curtain that ran the entire length of the trailer with a small knife. Carver then pulled himself up using the locking buckles and forced his broken body through the gap. The lorry gathered speed as it roared toward the motorway, causing Carver to smile, relieved to be leaving the carnage behind. It didn't take long before his body slumped on the cold floor of the trailer.

An attempt to check on his injuries is paused due to his lack of energy. Instead, he keeps peeping out of the damaged curtain, wondering where he's heading.

An assessment of the damage he did to the curtain worries him slightly. A keen-eyed police officer would easily spot the freshly sliced curtain. This tactic is typical of how migrants attempt, with some success, to cross into England, stowed deep inside an oily, smelly lorry, with the sole purpose of beginning a new life in rain-soaked London. In Carver's case, his purpose is to get back into the fight. To draw out Zhang and kill him. Everything that has happened in the previous week appears to Carver as a distant memory. The hunger is overpowering, sleep is calling for him, and his interest in Sarah has now deepened intensely. Carver considers this some more as he sits down and curls his legs up under him. Nestled between a couple of pallets containing what looks like buckets of paint, he folds his arms into a comfortable position across his knees and rests his head in the nook of his elbow. *How I would love to lie in her arms right now.* He sits there imagining that luxury and the touch of her warm skin. During this bumpy ride and the constant swaying, the lorry races unhindered down the road. Carver ponders how his life could be if Sarah was by his side.

***

The sound of the air brakes jolt a shot of adrenaline through Carver's body. Suddenly awake and alarmed, he quickly grasps at his situation, unsure of how long he'd drifted off for, and now he does not know his location. He fights the urge to curse out at himself for doing so. But now is not the time. He crawls forward and gently peels back the piece of curtain, which he had rudely sliced open. Not only is he avoiding a highly specialized tactical police unit, but he also wants to evade a furious truck driver once he realizes someone destroyed his plastic curtain. Carver's body aches when he moves. He hopes it's because of the low temperature inside the trailer, although he expects that's not the case. The blue sky overhead is a welcome relief. He lifts his head toward the sun and notes its position. He estimates he clocked up about three hours' sleep. With a glance at his watch, he confirms it exactly. Peak hour, which explains the traffic.

As the lorry rolls down the motorway, there are frequent stops for the traffic lights, then it resumes normal running. Carver reads all the billboards, looking for a clue of his location. Careful not to expose his face from the trailer, he notices the road he's traveling on is a double lane. A tramline separates the road, with a tram now coming in the other direction. The road signs are all written in German and some locations are recognizable; however, his location is not immediately clear. The key thing on Carver's mind is exiting the lorry without causing attention. He doesn't want to do it in full view of pedestrians, nor does he want to wait until the lorry enters a gated industrial park. As the streets pass by like a moving picture, his eyes dart from street signs to billboards to shop windows, looking for a clue. Then he sees something that could be very useful. *Oh, you good thing, now don't muck this up,* Carver mouths to himself. He peers out onto the street at the ground below while the lorry slows down for the next set of traffic lights. He squeezes the muscles on both legs and stamps his feet on the wooden floor of the trailer, attempting to force some blood around them. The lorry has now stopped, lights are red. Carver jumps and lands heavily on the ground, immediately going into a crouch to absorb his weight. Without pause, he walks behind the lorry and crosses the road. The red lights will change to green soon, so he jogs slightly until he reaches the other side, then resumes his pace. From the corner of his eye, he checks for police, or anyone causing a scene about a man exiting a trailer in the middle of the morning. He can't be certain that someone within the traffic hasn't called the police, so he walks off in the opposite direction from where he intends to go. He breathes easily as the lights turn green and the traffic moves off, slowly at first, then the efficient Germans have cleared the area and the traffic is light once again. Carver takes a side street and, once he reaches the end, turns back toward his intended target.

After a two-minute brisk walk, he arrives at a suburban railway station. The sign overhead provides a clearer picture of his situation: "Stuttgart-Feuerbach." He walks inside, and after a few minutes' wait, he climbs on board the first train to Stuttgart's main train station. Carver knows only too well that once he enters a European railway station, his choices of escape routes increase dramatically. As he rests his tired body on the train, the urge to drift off to sleep is overwhelming. Passengers sit all around, mostly staring into their electrical devices. Some use headphones with their eyes closed. A middle-aged woman applies lipstick and an older man sips on a coffee as he watches the northern suburbs of Stuttgart float past his window. Carver can smell the rich aroma of coffee, so too can his stomach, which awakens with a chorus of wild screams emanating from within. The last liquid to enter his mouth was river water, which was accidental at best.

During the time Carver spent looking around him and assessing his next move, the train had already reached its destination, Stuttgart Hauptbahnhof. With a parched mouth and rumbling stomach, Carver needs to refuel. Knowing that the police are searching for an escaped murderer, he pulls his cap down slightly and walks alongside other commuters through the large concourse. Spying a row of ATMs, he veers over and withdraws the maximum amount of euros using his legend, Charles Walcott. *Can never have too much money*, he thinks while folding the wad of cash in half, then shoving it into his trouser pockets. Next, he visits the ticket counter and picks up a first-class seat to Zurich. The seller is polite and fast, only looking up to say good morning and goodbye; other than that, it's all business. Zurich is chosen, as the wait time is only twenty-five minutes. Other locations such as Frankfurt, Munich, or Berlin would have been worthwhile options also if he was not being hunted by the German police. Leaving Germany and entering Switzerland is more attractive to the SIS man. His safe deposit box, which holds a collection of passports and various documents, will allow the British businessman to transform himself as a Canadian researcher, American hedge fund manager, Australian engineer, or an Italian architect. Charles Walcott's life has sadly come to an end.

With a handful of sandwiches, a liter of water, two coffees, a spicy sausage, and a can of beer to accompany his look, Carver heads to the platform. Checking the train ticket once again before slipping it into his top pocket, he marches quickly to the correct carriage. Once inside the train, the doors close behind him with a thud. Standing just inside the entrance of the carriage, he briefly casts his eye over his fellow passengers before trudging down the aisle toward his seat. As before, most people are addicted to their phones or laptops; telephone calls begin, movies start, and those indifferent about privacy are involved in work-related video calls. Ignoring these whispered conversations from his surroundings, Carver lowers his tired body down into his soft seat with a groan and scans the train platform with a suspicious eye. The sound of the train crossing points as it makes distance from the platform is a blessing in Carver's mind. With no idea how he managed to escape from the massacre in Luxembourg, or the police thereafter, he sits there quietly thanking God. Another promise is made, to visit a cathedral and shove some euros into the charity box.

Over the next four hours, as the train races towards Zurich, Carver, shovels down his food, coffee, and water, then he opens his beer and takes a couple of slugs. Observers would only see an alcoholic man struggling through life. Nothing unusual. The trip through the German and Swiss countryside is enjoyable for Carver, mainly because of the rest and getting some strength back. And although his anxiety had subsided for an hour or two, it is slowly building again as the train slows on the approach to the platform in Zurich. The destination has now been reached, on time and without fanfare. Everyone rises from their seats and collects their belongings just as the brakes are applied and the train eases to a stop. Once the electric doors open smoothly, the passengers all leave the train neatly. Carver once again follows the crowd, walking at their pace and mingling between those that are roughly dressed the same and have a similar build. Once he exits the building, he follows the path directly to the taxi stand.

Zurich is another city he knows well. Over the years, contacts of his came and went, settling in various cities or small towns around Europe. Zurich is one of those places that everyone has reason to visit for various motives. Some of which are legitimate, others may be more nefarious. Carver knows this trip he's undertaking will be the latter. Once in the taxi, he directs the driver to make his way to his bank on Marktgasse in the Altstadt of Zurich so he can quickly swap over his passports. Leaving the bank, which houses his safe deposit box, he jumps back into a taxi and this time heads to the Langstrasse district. The neighborhood of Langstrasse is a colorful area, locally known to be one of the worst areas in Zurich. The "long street" contained the red-light district, drug dens, criminals, and various entertainers of the gritty underworld, which all form the perfect breeding ground for multiple crime bosses. Despite some gentrification, the area would never move away from its past. This allows Carver to hang onto a thread of hope that his old friend is still peddling his trade. Directing the taxi toward the area, Carver can't help but check out the new businesses lining the street. A real transformation since the last time he was here. He orders the taxi to pull up on a side street next to a chemist, then he pays the man one hundred euros and leaves. A discreet "thank you" for riding without the meter and with no knowledge of his existence if the police should ask questions. The Iraqi driver knows how to play the game well.

Carver walks to a store that would sell cheap disposable mobile phones and SIM cards that will not require complicated activation, such as driver's license details or passport numbers. Calling his SIS encrypted mailbox to check for messages from Sarah should only be made using secure phones. Or those that will be disposed of soon thereafter. The whereabouts and safety of his English girl gnaws at him. Once he buys a couple of phones, he exits and walks across the street to a small Turkish restaurant. A place where he can drift in and out without someone sticking their nose into his affairs. Ordering a mixed kebab and a Coke, Carver turns and finds a quiet seat near the back. The place is filled with cheap metal chairs repainted in red-and-white colors, wooden tabletops covered with clear plastic, and yellow floor tiles that are cracked and have had years of grime worn into their surface. It is perfect. Carver slowly gets to work removing the SIM card from its plastic card and inserting it into position. The phones come with half a battery life, which is plenty for their sole purpose.

Clicking the power button on, Carver waits until the home screen appears. The restaurant staff have been bickering among themselves behind the counter ever since he arrived. A small television perched high above the fridge is tuned to a foreign channel. Whatever the news host is discussing appears to be the source of their frustration. A staff member arrives at the table to deliver his can of Coke and a glass, then turns and leaves again without speaking. Out on the street, a couple of touristy types stop and look inside the restaurant. They have a brief discussion with each other and keep moving. Across the road, a delivery truck is off-loading casks of beer for a small bar; the workers stop for a smoke under the sun, which appears through broken clouds. Other than those people, life in Langstrasse is peaceful. It quickly shatters Carver's serenity when his new phone rings. Thinking it is an automated message from the network provider, he taps the red "end call" button and opens the can of Coke. Cleaning the rim of his glass on his shirt, he soon fills it with the cold fizzing liquid. The phone rings again. Automated messages do not call back, and this is a new number. Annoyed at this persistent nature of the German network, Carver answers, for the simple reason to stop it ringing again. He presses the green button and waits for the network's automated advertising or marketing message.

"*Guten Morgen*, old bean," says the man with a cheeky English accent.

A lump appears in Carver's throat. He picks out the voice immediately. "Sorry, say again."

"I would have said good morning, Mr. Walcott, but I guess he has left the building some time ago," the voice speaks with a mock posh Etonian accent.

"Am I glad to speak to you! Where are you?" Carver speaks quietly, his eyes fixed on the street outside.

"In front of my computers, same place I've been for days, man, and it's lucky for you. Christ, I've been busy mopping up after your shit. Your digital trails are messy." Tommy is truthful. He spends every waking hour in front of a panel of screens deep in an office rented and funded by an old SIS friend.

"This phone is not secure; I can't be on it long, you realize that?"

"Relax, man, your number is on my screen. If anyone taps it, I will be the first to know."

Carver considers the confidence in Tommy's voice and appreciates the young geek's capability and knowledge of the hacking world, which is 100 percent. "How the hell did you find me? I've just bought this bollocks of a phone. If you can track me, then who else can?"

"You are old school, man. You rented a car under Charlie, which was involved in a car crash. Then you pulled money from an ATM. It wasn't long before I accessed the platform cameras. Then you disembarked and walked down the street in broad day light. It's not rocket science, like tracking a drunk clown through a forest."

Immediately Carver feels stupid, but what options did he have? "Listen, I need your help. As you know, I've been offline for a couple of days. I'm in the dark about what's happening with all our friends."

"There are a lot of dots to connect, and I'm working on that. Your friends are all in Monte Carlo. I guess you can meet up with them soon. As for your . . . what should I call him? Oh yes, your nemesis. Well, he is unaccounted for. Last known location, Zermatt. Likely to have left within the past twenty-four hours. One of our American friends traveled there to get eyes on, and reports coming in this morning lead me to believe the dead body, which was found in a burned-out hotel, was him."

"Wow, shit . . . that's too convenient for me to believe he is acting alone."

"Well, he isn't. The worrying thing is this high-level support is not coming from the Chinese. Their own president had been in contact with our PM. He warned about a renegade faction in the Communist Party trying to derail European relations and drive the West into a war with them. Take what you want from that, although doing something brazen like this is out of character for the Chinese. Europe is not mainland China."

"Yeah, they wouldn't have the balls to launch something overt, like bombings and shootings, outside their own borders. Okay, well, I guess you are tracking my little nemesis, buddy?" Carver asks. His kebab is now being carried to his table by the same impolite waiter.

"That I am. I have a few programs running, some of which are hooked up to the Israeli networks. They are on board with us. A bombing in Istanbul last night occurred around the same time as one in Berlin. Naturally, the Turks are pissed at everyone and have yet to nail down a strong suspect. We, as in the Brits and the Israelis, are looking at this Chinese team. So, our Jewish friends hooked me up with them."

Carver monitors the irate kitchen staff while chewing his way through the spicy doner and chicken mixed kebab. Between mouthfuls of meat and hot chili sauce, he gives Tommy his orders. "These guys love their bombs, taking a chapter out of the jihadi playbook. Righto, I will make my way down to our friends by the sea. I'll hook up with my lady friend and get back to you. Meanwhile, do your best to track down the shithead so I can end this. Find out who the hell is providing him with information. Obviously it's the Americans, so tread lightly."

"I fear it goes the entire way to the top. One of the CIA staffers hasn't been seen or heard from in Berlin since yesterday. Hoffmann wants to unleash hell. They have massive internal issues. So, it's basically you and your new bestie, Mr. Flynn." Tommy ends his words with a chuckle.

"What's so funny?" Carver asks while wiping the grease and sauce from his chin.

"That's not for me to say. Maybe your good friend will explain her X-rated show to you later!"

There is a period of silence for a moment as Carver worries about the pair. He takes a drink of Coke and tries to wash the fatty meal down his throat and wash away the image appearing in his head. "Okay, sod off, Tommy, you little Muppet, and go do your homework. Thanks again, by the way."

With an embarrassed acknowledgment that he may have overstepped his remarks, he goes to drop the phone, then he hears Carver speak again.

"How did you get this number?"

"Easy. I followed you on the street cameras and watched you duck inside the small phone shop, then go to the Turkish restaurant. I then pulled up the various networks in that area and waited for any new registrations to appear. It was a simple cell tower triangulation method. Child's play, really."

"Yeah, child's play," Carver repeats as he ends the call.

Before phoning an old friend, he fleshes out what Tommy said. A headache forms as Carver struggles to look at these evolving situations from various perspectives. Sitting uncomfortably on the hard plastic chair, he pushes the broken kebab bread around the plate with a fork. Casually observing the staff members as they annoy each other with their jibes and gestures, Carver then centers his thoughts on his own situation. He explores all possibilities between Zhang and Berlin. He lifts the glass and finishes the Coke, then thinks about Sarah. *No, push that matter to the side,* he thinks. Picking up the mobile, he dials the number for the SIS encrypted mailbox and enters his unique code. Once the tone beeps, he enters another code that describes his personal situation. He thumbs the four-digit code, allowing the software to record no injuries, no threats, and no need for backup. The last two mean nothing. There is no backup.

Once the beeping begins, Carver presses the phone to his ear and listens intently. *One new message.* Another beep followed by a short one-line statement. *Paris job well done; Luxembourg was an issue. Shared intelligence to the Americans made its way to the Chinese team. Unsure who is working against us. Next up Venice.* A beep once again. *Second message.* Once the next beep sounds, the unmistakable voice of Sarah comes through the cheap speaker. *Hey, I hope you are okay. Tommy is trying to track you down. If you can, please come to Monte Carlo. We will reassess and work on something. Plus, I really want to see you, Carver. To hold you.*

Then the line goes dead. Carver presses the pound key and enters a new code, speaking quietly after the beep. "I can't wait to be with you too . . ." He struggles to describe his feelings. Sitting in a dirty restaurant, the words don't come easy. The one thing Carver is sure of is his love for Sarah. He thinks about touching her face to watch how her eyes light up and how the bright smile . . . "I'm in Stuttgart, will speak with an old friend and make my way down real soon."

Carver tries to keep focused; his eyes focus on the street. Sharing his love into a voice mail feels like an empty task, but he must continue. "I'll join you for breakfast, okay. Take care, all my love."

He pulls the phone from his ear and hits the red button. *'All my love.' Did I actually say that?* Carver surprises himself. Maybe it's the fact he was almost killed or close to being locked up in a European prison for decades. No matter what, he desperately wants to see Sarah. And to kill Zhang. *Sarah first on the list, hopefully,* he decides.

***

The street is filthy. Fast food wrappers, beer cans, and cigarette butts lay discarded from the night before, yet to be swept up by the small council trucks that roam the streets. The top-floor apartment is near several nightclubs and twenty-four-hour cafés. Among the graffiti on the walls and stickers plastered on the brickwork, advertising various underground events and brothel discounts, there is a semblance of change. In the old days, rough-looking prostitutes used to stand by the doors beckoning to the depraved, drug peddlers would hang out on street cafés, while the low-life pimps and crime bosses would prance around like movie producers, making sure everyone was in their place and acting accordingly. Now the place looks almost respectable. Fresh hipster cafés, filled with enthusiastic university students, replace the old dark bars.

The brothel owners had dispersed, and new business ventures opened in their place, selling expensive racing bikes and tight Lycra, while the strip joints had removed the poles, replacing them with pianos and jazz bands. It wasn't yet Le Marais, but it was striving to lift itself up from the gutter. The influx of the wealthy middle-class slowly squeezed the poor into outer areas, sometimes forcing them to leave Switzerland behind altogether, where they would pursue other inner-city European haunts to sell their souls. The wealthy newcomers, however, still require a touch of darkness. Their high-pressure jobs are an excuse to reach for the buzz on weekends. Their drug of choice, cocaine, attracts a high price in a place like Zurich. Luckily for them, some opportunists are more than willing to dance with the devil. An old friend of Carver is centrally positioned to offer such services. A wealthy man. Well known in the arms trade around Eastern Europe and an owner of various properties throughout Italy, Croatia, and Greece. No one knows more about the Mediterranean than Jakov Kovačević. He earned his respect from the old men within the SIS. One of Harry's loyal contacts. It was Harry himself who confided in Carver, after meeting the Croatian for business in Rome, "If you ever screw up, Jakov will help you better than the service." Carver remembered those words clearly. Today was one of those days.

He approaches the blue-fronted building that sits between a bakery and a real estate shop offering multiple apartments for rent at exorbitant prices. Carver takes a casual look around the street before pressing the top intercom button.

***

Carver hears a buzzing sound after a slight delay, then pushes the door inward and climbs the stairs. Jakov Kovačević waits for him on the landing just outside his apartment door. He wisely sizes up the old friend from England before a gentle smile appears on his wrinkled face. Jakov offers his hand to the new guest, and to Carver's surprise, the octogenarian squeezes and shakes hands firmly. *His strength is still there but doesn't match his appearance these days*, Carver thinks. Wearing his trademark red circular glasses, perched delicately at the end of his nose, the eighty-plus-year-old man is an anomaly in the black-market trade. Arrested multiple times in various European countries over the years, the likeable and jovial criminal defense lawyer always walked free. Those years had been tough for Jakov Kovačević, finding himself the subject of intense scrutiny by Interpol and various smaller organizations. Despite representing himself successfully and frequently when he was before the courts, he found their agency to be more valuable to his operations than a hindrance. Understanding who the puppet masters were in Interpol and various other global organizations allowed him to undertake years of research and intelligence work. Once he found a way to corrupt or blackmail those high-ranking officials, or their family members, the Croatian could break the shackles of the international police organizations and their irritating methods. The crafty swindler also used their tools to his great advantage. When someone overstepped their mark or failed to deliver on a deal, Jakov Kovačević had his contacts in Interpol send out a yellow notice rendering their ability to jump countries incredibly difficult. The man had everyone in his pocket, and those contacts were priceless. This struck Carver as both a weird and wonderful situation. His knowledge was as valuable as it was dangerous. Yet here he is, living in a four-bedroom apartment, in the middle of a small city. Everyone knows the man has millions, enough to retire and live in peace, where or how he wanted. Carver watches as Jakov walks over to a large dining table by the window. He clears a few files, legal documents, and places them neatly in a tattered tan leather briefcase. Jakov sits in a high-backed chair and slides a bottle of brandy across the table, followed by two glasses.

"It is not too early, I hope?" he asks.

Carver feels obliged somewhat to join the man in a drink. He is, after all, looking for his help. "I will gladly join you, Jakov. It has been a long time since we last met."

The wheels turn in Jakov's memory box as Carver watches the street below, waiting for the reply.

"Oh yes, Rome." Jakov lets out a chuckle, more of a relief that his memory hasn't yet abandoned him, then he continues. "Yes, the Antico Caffè Greco, if I am not mistaken."

"That's correct, and you will be happy to know I still work with Harry, and he told me to send you his best wishes."

"Did he, now?" Jakov sits forward, his hands resting on the glass table. A smirk that he cannot suppress now turns to a laugh. "I am not long off the phone to our distinguished friend, Mr. Carver. I couldn't possibly string you along."

Carver feels somewhat embarrassed. The thought of Harry able to calculate his plan causes Carver to consider if he is being too predictable. Putting it to the back of his mind, he simply gives the man a nod of appreciation.

Jakov slowly pours a healthy amount of brandy into the two glasses and carefully places them onto padded coasters. He slides a glass over to Carver and says cheers. "*Živjeli*. Now to business, as I know your time is limited. Our good friend mentioned how you would like a safe passage south. I wasn't sure how I could really help. The very thought of someone of your caliber coming here looking for guidance appears strange. Is it not your expertise to move around unseen in full view? To tread with confidence and furtiveness? This is like inviting a pilot to build a paper airplane. You could be swimming in the Mediterranean Sea by now. What is your genuine concern, my boy?"

Carver looks down at his drink before committing himself. "Okay, as you are most likely aware, there have been several incidents recently."

"You mean the bombings in Istanbul and Berlin? That severely upset some plans of mine. Istanbul hurt me. Berlin! Well, that is none of my business," Jakov admits.

"No, none of those. Before that, Florence, Monte Carlo, Paris." Carver meets Jakov's eyes when he rounds off the list with Luxembourg.

Jakov rubs the edge of the coaster with his fingers while watching the young SIS officer speak. The intelligent and humble Croatian does not indicate acknowledgement or surprise from Carver's words. Just silence.

"A friend of mine from the CIA also dropped in unannounced, just like you. He arrived late last night. At least you had the decency to come during civilized hours." Jakov stands and walks to one of the other windows. "When he left a short time later, a car arrived. It has been sitting there all night and all day."

"CIA?" Carver asks.

"No, definitely not. These guys are making a statement. The CIA wouldn't be so blatant. I ensure my circles do not overlap with those of the Americans. I am very sensitive about what I do or to whom I offer my help." Jakov turns and looks into Carver's eyes. He can see no fear, no judgement or remorse.

Carver takes a sip of brandy. The smooth alcohol soaks into the partially digested kebab that is now rumbling in his stomach. "What's your best guess?"

"I don't like to guess. Nowadays there is too much to lose in guessing. We need to know the exact ingredients when cooking a new dish, yes? Well, I did some digging, and the Swiss intelligence provided me with limited information. The DGSE, however, well, they surprised me. The car was rented a few days ago. From Saint-Tropez. The name on the rental documents is that of a highly respected Chinese businessman. Nothing unusual, yes? Well, what if I told you the China man is in London? He flew there two weeks ago for a conference and hasn't returned."

"Okay, that sounds suspicious, but what have the Chinese got to do with you?" Carver assumes these men are part of Zhang's backup team. However, Jakov is not part of the problem, so why follow him? Suddenly, he feels uneasy. Is it himself they are waiting for? How can they be two steps ahead? This is beginning to stink, and Carver senses his world gradually closing in around him.

Jakov turns his face to an old mirror hanging on the wall. He stands there looking at the wrinkles, the blackness under his eyes, and the hairs growing wildly out of his ears. With a shake of the head, he says, "Where have the years gone?" Stepping back from the window slightly, he responds to Carver.

"I stayed out of China. Little interest despite their growth potential. Just didn't trust them. I did, at one point, provide the East Turkestan Islamic movement with a pathway to get some weapons and explosives for an uprising. Although I was well hidden from view. That was a long time ago, and I would find it strange if the Chinese Communists would come after me, especially in Europe. They lack the expertise and connections. Few people want anything to do with them. And we could say the same for the Chinese, they don't trust the West."

"I tend to agree with you. The Chinese steamrolled the Islamic movement a few years ago." Carver looks toward the window. "Is the car still there?"

"Sure is."

Looking around the apartment, Carver can see no obvious signs of security. "Do you have protection? A man of your standing, I guess, would have ruffled a few feathers over the years."

Jakov bursts out laughing. "Yes, yes, I have done just that. Ruffled a few feathers. I have indeed." The old man stands still, staring up at the ceiling while deciding if he should reveal a few tricks of the trade. Then he simply looks back at Carver and says, "All is not what it appears to be, my boy."

The room Carver sits in has limited furniture, only the dining table and a couple of leather armchairs. A walnut buffet table with a collection of antiques displayed on top runs across one wall, and a bookcase next to a filing cabinet takes up position on the wall opposite. As far as Carver can tell, the man lived alone. Two doors lead out of the dining room to his left, both closed. The door he used to enter on his right is still open, and that leads out toward the hallway. The wooden front door that opens to the common area of the five-story building is reasonably thick. Fitted next to it is a simple intercom, which Carver presumes must have been installed when the building was completed almost fifty years ago. The communication device, which also controls the lock on the front door, appears to be the most advanced piece of equipment he can detect. Carver needs to sort out his dilemma, although the prospect of another incident with Zhang's goons outside is disturbing his thoughts. "Do you mind me asking what the CIA was after?"

"No, not at all. We are all friends, aren't we?"

Before Carver can reply, Jakov continues to answer the question.

"A young CIA officer, Liana is her name. She was abducted off the streets in Berlin recently. Inside job. That was one thing we discussed. The next was the bombing in a café close to the American embassy. Whoever planted the bomb tried to kill a couple of embassy staff. Or at least that's what I first thought the targets were. They killed a high-ranking member of the European Commission, a brazen attack and, again, I am unsure if that was their intended target. Nonetheless, it has caused a huge fallout. The last subject we moved on to was more interesting. The inside job I mentioned. It has all the hallmarks of a corrupt team of the CIA special forces guys. The Americans have shut down their current operations in Europe. Therefore . . . well, how can I say this? The CIA man asked if I could lend a hand with some internal issues for them. Until they get back online."

"That is a lot to unravel," says Carver. "So, they want you to deal with this Chinese issue?"

"No, that's your problem, I guess. They only want me to keep an ear to the ground. If there are requests to purchase high-end weapons, then I'm to follow up with it. My organization is not what it used to be, I'm afraid. My best earner is information. And the Americans pay well." Jakov stops talking when his phone starts buzzing. He pulls it out of his pocket and taps the screen twice. Then he slips the device back into his pocket. "Come over here beside me," he says.

Carver walks over, leaving his drink on the table. He looks at Jakov, who is staring out the window at the car five floors below. Following his gaze, Carver can see the car parked with the windows partially rolled down. He never noticed the motorbike pulling up until the last moment. The rider is wearing full black leathers. The helmet visor is also deep black, which obscures his identity. The shooting happens extremely fast. A black handgun, with a suppressor attached, is pulled out from his jacket, then he points it toward the open window. The suppressor expels four soft puffs of smoke as the bullets leave the chamber. Once the killer secures the weapon back inside his jacket, he drives off calmly.

Crafty old bugger, thinks Carver. "I liked that," he says. As Carver turns around to face Jakov, he immediately knows repercussions will follow. The smile on Jakov's face, however, is one of deep satisfaction. A true master of the spy games, this old man will never retire; a disturbing love for the dark side and all the trappings that come with it is more alluring than material possessions. Carver finally appreciates why Jakov could never settle down on a beach somewhere. The minute he drops his guard, there would be a broad assortment of ghosts from his past racing to wipe him out.

"We don't have long, I guess. The Chinese will send more. Goons for hire, most likely. You should make your way. But first, what is it you require, my boy?" Jakov asks.

Chapter Twenty-Four

Milan, Italy

Zhang Xiaopeng walks east along Bastioni di Porta Nuova and takes a right turn down some steps leading to a narrow alleyway. After two hundred meters, the man turns left and appears on a larger street. Another five minutes later, he changes direction once again. With a high level of dedication and countersurveillance professionalism, Zhang keeps this up until he is sure no one is following him. The pace in Milan is similar to other large European cities, such as London, Berlin, Rome, and Paris. Just as much traffic and heavy-to-medium industries. Not as pretty as Paris, although the inhabitants love their fashion. Such details are not lost on the man as he removes the heavy black canvas from his left shoulder and swings it over the other one. Everything he needs is inside. His flight landed twenty minutes late, which doesn't matter, as he has plenty of time. The method is similar to Berlin. Once arrived, head straight to the metro station storage lockers to collect the bag, then proceed to the apartment and assemble the device. The weather is perfect, cool enough to justify wearing his jacket, as other pedestrians are doing. *Everything is smooth,* he thinks to himself when reading the street signs fixed on the wall above him. Once he makes the last turn, his apartment is now visible straight ahead. His next target lies only a few blocks away.

The apartment is exactly how he remembered it from the photographs. A rustic building, painted with an orange terracotta color, iron railings across the first-floor windows with planter boxes filled with green leaves. Zhang stops and considers if the plants have yet to produce flowers. *No flowers!* Zhang fears something is badly wrong. He fumes at himself and keeps walking. They organized this apartment for him only a day ago. His surveillance guys, arranged by the general, sent through the images only a few hours ago. Zhang had opened the file on his phone to view the photographs, then disposed of the device in Berlin. He swears to himself that the planter boxes contained red flowers, and the place should have been empty. It is little details that matter. Failure to act on instinct or sloppy behavior could see him killed. For this very reason, he rejects the apartment and strolls off to find a hotel. After about twenty-five minutes, he finds something suitable and is shown to his room.

***

Zhang looks around the bleak hotel room before crossing the carpeted floor to close the heavy curtains. Next, he switches on all the room lights. For extra illumination, he takes the two bedside lamps and carries them over to the small desk next to the kettle and teacups. A digital radio that once sat on the bedside table is removed and replaced by the kettle. He turns it to boil, then disappears into the bathroom to grab a quick shower. After drying himself, Zhang pulls on a pair of sterile gloves and seats himself at the small desk. Once he clears enough space, he opens the black bag and removes a shoebox-size container. Next to that, he sets down three mobile phones, a small box of electrical components, a few rolls of electronic wire, a soldering kit, and some flux. A cloth bag full of tools sits on the floor next to his freshly brewed cup of jasmine tea.

Zhang takes a couple of slow deep breaths to steady his fingers, then removes the plastic covers on a phone to expose the circuitry. Two minutes later, he opens the container and pulls out two small slabs of an advanced type of plastic explosive. The Chinese military added the compound bicyclo-HMX to the well-known Czech explosive named Semtex. The resulting explosive strengths of this mixture quickly became popular with their special forces, and because of the putty mix being relatively safe to handle, it soon replaced the earlier types of C-4. The military labs in China provided General Zhou Kai with tons of it, destined for the military engineers and selective training for his special forces. However, the general had better ideas for it. His plan of forcing the West into a new world war was unpredictable and evolving. The time had come for his men to take possession of this formidable instrument to generate mayhem. Istanbul went as planned, Berlin as well. Now Zhang will shut down the financial district of Milan and cripple the Italian economy.

Zhang feels his head spinning, then the pains begin. Slow and pulsating at first, turning slowly to a persistent ache. He needs fresh air. Breathing in the chemicals for over two hours leaves him nauseous. He has another shower to wash off any residue from the explosives, then leaves his room to get something for dinner and to clear his head. A "do not disturb" sign hangs on the room door handle, which is his first and only line of defense against the Italian intelligence agency. Walking along the busy streets is working; the fresh air washes out the chemicals and his vision becomes sharper. With each step, the hunger builds up inside him to the point his stomach starts rumbling. Zhang has been so totally engrossed in building the two bombs that he never noticed the time.

As he passes a restaurant, he stops briefly to read the menu fixed to the wall outside. As he runs his eyes down the mains comprising various types of pasta dishes, he pretends not to notice the heavyset man sitting inside reading the daily newspaper, the *Corriere della Sera*. Zhang looks around for alternative places to eat, then walks down the road a few meters and crosses the street. Once he finds a different restaurant, he chooses a seat set back slightly from the window and orders the osso buco. The restaurant is dimly lit, and a few candles flicker on the tables. A television, mounted on the wall near the back, is switched off, although there is Italian music coming through the small speakers above the bar.

Zhang sits alone in the neatly decorated dining area. The restaurant has about twenty tables, half of which are occupied. Most of them are couples and three business-type people, who most likely are staying in Milan for a couple of days. There are about five staff that Zhang can see, and the door to the kitchen swings both inward and out.

When the waiter arrives with the wine list, Zhang refuses and asks for a Coke, then he excuses himself to check the bathroom. Being the only person in the small room, Zhang opens the window and finds an alleyway filled with garbage bins and a collection of mops and buckets. He steps inside the toilet stall and checks his Smith & Wesson revolver. A weapon he now admires, simple and reliable. Tucking it inside his jacket, he checks himself in the mirror as he splashes some cold water on his face, wiping it off with his hands before opening the door and heading back to his table.

Shit! Momentarily stunned, Zhang wonders who the hell this guy is, sitting at his table. *Italian intelligence!* He glances around the room and notices everyone deep in conversation with their partners. Red wine is being sipped while the sounds of laughter and glasses clinking drown out the voices in his head. The fresh aroma of roasted tomatoes, oregano, and garlic fill Zhang's nose. He can feel his head spinning slowly. Standing in the middle of the room, absorbed in this thick atmosphere, Beijing now seems like a different world. As the waiters pass by holding plates of pasta and pizzas, his hunger no longer guides him. Those pains have long drained away, quickly replaced with anger and images of destruction.

"Excuse me, this is my table," says Zhang, contempt easily noticeable in his voice.

Gary Duval doesn't bother to look up. He's more interested in the wine menu he holds between his fingers. Just as Duval is about to speak, he slowly closes his mouth and, with a finger, he simply motions for Zhang to sit down. Zhang doesn't have the tolerance for this, but he can't just ignore him and walk back to a hotel room filled with explosives. Neither does he want to sit here playing mind games with someone that knows more than he does. Zhang thinks of what to say just as the waiter arrives with two glasses. Instead, he sits back and tries to look relaxed while Duval orders a bottle of red. Zhang notices that the uninvited guest speaks Italian well, yet he presumes him to be American.

"Excuse me, sir, are you lonely or something? There are many tables around."

Duval looks up and the two men lock eyes. It is then that Zhang spots the look of death in the man. Duval has an icy stare that speaks volumes. It is at this precise moment that the Chinese special forces member knows this man is no stranger to mass slaughter. The man equaled him in confidence and hardness.

"I won't apologize. In my world, I don't make reservations. I feel that is somewhat amateurish behavior. Much like sticking to procedures and following a well-known plan. Don't you think, Mr. Zhang?"

That last part stings Zhang. He does his utmost to hide his true identity; only a handful of men know his real name. Certainly, no Westerns should have been privy to such information. Once he became involved in the special missions unit, his commanders quickly erased his past. For years he used various names and backgrounds, carefully selected details that he spent hours memorizing and building on. These legends are tried and tested, not only in Europe but also in Southeast Asia and within China itself. Zhang tries to hide his frustration, but Duval can see how rattled the man is.

"Well, I won't apologize either. Tell me, who the hell do you think you are? You come in here and disturb my dinner, pretending to know me. So again, I ask, who the hell do you think you are?" Zhang tries to speak softly, yet the last words come out loud enough to cause some people to turn around and look at them.

"How about we maintain a sense of decorum, and I will unravel some of your concerns," Duval replies in a hushed tone.

Zhang sits there fuming. As his dinner is served, he watches other people in the restaurant. Some have finished their meals and settle their bills while staff clear the tables for new arrivals. When the waiter leaves their table, Zhang is the first to speak.

"So, you are an American? I presume you are not a businessman looking to open a factory in China. Maybe you are after a pleasant woman or a man. Who am I to judge? You look military. That is written all over your face."

Duval lifts his glass and smells the Barbaresco wine. "You are correct on one point. I am American, I will give you one point for that. Minus points on the other." The American sits back and stretches his legs under the table as he waits for Zhang's reply.

"You want to play games? Okay, maybe I will leave and you can eat my dinner; I suddenly lost my appetite." Zhang slides his chair out and stands up. With a sleight of hand, he slides his wineglass off the table. Instantly, Duval drops his arm and catches the glass before it smashes on the marble floor. The movement allows Zhang a fleeting glimpse inside Duval's jacket. The black handgrip of a pistol is plainly noticeable.

Duval realizes Zhang played his own game very well. "I'm impressed, okay, Zhang . . . Sit down, please, no more games."

Zhang knows he needs to know who this man is and what he wants with him. His situation and personal freedoms could be compromised if he doesn't sort this out. It only makes sense to stay and drain this man of his intent.

***

The sight of two men quarrelling causes quite a stir to some within the restaurant. Juliana Calabrese and Giovanni Lucchese have just arrived and are about to order from the wine list when the young brunette hears their outbursts. The two men appear to be testing each other through their egos and macho behaviors, which play out brusquely within the delicate surrounds of the traditional family-owned restaurant. Juliana sits facing the table while her colleague has his back to the men. Once the two young professionals order their drinks, Giovanni leaves to use the bathroom, leaving Juliana alone. She stands up and removes a navy jacket and hangs it on the back of the chair. After loosening a couple of top buttons on her green blouse, she unties her hair and lets it drop naturally over her shoulders.

Gary Duval can't help but notice the naturally irresistible looking woman. His eyes glance from her eyes to her chest and down to her tanned arms then back up again. Juliana catches him looking and pretends not to care. The head of the CIA's Special Operations Group is slightly embarrassed and self-consciously looks away. The distraction interrupts the American momentarily. Juliana can see him straightening his jacket and composing himself in front of his guest. Despite Juliana's distance, she can barely make out what they are talking about. They are keeping their comments short and sweet.

As she waits for her wine, Juliana wriggles out of her white tennis shoes and stretches her tired feet upward, then points her toes down and out. Today she had covered an estimated distance of almost ten kilometers, plus another five or six hours standing around. Her calves are tight, and what she really needs is a massage to fight off the annoying cramps that will set in later. The last thing she wants is those horrible stabbing pains occurring throughout her dinner. As she gently stretches her lower legs under the table, her mobile phone vibrates silently. She slips it out from her navy cargo pants as she enters the lock number and reads the message.

Everything is ready, confirmed to go.

Juliana deletes the simple message and selects a name from her contact list, then holds the phone to her ear. After a few seconds, the call connects. Within moments, Juliana rests her elbows on the white tablecloth with a look of anticipation. As she listens to the caller, a deeply traumatic expression sweeps across her angelic face. "*Cazzo*," she shouts before placing a hand in front of her mouth, an attempt to feign her embarrassment for using the curse word. Staring blindly at the mobile, she taps the screen a few times before setting it heavily on the table.

***

Zhang sits with his arms folded, smiling naturally at the serious face in front of him. "Well," he says, "what should I call you?"

"Brown," is all Duval offers, with one eye on Zhang, the other on the distressed young girl opposite him. "Listen, Zhang, I will cut to the chase. I am on your side; you wouldn't know that, and I don't possibly expect you to believe me. But understand my contacts are in direct partnership with your contacts. General Zhou Kai."

Zhang's eyes widened at the sound of the general's name. Duval can see he hit a nerve, so he presses Zhang's psyche some more. "We know what your job is here in Europe, and so far you have worked flawlessly. The incident with your foreign minister was not your fault. He was limp-wristed, all teeth and no bite, so there was no love lost." Duval takes a drink of wine, allowing his words to penetrate Zhang's thick skull, while not wanting to give too much away about his hand in that.

He doesn't have to wait long. Zhang looks as if he is about to reach across the table and crush Duval's throat. His eyes scan the room, looking for potential assassins. *Is this an attempt to have me admit something before being arrested and left to rot in an Italian prison?* His head stimulates worrying bursts of paranoia and thoughts of extreme violence.

"You must watch a lot of news, Mr. Brown. Perhaps you have me confused with someone else. I don't know any general."

Duval lets out a sigh. He hadn't eaten all day and doesn't have time to play footsie with this man. "Listen up, numbskull. If I was a regular cop, you would've been locked up a long time ago. You wouldn't have left this country after your first hit. Instead, your ass would be passed around to all the big hairy Italians in San Vittore prison." Duval taps the table with his middle finger to drive the message home on his last comment.

Zhang's head spins. His first thought is on his firearm. To pull out his cowboy Smith & Wesson and fire point-blank on this man's face was one option. The other was to hear him out, to figure out what the hell he wanted.

"Excuse me, gentlemen, sorry to bother you."

Both men are taken aback slightly. Zhang turns and looks up, while Duval quickly checks the beautiful woman from head to toe. Standing looking down at the two men seated in front of her, Juliana holds up her phone, showing a blacked-out screen, and apologizes wholeheartedly.

"It's my shit phone. The battery is old, and my mamma is having medical problems." She then bends forward at the hips with both hands resting on her knees. Speaking softly, she asks if they have a phone she can quickly borrow to make a local call to her mother. Duval is in awe at this beauty. The sight of her leaning into him almost causes him to enter a trance. As he takes a lungful of perfume, he reacts as any decent gentleman would. He reaches into his jacket and takes out his phone, and once he enters the passcode, he drops it into her soft hands.

"I cannot thank you enough," she says. With a gentle smile and a pout on her bottom lip, she turns and returns to her table.

"Don't get smart, Brown. You know so much about me and you think I am about to lay it all on the line. What's your game? What do you want from me?" says Zhang.

Duval takes his wine glass and places it to the side of the table, then he leans forward and speaks with a hushed tone. "The guy in Zermatt, he was only gathering intel. Two men are looking to upset your plans. You need to concentrate on them. Otherwise, you will get strung up somewhere, and this all goes to shit."

He doesn't like the fact that this American knows about Zermatt. Zhang takes a minute to figure this all out. He slowly pours himself a glass of wine and drinks almost half of it. *If this man is corrupt and on the payroll of the general, then he is speaking the truth. I would have been arrested a long time ago.* Zhang eyeballs the American, looking for a hint of betrayal. Out of the corner of his eye, he notices the waiter coming to the table. Leaning back, as his osso buco is laid out in front of him, he knows a decision is required.

Once the waiter leaves, the decision has been made. "If you want me to trust you, then you must answer something."

"Fine, what do need to know?" replies Duval.

"Why would you betray your country? Also, who else is involved? I want to know who or what agencies are spying on me."

"Good question." Duval considers how much he should tell the China man. As he forms the words in his head, he sees the young girl eyeing him. Then she finishes her call and gets up from the table. When she approaches

Duval, he notices a slight tear in her eyes. "Is everything okay with your mother?" he asks.

"Kind of. She will recover. My mum is old, and she has had a slight fall. Thankfully, my sister can look after her. Thank you again for allowing me to speak to her." Juliana sets the phone into Duval's hand, then turns around and moves back to her table. The American stares at her curves until she sits, then he faces Zhang again.

"It's all about the dollar, plain and simple. I could work for years, and for what? A pension! Bullshit to that. This information and assistance I can offer to your general is worth a lot of money. My small team of hard-core men does not come cheap. We are all in this together, and we have come too far to watch it all slip away. I have my orders, much like you do. My orders are to protect your back and ensure you have a clear path. We made some moves that you are unaware of. Protecting you in Berlin and looking for those men that are your biggest threats. What you and your cronies do later is none of our business. That's between your country and the Western armed forces. I, for one, will be tucked away enjoying my life." Duval can feel his temper rising. Not with Zhang, but with the thought of his dreams being pulled from under him. His plan to erase his whole life and start again in a South American resort will only come to fruition if this man in front of him can continue his quest to push the Western countries into a new world war. Duval reaches for the wine bottle to refill his glass, then remembers something. Val Olszewski had warned him previously about Zhang's tendency to leave behind forensic footprints. The last thing Duval wants is to share a cell with the Chinese renegade. "So, tell me, Zhang, when your part is complete, what do you plan to do? Settle down somewhere in China or disappear completely?"

"I don't betray my country. I will stay on and take control of the armed forces of China. I intend to remove the weak generals. Soon our country will not only be respected but feared."

With another full glass in front of him, Duval thinks back briefly as he recalls similar fantasies stated by Communist generals. "That's a fantastic plan; bravo, young man. Not sure how that will work, although I'll raise a toast for you."

In a display of sarcasm, Duval raises his glass and takes a large sip. "Now, to answer your previous question, our intelligence agencies are spread far and wide. We cover a lot of ground. Recently our tentacles have been pulled back so those at the top can check for leaks." Duval rolls his eyes at the thought of this. "The FBI will lead most of the investigations. Those guys are not on board with our arrangement. What I mean is, the general has his contacts within the DNI, and downstream from them leads you to the men on the street doing the hard work. I control those men, and therefore I am responsible for ensuring you have a safe passage. Now, this is the interesting part, the slightly problematic part. The British are operating more covertly than normal. They are calling the shots and working hard to derail your process. If you want success, then you will have to hit them hard. Wipe them off the map and make their superiors think twice before coming after you. If you are arrested, then there is no buffer between them and us anymore. You cannot fail."

"I don't plan to fail. I need to complete my mission here in Europe before going to New York," says Zhang.

"Yes, well, your time in Europe will come to an end very soon if we don't find these two men. You killed very important members from the European Council in Istanbul and Berlin. You got the executive vice president of the European Commission. Not too bad, in the space of a couple of days. From going after spies to blowing some European institution leaders to pieces in one week is quite something." Duval watches how Zhang hesitates slightly when cutting through his veal shank. His words appear to be annoying him. Soon he will leave him to eat in peace.

"Let's just say there are many more men just like me. Your traitors and those of other Western countries will still meet their fate. I have more pressing matters to take care of. These two men you speak of. I presume you don't know where they are, otherwise I would have my 'safe passage,' as you said."

Duval knows how much money he could make by taking out Carver and Flynn. The general pays well and promptly, and through Val Olszewski, Duval knows he has that extra layer of protection. However, the thought of killing both a CIA paramilitary officer and their SIS counterpart doesn't come easy for him. This is something he's juggled with for days. *What difference would it make compared to the countless others I put away?* He hunches over and pulls his glass to the center of the table. Clasping it in his two hands, he considers this question, and whether his men in Berlin can do it. They would have to keep their heads down and stay off the circuit forever. For that is what it would take. Duval knows if they ever surfaced and produced a link back to their old life, then he would be looking over his shoulder until he dies.

Looking into Zhang's lifeless eyes, Duval speaks, "I know where they are."

"Well then, go and chop them up," replies Zhang.

"I thought you would rather do the honors. After all, it's your ballgame, and from what I can see, you are still hurting from the bullet Flynn put into you."

Zhang never considered anyone else killing Flynn. This is personal. He is a man of war and has to protect his honor. Returning to China without taking his revenge would make him look weak. No one in the huge military would give him an ounce of respect. Killing this top CIA creature and the hateful Englishman would cement his reputation as a ruthless warrior in the modern world. Zhang sticks a piece of veal into his mouth and chews it noisily while he thinks about these two men. He can feel the six-and-a-half-inch barrel of the Smith & Wesson revolver digging into his waist. The large handgun is something he'd come to respect. This weapon is something Zhang believes could be useful in constructing his status symbol and a powerful reputation. Despite having access to a world of weapons, Zhang thinks it would be a classic challenge to blast their heads off with this piece of steel. "Yes, I wouldn't have it any other way, Brown. I'll take care of these two dogs. Tell me where they are and stand back. No need to follow me around like a puppy."

Duval laughs joyfully. "I just want to make sure you are not being tracked. Okay, give me your number and I'll pass on their movements. Flynn is in Monte Carlo, and Carver? Well, he should be there soon. He got spooked in Zurich and won't hang around too long."

Zhang looks up from his plate when Flynn mentions Zurich. Nodding approvingly toward the American, he then agrees to swap numbers.

"One more thing, Zhang, we don't have much time. We rubbed our people in the CIA the wrong way by kidnapping one of their own. She was the link to this British girl who oversees Carver."

"British girl? I'll slice her up if need be. Whatever it takes to smoke out these guys." Zhang reassures Duval of his ruthlessness. Without looking up, he taps the screen on his mobile to display his number, then spins it around on the table, allowing Duval to see it.

Duval types the number into Zhang's phone and hits dial. Once the phone connects, he hangs up and wipes his mouth with a napkin.

"Okay, Mr. Zhang, we are all done here. Hopefully, we won't meet again in person. You do your job, and I'll do mine." Duval then pushes out his chair and stands up.

"If you ever surprise me again, Brown, you better be ready to die," Zhang speaks with fire in his voice. Preferring to work alone, he despises the fact that this stranger walked into his life, treating him like a simple tool.

Duval smiles as he adjusts his jacket and slips on a pair of leather gloves. "I wish you a good night, Zhang." Duval steels a final glimpse at the attractive girl, who is busy eating her food, on his way past, then walks out of the restaurant.

***

Giovanni Lucchese had left Juliana at the table all by herself. It wasn't the first time he needed to do this. Sitting on top of the toilet seat with his laptop running, he tapped a few buttons, activating the hacking software. With a strong signal displaying and the program ready, he then typed a brief message and sent it to Juliana's phone. Once the message was received, his colleague faked a call, then asked to borrow the phone from the CIA officer. Giovanni waited until she dialed his phone, which was also connected to his laptop. The waiting was the worst part. The Italian intelligence analyst from AISE could handle any other aspect of his work except for waiting. Everything so far had gone smoothly until the bathroom door suddenly opened.

Giovanni's head spun and his heart began pounding in his chest. He listened as a man walked across the tiled floor, then stopped at the urinals to unzip. The tapping of the keys was hard to disguise in the silence, so he reached around to grab the handle and flushed the toilet. While the water roared beneath him, Giovanni quickly typed commands onto the screen. The programmed jumped to life and successfully hacked into the American's phone. Juliana had cleverly turned on the Bluetooth mode for a few moments, allowing Giovanni's malware to be transferred effortlessly. Once all the contacts, call logs, and messages were downloaded, Giovanni then finally broke the connection. He waited until the man on the other side of the bathroom stall washed his hands and left the room. Then Giovanni packed up his laptop and left the privacy of the toilet cubical. Checking no one was about to enter, he then quickly passed the device out the bathroom window and into the waiting hands of another colleague from AISE.

With his work complete, he turns on the cold tap and splashes some water on his face and neck, then dries himself off. Giovanni takes a couple of deep breaths as he grabs the door handle, then walks back out into the quiet restaurant to rejoin his pretend date, Juliana, for some pasta and wine.

***

Zhang sits there slowly finishing his meal, staring silently at the glass of red wine sitting in front of him. He knows he shouldn't have drank too much as there is sensitive work yet to be completed back in the hotel room. Looking around the restaurant at the happy diners, he feels somewhat relaxed knowing elements of the CIA, corrupt men, are providing a level of protection for this operation. When an Italian man with glistening wet black hair shuffles slowly from the bathroom holding his stomach, Zhang assumes nothing of it. *Weak stomach, weak man.* A smile flashes across Zhang's face. In a few days, he will have caused enough carnage within Europe before flying across the Atlantic to pull off one more bombing before heading back to the safety of his motherland. A life of extreme power and carnage will follow.

***

Duval crosses the street and walks to the end of the block to a waiting black Mercedes. He slides into the backseat and pulls the heavy reinforced door shut. With a slight nod to the driver, he then turns to the other man sitting in the rear with him and says, "Welcome to Milan. You are a busy man, so I won't keep you. It's all going to plan with our Oriental clown."

"Good work. But I didn't fly all the way from Washington to hear that. You need to monitor him, Duval. And don't turn your back on him. I will be in Switzerland doing some banking. I am not to be contacted, okay? Any issues that need addressed before we part company?" asks Val Olszewski.

"No, nothing. Although Zhang appeared shocked to discover we have been following his every move," replies Duval.

"Well, he should be. General Zhou Kai doesn't fully trust him either. I can read it in his eyes. This tap on Zhang's shoulder will remind him not to have any stupid ideas. A man like him should cover his tracks better. If this all goes pear-shaped and he comes after us, well, I will not have that possibility hanging over my head."

Duval eyes Olszewski with suspicion. "If Zhang pulls this off and returns to China and instigates a successful coup, then what's the issue? He got what he wanted. To overthrow the president and launch an attack on weakened Western nations."

Olszewski removes a leather cigar wallet from the center console separating him and Duval. As he slides out a Churchill-size cigar and gently squeezes it between his fingers, he turns around to face Duval. His view of the man's loyalty and ability to successfully conduct dirty operations is solid. However, Duval's lack of political sagacity in something so crucial would be his downfall. "Working with these corrupted Chinese renegades is like winning the lottery. But it comes with a price, and not a financial one. No matter what way you look at it, or what plans you have made. Understand one thing, we have entered this relationship at great peril."

Duval turns and looks out the window instead, watching a handful of pedestrians walk along the street and expensive cars weaving in and out of the traffic so gracefully.

The hardened CIA paramilitary officer always avoided the seriousness of these conversations. He knows there will be savage repercussions from his act of treason, yet he brushes it aside. The man is in pain. His inner secrets would never be revealed. Duval can't get over the fact that his only child had died at the hands of a terrorist. Years ago in Iraq, his first tour. The young private had been trapped in a building and dragged away, hooded, and beaten, while his section retreated and requested assistance. The backup arrived too late. The failed rescue attempt found an empty shell of a house and the young soldier dressed in an orange jumpsuit stained with his blood. He was slumped in front of a tripod, with the recorded footage aired later on social media. When Duval heard news that his son was missing, he knew the outcome was inevitable. Shortly after, he found, through a source, the details of the murderers and their whereabouts. Over the years that followed, he wiped out cell after cell of the Islamic terrorists.

By hiding his relationship from the agency, it allowed him to work away from the spotlight. His patriotism changed a few years back once he learned a CIA team had been in the same location where his only child was being held captive. The order for the paramilitary operatives to move in and snatch his son was never made. The hierarchy in the CIA did not want their presence known to other nations. For Duval, this translated into the country he'd fought for turning and walking away, allowing his son to be savagely murdered by the barbarians. *There would be consequences for the CIA.*

Now, all these years later in Milan, he hopes and prays for the ultimate punishment. Watching the traffic as he sits in the car with Olszewski, listening to him talk about Zhang, he can feel his palms becoming sweaty while his temper rises.

Through the years of violence and mayhem he committed, it was never enough for him. His contentment would never come. Duval realized the great war machine cared little for his boy, and likewise for many others. That was the cruel nature of war. Going behind everyone's back to kill Danny Lin was his part in bringing about World War III. *Let others feel my pain*, was his mantra. Nonetheless, he would continue to assist any bringers of death and destruction, hoping that this violence would visit those who left his boy behind. Duval would then leave his soul to the mercy of God.

Chapter Twenty-Five

Poznań, Poland

When Liana Peviani wakes from a deep slumber, her eyes focus on the bright light shining through a tattered curtain. From what she can tell, the room is either in an apartment block or in the countryside. She looks down at her silver Tissot; the time is now close to 5:00 PM. Laying on a mattress without a bedframe, she slowly makes sense of what had happened. There is no furniture in the small room other than large black plastic bags in two piles. The stained light green carpet emits a foul smell, and the decorative yellow wallpaper peels at the corners near the ceiling.

Liana tries to stand up to look outside the window. What she doesn't expect is the powerful wave of dizziness that forces her to crouch down on all fours. Trying not to black out again, the terrified CIA agent immediately recognizes her predicament. *Berlin, they took me . . . those men were Americans!* Liana quickly checks herself for injuries or signs of a sexual assault. Lifting her cream dress and undergarments, dreading the worst, she is relieved to see her skin is intact. As the seconds tick by, Liana understands why she is feeling so groggy. An image of the smiling man on the bridge materializes in her mind. Then she remembers how the horrifying pain in her stomach caused a paralyzing effect. The last thing Liana recalls is another man at the van with a gold chain before darkness fell upon her.

The shock of what happened to her grows into anger. Anger at those who swiped her off the street. Stretching her legs out in front of her causes some minor pains. Her black boots are still on, although she can see numerous scuff marks all along them. With sore ankles, she realizes that at one point they must have tied her up. Her mind races. *They haven't killed me, nor raped me, so what the hell do they want with me? Information or a ransom demand? Pricks!*

Liana fights will all her strength through the fog; she knows her head needs to be clear. Standing groggily to her feet, she allows a moment for the blood to settle, and as she waits for the dizziness to subside, her hearing picks up a muffled sound coming from outside the door. She can hear men talking, although the words are indistinguishable.

Gingerly, she moves a few steps over to the metal-framed window, which is partially covered by the stained, drab curtain. To her horror, as she looks outside toward the enormous concrete building opposite the room she is standing in, the chances of escaping drift away. The drop from the window is far too high. Liana estimates she is at least four floors high. The neighboring building has no windows. It looks like the end wall of a factory, which is separated from her building by a chain-link fence. There are no signs of life, no one to which she can scream out for help.

No, Liana knows from this point that she needs to help herself. She understands the men in the other room are waiting for the drugs to wear off, then they will press her for intelligence. And that is something she doesn't want to be subjected to. Tortured, questioned, then killed, her lifeless body dumped in a canal somewhere. "No damn way," she uttered silently.

Thinking back to her basic training at Camp Peary, what the CIA calls the Farm, she remembers what her instructor told her about escaping from a situation. *Speed, Liana, it's all about speed. Make a decision, regardless of whether it's the correct one. Whatever you decide to do, do it with speed and keep running.* Bracing herself for what is behind the door, Liana prepares for her exit, or more likely a fight for survival.

Limbering up quietly, her athletic frame pumps the much-needed blood to her extremities. With the dizziness finally gone, she looks for anything that could work as a weapon. Kneeling down, she gently tears open the black plastic bags, looking for hard or sharp objects. The contents are mostly old clothes and spare bed lining, so she gives up and moves to inspect the door. The flimsy internal door has no lock from the inside, and it is unknown if there is one on the outside. She will soon find out.

Taking a deep breath, Liana removes her cumbersome boots then cups the doorknob in her hand and slowly rolls it clockwise while staring at the nib retreating into its housing. As she pulls the door inward slightly, it relieves her to hear no squeaking from the old hinges. Through the slight gap she created, the sound of the men talking has now become more audible. Right away, she can see the long, dark hallway. The threadbare carpet is the same color as the bedroom, and the walls are painted a dull cream. Black scuff marks line the lower portions of the wall, and the wooden front door has two huge sliding bolts fixed without padlocks.

As Liana opens the bedroom door farther, she realizes the light from her room will illuminate the hallway. Understanding she has no other options other than to wait in the room for the torture to begin, her decision to run stands firm in her mind. *Run, and run fast,* she repeats to herself. Sliding her thin frame out between the narrow gap she created and gently pulling the door closed, Liana drops quickly to a crouch and scurries over to the front door. With a quick glance over her shoulders, she can see into the open living area where it is much brighter. In her view sits a man on a worn-out couch. The back of his bald head brings back more dark memories. Liana's heart pounds as she slowly slides the lower door bolt open, then she stands and puts her fingers on the top bolt. Turning to watch the man on the couch, she silently slides the top bolt across, then comes the moment of success or failure. An old olive-green Yale deadlatch is all that stands between her and freedom.

***

Chuck Lambert is on his third beer. He told himself two was enough but couldn't resist one more. Buchanan, meanwhile, is pacing back and forth, talking to Duval on his mobile. The situation in the room is tense. The two men in the house have years of experience in dealing with stressful situations. Lambert, though, has noticed too many deviations on the plan to let matters slide.

It has been thirty minutes since Marchetti and Kenn left the safe house in the inner-city area of Jeżyce to grab some food. During this time, Lambert sits quietly on the couch, trying to decipher Duval's intent. Each layer he peels from the dilemma, the more risks he finds. In his eyes, Duval, and Buchanan are leading the men down a dark alley.

Buchanan finally ends the call and looks over at Lambert, then glances at the two empty bottles by his feet.

"Well, what's the go with Duval?" asks Lambert.

Buchanan sits down on a dining room chair and puts the phone into his pocket. He holds up one finger at Lambert, then picks up a pack of locally made Fajrant cigarettes and taps one loose. "You want one?"

Lambert shakes his head.

Once Buchanan lights the cigarette, he tosses the lighter onto the table and blows out a puff of smoke. "Duval is about as helpful as a kick in the teeth. He is giving away nothing. There is a manhunt for our guest, and Berlin is locked down."

Lambert cannot hide his frustration. His eyes narrow as he shakes his head. "What about this chick? When is he coming to take her off our hands?"

"He wants us to press her for more information. But I want to know more about this British guy. He is a loose end and someone that can come back and hurt us. Duval told me not to worry, as the Chinese will take care of him. All we need to do is smoke him out," says Buchanan irritably.

"You said press her for more information! Are you serious, man? Those two ass clowns Marchetti and Kenn shoved so much shit down her throat I doubt she will remember her own name."

Buchanan shrugs. "Look, it is what it is. Duval said press her, so we will do that. Give her a cold shower and get some coffee down her neck, then we will see what's inside that cute head of hers."

"You know what I think? I think she is well out of the loop. If you believe the Brits tell us everything they know, then you must have rocks in your head." Lambert's face is turning red and the veins that run along his temple are pulsating. He can't hold in his doubts about this unexpected turn of events. "The longer we hold on to a CIA agent, the closer we are to receiving a full-on firefight with them. And guess what, Buchanan? That's our CIA comrades. The cavalry will burst through that door any minute. We were only meant to get the info and drop her off, not take her across Europe and keep her as a freaking hostage."

Buchanan is about to take another draw of his cigarette, but stops sharply and shouts back. "STOP BEING SUCH A PUSSY, LAMBERT . . . you knew exactly what you signed up for and were quick to accept the money transfers. Now you are becoming soft in the head. What the hell has got into you?" Buchanan has long grown tired of Lambert's complaining. From the surveillance and baggage of the hostage, then the three-hour trip west from Berlin to the city of Poznań in Poland, the man never stopped moaning. Marchetti and Kenn warned Buchanan that Lambert's mind is slipping from the end goal.

"I'll tell you what. Duval has us running around doing his dirty work. Yes, I signed up for it, but what I didn't sign up for was pissing off our own people. You know what they are capable of *because we are those people*," Lambert shouts before gulping down the rest of his third beer. He knows that venting his built-up anger on Buchanan feels good, but it isn't enough.

Buchanan sighs heavily, then stubs out his cigarette and goes to the fridge, returning with a couple more beers. "Look, man. I owe you an apology."

As he hands one to Lambert, he notices the man's eyes are dark and menacing. The same look men have when facing off with a dangerous enemy. Buchanan retreats to the table and considers how tonight will play out. *Lambert is becoming a weak link,* he thinks. His mind turns to the possibility that Lambert could destroy everything their small team has worked so hard to achieve. Buchanan speaks cautiously this time. "When the boys come back with the grub, we will sit down and iron this shit out. If we decide to cut and run, then so be it. Team decision, Lambert, okay?"

Lambert sits there motionless, staring at the window opposite him. He opens his can of beer but only takes a sip. He doesn't want alcohol affecting his judgement.

***

Liana hears the two men in the living area arguing and shouting at each other about Duval. Knowing there are two others in the street reinforces her mindset to be ultracautious once she hits the footpath. The small knob on the Yale lock turns easily. Now all she has to do is pull the door toward her, then squeeze out and run like hell. Looking behind her as she opens the door softly, she can see the man still on the couch. Then she sees the red mist. Stifling her scream with her free hand, she holds down a mouthful of vomit. Liana cannot believe what has just happened. The bald man on the coach who was drinking a beer suddenly had his head nearly blown off with a suppressed firearm. Now he sits there with his head slumped backward, staring at the ceiling.

Out of extreme fear, Liana swings the door open and runs. Heading toward the concrete steps and iron railings opposite the apartment door, she races down them to the next level. Terrified and filled with adrenaline, she grabs the railings and swings her body to the right and continues down to the next floor. Her heart pounds and the visualization of the kill shot before her eyes threatens to throw her legs off balance. "Keep running," she squeals as she rushes down another floor. Once on the ground floor, Liana has two options, left or right. She chooses left.

***

Dave Kenn and Tony Marchetti had spent their time checking out the suburb of Jeżyce, tasked by Buchanan to source some food and a couple of local mobile phones, plus a few beers for the long evening ahead. Kenn has been too busy being pissed off about Liana to notice

Marchetti trying to get his attention. The fact that she scraped his face when he bundled her into the van was annoying him. Two thin red marks run from his forehead to just under his right eye. As he checks out his reflection in a shop window, he never notices the young girl walk past on the other side of the street.

Marchetti is ropeable with his partner. He quickly walks across the bakery past a couple of customers and bangs on the window. When Kenn looks up with surprise on his face, he instantly realizes the day has turned to shit.

Kenn spins around and locks eyes on Liana. In that precise moment, she too catches the eyes of the man who kidnapped her in Berlin. Kenn doesn't wait for Marchetti to join him. Instead, he takes off running across the road. The cars honk their horns as he holds out his hands to stop them. Jumping over the tramlines, he races into a full-blown sprint. His target has a good twenty meters on him before she flees. Her arms bend at ninety degrees, swinging in rhythm with the movement of her hips as she runs for her life. Kenn stays on the road with the traffic now at a standstill. Some people get out of their vehicles to watch the crazed looking man chasing the woman.

Liana runs past stunned pedestrians, weaving past the street furniture and skipping over wet puddles. The words on the traffic signs or street names mean nothing to her. All that matters is the distance between herself and the threat. Afterward, she will work out where the hell she is. Liana gives little thought to her now badly bruised feet. Without footwear, her heals take a hammering from the cobbled streets. Up ahead, she sees a junction giving her two options. Quickly spinning her head around, she can see the man chasing her down like a bull in Pamplona. Dropping her right shoulder and taking the street to her right, she quickly finds another couple of options: disappear inside an area that contains a couple of huge gray apartment buildings or keep running toward the center of town. The street is quieter and she can make out the fast footfalls of the man closing on her. Liana keeps her strides long and fast as she scans an upcoming side road for any other potential escape routes. With a quick check behind, she notices the man has his firearm drawn at waist level. *Take the side road,* her mind screams. Just as she prepares to drop into the corner, she sees something about fifty meters ahead. *A taxi, or is it cops? Please be the cops.* Liana runs down the road waving her arms wildly. About twenty meters away, she screams at the car. It is unmistakable. The white letters spelling *Policja* run along the side of the silver-and-blue-striped car. Liana is overwhelmed with relief once the officer inside pulls the car onto the middle of the road and switches on the red-and-blue lights.

"Help me, there is a man behind me with a gun."

The two officers quickly deploy their firearms and point them up the street, shouting for her to get behind their car. When Liana looks out from behind the car, she finds the street empty. He is nowhere to be seen. Looking down the side street, she catches a fleeting glimpse of another man before he backs into the shadows and then retreats.

The distance back to the police station was short, yet the ride still filled Liana with fear. They were the CIA. She knew that now. *Duval.* That name fills her with dread. She couldn't believe the two men in the apartment talking about the deputy director of the CIA for operations. As she tries to piece it all together, the police officers keep asking questions. Their interruptions will have to be addressed.

"Hey, American, yes?" the officer in the passenger seat asks.

"Yes, yes. I'm sorry, I'm a tourist. Poznań men following me, I think?"

Chapter Twenty-Six

Monte Carlo, Monaco

Arriving in Monte Carlo just after nine in the morning is perfect for Carver. The sun is already high and some of the expensive yachts have left for a day of cruising. Traffic is predictably terrible, and his fellow travelers in the silver Audi look ready to fall asleep. Although this doesn't affect his mood, as he has the makings of a plan. A fluid and high-risk plan that involves putting his life in danger. A situation he is becoming uncomfortably used to.

Jakov provided the ride from Zurich. Which helped Carver stay clear of train stations and car rental offices. The old man of organized crime sorted everything. The crafty Croatian had come through as expected on Carver's two requests. Delivering him safely back into the hornet's nest was the first. The second would take a little longer to work out. Which suits Carver fine, as there is much work to be done in the meantime.

He gets out of the car before the driver reverses into a garage, which is attached to a small wine bar. Jakov told Carver he rented the place for the year and uses it to store certain items before moving them to one of his yachts.

From there, they would distribute the hardware around the various ports in the Mediterranean, unbeknownst to the authorities. The guests on board the chartered vessels would be unaware they were sailing the Med with kilos of cocaine or military-grade weapons stashed deep in the hull.

Carver wants nothing to do with their operations. It isn't his concern and gaining access to firearms is left to the good people of the SIS. He politely shakes hands with the men and takes off down the street, leaving them to their profitable criminal enterprise. After a twenty-minute walk, Carver finally arrives at his apartment on Rue Colonel Bellando de Castro.

He skirts the block, then doubles back and heads to the front door. If anyone is following him, he would have noticed. Showing his face is part of the plan, and Jakov is kind enough to gift him a ten-year-old Glock. In the event someone tries to take him out, he could at least get down to business. The firearm is well maintained. However, now that Carver is at home and has access to his own weapons, he wants rid of the thing. The likelihood it has been used in a wide range of killings or robberies and easily traceable by a ballistic forensic analyst is the reason to ditch it. *The priest can help dispose of it*, thinks Carver as he enters the door and makes his way up the steps to his property. It feels to him like weeks since he was last at home. The kitchen looks spotless. Obviously, the old priest had been back to check up on the place. He walked from room to room, checking for anything suspicious, then ensures the security equipment is working and online. Once he replaces the old Glock with his favored

Sig Sauer and slides it into his waistband holster, he sits down next to the window and phones his girl Sarah.

***

Sarah has just finished a briefing with Flynn when she looks down at her phone. The unknown number can only be one of a handful of people. Rerouted through the exchange in the SIS building, she desperately hopes it's Carver. She picks it up and walks to a quiet area inside the café.

"Good morning."

"Hey, beautiful, how are you?" asks Carver.

"My God, it has been ages. I should ask how you are? You certainly left a trail of destruction across Europe."

"I am fine, but my legend is screwed." Carver laughs.

"Don't worry about that. I guessed you would need another one. Listen up, I just had a discussion with Flynn. He left to scout out the area around Monte Carlo. It's a long story, but the CIA has narrowed down their list of men of declared suspects. There is a huge reluctancy to pass those details on to us Brits, partly because of embarrassment. Flynn told me enough to understand the situation. Now he is pissed off and wants to wipe them out. His fellow countrymen turned traitors," says Sarah.

"So he should be. It's about time he gets off his lazy ass and helps me out," says Carver.

Sarah smirks at Carver's response before speaking. "Whenever you are ready, Mr. Rambo, there is someone I want you to meet. He has proven extremely helpful to us in building the character profile of your new best friend, Zhang. Besides, I want to have you by my side."

"You need protection? I heard you are having quite a fun time in Monte Carlo while I am bleeding in ditches," Carver says with a smile planted across his face.

"That bloody Tommy spilling all my secrets, is he?" Sarah's hysterical giggling causes a few guests in the café to take notice.

"Tommy freelances to the highest bidder. You should know that." Carver laughs before continuing. "Okay, Sarah, all jokes aside, I need to draw out this bloody Zhang Muppet. He spent enough time flexing his muscles around Europe. And to do this correctly, I need to do it my way. Otherwise, he will smell a trap if the agencies try to block off Monte Carlo and corner him. He proved to us his ability in using the waterways to attack, now he could also use it to escape. So, it is my job to force him to come after me."

"Okay, what do you need from me?" asks Sarah.

"There is someone you need to locate for me, and also have Tommy work on the usual jamming of security and traffic cameras on my movements. Then pull out all the stops and locate Zhang. Or anyone connected to him."

Carver takes a moment to calibrate his thoughts before continuing. "Whoever took out the minister of state security did so for a reason. The reason why is something I haven't figured out yet. At first, I assumed it was a power move orchestrated by Zhang himself. However, I can't get my head around the timing. Zhang's motives and the fluidity of his movements are as clear as mud. I believe there are high rollers around Monte Carlo moving money for this mission. They would likely use multiple shelf companies and be looking for Western business partners in order to show legitimacy. Whatever it is, I need to sever that link," says Carver.

Sarah considers everything Carver told her, then looks over at the man sitting at her table.

"I will see what I can do. I have a strong lead, so leave it with me. When I give you someone linked to this Chinese team, what will you do?" asks Sarah.

"The Chinese team has a head. Once I remove it, the rest of the team will run like rats. Just make sure you give me someone big," says Carver.

"Don't worry, I'll get that done soon. And, Carver, when this is all over, do you remember the promise you made?"

Carver smiles at the thought of what he would like to do. Instead, he replies appropriately. "Roses, candles, wine, and laughter, yes!"

"Good boy. Please take care." Sarah cuts the connection with a heavy heart, then turns and walks over to the table and takes a seat with her guest.

"Okay, Eddie. Let's have a chat about who's who in Monte Carlo," says Sarah.

"I am more than willing, Sarah. Take out your notebook while I order us more coffee." Eddie Wu had wasted no time in working with the CIA and SIS once his embarrassment of being caught in a compromising position finally wore off.

Sarah and Flynn had been forthcoming in their assessment of his future within the Chinese political hierarchy. The NSA found Eddie's name added to a list compiled by the Chinese Communist Party after the recent shooting of Danny Lin. No matter what way Eddie tried to twist his story to the CCP, he would always be a suspect. With or without proof, Eddie would be looking at a death sentence. Now, with the American and British governments prodding him for information, he instantly decided his fate would be best left in their hands.

***

Flynn walks through the backstreets of Monte Carlo toward a safe house that Sarah organized for him. He's had enough discussions for now and the sea air is doing him good. Eddie was proving useful, although the nature of business and political ideologies was sending Flynn to sleep back in the café. He misses the real combat theater. A place where armed-and-dangerous men try to shoot or blast you to pieces. A world that makes sense to Flynn. If normal combat fails, the downside resorts to the enemy employing horrible tactics, such as blowing up their own people so they can blame the occupiers. Shaking his head at that murky side of war, he still finds close combat more appealing than the political assassinations Sarah wants. *Unless there is some female-on-female action,* he thinks to himself with a satisfying smile as he edges closer to the address.

Flynn also takes a moment to consider the elusive British SIS operative. He knows Carver is highly capable of looking after himself. He also imagines it would be nice to work alongside the man. Flynn is reflecting deeply about avenging Jackson's death and the Texan's small team, which he brought to Europe with him. He feels sick in the stomach that all those men died on one of his operations. *This slimy enemy needs to be put down,* thinks Flynn. As he makes his way through the narrow streets, he feels safe in the knowledge his firearm is ready for action. However, the ongoing threat of explosives makes him jumpy. A careful assessment of the surrounding street keeps his mind busy, as a plan is already set. Kill the Chinese man, then go after the CIA traitors. There isn't much more to it than that. Flynn checks his tail as he crosses the street to approach the safe house. He really hopes Carver has a more detailed plan.

***

Carver wakes in a panic from a deep sleep. He instantly grabs his firearm that lies next to his pillow and aims it toward the empty corners within his bedroom. Covered in sweat and breathing heavily, he climbs out of bed and takes a walk around his apartment. The nightmare was horrible. Pouring himself a glass of water, he stands there thinking about it with a strange degree of remorse. It began back in the Parisian apartment. Carver was laughing and screaming as his knife plunged in and out of Le Xing-Fu's body. The sensation felt hilarious, as much as it was addictive. Exhausted and covered in blood splatter, he ripped the soaked covers off the corpse, only to see Sarah's naked and lifeless body. She looked at him with pity and sadness. Telling him it was okay. *Don't worry, keep doing it?* she was saying. Carver shudders at the brutal savagery and vividness of the nightmare. The only helpful part was the four hours' worth of sleep he grabbed since returning to his apartment. To reset his mind, he slugs down the cold water, then takes a long hot shower followed by a heavy breakfast. Carver finally feels close to being a normal human again.

***

A couple of hours later, a brand-new smartphone is charging next to the kitchen counter when it abruptly beeps. Carver swivels around on his stool and quickly picks it up. The brief message on the screen reveals the name and address of his target. Under the message is a link attached to an image file. With a tap on the link, a recent mugshot downloads itself onto the screen. *Just another lucky Communist Party leader,* Carver jokes to himself. He figures this middleman between the CCP and all Chinese-owned businesses in Europe is a key threat. Someone who tried to overthrow each country through economic soft power. This is as much politics as Carver can handle. He doesn't care too much about the man or his dirty tactics, so he sits back in his chair and studies the photograph until the face is imprinted in his mind.

Carver had earlier considered how he would approach this task. He knew surveillance of someone's movements would naturally take a few months. He also considered how the method of assassination would depend on how close he could get to the man or if a message needed to be made to scare others. Such as a messy and painful slaughter. Sarah had advised on employing a discreet or accidental death. *Make it look like a suicide,* she had told him. Carver, in his mind, has no intentions of that. He wants to make a statement, and he knows how everyone within SIS is currently working outside of their borders of authority. Carver thinks he too could use the same level of abstract methods.

Eddie had mentioned to Sarah earlier that the purge of Western spies who are no longer useful to the CCP will probably continue unless the West can return the same level of hurt. This is something Carver would not have an issue with. The political fallout would be enormous, and the Western mainstream media would do everything they could to blame their countrymen and countrywomen for all the world's problems.

As Carver makes his tactical plans, he can't help but feel good about tomorrow. A smile appears effortlessly on his face. "Gentlemen's game of combat," he whispers while his fingers fiddle with a detonator as he carefully attaches it to one of his bombs.

***

The room isn't too shabby, although there will be no time to enjoy it. Zhang has made plans to leave Monte Carlo in a couple of days. His flight to New York departing from Côte d'Azur Airport in Nice cannot be missed. General Zhou Kai, the Black Bear, has ordered Zhang to tie up the loose ends in Europe, then make his way to the United States. It is well known that the UN Security Council is in turmoil and the media have reported great distrust between European nations and China. The general believes the moment has arrived in which to pursue World War III. Zhang stands shoulder to shoulder with the general as he relishes the thought of moving up the ranks and leading an army of hard fighters. He views the last bombing in Berlin as killing flies. The New York bombing will be spectacular, he promised to the general.

As Zhang gets to work preparing his instruments of death, he acknowledges the Black Bear will be no match for Zhang once he gets back to China. "That's a fight for another day," he mumbles to himself. His mindset now focuses on the assassination of the only two men who can prevent himself from success.

***

As the last of the sunlight falls over the horizon, the buildings turn a dull yellow from the streetlights. Shadows pop up all around Carver as he walks hurriedly to a blue Japanese car. He thumps a screwdriver-type device into the keyhole and twists it strongly. Now with a broken lock, he opens the door and deactivates the alarm system. Once he starts the engine, he sets his bag on the passenger seat and drives off. The roads are not too busy as the peak hour has passed. The thousands of workers who travel from France into Monaco every day for work have all retreated to their homes, leaving wide-open roads for Carver to zip around in.

He finds the address easily and parks outside. His thoughts turn to Luxembourg, when he was ambushed and needed a quick getaway. So tonight, Carver keeps the car a lot closer to the driveway with the nose facing the nearest road junction. "Be sure and be quick," he repeats to himself when leaving the car. The surrounding air is humid and still. Homeowners in this quiet suburb just outside the state of Monaco have larger properties and, therefore, use their back gardens for dinner parties. Tonight is one of those moonlit nights where the neighbors can be heard chattering lightly just above the sounds of music. The more affluent neighbors will, of course, have a brass band playing for social events. Carver enjoys the short walk and appears like a man who casually fits into such a noble area. With a smile on his face and humming a tune, he turns into the target's property and walks up the short path to the front door. Once on the doorstep, he promptly presses the doorbell. "Learn from Luxembourg," he whispers.

After a few brief moments, he can hear someone on the other side of the door, followed by a moment of silence. Then the sound of the door locks being eased before the door swings inward.

"May I help you with something?" asks the portly man, a look of displeasure on a round face for being confronted by a stranger at this hour.

"Oh, yes, Mr. Shuang. I believe you could. Just stand there a moment and don't move, okay?" says Carver.

The man is not only confused, he is also disturbed by the foolish and rude request of the stranger.

"Don't move? What the hell do you mean?" says Shuang.

Carver doesn't bother replying. His firearm will do the talking. Snapping it out of his jacket, he points it directly at the man's forehead and squeezes the trigger twice. The man falls heavily against the front door as Carver calmly turns and walks back to his car.

Chapter Twenty-Seven

Berlin, Germany

The hum of the fluorescent lights overhead and the clicking of the keyboard in the small room add to Liana's frustration. Her foul mood had started not long after arriving back at the American embassy. The CIA wanted to keep her abduction and subsequent escape under wraps until Hoffmann read her detailed report. It was he who met Liana at the Berlin airport a few hours after first being picked up by the police in Poznań.

After fleeing from Kenn and Marchetti earlier in the day, Poznań police assisted the terrified girl into their patrol car. When they found no such risk, they all returned to the station to begin the mandatory report. The two officers considered this to be another foreign tourist that got robbed or assaulted. Petty crime is not worth reporting. It had been the fourth of the week and was, as one officer commented to his partner, "A couple of hours of wasted paperwork to be filed in the bin." Nonetheless, the two officers enjoyed the company of the beautiful American.

The bitter coffee provided in the white polystyrene cups did little to help Liana's state of mind. Seated in the messy interview room, the younger officer quizzed her as the older one sat in the corner with a shameless leer on his face. After a few apologies, she convinced them of her earlier misunderstanding and misguided panic. When the paperwork was finally completed, they showed her the door and told her to be more responsible on her travels.

Fearing the prospect of venturing into the street, she spotted the public telephone in the tattered-looking reception area. Her first call was to Hoffmann. He cut short her stay at the police station by arranging for two local CIA contractors to pick her up and escort her safely back to Berlin. His instructions were simple: do not speak to anyone and get back in one piece. Liana overlooked the first one. The second she ended the call with Hoffmann, she immediately dialed Dallas Pope at Langley. The conversation with her close friend and mentor was the third such call she made during her time in Europe. Speaking freely to Pope allowed her to vent and seek reassurance that the abduction wouldn't hurt her career. She explained every detail to him and, through that conversation in the Polish police station, her confidence returned. Until she arrived back in Berlin.

Hoffmann, with his outstretched arms and a smile of reassurance, hugged her warmly. Then he preached a few lines about bravery and loyalty, which led Liana to believe her future in the CIA would be safe. During the ride back to the embassy, he spoke to her like a grandpa to a young child, acknowledging that her ability to run and keep her mouth shut was admirable. A sense of achievement overcame her embarrassment of being snatched so easily in the middle of Berlin over a day ago. Hoffmann acknowledged her account of what happened back in the apartment in Poznań was surreal. "The intelligence you supplied is like a golden egg to the agency," he mentioned again.

Her pride quickly turned flat when Hoffmann walked with her from the black Audi into the basement of the embassy, leading her into the cramped room to type a bullshit report that would most likely be wiped afterward. She could hear the door being locked from the outside when he left. The unpainted room with bare gray walls contained the table, plastic chair, and a cheap coffee machine with a small fridge. When Liana looked at the mirror in front of her, she knew the unknown people behind it would watch her every move.

***

Once Cain Hoffmann leaves Liana down in the basement and out of harm's way, he goes to the CIA office farther down the corridor. When Hoffmann steps into the small, soundproofed room within the office, he closes the door and calls Harry Woodward back in London.

"Harry, good man, I thought you would hide from my calls."

"Never a dull moment with you guys, is it?" says Harry.

"What do you mean?" asks Hoffmann.

"A question with a question! Typical CIA." Harry laughs before continuing.

"Right, listen up, old chap. We have a lot of movement down in Monte Carlo. I know you guys want hands-off.

But that cannot be avoided right now. You likely know some of your boys have gone off the reservation. Which means we need to clean up this mess. Which, I am afraid to say, will cause your agency some embarrassment. That, my friend, will be unavoidable."

Hoffmann knows where this is going. He views Harry as a kind of long-lost brother and feels somewhat foolish in his current predicament. He looks back at the door, making sure it is closed before speaking.

"Tell me about it. Luckily, the young girl escaped and is now safe downstairs. I have contained her until I figure out who's involved. Gary Duval is what I would consider the number-one guy. I cannot be sure how far his tentacles have reached. Although I have some details coming in related to his shady team of current CIA paramilitaries in Berlin," says Hoffmann.

"I need those names and everything you have for me," replies Harry as he skims over the sheet of paper on his desk marked *Agenzia Informazioni e Sicurezza Esterna.*

"That's not a problem. Just make sure my guy Flynn gets those names. I have a feeling he can be quite helpful. There will be a huge air gap between myself and the men on the ground. I have been exposed enough. Once my plane is ready, we will head back to the States. I have a sick feeling the media circus will set up camp on the White House shortly."

Harry Woodward can visualize the same media frenzy bustling around Number Ten anytime soon. He realizes once Carver and Flynn join forces, the entire world will scramble for information. He withholds the fresh information the Italians have provided him with until he connects more dots.

"Flynn will be catered to. Enjoy your flight, Hoffmann, and I hope to catch up with you for a proper drink once these matters get resolved," says Harry as he pours himself a glass of Blackwoods gin and pushes some tobacco into his worn-out pipe. After the pipe tobacco is glowing, he carefully reads through the intelligence report compiled and beautifully translated by Juliana Calabrese. One hour and three glasses of gin later, he finally looks up from the desk in the SIS building and peers out the window over the River Thames. "Crafty bastard," he says. Picking up a phone from his drawer, he selects the last call and hits "dial."

"Thanks for the report, Sarah. Pass my compliments to the Italians. And make sure Tommy has all those phone numbers."

"I have already thanked the Italians, Harry. After Florence, they were incredibly keen to join forces. And after Berlin, the Germans have now responded. They have offered to send some of their BND operatives our way," says Sarah.

"No way, Sarah. We cannot have that. Next thing, the Turks will be rolling down the streets to get revenge for Istanbul. Then the Chinese will send the North Koreans to do their dirty work. No, we clean up this mess, leaving the smallest footprint possible. Tell Carver to do exactly that. Get in and out. Make it clean. Take this guy Zhang out of operation. Leave Duval to Flynn, otherwise it will be a political nightmare if they finger us for killing a CIA operative." Harry feels breathless when speaking quickly into the handset. He tips the contents of the pipe into a glass ashtray on the table as he waits for Sarah's reply. Encrypted or not, he wants this call to be over.

"Okay, boss, I copy that. I'll do my best with Carver. You know how he is."

As Harry ends the call, he watches an Indonesian-built, green-and-white dredger moving slowly along the River Thames. The strange-looking vessel approaches Lambeth Bridge, a stone's throw from the MI5 building. Harry sets his glass down on the thick marble windowsill, then pours another from the almost empty bottle. The thought of these bombings and shootings coming back to London would destroy him. *Those men and women over the river in Section 5 would humiliate me. Don't screw this up, Carver. Tread bloody carefully.*

Chapter Twenty-Eight

Monte Carlo, Monaco

Duval finishes his breakfast of croissants, eggs, and cheese on the balcony of the hotel, then walks inside his room, locks the balcony doors, and grabs his Glock. He then switches off the lights in the room and walks out into the hallway, pulling the door closed behind him. The carpet under his feet has a familiar bounce to it. Subtle, but noticeable all the same. He chooses the fire escape to walk up the two flights of steps to the fourth floor. Once he arrives at the door, he holds up a device and places the lens over the peephole, which now gives him a sharp view on the small screen. Inside, he can see Zhang sitting at the table, working intently. With his other finger, he knocks on the doorbell and watches Zhang flinch somewhat before lifting a firearm and coming toward him. Duval slips the device into his pocket and takes a step back from the door.

"What the hell, asshole? Quick, step inside, out of the corridor." Zhang is furious with Duval for following him on his mission and appearing at his hotel.

Duval steps past Zhang, ignoring the dark hollow eyes staring at him. Instead, he walks over to the table and looks at the various pieces of equipment Zhang has been working on. Sticking out from under a towel is a vast block of plastic explosives. The amount causes him some delight.

"When we met in Milan, I told you I would kill you if you followed me. Brown, or is it Gary Duval?"

Duval, on hearing his real name, turns to face the man he hopes will cause destruction on his behalf. "You have been doing your homework on me. Good boy."

Zhang steps closer and interrupts the lying American, his face a couple of inches from Duval's. "You haven't been truthful to me, so why should I trust you. I could simply kill you and complete my operation. I would be out of the country before they find your worthless body," says Zhang.

Suddenly Duval swings his right fist in a tight hook, catching the top of Zhang's forehead. Zhang is stunned, but fights off the ringing in his ears. He crouches down and drives his shoulder with all his weight into Duval, causing him to tumble back onto the floor. Duval lands heavily with Zhang on top and immediately tries to wrap his arms around his attacker's neck. Zhang is waiting for this; he shoves his head up, colliding with Duval's jaw. A tooth shatters in the American's jaw, followed by a scream.

"You bastard," shouts Duval. With blood pouring from his mouth, he wrestles Zhang onto the floor and tries to use his weight to pin him down. The smaller man, however, is stronger and more mobile. He hooks his leg around the back of Duval and spins out from below him.

As he moves to free himself, his hand reaches inside Duval's jacket and grabs the butt of his firearm. Duval can feel the Chinese man fumbling and knows his plan.

With one hand, he struggles with Zhang, and with the other, he tries to slide out a small knife concealed in an ankle holster. Zhang rips the weapon free from Duval's jacket and presses it strongly into his forehead. The two men suddenly stop wrestling with each other. Duval has one hand on the barrel of the gun. His finger clasps tightly on the safety switch and his other hand pushes the tip of the blade on Zhang's throat. A light trickle of blood runs down the steel. The two men lock eyes.

No strangers to death, there is no fear in either man's eyes. It is the mission that becomes more important. Zhang is the first to pull back. He releases his grip on the Glock before Duval eases the knife away from his windpipe. Zhang stands up and backs off. Then he touches his neck to check on the source of his blood. Duval sits upright and re-holsters his knife in the sheath tucked under his trouser leg. Then he rises to his feet, still holding his gun.

"Perhaps we can put aside our differences and get down to business, Zhang," says Duval, who is breathing heavier than he would have liked.

Zhang is silent by the mirror that hangs next to the bed. "I don't understand you, Duval. We agreed to everything in Milan. Now you show up again like a ghost. This is my operation. You are only giving help, not guidance. Yet here you are pissing all over me."

"I hear you, Zhang. I also need you to know this is the most important part of your mission. These men are not to be taken lightly. The bombs are causing mayhem with the FBI and their European buddies. All resources are being thrown at their investigations. You need to act now, or risk being arrested. I am here to tell you not to come back to this hotel. And also, I have some regret." Duval paces awkwardly about the room as he attempts to reveal his real reason for the interruption.

Zhang senses bad news. He wipes his neck with a tissue, then walks over to the table full of explosives. "Tell me."

"That night in Milan. Remember the good-looking lass that wanted to borrow my phone?" Without waiting for an acknowledgement, Duval continues. "I now worry, or perhaps consider, that she is a spook. Italian or maybe even British."

Zhang's eyes grow redder. The sound of panic now enters his voice. "SHIT! You have a big dumb head full of horseshit. They can trace us here. You realize that?"

"I know, I know. That's why I needed to speak to you. I ditched my SIM card today. You need to do the same," says Duval remorsefully.

Zhang wastes no time. He grabs his phone and throws it against the wall, smashing it into pieces. "I need to get the hell out of here and head to the airport," he shouts while lifting the SIM card from the floor. Hurriedly, he cracks the SIM into two pieces between his fingers. Then he carefully picks up the explosive devices he prepared and attempts to slide them inside the pillowcases.

"Give me a hand quickly," orders Zhang, now furious with the American. He fights the urge to finish him there and then. Instead, he focuses on fleeing this hotel. He knows the *Golden Tiger* has been forensically examined by the authorities and has now been handed back to the traitorous Eddie Wu. That is one escape route he holds up his sleeve, if required. Or less time consuming, his diplomatic Chinese passport under a new legend is the other pathway back to China.

Duval grabs a face towel from the bathroom to stem the bleeding, then sets the items on the table into a black bag sitting on the floor. "Perhaps you could just as easily sink a bullet into the back of their heads," he mutters painfully.

"Do you want to do it yourself, then?" Zhang's reply is quick.

Duval doesn't respond. He knows this screw-up is on him. Moving briskly, the two men pack away the gear before Duval apologizes and walks toward the door.

"Duval. Next time there will be no hesitancy. If I ever see your face again, I will blow you away," says Zhang.

The CIA man stands with his back to Zhang and considers a response. *It's not worth it.* Without turning, he simply nods and leaves the room.

***

Sarah calls Flynn before breakfast, asking him to walk around Monte Carlo and look for signs of any suspicious activity by the Chinese. This means checking the yachts and piers, the lobbies and restaurants of the hotels, and the small cafés in the backstreets. Flynn will speak to some honey traps he noticed working the bars the past few nights, and the valet staff, who understand the price of worthy information. The plan is simple: push handfuls of euros into their palms and don't shy away from attention. Once he finds anything important, he is required by Sarah to phone Carver immediately. *We need to unsettle the prick*, were the words Sarah used, which suits Flynn perfectly.

A couple of hours later, the sight of the man walking across the harbor walkway in Monte Carlo sends shivers down Flynn's spine. He can't believe what he's seeing. The urge to go after his prey eats him alive. Luckily, he reminds himself, Duval is only half of the prize. *The Chinese shithead is also hiding around here and is about to meet his fate.* He pulls out his mobile phone and calls his new partner.

"Carver, it's Flynn."

"Good morning, mate. We speak at last. I have heard so many crap and boring things about you," jokes Carver.

Flynn laughs before responding. "Looking forward to a beer so I can teach you about English women. But first I have something of interest. I have spotted our mutual friend heading into a hotel. I need you to get your ass out of bed and meet up."

"That's what I want to hear, good man. I also received a trace on locations. Zhang switched his phone on this morning for about two minutes. Although they must have ditched their phones now; there is nothing since. Tell me where you are and I'll come right over," says Carver.

"By the way, this caught me on the hop. I have nothing other than my gun and a couple of mags," says Flynn.

"Don't worry about that. Keep your eyes on and give me a few minutes," says Carver as he races to the garage where he stored the stolen Nissan Micra. His safe house, five kilometers outside Monaco, is the perfect place to plan an ambush. The main road to the international airport at Nice passes by the property. If Zhang runs for it, Carver can cut him off. However, this is not his preferred option. He wants to catch Zhang, trap him like an animal, and make him suffer a slow death. Make him pay for Gabriella and all the others. For this to happen, he needs to venture back into Monte Carlo. A full-on attack, to catch him with surprise. *Controlled aggression wins the fight,* Carver thinks to himself as he swings open the door on the little red car. The voice of Flynn continues over Carver's earpiece.

"I'm on the corner of de l'Hermitage and Henry Dunant. Duval has left the hotel. Do you want me to tail him?"

"No, wait for me. It could be a trap to give Zhang an easy escape. He is in the hotel and is likely preparing to escape," says Carver as he connects the two exposed wires under the steering wheel to ignite the engine. After selecting drive, he speeds out of the garage onto Chemin des Eucalyptus before connecting to the main motorway into Monaco.

"What's your ETA?" asks Flynn.

"About five minutes. Do your best to blend in and follow him. I'll try to make it as quick as I can."

Flynn can hear the screeching of car tires and a revving engine coming through the phone speaker. No doubt Carver is punishing the car. "Okay, great. I'll let Sarah know." Flynn disconnects the call and crosses to the other side of the street, which now allows him a better view to the front of the hotel.

***

Zhang sets the black bag on the bed and sets two white bundles on top. The hotel-branded pillow covers each contain one explosive device. Two Daihatsu key fobs used for unlocking and locking cars are being used by him to activate the detonator. He modified the frequencies to work over longer distances and numbered each fob with a black marker. These crucial components are placed into the top pocket of his black jacket, and he puts a couple of boxes of ammunition in the lower pockets. His dark eyes scan the room for anything of importance. Zhang considers how stupid he had been in trusting Duval. The general had vouched for the man, no matter what he said. Zhang recalls the look of detachment when he told the general, *Trust no one but our own.* Both of the men's incompetency has now left him against the clock with no time to clean the hotel room. Evidence which would put an ordinary criminal behind bars for life. Disgusted at his inability to kill Duval, he promises never to hesitate again. *Today it begins, no hesitation,* he promises.

Before slinging the black bag over his shoulder, containing his few bug-out items, Zhang considers his weapons' layout. He first sets a QBZ-191 assault rifle, complete with a few loaded magazines, inside his bag and partially closes the zip. He considers this assault rifle will be his best choice if trapped, so it needs to be easily accessible. Tucked into his waistband is a Norinco-made handgun. The double stack magazine holds twenty armor-piercing rounds and will be his backup if a shootout occurs. However, Zhang hopes to take the fight toward the American and British men, blasting them with the revolver. *Perhaps the Westerners will appreciate the irony. Killed by their own weapon.* With a twisted smile, Zhang can visualize the Smith & Wesson framed in a glass box and placed above his desk in the war room back in China.

With no more space in the bag, Zhang slides the two pillowcases under his left arm, which leaves the right arm free to access the revolver hidden inside his jacket. A few test runs of drawing each weapon helps his confidence. Finally, he places a black hat on his head and a pair of sunglasses wrap tightly around his face. Before leaving the room prior to a SWAT team arriving, he prepares to face the two black ops men. With a few deep breaths to control his heart rate, he pulls the door open and steps out.

The hallway has a long corridor with a fire exit in the middle and one on both ends. Zhang ignores those stairwells, as they could be a location where his attackers could hide too easily. There are two elevators close to his hotel room, which he can access both the lobby and the car park beneath. He considers how the open area of the lobby would be too public for an attack by these Westerners. *Leave the brazen attacks to me,* he thinks as he presses the button.

When the lift doors close, the elevator drops smoothly to the next level. An uneasy feeling creeps over his body. He despises the fact they have turned the tables on him.

The Chinese president is in hiding, fearing the planned coup, so he will not help in securing Zhang's release if he gets arrested. Only the general will have the political power to do so once he topples the government.

These concerns tug at his mind, causing a distraction. *Snap out of it, Zhang,* he says to himself. *Understand the mission is only delayed. Fight to kill, then escape and come back another day.* Such thoughts of getting arrested threaten to disrupt his concentration once again. *The general will demand the weakened Europeans secure my release immediately. Of course he will. No one will stand up to our mighty power.* With his mind made up, a sense of optimism returns and fuels his thirst for blood.

The elevator stops on the third floor and a couple of older gray-headed guests step in and turn their backs to the armed and dangerous killer. The doors close and the elevator drops once again. Music by Léo Ferré plays softly in the background as Zhang considers the possibility there are younger and more capable men already in New York. *Perhaps the bombing of the UN will go ahead! Focus, Zhang, it's killing time,* he screams inside his head as the elevator stops on the ground floor.

***

Hotel staff scurry around the lobby tending attentively to the new arrivals. Expensive luggage and immaculately dressed Europeans wait patiently for the elevators as perfume and laughter fill the air. Stacked neatly at one table near the back of the lobby is a collection of local fashion magazines and glasses of coffee. An unlit cigar sits within an ashtray next to a gold lighter. The cigar's owner flicks through crisp pages of the *Monaco-Matin* newspaper.

The man has the appearance of a distinguished gentleman, unsuspicious, and blends in beautifully with his surrounds. Despite the earpiece that relays ongoing security updates from the street outside, he could be mistaken for a banker, a lobbyist, or a philanthropist. Not a CIA paramilitary officer turned gun for hire.

Buchanan never acknowledges his accomplice. Duval walks out of the lobby knowing his men would be in the vicinity, covering him and Zhang. He smiles to himself, knowing the men are all here to protect their cash cow. Zhang's survival and the death of Carver and Flynn will add to the men's fortunes. Money is key to living a new life, and Buchanan, like the others, will make sure no one is going to stop them now. He considers the outcome if Zhang gets arrested. *Nothing would happen to Zhang other than his safe return to China. It is very possible he would hang us all out to dry. There is no loyalty with those people.* With each thought bouncing around in Buchanan's head, he finally decides it would be better to shoot Zhang himself if he needs to, rather than see him arrested. The plan so far is working, and Buchanan ignores Duval, knowing he is a big boy and can handle himself. He considers that Flynn and Carver have their sights set firmly on Zhang. *They are close,* Buchanan tells himself. *I can smell them.*

***

Dave Kenn picks up his pace after receiving the call from Marchetti. The narrow streets around the old town are bustling with tourists, and if he breaks into a run, people will become suspicious. They occupy every table in the cafés and restaurants along Rue Emile de Loth, with the guests snapping photos all around them. He keeps his head tilted to the side when he passes them to avoid his mug shot being recorded. Kenn brushes past an old priest carrying a bag of oranges, then he glances down to his hand and checks the ink letters corresponding to the small lanes around him. *Rt. Vedel, Lt. Carmes, Rt. Eglise, Lt. . . .* An impromptu map allows him to find Carver's apartment, followed by the escape route. Turning right onto l'Eglise, Kenn familiarizes himself with the small lanes before turning back to zero in on Carver's apartment. As he gets closer, he wriggles a small wrecking bar down from his sleeve and holds it in his hand. He slows his pace to allow an elderly couple to pass by him, then he steps up to the doorstep and shoves the pointed wedge between the doorframe and lock and pulls forcefully on it.

Kenn moves inside hurriedly then replaces the wrecking bar with a Glock 17 complete with a suppressor. He holds his firearm in both hands, pointing up the staircase in front of him as he scans the area. Kenn rapidly climbs to the top floor, then stops at the side of the apartment door and listens cautiously for any movement from the other side. Within seconds, he slides a fiber-optic scope under the gap and twists the snakelike cable until an unrestricted view of the apartment shows up on his phone screen. After finding no threats in the apartment hallway, he retrieves the cable and stuffs it back into his pocket. The lock proves no problem to pick, and a short moment later, the metal rod slides carefully out of its housing. Kenn now regains full control of his Glock and enters the apartment ready to open fire.

His expression becomes stony when he swings around the corner and into the open-plan area of the apartment.

"Empty," he mutters nervously. Less than a minute later, he's checked each room, all with the same result. He then turns toward the kitchen and heads straight for the fridge. The milk is fresh, cheese, vegetables, all recent additions, yet something is strange and doesn't feel right. The walls are bare, and the tabletops are empty, which gives Kenn the false impression Carver's apartment was robbed of all its valuables. He pulls out his phone and calls Marchetti.

"Hey, man, this place is empty. It looks as if he skipped town."

"Okay, make your way back here. Zhang should make a break for it soon," says Marchetti.

"Copy that." He slips the phone into his pocket and walks back into the kitchen to grab a piece of cheese. A few seconds later, and with a lump of cantal clamped between his teeth, he reaches for the door. Then he sees something that sends a shiver up his spine. With a horrible lump in his throat, he is frozen on the spot. On the wall next to the door is a small baby monitor complete with a movement sensor. The small LED is glowing a bright green. *He is watching me. You devious bastard.* Kenn stares with dread at a small wire that runs from the device up and along the wall, then across the ceiling. Directly above his head is a cigarette-size box, taped securely in place.

A feeling of hopelessness descends upon Dave Kenn. His face turns gaunt and gray, the once powerful shoulders droop, and his heart sinks. What happens next is inevitable. The small green LED flickers slightly as the electrical current is bypassed from the monitor to the device above Kenn's head. Once the electrical circuit is complete, the bomb explodes with a deafening din.

Dave Kenn's head mostly explodes. He's dead before he hits the floor. Now his lifeless body settles unnaturally on the cold marble beneath him. His blood had splattered evenly over the bare walls, now running downward in straight lines. Fine dust of ceiling plaster breaks away and falls leisurely, covering him like icing sugar, as the smoke alarm pierces the calmness with its loud signal.

***

Not even one hundred meters away, a lonesome priest sits beside a small fountain as he peels himself an orange. In silent prayer, he chews a segment of succulent orange with deep contentment as small birds drink and bathe in the water beside him. Somewhere in the distance, the sounds of men and women shouting and screaming grow louder, while those around him march toward the commotion. The priest, however, isn't disturbed, nor shows any interest in the confused tourists. "No questions need to be asked when you have the answers," he whispers to no one while popping another piece of orange into his mouth. The small electronic transmitter tucked away deep inside the black fabric of his cassock holds all the answers.

Chapter Twenty-Nine

Monte Carlo, Monaco

Sarah promised Carver the previous night that she would stay out of harm's way. He wanted her back in London, or at least in Paris or Milan, deep within a British embassy. Sarah knew there was no easy way of refusing him. She also knew Carver needed the focus to do what he was good at. To kill Zhang and end the dangerous Chinese faction attempting to drag the West into a new world war.

There is no point getting sucked into something that could trigger a worldwide manhunt. Your role within SIS is back in Legoland, dealing with and appeasing those narcissistic politicians with the necessary mistruths. Please stay out of this one. Leave it to myself and Flynn. He spoke his words with sincerity and love.

Sarah thinks about how she wants to please him, although there is no way she will sit this out. *This is my circus, and I need to be here to pick up the pieces.* Parked in a car close to Hôtel Hermitage, Sarah hides behind a large pair of black sunglasses and a heavy amount of makeup. With her long blond hair up and tucked neatly under a baseball cap, she sits patiently, drumming her fingers lightly on the steering wheel. Within a fashionable black canvas day pack, a Sig Sauer handgun rests next to her passport and various pieces of makeup. A tablet perched on her lap displays the profiles on Duval and the three men he brought in for this mission. Her finger slides over the screen, zooming in on their features until she can almost identify them all by touch.

With no advanced warning, she catches sight of Duval exiting the hotel and moving toward the marina. Without taking her eyes off the corrupt CIA director, she swiftly switches off the tablet and throws it onto the passenger seat next to discarded food wrappers and a couple of newspapers. With a careful look all around the car, Sarah opens her door and steps out onto the tidy pavement. A cluster of happy tourists march past from one marvelous sightseeing point to another. Perfect timing. Immediately she joins the stream of middle-aged men and woman as they meander along Avenue des Beaux-Arts, passing all the luxury stores.

Once the group makes it to the junction, Sarah detaches herself from them and steps into an alcove of a small shop. She can clearly see the unmistakable figure of Duval hurrying away from the hotel and making no attempt to check on a tail. Sarah moves with conviction. *You need to pay for what you did,* she mouths through gritted teeth.

***

Zhang walks with confidence past the reception desk toward the exit. His eyes flicker behind his dark glasses, searching for any sign of a threat. He can visualize a convoy of black armored vans pulling up outside the hotel filled with specialized police gunning for him.

Once he walks through the magnificent doors of the hotel onto Square Beaumarchais, the heat of the morning engulfs him. The cloudless sky allows the sun to strike down without mercy. He can feel the increasing burning sensation on the back of his neck. The weather is too hot for a black jacket. *There is no time to back out*, thinks Zhang. He needs to keep walking and make it to the vehicle, which is parked on a street two blocks away, primed for an emergency such as this. A bead of sweat immediately forms on his forehead and runs down into his eye. With a few blinks, his vision is good again. On inspection, Zhang finds the surrounding area calm, filled with the usual members of society he grew accustomed to since leaving China. He conducts a fleeting scan of the rooftops to check for snipers. Nothing. Neither is there anyone hanging around for no apparent reason. *This won't last long,* he thinks as he makes his move.

He turns to his left and bolts past the line of cars waiting to be parked by the valet drivers. The patter of his feet on the pavement is a welcome relief. "So far, so good," he utters. Until he spots something: a man standing inside a shop looking toward him. When Zhang spins his head in the direction to get a clearer look, he is certain it is one of them. There is no doubt. The tall man with long wavy blond hair turns slightly and picks up some item of clothing from a rack, feigning interest in it. The thick shoulders and chest stand out from any others he's seen. *Okay, follow me, you asshole. Let's get this done.* Zhang wants to make good on his plan with the diminishing amount of time left.

Flynn, on spotting the Chinese assassin passing the shop, dials Carver and provides Zhang's new location and direction of travel. Next, he stores the phone inside his pocket and leaves the shop.

It doesn't take long before Zhang changes direction. Flynn keeps his distance from him to roughly fifty meters, then turns down Av. de l'Hermitage while checking to see if he too is being followed.

Zhang doesn't move any faster. He now strolls somewhat casually while his eyes dart across the street looking for threats. He knows one is following him and the other must be lingering somewhere close. Zhang looks back and shouts, "Where is your dumb friend? The British man I blew up once in Florence." Then he stops momentarily beside a row of parked cars before moving on.

This causes Flynn to hold back until he can assess what he's up to. Once Zhang moves, Flynn has no option but to close the gap. He can now feel his phone buzzing in his pocket. "Go ahead."

"I am a minute out. Where are you?" asks Carver.

"Forty meters behind. He is approaching Av. de la Costa . . ."

Before Flynn can finish his message, a tremendous blast sucks the air out of his lungs. It throws his body backward onto the windscreen of a parked car, and his phone lands down the road, smashing into pieces.

"FLYNN, FLYNN," shouts Carver. "You bastard, Zhang . . ." Carver knows instantly what transpired. The Chinese man led Flynn straight down death alley. Walked him into one of his bombs.

Carver downshifts and speeds through the streets of Monte Carlo. The small engine roars with pain as its wheels struggle to keep traction. There is no other option than to take the one-way streets. In doing so, he cuts the last thirty seconds of the trip. As he takes the last bend, up ahead he can see a body writhing on the ground. Carver keeps his foot on the accelerator and races up the street toward a man he spies coming closer to Flynn.

Zhang tosses the key fob into a pot plant next to a shop front and retraces his steps. On the ground is the American, bloodied and deafened by the explosion. When Zhang gets closer, he reaches into his jacket and pulls out his Smith & Wesson. "I have been waiting for this moment, you American pig," he sneers.

Just then, a volley of shots rings out. The bullets make a cracking sound as they narrowly fly past his head. Zhang frantically jumps behind a car whose alarm is screaming wildly, set off from the explosions. He stuffs the last pillow cover containing his bomb under the car next to its wheel. Once the second bomb is hidden from view, he lowers himself behind the next car. From this new position, he takes the risk of peering through its windows at the shooter. *The British one*, mouths Zhang.

Carver runs along the opposite side of the street, then crosses over in the hope Zhang failed to spot him. The shots he fired would only hold him off for a few seconds before he came back to finish Flynn for good. He needs to gain ground to obtain a sight picture of Zhang before unleashing another volley of accurate fire.

The explosion was so sudden and loud it caught Flynn by complete surprise. Sprawled on the ground, his senses are overwhelmed momentarily. The car alarms and those from the shops in the narrow street reverberate off the sandstone walls. His instincts fight against the shock and attempt to force his sight and hearing back into play.

As the dust settles, he fumbles with his shredded clothing, a wasted attempt to locate the grip of his gun. Temporarily blinded, he cannot risk firing in case he kills a pedestrian. Flynn tries, with all his strength, to crawl behind the nearest car and remove himself from a possible fire lane. He blinks repeatedly in an attempt to remove the fragments in his eyes and to restore some kind of vision. After what seems like an eternity, he finally drags himself next to a car and sits himself upright against its rear wheel. The ringing in his ears still dominates and his vision is now a mess of blurriness.

"Flynn, don't move. I have you covered. Flynn, lift your hand if you can hear me," shouts Carver from the opposite side of the street.

Carver moves up closer, inching toward the last car he saw Zhang duck behind. The distance between the two men is less than twenty meters. Carver drops onto his chest and levels his firearm across the surface of the road and searches for Zhang under the vehicle. "Gotcha," whispers Carver. Zhang's leg sticks out a fraction and is now in the sight of a Sig Sauer.

Bang. Bang. Two quick shots from Carver drown out, only for a second, the sounds of the security alarms all around him. A quick scream follows the gunshots. Zhang's ankle has exploded. Carver's first bullet found bone, splintering it completely. The second bullet bounced off the curbside, smashing fragments of concrete against the shop walls.

Carver now springs to his feet and crosses the street to close in on Zhang. Just then, a burst of gunfire from behind forces him back to the ground. He rolls quickly back toward a parked car as he tries to figure out where the shooter is. *Two bloody shooters now.* The bullets whizz all around him. "Flynn, keep down, they are putting down suppressive fire for Zhang."

Buchanan and Marchetti have joined the fight. Both men armed with M4 carbine assault rifles approach from opposite sides of the street, closing in on Carver and Flynn.

Carver pounces up and sprints across the street, letting off another volley of shots toward Buchanan. Bullets from their weapons respond instantly, ripping into car doors, shop windows, and the surrounding buildings, causing carnage and destruction.

Carver dives behind a car and immediately crawls over to Flynn. He grabs him by the collar and shouts into his face, "Wake up, Flynn, we need to fight our way out of this."

Slowly Flynn responds, "I'm with you, brother," his voice broken and the faint words gargling in his mouth. Despite his bloodied and bruised appearance, a glint of light begins to sparkle in his eyes. He rotates his head from side to side, then stretches his arms and legs before pulling out his compact Glock 19 with bleeding hands. After a quick check of his weapon, he gives Carver a wink. "Nice to finally meet you. Now let's kill these bastards."

"Can you move?"

"Yeah, it's all surface damage. I'm good to go," says Flynn, the adrenalin now fueling his body.

"Okay, I shot Zhang in the foot. He isn't mobile, but his backup arrived. Coming in opposite directions." As if to prove his point, a stream of bullets begins pounding the cars next to them. Controlled bursts by experienced men. Carver ducks down under the cars to check for Zhang.

"He moved; the bastard has left. Okay, Flynn, time to get to work. I'll go after Zhang and the man covering him. You protect my rear."

Flynn now has pulled himself up into a crouched position and gives Carver a nod. "I'm on the rear, copy that."

Carver replaces his weapon with a fresh magazine and creeps around the front of the car, the engine block providing the only cover. He drops his head quickly as another volley of lead pierces the skin of the vehicles all around him, forcing a withdrawal. Carver quickly ducks behind the car once again. Time is running out, and he knows both he and Flynn are sitting ducks if he doesn't do something. Then he hears a clunk of metallic sliding against metallic. *Someone is reloading.* Carver springs to his feet and charges along the pavement, shooting at the car windows up ahead as he looks for his next cover position. As he passes a couple more cars, he drops quickly and rolls awkwardly, crashing into a scooter just as four bullets rip past him. With his chest flat on the pavement, he pushes his weapon in front of him and scans the area. A final search under the cars fails to catch sight of Zhang, only a beautiful blood trail to follow. As Carver forms a plan, he spots a suspicious object. *Devious bastard!* A bomb. Carver doesn't have time to wait for the shooter to reload. It's either risk being shot or get blown to pieces. Already on his feet, he charges up the street, trying to put distance between him and the device, knowing Zhang will be watching him.

***

Flynn watches for Carver to make a break for it down the street before he unleashes a few rounds toward one of the shooters. In doing so, it allows himself to get into a better position to cause a distraction.

He reaches his arm through the broken window of a car and opens the door. Then he pulls off the handbrake and shifts the gear into neutral. With all his strength, he pushes the car out of the parking space and adjusts the steering, the vehicle rolls slowly down the slight hill, slowly picking up speed. A smile covers his face when he notices movement about thirty meters away. As the car rolls down the hill, the shooter fires into the empty interior. This allows Flynn a moment to make his move. He darts inside one of the buildings along the street and allows his eyes to adjust for the darkened rooms while searching for a staircase. Ducked down beneath the windows, Flynn spots several terrified staff, all huddled together, crying, and pleading with him not to kill them.

"It's okay, I'm American, I am here to save you, please stay where you are."

Some of the staff are nodding, others are frantic and attempt to crawl away. "Listen, I need to get upstairs so I can stop those men from killing people. Don't leave or try to be a hero, okay? Just relax."

One man dressed in a fine black suit and a deep-blue shirt points a finger toward a door to his right. Flynn turns and immediately walks through the door, finding a set of steps leading up to the second floor. "Okay, everyone follow me, and keep low. Once upstairs, I want you all into one of the back rooms away from the street." Flynn has now positioned himself by a window looking down toward the carnage below. His vantage point gives him a picture of the battle space, and within it, he spots his man. Dressed all in biker leather, the shooter approaches the car that Flynn pushed down the street. With his M4 held up against his shoulder, he peers into the empty car and immediately withdraws. Clearly upset, the man now sweeps his weapon to all possible hiding areas, looking for his target.

Flynn now has the tables turned in his favor, so he slowly opens the balcony door, keeping his movement slow and deliberate. The Glock in his hand now points at the center of the shooter's chest down below. Flynn watches as the man gets closer, each step providing a better shot. *That's it, boy, keep coming, keep coming.* His finger is now ready to squeeze the trigger.

BOOM. The second bomb goes off, the shock of which causes the shooter to flinch and crouch down. Flynn, however, doesn't falter. Two shots enter the shooter's back. Then two more. From his position, Flynn can see the blood spurt out of the newly formed holes in the black leather jacket. The shooter's face looks upward toward the blue sky. Flynn stares down at his fellow American, Marchetti, the traitor. *You switched sides, wrong country, wrong choice. That's on you.*

An almost happy feeling about surviving the bomb and killing the shooter instantly changes. He suddenly snaps his attention as his thoughts turn to Carver. *Shit! The second bomb.* Thinking Carver has been blown to pieces, Flynn races back down the stairs and runs out into the street.

He keeps himself tight against the parked cars and moves quickly along the pavement, sliding slightly on the pieces of crushed glass. From the damage up ahead, he can gather vital information. The two shooters have used the carnage to retreat to a safe position. The blast caused the same damage as the previous one, and there is no mangled body or blood splatter nearby. As he passes the bomb site, his feeling of urgency relaxes slightly. Then, about ten meters from the end of the street, he hears someone calling him.

"They turned west, about one hundred meters down the street." It's Carver speaking. Flynn looks over to see Carver leaning up against a tree, pulling twigs out of his hair. The clothes on his body are torn, his face is bruised, and blood runs from his nose. "I was wondering when you were going to turn up," says Carver.

Flynn laughs at the state of the British man with his relaxed attitude and slowly shakes his head. "Are we going to finish this, or what?"

"By all means. Two left," says Carver as he climbs out of the small garden bed and brushes down his clothes before smiling at Flynn. "Here we go again." Carver takes off running with the American by his side.

Bystanders peer through their blinds with some venturing down onto the street to witness the action. Most members of the public associate the gunmen fleeing as bad and the two men chasing as good. This is apparent by a strange round of applause that Flynn and Carver receive as they hunt down Zhang and Buchanan.

"Flynn, you take this side of the street, and I'll take the other. If I get hit, you keep up the fight. There is enough support here to get medical attention."

"Sounds good," says Flynn as he changes position, the newly acquired M4 in his hand ready to unleash a world of pain. "We must be getting close."

"Right. We will walk from here. Keep that weapon up," Carver says before asking some bystanders if they spotted the men. Some don't speak, others point ahead toward Av. de la Costa. Flynn looks across at Carver to see him give the hand signal to keep moving. After a few minutes, both men worry Zhang and Buchanan escaped them. Their eyes sweep the side alleys, rooftops, and inside cars parked on the narrow street. All the doors that lead out onto the streets haven't been kicked in, nor are there any signs of blood. "Zhang must have stemmed the bleeding," says Carver.

As they approach a tight bend, Flynn breaks his silence. "I'll be damned. This is where Zhang shot me. He took off on his motorbike, and I think a couple of my rounds hit him. He knows these streets well."

Carver knows the area also. "He could hide anywhere. They built this place on a hillside. Alleyways and steps leading up and down the hill to other streets. Impossible to trap someone."

"GET DOWN," shouts Flynn.

The two men drop onto the hard pavement as gunfire erupts from down the street. Carver lifts his head and spots Zhang leaning against a car with his Chinese assault rifle spitting out round after round. As he turns to update Flynn, it surprises him to find the American has disappeared. Then he catches movement in the corner of his eye. Flynn races down the side of the narrow street behind the parked cars, about fifteen meters, then stops and spreads his feet into a wide stance, the M4 snug against his broad shoulders. Carver needs to time this perfectly.

Flynn opens fire on Zhang, who is maneuvering for another attack. This allows Carver to race down the street. He passes Flynn and runs on using his cover fire, then he stops and lets off a few controlled shots toward Zhang. Once Flynn passes by and adopts a firing stance, Carver repeats his movement. Both men now use the same side of the street because of limited cover on the opposite side. Now they have closed the distance to about thirty meters. There is no way Zhang can make a run for it. The gunshot had smashed his ankle, and because of the increased activity, it had resumed bleeding. His makeshift tourniquet had unraveled, leaving a trail of blood-soaked cloth scattered around the road. Carver points to the blood trail from the back of the car they are using for cover. Flynn looks down and follows the trail with his eyes toward a large sandstone archway. Under the arch is a large wooden door. The very door he had run through days before. A feeling of fear now runs through his body, which he channels into aggression.

Zhang curses silently. The realization that he is cornered almost smothers him. With no way out of this, he considers the last option, one final trick up his sleeve, if only for dignity. He clips in a fresh magazine, points it up the street toward the men, and empties it in one continuous burst. Once the mag is empty, he unclips it and throws it along with the rifle across the road.

On hearing the metallic action, both men know Zhang's weapon is empty. Flynn is the first to pop his head out from behind the car. "He chucked his weapon on the road."

"Let's get this done. Remember, Buchanan is out here. Cover me!" says Carver.

"Hey, hold it. Let me kill him."

Despite having been almost blown to pieces, twice, Carver knows what it means to Flynn. This animal brutally slaughtered his men. "Okay, I'll cover you."

"Here, use this." Flynn hands over his M4, which Carver takes and begins sweeping the area.

Flynn wastes no time. With his Glock in his right hand, he races along the road toward the archway to find Zhang waiting for him. As he closes in, Zhang quickly pulls out his Smith & Wesson and fires it toward Flynn. Carver is too quick. The M4 sinks into Zhang's shoulder, causing him to scream out. The Smith & Wesson falls from his limp grip onto the road.

Flynn stops running and takes a quick look around as he approaches the Chinese man. Face-to-face with Zhang, Flynn holsters his Glock. "Zhang, nice to finally catch up with you. I have some unfinished business . . ."

"To hell with you. You piece of dog—"

Zhang doesn't have time to finish. Flynn catches him by the throat, his grip squeezing the windpipe while his other hand works its way to the back of Zhang's head. Flynn's breathing has now returned to normal; his eyes, the color of the sky above, sparkle brightly while his face denotes a man in prayer.

"This is going to hurt you more than it will hurt me. I presume you have no faith, no one to grieve for you or exact revenge for you. Which means you are worthless. However, you will die, not with honor but with disgrace." Then, with a sudden jolt of his powerful arms, Flynn twists Zhang's neck forcefully to the left and then jerks it back. The sickening sound of the neck being snapped signals Carver, who closes in from his position farther down the street.

Flynn drops the corpse and spins around with the Glock now firmly back in his hands. "One more down, one left."

Carver motions toward a small black gate that has been kicked free from its hinges. The steps lead down toward the lower street, which allows access to the marina. The overpass Bd. du Larvotto, which runs adjacent to the steps, also provides Buchanan with a further escape route.

Flynn nods and leads the way. Both men are in sync as they cover each other in their movements. Descending the old, worn-out stone steps only takes a couple of minutes as they clear each vantage point before proceeding to the next open area. Both men know Buchanan will do anything to avoid being arrested. Which could mean a fight to the death or a kidnap scenario. For Carver and Flynn, this is a dangerous seek-and-execute job, which they desperately want to complete before disappearing from Monaco. Buchanan is a man too dangerous and volatile to be allowed to roam freely. His connections within the underworld mean he could resurface years later to resume the traitorous life.

"Flynn, cover me a second," says Carver as he stops and kneels down behind a stone column. He digs into his pocket and pulls out his phone and earpiece. Once he places a call and attaches the earbud, he gives Flynn a hand signal to proceed.

Flynn creeps down each step, his eyes and weapon moving as one. Abruptly, Flynn holds up his fist and Carver takes up a defensive position, his M4 searching for Buchanan. He waits as Flynn secures his weapon and climbs up onto the overpass. Once in position, he runs across to the other side of the road and looks down onto Pl. Sainte-Dévote, which leads out toward Port Hercules.

As he runs back and clambers over the side railing on the overpass to join Carver, he whispers, "I saw him. He is moving down to the marina. We need to be quick."

Carver takes the hostile-looking M4 and quickly strips it, then tosses the various parts into the bushes. Both men now keep their handguns tucked under their shirts and launch into a run down the steps and out toward their target.

"Take the lead, Flynn," shouts Carver.

Flynn runs across the road, almost colliding with the traffic as he focuses on the last know position of Buchanan. He climbs over a small wall that separates the main road from Route de la Piscine and drops down the ten feet onto his haunches and immediately scans the area. Carver hurries across the street about forty meters and drops onto the same road, keeping visual with Flynn. Both men stand in concentration, their eyes searching the sea of bodies going about their daily business. After a few seconds, Flynn jogs toward Carver and signals him to follow. His icy glare contains enough information for Carver to realize the man is on the hunt. Despite their tattered clothes, ripped from the bomb blasts and specked with dried blood and shards of glass, the two men jog past tourists and locals as they search for Buchanan.

"Hold," shouts Flynn. His eyes lock dead ahead. Carver can plainly see the CIA traitor. Buchanan's back is turned, and he has a phone against his ear. It is clear he is looking for someone as he walks along Quai des Etats-Unis. A row of about twenty magnificent yachts, berthed with their sterns toward the marina, sway gracefully as their owners busy themselves on deck.

"He is looking for a boat, or for someone," says Flynn.

"Maybe he is going to commandeer a vessel."

"That's likely. That's what I would do. How do you want to play this?"

"If he takes a yacht, we could follow him out to sea and finish him there, away from the crowd," says Carver.

"Or we get closer and end it now."

"I like your style, brother," says Carver as he breaks into a jog.

The two men run side by side, trying their best to blend in despite their appearance. As they gain some ground, Flynn hesitates somewhat. He grabs Carver lightly by the arm, then he pulls back harshly and drops his head. Carver follows his lead by jumping off to the side before leaping across onto the stern of the closest yacht, his legs getting tangled up in the sailing lines.

Buchanan swings around on hearing the footsteps, instantly drawing his weapon. He quickly fires off about ten rounds toward Flynn and Carver. The surrounding people run off in all directions, their bags of fresh supplies and bottles of water thrown to the ground. His plan has failed. Not only has Duval screwed him, he is now left with a risky escape plan. "You bastards," he shouts. The man from Wyoming feels the world around him start to crumble. "Think you can screw me over. How about this?" He jumps on a yacht and grabs a middle-aged lady by the hair and drags her off onto the walkway. With the barrel of his weapon digging into the crying woman's hair, he quickly manhandles her to stand in front of him. "Flynn, Carver, show yourselves or I'll blow her head off and grab another one."

The two men look at each other, their expressions dark and calculating. "Can you get a shot at him?" whispers Flynn.

"No, not from this distance, too risky," says Carver.

"Five seconds," screams Buchanan, "four, three . . ."

"Okay, okay, let the woman go," says Carver as he stands up and leaps off the yacht and onto the marina. He speaks with an air of confidence that Flynn can't match.

As soon as Flynn joins him, Buchanan gives his next order. "Drop your weapons into the harbor. Do it now."

"How many rounds do you have left?" asks Carver.

The question infuriates Buchanan, who screams back, "Enough to kill us all. Toss your weapons before you see this woman's head blasted off her shoulders."

Flynn immediately throws his Glock into the water, resulting in a large plop. Carver casually walks over to the water and releases the magazine out from its position.

"What are you doing?" screams Buchanan. "Don't test me. Chuck the bloody thing into the water and step back."

"I'm making it safe," says Carver while popping the round out of the chamber.

Without warning, the sound of a loud bang from a single gunshot echoes around the marina, catching Flynn by surprise.

Carver doesn't look up. He simply slides the round into the magazine and pops it back into the weapon, then tucks it into his waistband.

Sarah throws her handgun into the marina and keeps on walking. Shooting Buchanan at point-blank range wasn't part of her plan, although it was the best decision she made that day.

Buchanan had dropped like a stone onto the hard marina pavement. His hostage doesn't understand what happened. Instead, she wanders around the dead body, freaking out. Splashed with blood and brain matter, she screams and yells to an ever-increasing crowd.

Carver nods to Flynn and the two men immediately make their retreat down the marina and disappear into the backstreets. Flynn keeps on Carver's tail as they run through the winding streets. Carver concentrates on his phone calls while Flynn checks their surroundings for any surprises. Despite the sirens intensifying back at the marina, Carver's mood is relaxed and his attitude jovial. "Where's your weapon at? You need to go back to basic training." Flynn follows behind, shaking his head at his new mate's sense of black humor.

They walk and run for several minutes, crossing from one street to the next via alleyways and gardens until Carver speaks. "There he is." Carver steps out onto the road to signal the car to pull over.

When Flynn jumps into the backseat, he looks toward the driver behind the wheel. With a skeptical voice, he acknowledges the man. "Good morning . . . Father."

Chapter Thirty

South Lombok, Indonesia

The sweet notes of jazz music spill from a cozy beach bar at Selong Belanak and filter through the palm trees out onto the sand. The live band started their gig early, eager to please the growing crowd of a pleasant mix of expats and tourists.

Bottles of imported wine and canapes are presented while, out on the beach, relaxing around a sunburnt table, Carver and Flynn sit in comfortable silence. Their eyes locked on the vivid orange sun as it sinks lazily over the horizon. In front of them, Francesca Vecchiarelli and Sarah Fontaine frolic in the warm salt water of the Indian Ocean, enjoying the last minutes of daylight.

The playful Italian had accompanied Sarah on the long flights to Lombok from Nice, via Singapore and Bali. Between them, they had concocted a plan to work together and redesign future missions. Without consulting the two men, Sarah had offered Francesca a job working with SIS. When Flynn and Carver went to the airport earlier in the day to pick up Sarah, Flynn was in disbelief. He thought the Italian would have disappeared and kept on the run around the European cities, vanishing out of one shadowy life until she found another. That wasn't to be. The pair had been inseparable during the few hours back at the villa, and the prospect of spending their future together was the icing on the cake for Flynn. To celebrate a new chapter unfolding, they had made the short trip down from the hilltop villa to the beach for a night of seafood and vintage jazz.

Carver's reaches down and picks up a handful of fine white sand. While inspecting the grains with a slight interest he speaks softly, "So, you think you can keep your mind on your work, instead of Francesca?"

Flynn laughs. "I will have to try. It seems to work fine for you and Sarah."

A young Indonesian waiter approaches the table and excuses herself as she lights a few candles, then collects the empty beer bottles.

"*Dua lagi, termiah kasih,*" says Carver, asking for two more beers. He reaches her a generous tip, and when she heads back inside, he turns to face Flynn.

"Sarah told me today that she watched Duval leaving the hotel back at Monaco. The bastard walked down toward the marina, then a black car pulled up and the back door swung open."

Flynn realizes that until this point they never mentioned Duval. As if his part was no longer relevant. He looks over and pauses for a moment, then asks, "Did Sarah see who was driving?"

"No, but she saw who thrust open the door… It was your good friend Eddie Wu."

A look of exasperation falls on Flynn's face, his eyes search for answers but find only darkness. "You got to be kidding me! Eddie was in on this?"

Carver drinks the last of his beer and sets it on the table. "Afraid not, buddy. The fat degenerate piece of shit played us all. Duval had been shadowing him for some time. He wanted to find a way to pull Eddie into the underworld. Obviously, he found something dirty on him."

"Don't tell me the shooting in the marina was Duval's work?" Flynn asks.

Carver leans in closer and speaks quietly. "If his agreement with that crazy general falls to pieces, Eddie's wealth and connections will be his backup plan. He has the bloke wrapped around his little finger. If Eddie doesn't play ball, then Duval will finger him as the financer of Danny Lin's death."

Flynn sits in stunned silence, trying to figure out what was said, and what was missed when he debriefed Eddie.

Just then, the young bartender returned with the ice-cold Bintangs, Carver quickly grabs the bottles off her tray and hands one over to Flynn before speaking. "Hey, don't beat yourself up. We play with the cards we are dealt with. These guys are a different breed. Men like us need to step into their world. We must figure out their intentions, their plans, and who is pulling the strings. Then we do what we do best, by removing them one by one."

Flynn nods slowly while contemplating the high-risk work it would involve. He removes his sunglasses and sets them on the table and rubs his face to relieve the built-up tension, then takes a swig of the cold beer. Once the alcohol settles, he removes a couple of Indonesian *Dos Hermanos* cigars from their wrappers and hands one to Carver. Flynn gently squeezes the thick cigar between his fingers, testing it as he looks down toward the shoreline at Sarah and Francesca. The two women are now leaving the warm turquoise water and are making their way back to the table. "There's a lot of powerful and connected people wrapped up in this shit, Carver. We don't know how high this goes."

"I hear you, brother. But if we don't do something, then who will? Plus, we can work as a team. Did you ever have team members that looked like this?" says Carver with a grin as he waves toward the girls.

"How is the water?" asks Carver.

Sarah and Francesca giggle like teenagers as they approach the table and slip back into their bikini tops. "The water is beautiful. We can all have a swim together after dinner." Sarah bends over and wrings the salt water out of her long blonde hair, then takes a sip of Carver's beer before asking, "Well, did you tell him about our friend Eddie?" says Sarah.

"I did. Duval and Eddie, two men on my list of doom."

Francesca sits down on Flynn's lap, her warm and wet body sliding between his thick arms. "So..., are we going to hunt down these ass men, or what?" she asks.

Laughter erupts from the table and continues for some time until Flynn raises his hand. Through watery eyes, he gazes at the hot, bubbly Italian and gives her a wink, then he leans over towards Sarah and Carver and says, "This girl speaks my language. Let's do it, fuck them all, we will unleash hell on every piece of shit involved."

Carver smiles and nods his approval then toasts his cigar slowly until it begins to smoke. He passes the matches to Flynn, takes a couple of puffs and sits back to peacefully watch the small fishing boats sailing across the calm bay. The two girls move to their chairs and quietly discuss possible adventures and destinations. A small brown and white dog lays down at Carver's feet and wriggles itself comfortably into the soft cooled sand. Flynn carefully lights his own cigar and throws the matches onto the wooden table. The two men sit once again in silence, a cold beer in one hand, cigar in the other. Nothing more needs to be said. Both have been through many theaters of war, perfecting their own style of killing as the bodies pile up. The dice of danger and fortune have just been rolled, and only fate determines how they land.

Printed in Great Britain
by Amazon

76114292R00215